EXCHANGE STUDENT

Also by Michael R. Lane

<u>Mysteries</u>
The Gem Connection
Blue Sun
The Butcher
Six Weeks

<u>Fiction</u>
Emancipation
UFOs and God
The Family Stone
Long Journey Home

<u>Poetry</u>
A Drop of Midnight
Sandbox
Mortal Thoughts
Love & Sensuality
A Leap Year of Haiku

EXCHANGE STUDENT

Michael R. Lane

BARE BONES PRESS
P.O. Box 9653, Seattle, WA 98109

Published by Bare Bones Press, Seattle, Washington.

The characters and events in this book are fictitious. Any similarity to real persons, living or dead is coincidental and not intended by the author.

Design: Bare Bones Press
Production: Bare Bones Press
Cover Art: Michael R. Lane

Bare Bones Press
P.O. Box 9653
Seattle, WA 98109

www.michaelrlane.com
www.barebonespress.com

First Edition: March 2024

"How was your journey?"
"Lonely."
"Find many lights?"
"Some."
"Ends your story as begun."

— Michael R. Lane, "Welcome Home"
from *A Drop of Midnight*

CHAPTER 1

"Wick! Mae! Hurry up!" Dan yelled from the foot of the living room stairs, his bass voice nearing a baritone when he yelled.

Daniel Samuel Bluford was an imposing figure. At six-six of rock-solid muscle, plank-wide shoulders, and sporting a barrel chest and hands as big as catcher's mitts, he was nonetheless a gentle giant to his family, friends and peers, with twinkling brown eyes and a generous smile. He was also an asshole to his enemies, who knew those eyes as dark and piercing, containing a predatory snarl.

When asked if he played sports, Dan admitted that he had. Not American football or basketball, as most people assumed, but tennis and track (100, 200, and 400 meter races). He had been offered numerous athletic college scholarships that he elected to pass on, accepting, instead, one of numerous academic scholarships offered to a 4.0 student who attended a private school (although he did compete as a college walk-on in track and tennis, with some success). They were accomplishments he failed to confess unless prodded.

"We don't want to be late for school!"

Wickliffe Arnold Bluford (nickname 'Wick') walked down the stairs with an arm draped over his little sister's hunched shoulders. Dan's ten-year-old son was a solidly built, handsome, bronze-skinned boy who was the spitting image of his father at that age (except for a nest of dark, curly hair that he inherited from his mother).

His seven-year-old daughter, Mae Carol Bluford, had her brother's skin tone, along with petite, feminine features and her mother's big brown eyes and dimply smile. Her thick, dark curls fell to the small of her back.

The children were dressed for school: Wick in jeans, designer sneakers, and a hoodie with printed colored interlocking plastic bricks; Mae in jeans, designer sneakers, and a graphic tee with unicorns. Though Wick and Mae attended a private school, the specter of school uniforms did not exist at Pearson Academy.

"Mae's not feeling well," Wick said.

Dan immediately noticed that his daughter's face was flushed. Her normally laughing eyes were dull. "What's wrong, honey?" Dan asked his youngest child.

Harvey and Pearl had trailed the children down the stairs. The Odd Couple appeared equally concerned about Mae's condition as they looked on from seated positions.

A couple of years back, the children had been permitted to adopt a single pet from the local animal shelter. Wick had chosen a Doberman puppy. Mae, a Bengal kitten. The two domesticated enemies got along from the start like brother and sister—to the point where, at times in their youth, Pearl behaved more like a dog and Harvey more like a cat. It was a peculiarity that earned them the family nickname The Odd Couple.

Harvey and Pearl had unusual sleeping habits, as well (at least, as far as the family was concerned). Harvey preferred sleeping in Mae's room, while Pearl preferred sleeping in Wick's. No one knew why. In the end, the question of why didn't seem to matter.

"My tummy hurts," Mae whimpered.

Dan placed the back of his meaty hand on his daughter's delicate forehead. Mae was running a fever. The practicing physician of the house, his wife, Toni, was away at a medical conference.

As a scientist and engineer, specializing in environmentalism and geoengineering, his medicinal knowledge was limited. What he had learned about diagnosing and treating human illnesses had come primarily from Toni and firsthand experiences with family.

"Come with me," Dan told Mae, gently placing his large hand on top of his daughter's small head.

"Wick, where's your science project?" Dan asked as he and Mae walked away.

"Oh, snap!" Wick raced up the stairs to his room to fetch his school assignment. Dan led Mae to the downstairs bathroom. Harvey and Pearl parted, Pearl dashing up the stairs alongside Wick and Harvey trailing Dan and Mae as if the two had reached some sort of agreement to be the guardians of each other's primary caregivers.

Closing the bathroom door to keep out Harvey, Dan opened one of the medicine drawers, found a box of mercury-free oral thermometers, ripped open the package, extracted one, and asked his daughter to open her mouth.

Before Mae could do as her father asked, she whirled to the toilet and vomited. The sight of vomit did not bother Dan. He had seen enough barfing during his partying days at university, though the sour smell did give his stomach a queasy momentary turn.

What troubled Dan most was seeing his daughter puke. Dan held Mae's hair while she finished. Miraculously, Mae avoided getting any on her clothes. When Mae was done, Dan closed the lid and flushed the toilet. He then sat Mae gently down on the toilet, dampened a clean washcloth with warm water, and wiped away the vomit that speckled his daughter's mouth and chin. Dan rinsed clean the tainted washcloth in the sink, wrung it damp, and draped it over the towel rack in case the washcloth would be needed again.

"Feeling better?"

"A little," Mae responded, still clutching her stomach and rocking back and forth.

Taking her temperature was no longer necessary. Dan had already decided he was taking Mae to the hospital. Dan grabbed another clean washcloth, dampened it with cold water, and pressed it against his daughter's forehead.

"Can you hold that there, honey?"

Mae nodded and did so.

"I'll be right back." Dan kissed his daughter on the top of her head. Her soft hair held the sweet, mild scent of coconut, a byproduct of her mother's homemade coconut milk shampoo. It was a pleasant distraction from the curdling sour smell of vomit that had yet to dissipate.

He made sure to close the door behind him after he stepped out, so that Harvey and Pearl did not slip in.

Wick was standing outside the bathroom door holding a white cardboard storage box that contained all he needed to demonstrate how acid rain affects aquatic life. His anime backpack, filled with school supplies, books, and laptop, was perched on his back.

Dan and Toni were pleased and impressed by his choice for a science project. They were always lecturing their children on the importance of a healthy ecosystem, instructing them at every opportunity on how they could personally contribute to improving and protecting the environment that was so vital to all. It was good to know that Wick was listening.

"Is Mae alright?" Wick looked worried. His forehead furrowed, a habit he had picked up from his father that Dan wished he could break for the both of them. As much as Wick enjoyed picking on his little sister, everyone (including Mae) knew how much her big brother was protective of her. He would rather lose a limb than to see Mae suffer a hangnail.

"She will be, son. I'm going to ask Mrs. Czarnecka to give you a ride to school today while I look after your sister. Is that okay with you?"

The Czarneckas had moved into the neighborhood six months after Dan and Toni. The Czarneckas and Blufords became instant friends and great neighbors. The Czarneckas had three children. Twin daughters Lacey and Nicole were Wick's age. Their youngest son Charlie was a few months younger than Mae. All attended the same neighborhood private school.

"Sure, Dad," Wick said. "As long as Mae's going to be okay?"

"Don't worry, son. She'll be fine."

"Catch you later, Mae!" Wick yelled to his sister through the closed door.

"Okay!" Mae weakly replied. "Good luck on your science project!" Mae concluded with a string of coughs. Wick looked at his father as if he were ready to burst through the bathroom door.

"She'll be alright," Dan assured Wick in a low voice, touching his son on the shoulder. Wick took a couple of deep breaths.

"No problem," Wick yelled at the door with a nervous smile. "I've got this science thing nailed!"

"I know," Mae said. Her voice sounded clear, as if she'd had a rush of strength. "You take after Dad!"

Dan looked at Wick with pride. Wick appeared to feel the same. Dan was astonished that Mae could draw such a conclusion at such a young age. Then Dan thought of Toni. How many times had his wife said to Wick that he was just like his father?

"Love you, Marshmallow Head!" Wick yelled.

"Love you too, Pea Brain!" Mae yelled back.

Dan and Toni had no idea how they came up with their ever-changing pet names. When they asked their children about them, they appeared equally puzzled, answering "I don't know" in tandem with a shrug of their shoulders.

Dan called Sandy Czarnecka. He briefly explained the situation with Mae and asked if Wick could hitch a ride with them to school. Sandy said it was no problem, wishing Mae a speedy recovery. Sandy asked if Dan would like for Marek, her husband, to bring Wick home.

The Czarneckas and Blufords had the same arrangement: one spouse dropped the children off at school; the other picked them up. Dan was temporarily pulling double duty for the delivery and pickup of the children, with Toni away.

Dan told Sandy that would be best. He would let them know if anything changed. Wick left for the Czarneckas, still appearing worried about his little sister. Dan returned to the bathroom to attend to Mae.

"I want you two on your best behavior," Dan lectured Harvey and Pearl. The pets obediently looked up at Dan, Harvey barking and Pearl meowing as if they understood.

Dan opened the bathroom door. Harvey and Pearl rushed in. The two appeared to be taking a physical inventory of Mae rather than jockeying for attention, as they normally would. Harvey laid his head in Mae's lap and Pearl leapt atop the toilet tank. Pearl sat and rubbed her cheek against Mae. Mae returned the gesture. Mae stopped rocking and rubbing her stomach, petting Harvey instead.

"How are you feeling, honey?" Dan asked after Mae took a couple of healthy drinks from the glass of water her father had fetched from the kitchen.

The Blufords did not buy bottled water, out of respect for the environment. Their home was equipped with an excellent water filtration system, engineered by Dan's company Single Organism, that served them well.

"Better," Mae replied.

"Good." Dan noted that while Mae was momentarily looking better, he was not convinced that whatever illness she was experiencing had subsided. Dan telephoned Mae's pediatrician. She advised Dan to bring Mae to the hospital right away.

Dan made certain Mae was feeling healthy enough to travel—meaning Mae was not experiencing any inclination to vomit or any other condition that might require her to make immediate use of the toilet.

"Ready for a road trip?" Dan asked Mae.

Mae, Harvey, and Pearl stared at Dan as if they had no idea what he meant.

"You two behave yourselves while we're gone," Dan commanded Harvey and Pearl as he turned to face them at the front door. Their pets stopped walking with Dan and Mae, looking up at Dan, then at each other, then back at Dan as if to say: *don't we always?*

For the most part, The Odd Couple were well behaved. Their destruction of property days were mostly behind them. Obedient, they still possessed enough of a mischievous streak to keep the family on their toes.

Mae kissed Harvey and Pearl on top of their heads, her breath the minty smell of the mouthwash she used to wash away the "gross taste in her mouth."

"Listen to Daddy," Mae warned, wagging her finger at her captive audience. Harvey barked. Pearl meowed, resting on their haunches as they watched father and daughter leave before setting off together to roam the house in search of adventure.

CHAPTER 2

"It appears that Mae has already purged most of the toxins out of her system," Dr. Arella Elkin, Mae's pediatrician, said to Dan out of earshot of Mae after her physical exam.

Dr. Arella Elkin and Dan's wife, Toni, had been friends since medical school. Over the years, Arella and Dan had become friends, as well. Dr. Elkin and Toni were also colleagues. Both Toni and Arella specialized in family and emergency medicine and anesthesiology. Arella also specialized in pediatrics and dermatology, while Toni had additional specialties in cardiology and pulmonary critical care.

They had done their residencies together at McCune General Hospital, where Dan had taken Mae. It was a state-of-the art hospital that encompassed an entire city block and provided five-star care.

The good friends were offered full-time staff positions at McCune upon completion of their residences: Arella as a pediatrician; Toni as a cardiologist—full-time positions they had held just outside of seven years.

During her exam, Mae confessed to eating some leftover moo shu pork, one of her favorite foods. She sat on the examination table nervously looking around, her fawn-brown eyes avoiding eye contact with the doctor and her father. Her arms were wrapped around her waist, as if readying herself for another tidal wave of purging. She appeared more embarrassed, now, than ill.

Diarrhea had seized Mae shortly after they arrived at the hospital. Her vomiting had turned into dry heaves. Dan's usually-energetic child appeared spent and pale.

"Then it was food poisoning," Dan said to Arella.

"Yes. Be sure she gets bed rest, drinks plenty of high electrolyte fluids such as sports drinks, and that she only eats easily digestible foods: soups, bananas, oatmeal, and such, for the next few days. Avoid milk and milk byproducts.

"Keep a close eye on her. Make sure her fever doesn't return. If her condition does not improve within the next couple of days, bring her back and we'll take a closer look."

Arella and Dan walked over to Mae with sympathetic faces.

"Sweetie, you're going to be okay," Dr. Elkin said in a convincing voice, lightly cupping Mae's cheek and then doing the same to her shoulders.

Arella turned to Dan and said, in a professional tone, "Call me if you need anything, day or night."

"Thanks, Arella."

"You're welcome. Take care, Mae—and no more eating leftovers without checking with your parents. Got it?"

Mae weakly nodded.

"Alright." Arella gave Dan a reassuring smile as she patted his chest before she left, causing his wrinkled forehead to relax.

"Ready?" Dan asked Mae. Mae looked up at her father and nodded more vigorously than Dan expected. Dan hoisted his daughter from the exam table and settled her onto one arm as easily as if Mae were still an infant. Mae wrapped her spindly arms around her father's thick neck, resting her head on his broad shoulder.

Dan would have traded places with his daughter, if he could. He'd have suffered any medical malady to rescue Mae from what had moved from pain to discomfort. Dan knew, as every parent comes to understand, that life does not work in that manner. Parents learn to navigate through their children's suffering like potholes on an often-pitch-black road.

Mae fell asleep on the drive home. Dan thought of Toni. He decided to wait until they spoke, tonight, to tell her about Mae. He'd assure Toni everything was under control and that there would be no need for her to cut short her conference and rush home. He hoped Toni did not talk to Arella before him.

Would Toni have taken Mae to the hospital, or would she have diagnosed the problem and treated their daughter at home? Dan thought. He felt certain Toni would have diagnosed and treated Mae at home. Again: he was not an MD, and was not about to take chances with their daughter's health.

Dan carried Mae into the house still asleep. Harvey and Pearl enthusiastically greeted them, but not making a sound, as if sensing that Mae needed her rest.

Dan hated to wake Mae, but knew she needed to hydrate. He coaxed his daughter into drinking as much water and sports drink as she could stomach. He checked her temperature with both the back of his hand and a digital thermometer that he cleaned with cold water and alcohol, as Toni had instructed him in the past. Just a little high of normal.

Mae's resiliency amazed him. The last time Dan had food poisoning, it took him almost a week to fully recover. Dan carried Mae to her bedroom, her arms and legs draped loosely about him and her head quietly resting on his chest.

He helped Mae slip out of her clothes and into her pajamas. Every movement seemed to exhaust her.

Dan managed to put on a brave face. Giving Mae a reassuring smile, he tucked her in. It appeared to work. Mae smiled back at him before she drifted off. Harvey camped out in Mae's room while Pearl followed Dan.

His daughter was sound asleep when Dan returned to place lidded tumblers (with straws) of sports drink and water on her nightstand. He watched Mae while he petted Harvey. Pearl observed the entire scene from the foot of Mae's bed.

His daughter appeared at peace. It eased his concerns a bit, but not totally. Dan left Mae's bedroom door open. He seriously considered putting one of their old baby monitors in her room, but knew Mae would be furious if she woke and found it there. Instead, Dan opted to move his laptop from his office into the living room near the foot of the stairs so that he could hear his baby more easily if she called.

Dan knew that Mae liked bananas and most soups, but she hated oatmeal. He made a list of Mae's favorite foods—excluding moo shu pork, of course. He picked from the list those that were easily digestible, then did a search of the kitchen to see what they had in stock.

After disposing of any takeout leftovers in the refrigerator, Dan realized he would need more of everything on that list, including sports drinks. He put in an online order to his local market to have them delivered.

Dan had phoned his executive assistant from the hospital to inform him of his family emergency. Amiri Hayden was named after the famous American writer and activist Amiri Baraka (who his father was a huge fan of). Already in possession of the surname of the international renowned poet Robert Hayden, Amiri could not help but wade into the lake of creative prose. Not possessing the talents of his namesakes and holding a Masters in English, he saw himself having two options: immerse himself in academia, or explore opportunities in the private sector.

Putting his enormous organizational skills to good use, Amiri found work as an executive assistant. These jobs paid better and were a lot less stressful than teaching. He hopped from one higher-paying job to another until finally landing at Single Organism, where he was paid top dollar for his considerable talents.

The atmosphere suited Amiri, as well. Single Organism felt more like a community rather than a business. The people at Single Organism really liked each other. They worked hard and enjoyed what they were doing. They were committed to their mission statement; part of which read, "Better environment through industry." Even their squabbles were handled like family affairs, through counseling rather than edicts or demands.

Amiri liked being a part of that community even if the intricacies of science and engineering were lost on him. He made no secret that he continued to write poetry, screenplays, and fiction in his free time, which most of his colleagues found equally impressive.

Dan later followed up with Amiri to notify him that he would be working from home for at least the next couple of days in order to keep a close eye on Mae.

Dan wasn't expecting this new development to be a problem. Every office worker at Single Organism, company-wide, worked from home at least fifty percent of the time. Amiri assured Dan that he would take care of everything. Dan knew that he would. Amiri was the most efficient person he knew. Amiri wished Mae a speedy recovery and prompted Dan not to worry.

The groceries arrived within the hour. Dan put everything away and started planning Mae's meals for the next couple of days. He had ordered clear vegetable broths that he would season with fresh herbs in order to start Mae on retrieving her appetite.

Dan had texted Arella to asked if it would be okay for him to give Mae a daily children's vitamin for the next few days until Mae regained her appetite. It was something they did not keep on hand, as he and Toni believed that nothing took the place of a healthy, nutritional diet. Arella said it couldn't hurt, then recommended a couple of brands.

Dan heard Mae in the upstairs hall about two hours later. He looked up to see his daughter walking toward the upstairs bathroom with Harvey by her side. Pearl darted up the stairs from nowhere to add to Mae's escort, having roamed the house after getting bored with Dan ignoring her.

"Up already!" said Dan, surprised to see his daughter walking about.

"I need to use the bathroom," Mae responded, as if walking in her sleep.

Dan went upstairs and waited in the hall with Harvey and Pearl. He listened. Mae would call if she needed him. He heard the toilet flush, then the sounds of Mae washing her hands. His daughter emerged, looking weary, but color was already returning to her face.

"You okay?" he asked.

"Better." Mae sounded exhausted.

The result of a hale body purging itself, Dan thought.

"Can I get you anything, Pumpkin?"

"No thanks, Dad. I'm going back to bed."

Dan, Harvey, and Pearl escorted his sleepwalking daughter back to her room, where Dan again tucked her in. It was an act he took great pleasure because, unlike her brother, Mae had not outgrown it.

"Sleep tight, Precious," Dan said, kissing Mae gently on her cooled forehead.

"Good night, Daddy," Mae yawned from her dreams.

CHAPTER 3

Mae was sound asleep in her room. Dan was in the living room, working on a research proposal on the effect of zero gravity on agriculture. Pearl wondered off, occasioning a visit with Dan for a moment's attention. Harvey took quick breaks from guard duty for food, water, and to use the outdoor dog potty.

"*Where is she?*" Wick said bursting through the front door as if his pants were on fire. Dan stopped working and turned his head to eye Wick. Pearl came out of nowhere to greet him and Harvey bolted downstairs to do the same. Wick waded past them on his way to his father.

"Keep it down, son. By 'she,' I assume you're referring to your sister."

"Of course."

"Mae's asleep in her room, and don't wake her. She needs her rest."

"Is Mae okay?"

"She's fine," said Dan, returning to work on his proposal. "In a few days, she'll be back to normal."

"That's good." Wick plopped down beside Dan on the living room couch, not bothering to unsaddle his anime backpack. He petted Harvey and placed Pearl in his lap. Harvey returned to Mae after a minute of attention. "What's wrong with Mae?"

"Food poisoning."

"*How?*"

"Mae got her hands on some bad leftovers?"

"Knucklehead," Wick said, shaking his head.

"I'm sure Mae would agree with you, right now. How was school today?" Dan asked, dividing his attention between Wick and his proposal.

"Fine."

"Did you present your science project?"

"Sure did! Nailed it! Got an A!"

"That's great, son!" Dan stopped what he was doing to give Wick a high-five. "Congratulations!"

"Thanks." Dan noticed that Wick kept glancing upstairs toward Mae's room.

"You can look in on Mae, but don't wake her. Put your phone on vibrate."

Wick bounded up the stairs two at a time with Pearl matching pace as he changed his ringtone to vibrate. Dan returned his attention to his proposal while keeping an ear out for any sounds coming from Mae's room.

A few minutes later, Wick sauntered downstairs, appearing relieved about Mae and carrying and petting Pearl after depositing his backpack in his room.

"Mae looks funny."

"It may take a couple of days for Mae to get her color back."

"But she's going to be okay?"

"Yep. Did you know your sister had gotten her hands on some leftover moo shu pork?"

"I went into the kitchen last night for some juice and saw Mae eating at the table."

Dan gave Wick his full attention. "And you didn't say anything?"

"Why would I?"

"Didn't that seem strange to you?"

"Mae eating at the kitchen table—what's so strange about that? We all do it."

"I mean, seeing your sister eating food that old?"

"I didn't notice what Mae was eating. Guess I was distracted. I was in the middle of reviewing my history notes for today's quiz. I assumed you'd heated it up for her."

"I didn't."

"*Whoa*—how was I to know Mae would go rogue over some moo shu pork? She's the only one in the house that likes that stuff."

"Where was I?" Dan asked.

"On a conference call in your office. You had the door closed with the 'Do Not Disturb' sign hung on the doorknob."

Dan remembered. He was hosting a virtual international kickoff meeting with his research lab partners in Brisbane, Lagos, Tokyo, Paris, Stockholm, Berlin, Vancouver, London, Mexico City, and Seoul to discuss what projects they were going to focus on in the coming year.

Dan knew Toni was not going to like hearing about how Mae became ill on his watch. There was no sense trying to finagle his way out of it. He was going to tell Toni straight out how it happened, and suffer her wrath. Mae wasn't the only one who was going to learn a lesson from her food poisoning.

"Dad, you want to play some ball?"

Wick meant tennis. They had a tennis court out back. For some reason, Wick used the term "ball" to refer to both tennis and basketball, in their home. Perhaps it was because Wick had wanted a basketball court. It was his way of reminding Dan of that fact.

"Not while your sister's sleeping. It might wake her."

"What about Roll Call?"

Roll Call was a video series of first-person shooter war games. Toni and Dan disliked violent games. They aspired to the thinking that violent games made children more aggressive. They controlled what video games Wick played, and for how long, at home. They discovered Wick had been playing online war games at his friends based on conversation snippets they overheard. How other parents chose to raise their children was their prerogative, he and Toni declared. They would not concede.

"You mean, the war game you're supposed to be eighteen to play."

"Yeah, I know. I'm just messing with you, Dad."

More like rubbing it in, Dan thought. "Is your homework done?" Dan said, returning to his proposal.

"I still have a little math and an English paper to get started. Other than that, I'm good."

"What are you doing your English assignment on?"

"Don't know yet. We've been given options. Choose something from a list of topics the teacher handed out, or one of our own that meets with the teacher's approval."

"Let me know if you need any help."

"On math or English?"

"Either one."

"Will do. I'm hungry. What's for dinner?"

"Salmon."

"And?"

Dan had to laugh. "What do you mean, 'and'?"

"You know I love salmon, Dad. But I'm not always crazy about the side dishes."

"Asparagus."

Wick made a face as if he had just bitten into a lemon.

"I know you don't like asparagus, but it's good for you."

"Why is it that some foods that are good for you taste so bad?"

"Could be worse."

"How?"

"Could be okra."

"Now you're just trying to gross me out."

"Eat your veggies and you get dessert."

"What's for desert?"

"Chocolate cake."

"Now you're talking! Is Mae going to join us?"

"We'll see. If she does, Mae won't be able to eat what we're having."

Wick nodded. Dan knew that Wick understood what he was getting at, but he decided to elaborate nonetheless. "Mae is going to be on a strict liquid and soft food diet until her system is cleared of the bad food she ate."

"Gotcha."

Wick's phone vibrated. Under normal settings, Wick's phone chirped when he received a text message and dinged when he had an email. It played ever-changing music when he had a call. This vibration signaled he had a text.

"Donny wants me to come over."

"To play video games?" Dan asked.

"Doesn't say." Wick texted Donny. Vibration. "He wants to play basketball."

It was a nice day. Most homes in their neighborhood had backyard basketball courts, tennis courts, or built-in swimming pools. Dan had no problem with Donny or his parents. The Underhills were good people as far as he was concerned.

Donny was a good kid. He was Wick's age, and one of his closest friends. Dan's primary concern was that Donny's parents did not regulate their children's play of video games as strictly as he and Toni.

Donny was a war games aficionado—not something to be proud of, in Dan's opinion. Video game rating systems were their go-to prevention excuse barring their children from playing blood-soaked, gory, and at times immoral video games that they did not agree with.

Kevin and Janet Underhill did not regulate or monitor their children's play, as they discovered while at a backyard barbeque at the Underhill home.

Donny, Wick, and a few other children their age had slipped off to the game room. Dan happened to pass by on his way from the bathroom. He peeked in to discover Wick and Donny in an intense competition over a game Dan did not recognize. There was a good deal of gore and blood, and even some nudity.

Dan rushed in and stopped what they were doing. He checked the game rating. M18+. None of the children in that room was old enough to play. Dan marched the disgruntled children out of the game room after shutting the online game down.

The Underhills shrugged it off when Dan quietly mentioned to Donny's parents what they were doing. They believed the games did children no harm, and considered the video game rating system only a suggestion, not the law.

Janet and Kevin confessed to playing them with their children. They were convinced it was an innocuous way for people (not only children) to exorcise their aggressions.

Dan knew that there were studies that presented strong arguments for both camps. He and Toni were not anti-video or interactive gaming. They also participated in those types of entertainment with their children. Their concern was content.

They agreed with the Underhills that video game age restrictions were not legally enforceable, but he and Toni made it clear that they did not condone that thinking when it came to their children. They did not permit Wick and Mae to play those games.

The Underhills accepted their concerns, agreeing to keep Wick and Mae away from such video games when they were in their home.

One of a number of characteristics Donny and Wick shared was they could be annoyingly clever when it came to circumventing adult authority and oversight in order to play those forbidden video games.

Basketball could be a ruse. Dan and Toni knew they could not monitor their children twenty-four/seven. Wick would have to make his own choices. If he decided to do like so many of his peers by playing those disturbing games, Toni and he could only voice their displeasure, explaining to Wick why they felt those games could have a detrimental effect on his development.

Of course, not in those words. It would be Wick's choice whether to heed their advice. Dan's hope was that basketball was all Wick and Donny played—if they played basketball at all. After Wick promised he would finish his homework right after dinner, Dan let him go.

"Dinner won't be ready for another couple of hours," Dan said. "Get an apple and banana before you leave. Don't eat any junk food while you're over there. It'll spoil your dinner."

"Heaven forbid I won't have room for asparagus."

"Ha, ha, funny guy. No room for asparagus, no room for cake."

Wick headed for the kitchen, still lavishing Pearl with attention. "You want anything, Dad?"

"I'm good, son. Thanks."

*   *   *

Dan's phone vibrated a few minutes after Wick left. He checked the caller ID.

"Hey, baby, how's the conference going?" Dan asked Toni.

"Mixed reviews," Toni said in her velvety soprano. "Some of it is stimulating, introducing new and exciting advancements. Some is boring, for lack of a better word. I'd say it's a winner, overall."

"Sounds typical of most conferences."

"I'll give you the highs and lows when I see you."

"Miss you, sweetheart."

"Not half as much as I miss you, Teddy Bear." Toni came up with that pet name for Dan when they were dating. It best described his cuddle factor, according to Toni.

Dan couldn't agree more. Dan was still working on a similar affection. Aside from his usual terms of endearment for his wife, her name Toni summarized the same fondness for him.

"Next time, you should come."

"You've never invited me."

"Consider this my official invitation."

"Next time, I will accompany you, Mrs. Bluford."

"Promise?"

"Promise."

"How are things at home? Are our kids behaving themselves while Mom's away?"

"About our children..." Dan paused to gather his thoughts.

"Oh no, what's Wick done now?"

"It's not Wick."

"Mae? What's going on, Dan?"

Dan hesitated, searching for the right way to tell Toni and shoring himself up for what was to come. "Mae has food poisoning." He sounded like a detached reporter stating the obvious.

"Is she alright?"

"She's going to be fine."

"How'd it happen?"

Dan let out a heavy sigh, then explained to Toni how Mae had contracted her illness. Toni burst out laughing, to his surprise.

"Poor baby," Toni said when her laughter died down.

"What's so funny about our daughter being sick?"

"That's your daughter."

"Why is it, when she does something bad, she's *my* daughter? When she does something good, she's *yours*."

"It's very simple, darling. Our children get the good genes from me and the bad ones from you."

"Well, honey, regardless of your totally illogical and scientifically implausible assertion, Mae's recovering well."

"Good," Toni said, sounding like a physician who had just received a favorable diagnosis for one of her patients.

"No lecture on how I should be keeping a closer eye on our children, or threats that you'll take the next flight home?"

"A lecture—as you put it, darling—does not appear necessary. How Mae got food poisoning probably would have happened had I been there or not. You underestimate your daughter's cunning."

"I won't, after this."

"Sure you will. Mae has you wrapped around her little finger."

Dan laughed. He knew what Toni said was true.

"Sounds like you've beaten yourself up enough about Mae already, Dan. As far as cutting my conference stay short, no need. You've got it covered."

"Thanks for the vote of confidence," Dan said, surprised at Toni's calm reaction.

"Let me talk to Mae."

"She's sleeping right now."

"Poor baby," Toni repeated with the same genuine sympathy. "What about Wick?"

"He's over at Donny's."

"Not playing any of those vile video games, I hope."

"We can only hope." Dan heard someone mention to Toni that the 3D transplant demonstration was about to begin.

"I've got to go. Call me when both our children are available. I at least want to wish them goodnight."

"Will do, sweetheart."

"I love you, Dan. Don't worry about Mae. She's going to be fine."

"Love you, too, Toni. Be good."

"I'm only bad with you, Teddy Bear," Toni growled before she hung up.

Dan went upstairs to check on Mae. Harvey greeted him and Pearl sauntered in. His precious little daughter was sound asleep, clutching her stuffed rainbow colored unicorn to her chest that, at some point, she must have retrieved from her bookshelf collection of stuffed animals. Her face was serene; her breathing relaxed. Dan was finally able to relax, as well.

CHAPTER 4

Mae was feeling better. It was Friday, the day after her food poisoning episode. Mae staying home from school was a no-brainer, to Dan. The extra day and the weekend would help Mae regain her strength.

Mae and Dan saw Wick off to school, having made the same arrangements with the Czarneckas as the day before. Dan informed Amiri he would be taking a vacation day to remain home with his daughter during their chat.

Amiri suggested that Dan not use a vacation day, since his boss had compiled a mountain of sick leave and had not used a personal day in years. "Vacation days are precious," as Amiri put it.

Dan opted to take a personal day, instead. Amiri agreed, and placed his personal day information into the corporate calendar. Amiri rearranged Dan's packed schedule of internal and external meetings, internal project consultations, and reviews, blocking out time for Dan to write progress reports on ongoing projects and proposals.

The girth of Dan's work had become managerial and marketing since his promotion to Director of Polar City Research Lab Facilities. Overseeing everyone and everything in his division through various research projects in different stages of development, his time was not his own.

Gratifying as it was to be part of the bigger picture, Dan missed doing actual research—running his fingers through the soil of discovery, so to speak.

Roger Shell and Michelle Tinder, the newest research scientist and geoengineer to join their research teams, were attempting to introduce a couple of items into Dan's busy schedule that, according to them, required his immediate attention. They were reports on research projects requiring his review.

Roger and Michelle had graduated at top of their classes from John Hopkins and Penn State. They were accustomed to receiving special attention, and were also seeded with the impatience of youth. Project time frames were more suggestions than deadlines.

Single Organism understood that scientific discoveries and breakthroughs did not happen on a set schedule. Once a research project was underway, unforeseen developments often emerged that required an alteration to the original timeline.

Roger and Michelle's proclamations of urgency were not even lukewarm. Their reports were not pressing and their conclusions were not due for another month. Dan had seen this behavior with newbies on a few other occasions, personal ambition and ego usurping team objectives.

He speculated that Roger and Michelle were of a mindset that submitting their reports early would open doors for them to be presented with more interesting research. 'Spotlight projects', as some have come to call them: the type that would fast-track their careers (not to mention the brownie points they believed they would score along the way).

Roger was part of Jacinda Steward's team. Michelle was part of Wyrain Gamble's. Jacinda and Wyrain were their research captains. Roger and Michelle were supposed to report their findings directly to their research captains. Jacinda and Wyrain would evaluate their conclusions and either confirm or discredit them, providing their crew with insight, guidance, and working knowledge as they progressed.

Jacinda and Wyrain were topnotch researchers, brilliant and intuitive. They were destined to head research facilities of their own, if they choose. Their research captains had earned their way into their positions.

Dan disliked Michelle and Roger attempting an end run around their team leaders. The concept they had yet to grasp about Single Organism is 'thoroughness and accuracy; above all else, teamwork was cherished,' not speed or mavericks.

As Dan had so often said (and his colleagues agreed), "Single Organism is not an assembly line nor a corporate battlefield. We are a visionary research facility whose mission is to do all we can to contribute to our planet's health. Results achieving those goals are what we relish.

"Add respect to that cherished list, and those are the most relevant factors we consider when assigning research projects."

Dan would be forwarding Roger's report, unread, to Jacinda and Michelle's report to Wyrain.

"Amiri, pencil in meetings with Roger Shell and Michelle Tinder on Monday morning. I'd like to have a talk with them. Fifteen minutes each should do."

"Someone's being called into the principal's office."

"You know it."

Amiri shifted a couple of things around on Dan's schedule, confirmed Dan's coming workweek with him, and locked it in.

"Thanks for your help, Amiri."

"No problem, Dan. It *is* my job." It took a couple of months to convince Amiri to call Dan by his first name—not sir, boss, or Mr. Bluford.

"You do it well."

"Thank you. How's Mae?"

"Doing much better. Thanks for asking."

"Tell the little princess I said 'hi and get well soon.'" Amiri had met Dan's family, as they had met Amiri's live-in fiancée, Gianna, at one of the company's family outings. Their wedding was still five months out, but Dan received daily updates from Amiri about its progress. To hear Amiri tell it made Dan's wedding drama seem like a breeze.

"I will," Dan said to Amiri's request. "Have any plans for the weekend?"

"Gianna's folks have invited us up to their home for the weekend."

"Sounds like fun. How are you and Gianna's parents getting along?"

"Fantastic. They call her Ginny. She's their only child, so they're always ecstatic to see her. I get a kick out of how her parents fall into mommy and daddy mode, catering to their little girl's every whim."

"Sounds like Gianna's spoiled."

"You know it. I wouldn't have her any other way."

"I know what you mean." The two men laughed, compatriots in their complexity of indulged spouses.

Dan closed by telling Amiri that unless the facility was burning down or under attack, he did not want to be disturbed. Amiri said he would handle everything. Dan was confident that he would.

It was standard procedure for Pearson Academy to post class work assignments on the school's website. All classroom lectures were recorded and available online, as well. Wick and Mae had restricted laptops that allowed them to do school work and little else. Mae enjoyed school, both academically and socially.

Social was a forced hiatus. Dan felt that Mae's schoolwork could wait. The weekend would be soon enough to ease his daughter back into her homework routine.

Dan and Toni wanted to put off getting their children cell phones for as long as possible. They caved to Wick's relentless peer pressure argument of "Why am I the only one of my friends without a phone?" grievance, allowing Wick to get his first cell on his tenth birthday.

Wick's cell was inundated with parental controls that Dan and Toni spot-checked without warning to make certain they were still properly functioning. When their son complained about either the controls or their spot-checking, they threatened to take away his phone. That always quelled any further discussion on the matter. It also set the bar for what age and by what conditions Mae would receive her first phone.

Gina and Tina, a couple of Mae's friends and classmates, called Mae on Dan's phone. Both seven-year-old girls had their own phones. They were nice girls. Dan was not surprised to hear from them. All of the parents in Mae and Wick's grade had willingly exchanged phone numbers.

If they hung out with his daughter, that meant Gina and Tina were smart and resourceful young women. That wasn't boasting, to Dan— simply fact.

Dan speculated that the girls probably got his phone number from one of their parents. Dan didn't ask whether they asked for or lifted his number. The girls were checking to see if Mae was okay, and to ask if there was anything they could do to help.

Dan could not imagine what a couple of seven-year-olds could possibly do for a sick peer except tell an adult, but they sounded genuinely concerned. Dan assured Mae's friends that Mae was fine and allowed Mae to talk to them for a few minutes.

Hearing their voices uplifted Mae's spirits and reeled her closer to the exuberant young woman Dan was accustomed to seeing.

"Attention and affection from family are nice," his mother once told Dan when she had returned from a weekend outing with her girlfriends. "Family is supposed to love and care for you, especially in times of need. Being with people who show the same fondness with no familial ties warms a different place in your heart." Eavesdropping on Mae talking to her friends was evidence of that assertion, to Dan.

The Blufords did much together as a family. Wick and Dan shared sports (both playing and watching) and their passion for science. Toni and Dan made time for each other. Mae and Dan's one-on-one quality time together had fallen off since Mae started school.

Although brought about by unfortunate circumstances, Dan was determined that today would be their day. Even work would be put on hold.

Harvey and Pearl set off on quests for entertainment, having been ignored by Dan and Mae, whose attention was focused on each other.

Misery loves company, even when it comes to dining. Dan warmed up some vegetable broth, tossed in some parsley, cilantro, tarragon, sage, and thyme, and let it steep like tea, fishing the herbs out after a few minutes.

Dan reminded Mae about some of the house rules while he and Mae shared black lacquered Japanese soup bowls of the flavored broth.

"Did you microwave that moo shu pork by yourself?" Dan asked, creating a riff in their placid father and daughter moment.

"Don't remind me," Mae said, moving uneasily in her chair and looking squeamish.

"Did you?" Dan's tone was gentle but firm.

"Yes, Dad."

"You know you violated a couple of house rules," Dan said. Mae sipped her breakfast from a ramen spoon. Later, Mae could have a banana.

"I know," Mae said, managing to swallow a steaming spoonful of broth after repeatedly blowing on it to cool.

"What are they?" Dan asked.

"Huh?" Mae was playing dumb and Dan knew it.

"Which specific house rules did you violate, Mae?"

"Don't eat any leftovers without checking with you or Mom first," Mae said with a huff, as if speaking the words was exhausting.

"Right. When in doubt, check with us regarding leftovers. What's the second?"

"Don't use the microwave," Mae said in a *blah, blah, blah* tone. "Ask you or Mom if I need something heated up.

"Why does Wick get to use the microwave on his own and I don't?" Mae concluded with a perky jolt.

"You already know the answer to that question, Mae."

"Wick's older. Why couldn't I have been born first?" Mae was trying to change the subject. Dan's daughter was good at switching topics in her favor. It worked on Wick half of the time.

Dan was certain Mae successfully manipulated others, as well, judging by how often she employed the tactic. Dan sometimes wondered where that gift might lead Mae once she honed the craft and became more sophisticated in how she instituted her track shifts. If used wisely, anywhere Mae wanted to go, was his conclusion.

"Not only older, but what else?" Dan said.

"When I turn ten, I will be able to use the microwave on my own." Listening to Mae spell things out made Dan wonder. Why *was* ten the age of ascension for their children in their home?

"Or any kitchen appliance," Dan tacked on to Mae's response.

"I know, Dad."

If you knew, then why did you do it? Dan thought. He didn't press. Mae's illness had taught her those lessons—at least for the next couple of weeks, before illness amnesia set in.

"How did you even know how to use the microwave, Mae?"

"Dad, I have eyes. I've seen you, Mom, and Wick use it enough times to know how it works. Some friends my age use the microwave at their house all of the time. They showed me how to use theirs. Tina has one in her room. They have them in the school cafeteria. I use them at school all the time."

Mae's admission struck Dan like a revelation. Why hadn't he and Toni thought about microwave usage at school before? Makes the whole 'not using the microwave until ten' rule seem even sillier.

"The way things work at school and with your friends is a whole other matter. Honey, we have rules in place not to punish you, but to try to keep you safe so things like food poisoning won't happen."

"I'm sorry."

"Where did you even find that moo shu pork?"

"It was in the back of the fridge."

"We had that like three weeks ago," Dan said. "I can't believe we didn't dump it. It must have kept getting pushed toward the back of the fridge. Out of sight, out of mind."

"Not to me, it wasn't."

"Obviously," Dan said with a chuckle.

"It still looked good … and smelled okay," Mae said, sounding guilty and embarrassed.

"You're telling me three-week-old moo shu pork looked and smelled okay," Dan said in total disbelief.

"It might have looked and smelled a bit rank," Mae admitted.

"Why would you even bother, then?"

"It was moo shu pork, Dad. You don't just throw something like that away."

"Baby, any food that old is suspect," Dan said, sounding more reassuring than accusatory. "Again, when in doubt, check with me or your mother."

"I thought the microwave would kill anything bad."

"Microwaves don't actually kill harmful bacteria, honey. And they certainly don't make bad food good."

Dan considered giving Mae a lecture on the basic workings of a microwave oven, then thought better of it. Mae was smart. She would easily grasp the basic principle if she were interested. Dan had learned not to push his engineering or scientific knowledge onto his children. They would ask if they wanted his input. Mae let the subject drop.

"Sorry, Dad."

"Come here," said Dan. Mae slipped out of her chair and walked over to her father. Dan hoisted his daughter onto his lap and hugged her. Mae curled into a ball within his embrace. "Mae, you have nothing to be sorry about. We simply don't want you to get sick."

"Neither do I."

"Sounds like we're on the same page. How are you feeling?"

"Much better."

"Good." Mae's color had already returned.

They sat silently for a bit. Dan rocked Mae back and forth, tempted to sing her favorite lullaby, *Dreamland*. At least, it was her favorite when Mae was five. He wanted to soothe her troubles in the same way his mother used music to soothe him when Dan was Mae's age and was distressed about something paramount to a child.

"Any news from outer space?" Mae asked. The question made Dan laugh.

"Nothing last I checked. Want to go see if anything's changed?"

"Yeah!"

"Let's finish our breakfast and we'll check it out."

Mae bounced down from Dan's lap, plopped back into her seat, and began slurping down her broth, which had cooled.

"Mae," Dan said, giving her his best parental warning face, "sip, no slurping. Take your time. If the aliens have waited this long to contact us, then they can wait another few minutes."

"Sorry, Dad," Mae said with a giggle. His daughter knew exactly what Dan was doing. The sparkle in her eyes returned. Dan slurped down his next spoonful of broth, inhaling it as if drinking the last of his broth through a straw. Mae burst into an uncontrollable laugh.

"Dad, sip—no slurping!" Mae said, still giggling. Dan slurped down another spoonful of broth. Mae followed, doing the same. The battle for who could slurp the loudest had begun. Belching did not count. Without Toni there to reel in her husband and daughter's juvenile behavior, they slurped down their broth to the last spoonful.

CHAPTER 5

Omari Bluford is Dan's cousin. They are the same age, born one day apart—something the family still considers a big deal. They were raised in different parts of the United States: Dan in Connecticut and Omari in Georgia. The two still managed to build a relationship by phone and post, hanging out at the yearly family gatherings. Cell phones aided in strengthening their relationship as good friends.

Omari's father, Gordon, is Dan's paternal uncle and the CEO of Bluford Real Estate. Omari is a member of the board and is their top real estate agent.

Gordon Bluford built a real estate empire began by Grandpa Bluford after the Second World War. It involved commercial and residential properties. Bluford Real Estate established a reputation for quality and honesty, and that became their trademark.

Dan learned at their yearly family reunion that Omari had purchased twelve acres of land in his neck of the woods on behalf of Bluford Real Estate. It was an area that had been owned by a combination of banks and county, and consisted mostly of abandoned farmlands and open fields. While the property itself was being optioned at pennies on the dollar, the extensive cost of real estate development kept investors and buyers away.

Bluford Real Estate divided their purchase into 100 equal parcels. The Bluford family was given first consideration when feeling out the market for buyers.

Dan and Toni were doing well financially. Toni was pregnant with Mae. They were looking to move out of their two-bedroom bungalow into a bigger house.

Omari had a vision. His ideal was rather than to stock the property with cookie-cutter suburban homes. Bluford would grant each lot owner freedom to realize their own vision. Omari even had a name for the community: Golden Meadows.

No other family members showed interest, at the time, due to financial constraints or being comfortable where they were. Dan and Toni were the only ones who took Omari up on his offer.

His cousin let them in on the ground floor on the cheap. Omari sold them their lot for one thousand dollars over total cost—much less than everyone else paid. It was a secret Dan and Toni intended to take to their graves.

Golden Meadows became a reality, better than Omari had imagined. Within a few months of being placed on the market, 76 of the 100 lots were sold. It turned out that modern home buyers were drawn more to diversity and individuality than conformity.

Each lot was sold with a proviso that only residential housing would be built, as agreed upon by the county. Bluford added a clause that construction would have to begin within a specific time frame from purchase. The purchaser would be obligated to sell back the parcel to Bluford Real Estate at half the cost if the owner failed to meet that stipulation. That condition inhibited procrastination or poor planning.

Dan and Toni built their contemporary, two-story, 3,000 square foot home using Bluford Real Estate connections in every aspect of design and construction. Some of those connections happened to be family, as well. Mae was one when their dream home was completed. They moved into their new home, chock full of modern conveniences, in time to celebrate Wick's fourth birthday.

Dan believed in intelligent extraterrestrial life. He began pursuing his belief when in the third grade after being introduced to the Star Trek television series franchise. He had watched other alien-based television shows such as Babylon 5, Sliders, Andromeda, and The X-Files. Dan enjoyed them, especially The X-Files; Star Trek, The Next Generation; Deep Space Nine; Voyager; and Enterprise.

Something about that television franchise grabbed him—how they often presented advanced alien life forms and humans as peaceful explorers of space. "Seeking out new life...," proclaimed the opening mantra. There were often conflicts in a constant thrum of combat (albeit for justice or survival).

It was the alien life forms they encountered that Dan found most fascinating—the moments of diplomatic interaction when honest efforts were exerted and amity was achieved between different species.

Dan believed in diplomacy and cooperation, not dominance and war. The Star Trek television series contained ample moments that reinforced his beliefs. Beings could communicate with one another no matter the differences; could share in a universal council or government. The possibilities seemed endless.

Back in high school, Dan was president of First Contact, a science club sponsored by his science teacher, Mr. Atuegbu (who, ironically, did not believe in extraterrestrials). First Contact followed the siren belief that there existed intelligent alien civilizations.

It consisted of a band of like-minded misfits—an odd mesh of geeks, nerds, popular kids, stoners, and jocks. Dan was a straight-A student and a budding track and tennis star. That gave him firm footing in the nerd and jock camps.

They diligently scanned the heavens with their telescopes, combing the airways with their radio transceivers in desperate search of signs to support their verdant claims of extraterrestrial life. Considered crackpots by most, they were subject to verbal and occasional physical harassment by non-believers.

Dan learned early on to keep close to his vest their club's activities. By the middle of his sophomore year, they weren't even an afterthought in the minds of their most ardent persecutors.

First Contact was unable to manufacture any concrete evidence that lent credence to their extraterrestrial claims during their entire four-year term. Whatever celestial proof or theories the group presented to Mr. Atuegbu, their cynical science teacher dismantled with solid facts and plausible models anchored in real world knowledge which, the group began to suspect, was Mr. Atuegbu's objective—to get their heads out of the clouds and root their toes into scientific approaches of discovery.

Dan would have to say, in retrospect, that if that were Mr. Atuegbu's overall plan, it worked. Their thinking became more pragmatic. Their methods stemmed more from discernable thought to substantiate their suppositions. Deductive reasoning took center stage within the group.

First Contact internally weighed what they encountered against credible theories and scientific facts before presenting their findings to Mr. Atuegbu. Even amongst themselves, their debates—for they never argued—became more analytical and refined. Bottom line is: they had fun. They learned a lot about science, their planet, and the galaxy in the process.

A few members of their club followed science fiction as if it were a religion. Dan did not go that far. The existence of extraterrestrial life was a foregone conclusion yet to be proven, to him. While Dan pursued irrefutable evidence of such life, he did not obsess over its discovery. It would happen when it happened, was his attitude. Dan did not feel the need to hammer home that point.

His parents had no issues with his alien pursuits, although they did not share his views. Looking back, Dan could see why they did not object. Applying his energies toward his studies, First Contact, and sports left him only enough free time for a social life centered on his close friends, girlfriend, and family, leaving no time for mischief.

First Contact disbanded after high school. They gave up their extraterrestrial pursuits and planted their feet firmly on terra firma with their eyes fastened on their futures. Dan remembered that there was not a dry eye at their members-only Aloha Party, with Mr. Atuegbu as their special guest.

It had struck him only recently for what Dan recalled as his first time, as is often the case when one of life's worthwhile experiences comes to what feels like an abrupt end.

They were more than like-minded misfits indulging in a shared passion. They had grown to genuinely like and care about one another. First Contact had morphed into a family. Dan believed they were not saying goodbye—they were merely transitioning into another phase in their lives, which was why he called what many would have termed a farewell party, Aloha. Goodbye until they met again.

Members of First Contact have stayed in touch over the years. Through highs and lows, achievements and losses, their bonds have endured. Members embarked on a variety of careers ranging from sporting-goods manufacturer to NASA scientist.

When Mae was four, Wendy, their NASA scientist (as they took pride in calling her), sent Dan two great birthday presents, one of which was Neil DeGrasse Tyson's video lecture on 'The Unknown Universe.'

Wendy no longer believed intelligent alien life existed in their Milky Way galaxy. To be honest, Dan had not given the topic much thought since their high school days. Listening to Professor Tyson's brilliant depiction of scientific understanding on the mysteries of the universe was not only educational and insightful but also very convincing.

The second of Wendy's gifts was best summarized by a partial quote from her birthday card inscription, "A blast from the past. When we believed anything was possible." It was the amazing PBS series *Cosmos*, hosted by the indomitable Carl Sagan, dressed in his trademark turtleneck or corduroy jacket. His voice was mesmerizing, measured, and effective as he served up complex scientific facts and well-drawn hypotheses as sumptuous dishes of a momentous galactic feast.

For some unknown reason, the combination of those two amazing documentaries rekindled Dan's fascination with the universe, reigniting his conviction that intelligent life existed within the galaxy.

Wick and his mom were firmly in DeGrasse's camp. Mae and Dan accepted DeGrasse's facts, but leaned more toward Sagan's possibilities. Mae was a future First Contact president if there ever was one, in Dan's opinion (although he was confident Mae would come up with a cooler name).

The Bluford basement is a spacious and well-lit rectangle. A straight wooden staircase descends at its middle to an engineered oak herringbone floor. Along the east wall off to the right is a game room complete with a kitchenette. Sectioned off to the left by interlocking blueberry rubber floor tiles is a complete home gym. Further left, along the west wall, is an enclosed bathroom complete with shower and dressing room. Hooking in behind the exercise area is an open laundry, also sectioned off by interlocking blueberry rubber floor tiles.

Beside the laundry behind the stairs is an open area used for temporary storage. It is also where the astronomical telescope is housed, used individually and collectively by the family to gaze at the heavens. It's a top-of-the-line catadioptric telescope—a far cry from the affordable reflector telescope Dan had in high school. It was a Christmas gift from Max, former First Contact member and current family friend (now full-time economist and part-time stargazer).

Max still believed there was intelligent alien life within the universe, waiting to be discovered. Happily married with a son, his intergalactic pursuits had dwindled from fervent to mild curiosity.

Dan piggybacked Mae down the stairs, her arms hugging his neck and her skin scented from cocoa butter.

Mae was grinning and gloating from having won their slurping contest. Dan had thrown the contest, which wasn't easy. He knew Mae liked to win. His daughter took offense when she knew she was being handed a victory.

"A hollow victory" is a phrase Mae has actually used to describe such an event. Charitable conquests make Mae irritable. They rankle her competitive spirit.

Normal parents want to instill confidence in their children. Dan has a soft spot for Mae, falling into the typical father-daughter relationship in that regard. Toni has repeatedly warned him against taking it easy on their daughter. "In order to prepare Mae for the outside world, sometimes we need to be tough." That advice ping-ponged back and forth between Toni and himself, who had an equal soft spot for Wick.

Dan would have given it his best had it not been for Mae's recent illness. He believed most parents would have leaned toward compassion under the same circumstances, even if it manifested itself in allowing their child to triumph in a silly slurping contest.

Straight-ahead due north at the bottom of the stairs was First Contact, a 12x14 rustic wood-paneled room furnished with a six-foot rectangular metal conference table, two high-back ergonomic desk chairs, and a state-of-the-art radio transceiver and affiliated equipment. The alder arched glass door with "First Contact" etched in the glass was rarely closed and never locked. Dan built First Contact inspired by Wendy's insightful gifts.

His free time was scarce. Dan spent the majority of it with family and friends. On rare occasions, he got lost wearing the noise canceling headphones, combing the airways for signs of extraterrestrial life.

Any member of the family was welcomed to use First Contact. They all had been instructed on how the radio transceiver worked and what to listen for over the airways. Toni and Wick were curious about the equipment, but little else. Mae absorbed everything like a sponge. Dan would find his daughter engrossed at least a couple of times a week, listening intently with her pink glowing cat ears through noise canceling headphones (the adult headphones were too large for Mae to position the ear cups properly on her small head).

Sometimes he would join her. Other times, Dan would leave her to her own devices. He knew Mae would ask, if she had any questions. Dan wasn't concerned about anything being broken or thrown out of kilter. Anything broken could be replaced or repaired, was his view. Whatever settings became skewed could be righted. What knowledge Mae gained from her experience was priceless.

As Dan had said before, "I'm a believer who is not obsessive. First contact will happen when it happens."

Dan gently placed Mae on the basement floor. Mae took his hand and led Dan into First Contact. Claiming the captain's chair, even though the two chairs were identical, Dan settled in next to his daughter. They decided to put the transceiver on speaker so they didn't have to use their headphones. Dan let Mae take command of the transceiver controls with only occasional advice or instruction here and there. They broke off to eat after a couple of hours of white noise.

Mae asked if she could have a burrito. Dan took that as a good sign. Her appetite was returning, albeit prematurely. Unless exposed to the food that made you ill in the first place, your mind could dismiss all other possible food contaminant threats, Dan reasoned. Dan would have to check his theory with Toni.

Dan explained to Mae how her stomach was not ready for solid foods like a burrito—how her body was still clearing out toxins (the bad stuff) out of her system. That did not stop Mae from making other suggestions like pizza or chicken or even a green salad, all of which were a negative.

They dined on carrot soup and saltines smeared with organic peanut butter. Mae sipped on unsweetened coconut water—a more natural alternative to replenishing electrolytes as suggested by her mom which, to his surprise, his daughter liked.

The rest of the day was spent reading stories to each other, playing cards, board, and video games, watching an animated Disney movie, talking to Toni on speakerphone, and laughing and being silly as often as they could.

Spending a day with his daughter was amazing. There was a time early in their careers when Toni and Dan set aside one day out of the month dedicated exclusively to Wick or Mae. They would do whatever their children wanted (within reason, of course). Dan made a heartfelt mental note to talk to Toni about resurrecting that tradition rather than waiting for an unfortunate event such as illness to force the issue, as was often the case in their hectic lives.

Although Mae appeared to be her old self, Dan kept a close eye on her, looking for signs of a food poisoning resurrection. Mae dozed off during the animated Disney film, fatigue having set in. His daughter agreed to take a nap only after Dan promised to wake her in an hour. He kept his promise.

Dan gave into a lurking guilt and snuck in a little work during Mae's naptime. Wick was home from school before they knew it. Mae abandoned her old man to hang out with her big brother. Dan returned to First Contact rather than diving back into work.

CHAPTER 6

Dan had wanted to pick up Toni from the airport, as he typically did. Toni insisted that he not, this time, knowing that Dan would bring the children along. Toni did not want Mae out until she was certain her daughter was up to an excursion.

Even though Wick was ten and was perfectly capable of looking after himself and his sister for a few hours, Toni still preferred not to leave them alone.

Placing them in the care of a trusted neighbor was an option, but seemed a frivolous favor to ask for an airport pickup. Toni grabbed an airport shuttle, then a taxi from the shuttle drop-off. In other words, she returned home in the same manner Dan always did when he came back from a business trip.

"Mom's home!" Wick yelled after spotting Toni Wilma Bluford exiting a yellow taxi that had pulled into their driveway late Saturday morning. Tall, straight, and athletic, with radiant espresso skin, she made a pair of jeans and a blouse appear elegant. Her cascading shoulder length curls, the same gleam, texture, and color as Mae, framed her high cheekbones, enchanting brown eyes, and dimply smile.

Wick and Mae rushed to their mother, accompanied by Harvey and Pearl. Dan followed the pack at a casual pace. Toni gave a modest regal lift to her chin as her family stampeded toward her.

Wick and Mae squeezed their mother in a hearty greeting. Wick's arms wrapped around her waist and Mae's arms wrapped around her thighs. Harvey's barking and Pearl's meowing added to the happy reunion.

Toni hugged her children to her, one in each arm, accepting their joy as sun to a flower. Dan managed to squeeze in a quick kiss and a "Welcome home, sweetheart."

"Help me with my luggage," Toni said, breaking into the flood of questions and comments coming from her brood.

The taxi driver handed out luggage from his open trunk like Santa Claus delivering Christmas gifts, referring to Mae and Wick as "young lady" and "young gentleman." He sounded more like a seasoned diplomat than an urban taxi driver. He was in his early thirties. His accent was Kenyan. Dan recognized it from his travels for business and pleasure throughout Africa.

The driver saved the heaviest suitcase for Dan. Dan paid the Kenyan gentleman in cash, giving him a generous tip. The driver nodded with appreciation and a gracious smile, saying a genuine "Thank you, sir" to Dan before getting into his taxi and driving off. Toni and Dan walked into their home holding hands, Dan effortlessly carrying Toni's weighted suitcase in the other.

The children took Toni's other luggage up to their parent's bedroom. Toni released Dan's hand in order to give Harvey and Pearl proper attention. Their children were well trained in what to do when one of their parents returned from a business trip, which happened often.

Dan pondered briefly if their having that awareness was a good thing. Wick and Mae rushed at their mother again when their deliveries were done. Dan stepped aside to make room for the circle of children and pets around his wife. This time, Wick and Mae did not squeeze Toni quite as tightly. They chattered over each other as they vied for their mother's attention.

"Alright, you two," Dan said, stepping further away from the scene and setting Toni's suitcase down near the stairs. "She's only been gone a week. Let's not act like Mom's just returned from a tour of duty."

"Tour of what?" Mae asked.

"Coming home from war," Wick said.

"Oh," Mae said, clearly not getting the connection.

Toni squatted down, placing herself eye level with Mae. "How are you feeling, honey?"

"Much better."

Toni eyed Mae closely, feeling Mae's forehead and cheeks with the back of her hand. "Do you mind if I give you a little exam later? It'll make me feel better."

"Sure, Mom, if it'll make you feel better."

"That's my girl." Toni paused for a beat. She put an arm around Mae's waist, pulling her closer. "I'll bet it was scary, huh?"

Mae nodded.

"That's what can happen when you break one of our house rules," Toni tenderly said, sounding maternal and not accusatory.

"I know. Daddy told me," Mae said with clear disappointment in her face and voice. Whether her displeasure was directed at herself or her parents, Dan was not sure.

Toni looked up at Dan, giving him an approving smile. Toni glanced over at Wick, who was standing beside his sister. "Wick, have you been behaving yourself?"

"Of course," Wick answered matter-of-factly. Wick was a good kid, although his parents knew he had a thread of mischief woven into his personality. Toni always put that question to him as more of a tease than an expectation of any wrongdoing.

"Don't look at me," Wick added. "I had no idea the munchkin was eating bad moo shu pork."

"I'm not a munchkin," Mae retorted.

"My fault, pipsqueak," Wick said.

"Potato head."

"How original."

"Neither is munchkin or pipsqueak."

"Still fits."

"Okay, you two!" Dan said. "That's enough of that."

"Sounds like things are pretty much back to normal around here," Toni said, straightening to her full height but giving a peck on the cheek to Mae before she did, then leaning over to cup Wick's cheeks before giving him a kiss on his forehead.

Toni sauntered over to Dan, embracing him in a body hug. "And what about you, Mr. Bluford? Have you been behaving yourself?"

"Of course," Dan said, mimicking Wick.

"Don't pretend you didn't miss me." Toni swayed her body into Dan's arms, not going as far as to create enough friction for unwarranted arousal.

Dan had missed her a lot. He'd missed hearing her voice and laughter as a part of his daily mix. Dan had difficulty sleeping in their bed when Toni was not lying beside him. Toni had confessed to Dan that she felt the same. Toni kissed Dan.

"Maybe I missed you just a little," Dan said.

Toni kissed Dan again with more passion. A preview of what was to come, Dan hoped.

"Yuck!" Wick exclaimed.

"There are children present," Mae added.

"*Your* children," Wick said. "We don't want to see that mushy stuff."

"Then close your eyes," Dan said, kissing Toni with as much passion as she had him.

"Why do grownups kiss like that?" Dan heard Mae ask Wick.

"Beats me," Wick said. "It's so unsanitary."

"Unsanitary!" Toni and Dan said at the same time. The parents rushed at their children. Toni had Wick in a bear hug, planting frisky kisses all over his face with "mmm" sounds as if she was gobbling up a delicious dessert. Dan did the same to Mae. Their children squirmed and barked for release through their hysterical laughter. When their parents finally stopped, Wick and Mae gave each of them a kiss on the cheek—an act of affection Dan thought his son had outgrown, when it came to his father.

"Come on, Mae," Wick said, taking Mae's hand. "Let's give our *parents* some alone time."

"Yeah," Mae said, "before they go on another smooching attack."

Toni and Dan feigned another attack. Their children raced up the stairs, followed by Harvey and Pearl, laughter trailing them. "Welcome home, Mom!" Wick and Mae yelled in unison over the upstairs banister before making their way into Mae's room. Toni and Dan kissed again after chuckling at their offspring, toning it down from what Wick and Mae had witnessed.

"I'm beat," Toni said. Her body hug created a sense of home for Dan that none of their rooms and furnishings could match.

"The medical conference was that grueling?" Dan asked.

"This one was more informative than fun. Lots of great information. Some of it, I'm still processing."

"Are you hungry?"

"I could eat a little something. I don't eat airplane food."

"I know," Dan said. Toni only ate airplane food in a pinch even on business or first class flights, as she had flown for her recent medical conference. Airline meals always tasted bland to her. Her stomach could wait, unless it was a non-stop flight of ten hours or more. "Care to join us for lunch?"

"What's on the menu?" Toni asked.

"Homemade soup."

"Consisting of?"

"Bone broth, onion, carrots, zucchini, and garlic, with a pinch of sea salt. I found the recipe online."

"Sounds just right for Mae."

"Wick and I are eating what Mae's eating."

"A show of solidarity."

"Precisely," Dan said.

"I'm not up for that," Toni whispered. "I'm feeling a little famished."

"How does a pastrami sandwich sound? Made with smoked turkey pastrami, toasted rye, Swiss cheese, spicy mustard, and sauerkraut. Along with a mixed green salad." Two of Toni's favorite foods.

"Delicious," Toni growled.

Dan whispered, "I'll smuggle your rations up to our bedroom."

"Thanks," Toni whispered back, tilting her head slightly to the left and giving Dan one of her alluring smiles. "You're such a sweetheart."

"Pleasing you is my greatest pleasure."

"You are so corny sometimes," Toni said with genuine affection.

"Yes, I am," Dan shamelessly retorted.

"Then why do you keep saying stuff like that?"

"Because it's sincere. And sincerity has a right to be corny."

"If you say so, darling."

"I do. One day, you'll appreciate my cheesiness."

"'Appreciate' might be a bit strong, my dear," Toni said. "'Accept' or 'tolerate' may be more accurate."

"Too late to back out now, *sugar*," Dan said, emphasizing "sugar" with a southern twang. "You're stuck with me. We made a promise for a lifetime. For better or for cheesiness."

"That's not quite how our marriage vows went, honey," Toni said. "I'm stuck with this corny guy who happens to be my husband."

Dan chuckled. "My darling wife," Dan's voice returned to normal, "let's get you unpacked."

"Sounds good," said Toni, matching Dan's tone and changing the mood of her smile from alluring to pleasant. "Don't forget about my rations," Toni finished in a whisper.

"Of course," Dan said in a clandestine response.

"Feels good to be home." Her words were as soothing as soft warm spring rain.

Toni dropped her arms from about Dan's neck in what seemed like a reluctant gesture and she led the way up the stairs, taking her time. Dan followed, carrying her suitcase, his other palm resting gently on the small of his wife's back. It was a habit he had adopted when Toni preceded him up a flight of stairs—a show of physical support that started when Toni was pregnant with Wick.

"What's going on in there?" Toni said as she passed Mae's room, in order to shake things up. Wick took more after his mother than Dan, in that regard.

"Nothing!" Mae and Wick responded in concert.

Toni and Dan both knew their answer could be literal. Either nothing was amiss; or it could mean something quite the opposite. With their children's digital connection to the outside world, anything was possible.

Wick had a natural tendency to corrupt Mae with any discoveries on how to usurp their adult restrictions although, in his mind, they were certain Wick viewed it as passing along knowledge—opening up avenues that he (and certainly not his baby sister) were equipped to explore.

Innocent curiosity was desecrated by access to adult information and, candidly, garbage hurled at them from digital gods and demons.

They weren't naïve. Toni and Dan knew their children were becoming more tech-savvy then they were. They also knew that, outside of their home, much of what they tried to shield them from could be accessed through other resources, mostly from their friends and classmates.

In their home, their sanctuary, their children knew there were boundaries they were not permitted to cross.

Dan placed Toni's suitcase next to her other luggage their children had deposited on their tidy king-size bed. Dan offered to help Toni unpack.

"I'll do this," Toni said, "while you rustle me up some rations."

"Vittles," Dan said.

"Pardon?"

"Rustle me up some vittles. 'Vittles' works better with 'rustle me up.' Didn't you ever watch any of the old American westerns?"

"No, I didn't," said Toni looking at Dan as if to say it didn't matter. "Food, please, Mr. Bluford."

"You know the kids are going to be in here as soon as I leave," said Dan.

"True." Toni thought for a minute. "Text me when you're ready. I'll handle our children."

Dan chuckled. "We don't have to go through all of this. Mae will not be upset if you don't join the band."

"I know. It's more fun this way," Toni said with a mischievous grin. It was one that reminded Dan even more of her similarity to Wick. "I can still join the band. I'll leave enough room for soup."

Dan smiled and nodded his consent. "Vittles coming right up, Mrs. Bluford."

Dan hurried down to the kitchen. He whipped up the turkey pastrami sandwich and green salad, drenched in his homemade Italian dressing.

"Deploy operation shooing," Dan texted Toni when he was done. Moments later, the response came. "The coast is clear."

Dan left the kitchen with the items stowed away in one of their reusable grocery bags. As Dan slipped past Mae's room, he heard a snippet of their conversation. Mae was explaining to Wick something about her neatly arranged stuffed animal collection.

Dan entered his bedroom, easing the door shut behind him as if having successfully made it through enemy territory. Toni was in the midst of unpacking.

"Is that it?" Toni said, as if the bag Dan was carrying contained some sort of top secret. Dan had to confess that he was having as much fun sneaking around as Toni. He nodded and handed his wife the vittles. Toni gave him a thank you kiss, sat down on the bed, and scooped out the sandwich and salad he had placed in plastic containers. Wasting no time, she dug in. Dan eased over and locked their bedroom door.

"That is so good," Toni said after a couple of forkfuls of salad.

"You act as though you have been starving."

"The conference food was okay."

"Didn't you go out to eat? There are plenty of great restaurants in Toronto."

"Ordered in. There was so much quality material that I hunkered down in my room. I wanted to recap and digest it as soon as possible."

That was typical Toni. Once she focused on something, just about everything else faded to gray. For better or worse, that was a characteristic they shared. Dan looked on in silence as Toni devoured the salad.

"I'm going to check on the kids," Dan said.

Toni nodded, choosing not to answer with a mouthful of sandwich.

Dan walked in to find his children playing Battleship the old-fashioned way with pegboards, miniature ships, and red and white pegs marking hits and misses. Wick must have grabbed the vintage version from the game room where it was normally kept. They looked up at Dan for a moment before redirecting their attention back to their grids.

"Mom settling in okay?" Wick asked.

"Yep," Dan said.

"Are you two finished smooching?" Mae asked. The two laughing, then, making kissing sounds and moving their mouths like suffocating fish out of water.

"For now," Dan said, ignoring the joke. "Who's winning?"

"Too early to tell," Wick answered. "E4."

"Hit," Mae said. Wick recorded the hit with a red peg on his board.

"F3," Mae continued.

"Hit," Wick said, marking the strike to his submarine with a red peg. His submarine in danger of sinking with one more strike.

You could tell they were in full out competitive mode in an effort to destroy the other's fleet. Mae and Wick did not take their eyes off their boards, their brown eyes teeming with concentration. Neither of them talked smack.

"Wick, let me see your phone," Dan asked. Wick nonchalantly handed his phone to his father. Wick did not bother to ask, because he already knew why his father wanted his phone. Dan checked to make certain all of their parental controls were still in play. They were.

A part of Dan found that a good sign. Another, less optimistic part of him reasoned, *why bother tampering with your own phone when you could find what you sought elsewhere?* At least house rules were still in place. Dan handed Wick back his phone. He went over and checked Mae's laptop. Mae never minded when he did.

Dan settled in behind Wick when he was done. Dan could see Wick's board. He didn't know what was happening with Mae, but she had not located Wick's battleship.

"F1," Mae said.

"Miss," Wick said. "E5."

"Hit."

Dan went to Wick's room and powered up his son's laptop, intent on doing a thorough examination of its contents. The software appeared normal. The apps appeared acceptable. Protocols were untampered. The search history spotless. A quick perusal of his files did not send up any red flags. Wick's laptop was clean.

Almost too clean, as if it had been scrubbed. His son had changed app links on parent-approved apps before while leaving the icons unchanged. The *Monster Physics* icon app linked to the video game *Call of Duty: Modern Warfare*. The *Orchestra* icon app was altered to link to the *Mech Warrior 5: Mercenaries* video game.

Dan discovered Wick's deception by sheer luck. He had clicked on the *Monster Physics* icon, curious to see what material the software was covering. Imagine his surprise when the war video game login popped up, instead.

Wick explained to Dan how he'd usurped their parental controls when Dan confronted him about being capable of accessing the over-aged games. Wick jockeyed between being both proud of his achievement and embarrassed about being caught. When pressed about whether he had done it on his own, Wick claimed full responsibility.

Which could have been true. On the other hand, Wick could have been taking the blame in order to protect his source. His punishment was no cell phone for a month and use of his laptop only under strict supervision by Dan or Toni.

Dan double-checked all of Wick's apps and released and reinstated his parental controls, returning all checks and balances to their initial settings.

Dan was unable to detect if Wick had found a way around them. At least he would have to start from scratch, if he had. That was probably the best Dan could hope for from his oldest child.

The door was still closed by the time Dan returned to his bedroom. Toni had finished eating and placed the plastic containers, used cloth napkin, and silverware in the reusable grocery bag near the door. Dan helped Toni finish unpacking as she told him about her medical conference experiences, both professional and personal.

CHAPTER 7

Toni gave Mae a private physical exam after she finished unpacking. Mae was progressing well as far as Dr. Bluford was concerned. Toni contacted Arella to hear her diagnosis firsthand. Mae's pediatrician recommended that Mae stay hydrated and avoid solid foods for a couple more days as a precaution. Toni concurred. Mae's body needed more time to recuperate from its recent trauma.

The Blufords ate in the dining room rather than the kitchen, the kitchen table being their normal rendezvous area for joint breakfasts and lunches. A lingering hint of the spicy aroma of smoked turkey pastrami still hovered in the kitchen. If the children caught wind of it, they remained mute on the development. Knowing Wick and Mae as well as their parents did, that would be a secret discovery the children would only share amongst themselves, for now, waiting for just the right moment to spring their query regarding the curiosity upon their parents.

More often than not, their children worked as a team when confronting their parents. Toni joined the band, eating a bowl of homemade soup in support of Mae. She had to admit it was delicious. Toni abstained with a polite "No thank you" to offers of hard-boiled egg whites and saltines, never letting on what she had eaten earlier.

Mae, Toni and Wick dominated the lunchtime conversation. Wick and Mae caught Toni up on what was happening in their world and Toni gave them a simplified version of what she believed the children might find fascinating about her medical conference. Dan remained quiet for most of their lunch, enjoying the vibrant conversation and laughter and overall bliss of family.

The Blufords cleared and cleaned up after lunch together, then made their way to the game room to play video games.

The afternoon weather was crisp and sunny. Wick and Dan peeled off for a set of tennis in their backyard court. Wick was getting better. His son still had a ways to go before he would be able to defeat his old man, if Wick ever decided he wanted to become that good.

Dan took it easy on him and gave Wick pointers on how to improve his game as they played. Pearson Academy offered sports programs for soccer, volleyball, swimming, diving, golf, tennis, baseball, lacrosse, gymnastics, fencing, basketball, ice and field hockey, water polo, wrestling, and track & field.

Dan and Toni had asked Wick and Mae if they were interested in playing any sports for their school. They were. Mae fancied soccer, volleyball, and tennis. Wick gravitated toward basketball, soccer, and track & field.

Dan had already lined up a private tennis instructor for Mae. The Pearson tennis coaches were excellent ex-pros who had a passion for teaching. Dan knew from personal experience that private lessons were the best, just as he knew from eyewitness examples that parents attempting to coach their own children more times than not yielded disastrous results.

Around the same time, Toni and Dan had asked Wick and Mae if they were interested in playing any musical instruments. Their children were still lukewarm on that idea.

Wick put up a good fight, but his inexperience and nominal skill level were too much to overcome. Dan won 6-2, 6-3, and 6-3. Dan threw every match that he lost. By mostly hitting balls out, Dan could have easily kept in, but he didn't want to humiliate his son.

Dan and Wick returned to find that Mae and Toni had commandeered the living room where they caught up on what they referred to as 'girl talk.' No boys allowed. This primarily meant Toni listening to Mae dispensing the latest gossip of what was happening in the secret lives of Mae and her besties.

Dan had not gotten around to mentioning to Toni about his idea regarding resurrecting their past practice of spending solo time with their children. The splitting of their attention with Wick and Mae had organically occurred.

Evening rolled around before they knew it. Everyone ate what Mae was having: a meal that consisted of the BRAT diet, bananas, rice, applesauce, and toast.

They debated what type of film to watch for their impromptu family movie night, after dinner. Wick wanted an action flick. Dan was stoked on sci-fi or a mystery. Toni was partial to mystery, but leaned more toward a romantic comedy. Mae wanted Disney (or something Disneyesque).

Since Mae was recuperating, her choice was given priority. *Pocahontas* it was. Dan wasn't a fan. He knew that the real story of Pocahontas (whose real name was Amonute) was a horrible tragedy; one that John Smith (whose real name was John Rolfe) played a big role in creating. Dan would pass that history along to Mae when Mae was old enough, if she hadn't discovered the truth on her own by then.

Mae had cherry Jell-O that she made herself with a little help from Toni. Mae permitted the rest of the family to have popcorn, insisting that it would not bother her if they did. Wick was still feeling compassionate toward his little sister, because he did not once taunt Mae with his popcorn.

*   *   *

Dan and Toni put Wick and Mae to bed without any of their usual fuss. The children were exhausted, leaving their resistance to slumber nil. Being good for their mother on her first night back may have figured into their cooperative behavior, as well, was Dan's guess.

Wick and Dan had showered before dinner after their tennis match. Mae decided to take a bubble bath before dinner. Dan heard running bath water coming from the master bathroom when he entered his bedroom after the children were in bed. Toni was humming the song "Try A Little Tenderness," the musical genius Al Jarreau's version being their favorite.

Dan considered asking Toni if there were room for him, as Jarreau had suggested in his live version of the song. *Maybe next time*, Dan thought.

Dan slipped downstairs and retrieved his laptop. He was propped up on the bed going through work emails when Toni emerged from their master bathroom looking refreshed and relaxed, wearing a rose red, satin lace, chemise nightgown that Dan had never seen before.

Her espresso skin was aglow from lotion, her nipples budding beneath the satin as if attempting to poke their way through. Toni sat on her side of their king-size bed. Propping up her pillows against the headboard, she stretched out, resting her back against the soft wall she had formed and duplicating what Dan had done.

Toni grabbed her laptop from atop her nightstand, flipped it open, and started reading medical conference material she had not gotten to.

An intriguing thought interrupted Dan's work. *Strange, how people fall into a resigned and often stale routine. Here I am, next to my wife—the love of my life whom I have not seen for a week. The same woman whose absence at bedtime kept me awake and longing for her presence. The same woman who, on a daily basis, invaded my thoughts.*

Yet here we are, behaving as if the week of absence never happened and exhibiting what some would refer to as a comfortable state.

Toni closed her laptop and placed it on her nightstand, then scooted over next to Dan.

"What are you doing?" Toni playfully whispered into Dan's ear, as if she had read his mind.

"Reviewing a preliminary report on one of our latest R&D endeavors."

Toni had faded into the gray of his focus despite his recent revelation. About fifty-percent of what Single Organism did corporate-wide was top-secret research and development. Dan never concerned himself with sharing sensitive information with Toni. He never volunteered that info, either.

Whenever Toni was intrigued by something he was working on, she would encourage him to elaborate. Toni never discussed in detail anything about their work with anyone. When asked about the type of work Dan did, Toni responded with a primed general statement. If queried for more details, Toni claimed repeated ignorance until the person dropped the subject.

It was not because Toni did not care about or was not proud of Single Organism. Quite the contrary. Toni had come to realize that nothing said about what Dan told her was better than letting slip something that Single Organism did not want publicly known. Vital information could fall into the hands of their competitors. Being aware of giving away any particulars could amount to the equivalence of loose lips sinking ships.

Toni reached over and closed Dan's laptop.

"Not tonight, you're not, Teddy Bear," Toni said in a sensual whisper in response to his answer. She was so close, her full, moist lips nearly brushed his ear, the warmth of her breath grazing his cheek and a mild, delicious scent of cherry almond coming from her skin.

Toni gave Dan a peck on the cheek. It took a few seconds for Dan to disengage from the fascinating report he was reading and fully grasp the situation. Toni turned his head and kissed him with the same passion she had displayed in front of their children that afternoon, upon her homecoming. She gradually turned up the heat like the concentrated flame on a Bunsen burner.

Dan blindly placed his laptop on his nightstand and took Toni into his arms. Then he tickled Toni. He didn't know why. The impulse came over him, and he went with it. Toni giggled. They kissed again. Dan tickled Toni again.

"Oh, so that's how it's going to be," Toni said after a second spurt of laughter.

"Um hmm," Dan said, with a nod, randomly attacking Toni's ticklish spots (her feet, stomach, armpits, sides, and belly button). Toni attempted to retaliate. Her frenzied laughter made her disjointed counterattacks futile. Dan stopped as suddenly as he'd started.

Toni's face was glowing. Her eyes were as radiant as the stars; her smile the white flag of surrender. They kissed—playful kisses that leisurely intensified. The lovers drew each other close in an ever-tightening embrace.

Toni and Dan knew each other's bodies well from years of exploration and experimentation. They had entrenched cerebral and visceral notes of each other's erogenous zones and variant maps of foreplay. Sometimes they made love. Sometimes they had sex. Sometimes they did both. They even occasioned a quickie.

Whether their engagement would be primal, lovemaking, or both was too early to tell. One thing Toni and Dan had mastered over the years when it came to sex was to be in the present. They responded to each other's desires without words, a spontaneous dance of intertwined bodies becoming one and culminating in an explosive crescendo of ethereal tranquility. It was an erotic experience they would repeat before the night was through.

CHAPTER 8

Toni elected to stay home with their daughter during Mae's down time. Toni had cleared taking additional leave with the health care providers handling her patients during her absence to attend the Toronto medical conference. Toni also wanted to use this time to help her daughter catch up on her schoolwork and homework assignments.

Dan dropped Wick off at school and arrived at work at seven-forty-six on Monday morning, around his usual time. Toni would be picking Wick up after school if all went well with Mae.

The Single Organism campus spanned three million square feet of space located on 150 green acres thirty-four miles east of Golden Meadows. It was a solar engineering marvel, containing its own underground substation and standby generator plant. The campus was divided into three fully functioning, self-contained sections. A fourteen-story circular glass tower for offices was where Dan worked: a Research and Development Center fully equipped with high-end technology and infrastructure capable of accommodating twelve-hundred people.

It had a manufacturing district that built Single Organism products. Each section had ground level, plant-rich courtyards often used as break and lunch areas. Indoor exercise facilities were also provided for each section, that were open 24-7.

While Single Organism promoted bicycling and the use of public transportation, and provided hybrid shuttle buses to get to work, free parking was available for all their employees in any of three concrete parking structures.

Single Organism preferred to keep all aspects of its organization within close proximity of each other. The company believed—and their record of accomplishments bore it out—that by doing so, they efficiently maintained a quality and commitment to their clients that was second to none in their unique and forward-thinking industry.

Security at Single Organism was very tight. Security cameras and motion sensors were everywhere except for restrooms and private offices such as Dan's. There were two main entrances staffed by two receptionists and armed security. Every employee had a card key that allowed him or her access to any building during the core hours of 7 a.m. to 6 p.m. Outside of core hours, one had to sign in with security. Each card key was coded as to what segments of the building an employee was allowed access.

Certain departments deemed sensitive (such as accounting, IT, R&D and executive offices) required face and voice recognition in order to enter. Guests were to be accompanied by at least two Single Organism employees at all times. No one without clearance was permitted into sensitive areas without expressed permission from Dan or his assistant director.

Dan entered his outer office, where his personal assistant Amiri Hayden was seated at his station. Dan was drinking a turmeric chai latte made with coconut milk from his 20-ounce insulated stainless steel tumbler—a free latte from the café on their floor and his favorite office drink. Free (as were all food and beverages for Single Organism employees from the food court) café or espresso bars were located in various sections and floors throughout the campus.

A shade under six feet, with brown skin, brown eyes, and clean cut with a meticulously groomed doorknocker beard, he was always dressed in stylish attire. A former track star in high school and college, the stone gray glen-plaid, three-piece skinny suit fit his toned body as if it were tailored for Amiri. It was topped off with a white dress shirt and solid black plum tie.

Single Organism had no formal dress code. Their only documented requirement was whatever you wore was office-appropriate, clean, and pressed.

Beneath Dan's open tan trench coat was an ensemble centered on a classic charcoal two-piece suit, accented with a white cotton dress shirt, blue Oxford stripe tie, and polished brown leather shoes—clothing Dan regarded as befitting his position.

"Good morning, Dan," Amiri said in his baritone voice with a welcoming smile, standing tall behind the full height of his adjustable desk.

"Good morning, Amiri. How are you?"

"Doing well; thanks for asking. How are you, sir?"

"Doing well," Dan said with sincerity. When anyone within his circle of trust asked Dan a question regarding his well-being, he always answered honestly. With Mae on the mend and Toni home, life was good. For those outside of his trusted circle, his stock response was, "Fine."

"How's Mae?" Amiri asked.

"Doing much better. I'll tell Mae you asked about her." Mae had a crush on Amiri, a craze Dan was certain his PA was accustomed to encountering from women of all ages. It was a fondness Wick sometimes teased his little sister about. Dan kept a close eye on the matter, as fathers have a tendency to do when it comes to their daughters.

Amiri treated Mae's infatuation delicately in accordance to what it was. As every adult involved knew, Mae would move on to some other romantic attraction, probably before anyone realized that her infatuation for Amiri had passed.

"That's great news," Amiri said. "I'm glad the little princess is feeling better." Amiri had a flair for false sympathy and concern in matters on which he was apathetic or which were of marginal concern to him. Dan had known Amiri long enough to recognize that he was sincere regarding his sentiments regarding Mae. Dan nodded.

"Anything new on the docket for today?" Dan asked.

"Not much you haven't already addressed, that I can see. I thought you were not working this weekend," Amiri said with a needling grin. Amiri was referring to Dan's not heeding his own directive, having spent part of Sunday catching up on some of his digital paperwork and reading and addressing as many of his trunk load of emails as he could sneak in before being caught by his family.

"I got the itch," Dan replied, smiling back.

"I know what you mean."

Amiri, Dan, Toni, and most of the people within his sphere were workaholics. They knew it, freely admitted and accepted it, and didn't see any reason to change that fact. Perhaps it was because most of the people Dan knew loved what they did for a living.

"Keep me posted, Amiri," Dan said as he headed for his inner office.

"Don't forget, you have back-to-back meetings with Michelle Tinder and Roger Shell, starting at nine this morning," Amiri said to Dan's back as he was walking away. Dan had not forgotten about the meetings with his ambitious newbie geoengineer and research scientist.

"I'm all set," Dan said over his shoulder.

Dan stepped into his top floor office, leaving the large oak doors open. His office was eight paces wide by fifteen paces deep with a shallow coiffured barrel vault ceiling, handmade contemporary chandelier, and seashell wall-to-wall carpeting. Oyster floor-length, remote-controlled custom drapes framed the gray morning light peeking through the glass exterior of the east wall.

The other three walls consisted of warm brown natural walnut with a bookshelf, mantles, cabinets, drawers, and a coat closet seamlessly built in.

Centered in the farthest portion of his office closest to the glass wall was a cubed, brushed, gold stainless steel coffee table. North and south of the coffee table were two pairs of cream cushioned, pine wood, upholstered armchairs divided by walnut end tables.

Stepping away from the coffee table area and nearer the doors were two freestanding handmade hardwood desks forming an L, the shorter leg of the L being an adjustable-height desk facing the glass wall, where his office computer and phone were situated.

Across the longer leg of the L, facing south, were two visitor black leather butterfly chairs. 'Cozy' is how his office had been described on numerous occasions.

Dan would have to agree. He could not deny it felt like home away from home. Comfortable, elegant, and spacious were what Dan had in mind when working with his interior designer on the vision of his director's office. Mission accomplished. His ergonomic office chair was the only item that looked out of place.

Dan grabbed a square cotton coaster from the coaster caddy on his desk and placed his tumbler on it. He set down his vintage bison leather briefcase—a gift from his parents—on the long leg closest the framed photographs of his wife and children.

Dan hung up his raincoat in the closet and stepped over to the glass wall. He could still see through the rain-beaded glass. His office smelled of lavender—his favorite. A fresh vase of deep purple lavender was centered on the coffee table. Fresh flowers—or in this case, herbs—were delivered daily by Single Organism's in-house florist.

Dan always took a moment out of every workday to look out over their complex. It served as a reminder for not only what Single Organism had accomplished, but reinforced the magnitude of his responsibilities. Dan believed it his solemn duty to keep his employees safe on their campus.

He provided them with a comfortable, productive work environment, made certain they were generously compensated for their efforts, and motivated them to do their best. He ensured every member of their team knew they were respected and appreciated as part of the Single Organism family.

Sounded like canned corny corporate bullshit, he knew, but not for one who truly believed in that commitment, such as himself. Dan would say that most Single Organism family members believed it, as well, judging by the large, enthusiastic turnouts at their social events.

Dan met with Michelle Tinder at nine sharp. Michelle sat in one of the butterfly chairs across the desk from him, confident, poised, and determined. Dan listened to her report without interruption.

Michelle was once again attempting to usurp their chain of command. Dan had repeatedly tried the diplomatic approach in an effort to align her ambition with their teamwork policies, but that tactic was not working. Michelle's repeated dismissal of company protocol, as if the rules did not apply to her, was clear evidence of her contempt.

Dan scolded Michelle over how things were done at Single Organism. He firmly drove home his point that he expected her to get on board with their conventions or start looking for other employment, stifling any further attempts at extending their conversation by standing and issuing an unequivocal "Thank you. Have a nice day," while gesturing toward the door for her to leave.

Michelle exited, stunned and speechless. Dan doubted anyone had spoken to her in that way for some time.

His meeting with Roger was a repeat of what had transpired with Michelle. Dan could not be certain how the two of them would react to his ultimatum. He already had a shortlist of replacements in mind if they decided to quit.

Dan gave a teleconference presentation on their fiscal plans for the next four years to the Single Organism Board of Directors (of which he was a member, that included their CEO) at ten-thirty. His presentation was well received, as expected. The only part of his presentation that was greeted with resistance was his proposal for expanding their roles in CSR (Corporate Social Responsibility). It was not surprising, but still, nonetheless, disappointing.

The current board, while still committed to saving their planet through science and technology, was tightfisted and squeamish when it came to matters of philanthropy, activism, volunteering, and charity. The majority of the board felt those were problems best suited for communities to invest their time, finances, and energy in resolving.

Single Organism, as a corporation, did the bare minimum for tax breaks and public relations.

Pending an accounting review that bore out his figures and then their fiscal budget—discounting Dan's CSR proposal—would be unanimously approved. Dan had no concern over the accounting assessment. He had been ultra-conservative in all of his estimations. Even if the board approved less than what he posted, then that would still be more than enough.

The rest of his day was routine. He had productive video chat conferences with two new clients and calmed the concerns of an existing municipal client regarding the installation of their new state-of-the-art smart sanitation system.

He addressed more emails and had a catered late lunch in one of their private conference rooms with his assistant director and department heads, that served as an informal round table discussion.

He approved the latest production schedules, approving one and rejecting the other with improvement suggestions for potential client pitches. He gave the green light to a new R&D project and paid a visit to R&D labs A and B to get firsthand looks at their progress after having read their sparkling updated reports.

Before Dan knew it, the virtual whistle blew and Dan found himself driving home.

CHAPTER 9

It was a little after six. Pitch-black. A starless sky. A heart-of-winter night. The highway traffic was start and stop. Rain was a steady downpour, further affecting poor visibility.

Dan drove with caution. Conditions merited he do so. He listened to a mix of modern and old-school jazz from one of his Cloud playlists: a blend of music that allowed Dan to relax while staying alert.

Dan had felt the punch of exhaustion when he left the office. When one gives ones all to something, you typically do not realize how draining the experience is until you come up for air. Today, for whatever reason, Dan was having trouble keeping his eyes open on the drive home.

Perhaps he was feeling more stress over Mae's bout with food poisoning than he had realized. His father always said that his premature gray was a direct result of worries over Dan and his younger brother by five years, Benjamin (whom everyone, including their parents, called "Ben." It was a contraction Dan hated in regards to his brother, for some reason, and never used).

Dan kidded his father that his premature gray hair was simply genetic. Genes or circumstance, Dan noticed his first strand of canities this morning. One thing was certain: he would not be doing his typical Monday cardio workout when he got home.

Dan was losing his fight with drowsiness. Maybe it was the darkness. Maybe it was the steady drumming of dulcet rain soothing as an ancient lullaby. His mind typically hashed over matters, be they work related or home. It was a curse, at times, having little control over his barrage of reasoning.

Dan was only a few nods from dreamland. He needed a strong cup of coffee and could not wait until he got home. Dan decided to take the next off ramp. He pulled into the empty parking lot of a coffeehouse about a quarter of a mile after taking the off-ramp exit.

"Kind of slow tonight," Dan said in jest to the barista who wore a jean apron, pink button-down shirt, and casual jeans with glowing tan skin, bright brown eyes, and wavy brown hair pulled back into a ponytail that reached her round hips.

She had a sacred Maori chin tattoo—something Dan had become familiar with from his time in New Zealand and Australia for both pleasure and business. Her name tag read "Aroha."

"Very," the barista said in a chipper voice. Her smile was contagious. Dan thought of offering Aroha a job at Single Organism. *Someone with her personality would be an asset to our organization*, he thought. He immediately shunned the idea. Poaching employees was not his style.

"We were closed for renovations for a couple of weeks," Aroha continued. Her smile diminished, but not the glint in her eyes. "Just reopened today. It is going to take time for customers to realize we have reopened."

"I get that," Dan said. After glancing around the large coffeehouse filled with pristine empty booths and neatly arranged tables and chairs, he asked: "How many people are usually in here at this time?"

"About three-quarters full." Her gaze was steady and patient, as if she were on the cusp of deep meditation. Dan glanced around again. He had been to this coffeehouse on a few occasions over the years, for the same reason that he was there now.

He remembered it always brimming with energetic people and the lull of commercial background music. Dan did not notice anything different about the place. Aroha must have read something along those lines in his face.

"Back room renovations," Aroha said, smiling.

"I see," Dan said with an understanding nod.

"What can I get for you, sir?"

Dan looked at the overhead display menu. "A tall Ethiopian coffee."

"Room for cream and sugar with that, sir?"

"No thanks."

"Coming right up."

The place was quiet, but not in a disturbing way—rather, it was calm and serene. If peace were a room, it would feel a lot like this. The sound of the coffee pouring into the cardboard cup was like a drum roll in an empty field.

Dan listened closer. He could swear he could hear the young woman's heart beating, the buzz of the lights, and wind whispering through the crack where the front entrance doors met. The brightness of the lights seemed to intensify and air danced liked light kisses on the back of his neck and face.

The moment passed in a slow motion montage. The aroma of the coffee. The rhythm of his breathing. The pulse of his blood. The passage of time. Dan felt one with the moment. A deep serenity cupped his soul and he experienced tranquility. The young woman broke Dan's trance when she placed his order on the counter in front of him, capped and ready for consumption.

"Here you are, sir," Aroha said with what now appeared to Dan to be a mischievous glint in her clear brown eyes. It made Dan believe, for a moment, that Aroha knew something that he didn't.

"How much do I owe you?"

"Because you are our first customer since our renovations, this one is on the house," Aroha said with a prideful grin.

"That's awfully generous," Dan said. "I trust that tipping is still allowed."

Aroha laughed. "If you insist, sir."

"I do." Dan placed the ten-dollar bill he was going to use to pay for his coffee in the tip jar.

"Thank you!"

"You're welcome." Again, the thought entered Dan's mind to poach this energetic young woman for Single Organism. He moved on before the impulse overtook him.

Dan decided to sit a while inside the coffeehouse instead of going back to his car. He wanted to enjoy his coffee and give the caffeine a moment to kick in.

He chose a booth near one of the windows, where he could keep an eye on his car, and took off his coat and made himself comfortable. Dan texted Toni to let her know he had stopped for coffee, explaining his reason. Toni texted back, "Smart move. Can't wait to see you. Love you." Followed by hearts and kisses emoji.

Dan stared aimlessly through the rain-blurred windows feeling more like an observer rather than a participant in life. His car looked sad and lonely in the well-lit empty parking lot. He could make out a phalanx of vehicles on the drenched, two-lane paved roads heading north and south. Mini-cabins on wheels, transporting humans from place to place, their headlights pointing the way and their rear lights marking their journey.

The coffeehouse remained empty except for the two of them. Dan sipped his coffee. It was velvety smooth with hints of dark chocolate, zesty spice, and honeyed citrus. Dan felt relaxed, rather than gaining a jolt from the coffee, as he had expected.

He looked over at the counter. Aroha's back was to him. The barista was busying herself with whatever baristas do when not serving customers.

Dan turned to stare back out of the rain-blurred window. He sipped his delicious coffee on a four-four half-note downbeat of every third measure.

Dan—and the other acting board members—had pioneered Single Organism. They were visionary college grads who became fast friends and were now directors of their own Single Organism campuses disseminated around the world. They'd built Single Organism into the number one global eco-business that it was today. They had constantly discussed the importance of community involvement and social responsibility as being an engrained part of their company doctrine, during their fledgling years.

For a while, it was, when they were huddled together in one office, then the same building, and ultimately, their first campus. The broader mission of philanthropy and social responsibility had narrowed as they branched out and profits ballooned beyond their wildest dreams.

Enjoying the spoils of their hard labor took precedent. There was more talk about new homes, yachts, private planes, and expensive vacations rather than community and social responsibility. Most of the founders' priorities had changed.

That disturbed Dan. Their worldview had tapered to family, business, and perks. Dan was certainly guilty of the first two, perks never having been important to him. That left him and Seo-yeon Hong allied as annoying reminders to the rest of the founders of their forsaken promises.

Dan reflected on his most recent CSR proposal. This time, Dan had hashed out the numbers from every conceivable angle. His footing was sound. In the short run, Dan had projected that there would be an outlay of ten percent of corporate profits needed to be set aside to institute his philanthropic and community involvement programs.

Within four years of their corporate outlay, Single Organism could expect a substantial goodwill return on their investment, along with a twenty-to-twenty-five-percent profit from ecologically conscientious clients who made up seventy percent of their growing customer base.

Citing numerous examples to the board of how good CSR directly translated into new and repeat business, Dan had clear and decisive answers to all of their questions. Every objection they raised was aimed toward the short-term profit margin. It was an attitude that disturbed him about corporate culture: fixation on the immediate bottom line. Dan kept bringing the argument back to long-term goals.

A wave of disappointment washed over Dan when his proposal was voted down 8-2 against, Seo-yeon being his only advocate. "Not fiscally prudent at this time," the CEO had gleefully summarized.

The CEO was the only person present at the meeting who was not a founding member. The board was unanimous in their belief that it would be best to hire someone outside of their circle who was well versed in corporate organization to manage their hulking empire. It was a monumental task that they had been doing by committee.

The CEO kept a close fiscal eye on all of their campuses and affiliates, monitoring campus activities to make certain there were no overlaps or redundancies. He did a good job, from that prospective.

What Dan disliked about their CEO was: he was too much Wall Street and not enough Single Organism, to him.

They were a multi-billion dollar international corporation with profits expected to catapult them into the trillion-dollar atmosphere within the next five years. They did a lot of good in this world, on one hand, with their eco-products, but slapped away the needy with the other.

It made no sense, and was hypocritical in fact on both social and ethical grounds. Dan had argued those points repeatedly, in the past, only to be met by obstinate opposition from the majority of his peers.

The CEO's rigid thinking had won them over—something Dan and Seo-yeon had failed to do. Dan had not lost faith in his friends, despite another defeat. Dan was pondering what he could do to bring them back to their original doctrines when the rain-blurred window he was absently staring at faded to black.

CHAPTER 10

Dan awakened disoriented. He called for Toni in a hoarse voice. No response. Feeling drowsy, he eased open his heavy eyelids. His vision was clear.

Dan looked around what appeared to be a private hospital room. It had the sanitized smell of one, too. Toni was nowhere in sight. A woman entered, dressed in a cherry blossom print scrub top and white scrub pants with a stethoscope draped around her neck.

"Hello, sleepyhead," the woman greeted Dan with a warm smile.

"Who are you?" Dan asked in a groggy voice with his eyes shut.

"We are who you could have become. Maybe it is not too late."

Dan opened his eyes. "Aroha?" Dan said, shaking lose the cobwebs. "Is that you?"

"It is, Mr. Bluford."

"You're a doctor?"

"I am."

"I thought you were a barista."

Aroha smiled briefly, as if at a child to whom she was about to shatter some long-held childhood folklore.

"The coffeehouse you happened into will not reopen for another week. The Aroha who is a barista and my star-twin will be returning to work there when it does."

Aroha looked the same, except for the uniform. Her demeanor was more serious, accented with a passive intensity—the same as Toni when she was in doctor mode. Her brown eyes remained bright and clear, but were less cheerful and more clinical. Her smile had turned into a tight, sharp line.

"Star who? What are you talking about, Aroha?"

"I was at the coffeehouse for you, Mr. Bluford," Aroha said in a pleasant matter-of-fact tone.

"I don't understand."

"All will become clear in time."

Aroha pulled down the soft Native American print polar fleece blanket that had been pulled up to Dan's chin as if he were about to submerge his head underneath to escape the boogey woman. She undid the top two buttons of Dan's pajama top.

Dan felt physically powerless to stop her. Dan noticed he was no longer hypersensitive, as he had been in the coffeehouse. Nothing about him seemed beyond the pale. Aroha placed the cold resonator disc of her stethoscope over his heart.

Dan noticed for the first time that he was wearing pajamas as Aroha moved the disc around his chest, stopping to listen closely each time she did. They were his favorite pajamas: grass green 100% cotton, with giraffe animal prints (his spirit animal, or so Dan believed). A birthday gift from his children.

"Your heart is strong; lungs are clear," Aroha said.

"What in the hell is going on here?"

Aroha ignored Dan's question, extracting a digital thermometer from her right smock pocket. Dan opened his mouth and lifted his tongue without question. He could not say why he trusted this woman, but he did—call it instinct or gut or whatever signals that cause the mind to dismiss the rantings of common sense and take a chance.

Aroha eased the thermometer probe in place under Dan's tongue. Whenever Dan attempted to talk with the thermometer still in his mouth, Aroha silenced him with a firm, motherly *"Quiet."*

The thermometer beeped in less than a minute, but it seemed longer to Dan.

"Good," Aroha said, after checking the temperature reading before putting the thermometer back into her smock pocket. Aroha moved on to check Dan's heart rate, respiration, and blood pressure.

"You are doing great, Mr. Bluford," Aroha said when done, flashing a cheery smile similar to the one she had greeted Dan with at the coffeehouse, but backed by a more mature confidence.

"How are you feeling?"

"I feel weak."

"Transformation Fatigue. That is normal." Aroha buttoned up Dan's pajama top.

"Transformation what?"

"All will become clear in time, Mr. Bluford." Aroha pulled Dan's blanket back up to his chin.

"You said that already. Where am I?"

"You need your rest."

"I don't know what's going on, but I'm getting out of here." Dan tried to sit up, but could only move his head an inch off the soft pillow. He felt as though his voluntary muscles were so relaxed, they simply wanted to chill. Aroha placed a gentle hand on his chest, holding Dan down with no effort.

"You need your rest, Mr. Bluford." Dan drifted off to sleep as if Aroha's soothing words were a sedative.

*   *   *

The door opened. Dan woke to find a young man pushing a shiny metal food-serving cart, coming toward him. He was the spitting image of his neighbor, Marek Czarnecka. Both were the epitome of what some would consider handsome Nordic males: tall and fit, with short blonde hair, clear white skin, and icy blue eyes. He wore a green hospital uniform. On top of the cart was a large shiny metal tumbler with a doglegged white straw sticking out from its sealed lid.

"Hello, Mr. Bluford," he announced, parking the cart a little off to his right. His visitor stood next to the bed.

"Hello," Dan said, still staring at the man as if he were an odd curiosity he could not quite discern.

"Do I remind you of anyone?" The man asked in a cheerful tone. His voice was the same husky and clear pitch as Marek Czarnecka.

"As a matter fact, you do."

"Marek Czarnecka."

"How did you know?"

"He is my star-twin."

"What is a star-twin?" Dan asked, recalling that Aroha had used the same term to describe the barista.

"What you may refer to as a doppelganger."

"What is going on here?" Dan asked, attempting (and failing) to sit up.

"All will become clear to you in time, Mr. Bluford. My name is Bartek Sokolowski."

"Where's Aroha?" Dan asked, feeling apprehensive, for the first time, about his situation.

"Aroha is your GP or General Practitioner."

"I know what a GP is," Dan snapped. "I'm married to a doctor."

"Of course," Bartek said without the hint of an apology. "My point being, Mr. Bluford, that Dr. Ngata—Aroha—is your medical physician. I am your attendant. How are you feeling?"

Dan felt fine from the neck up. He was able to move his arms and legs a bit, but the effort exhausted him. "Still weak," Dan said, after his exertions.

"That is to be expected," the attendant said, giving Dan a sympathetic smile. "The major muscle groups are typically last to recover."

"Where am I? What am I doing here? Was I in an accident or something?"

Bartek snapped off a "No, you were not in an accident," to Dan's third question, choosing to ignore questions one and two.

"Then why am I here?"

"What is the last thing that you remember, Mr. Bluford?"

"Driving home from work."

"Do you recall stopping at a coffeehouse on your way home?"

"Yes, how did you—"

"How was the coffee?" Bartek said with amusement. "A tall Ethiopian blend, was it not?"

Dan thought for a moment before answering, in a puzzled tone, "Delicious."

"Do you remember any other details?"

Dan thought hard. He recollected pulling into the coffeehouse parking lot. Ordering coffee. Aroha cheerfully filling his drink order. The solemnity of the place. The emptiness of the coffeehouse, giving it breathing room. His heightened senses absorbing every detail. A calm embracing him. Peace.

"Excellent!" the attendant blurted out with a wry smile.

"But I didn't say anything," Dan said. Dan attempted to rise from the bed, with no more success than before. He felt as if every molecule of his physical strength had been drained from his body. His mind was alert, making him restless and starved for answers.

"You are experiencing minor transformation side effects. We are administering the Purification Process to nurture you back to full strength," the attendant said, as nonchalantly as if giving Dan routine instructions on how to navigate a new phone app.

"Transformation Fatigue, Purification Process. What are those? What's happening to me?"

"All will become clear in time," the attendant said, adding, "Are you hungry?" before Dan could pursue the matter further.

"Famished," Dan said. And he was.

"Let us get you propped up into a more comfortable position so you can enjoy your drink."

The armless bed slowly rose without Bartek touching any controls.

"There we are," Bartek said as the bed settled Dan into a comfortable upright position. Bartek made a few minor adjustments, positioning Dan's pillows behind his lower and upper back.

"How is that, Mr. Bluford?"

"Fine."

Holding the tumbler and placing the flexible straw near Dan's lips, Bartek said, "Drink up."

"What is it?" Dan asked, jerking his head away like a child avoiding a teaspoon of unwanted medicine. Dan suspected that his coffee had been spiked with some sort of knockout drug. Whatever Bartek was trying to feed him could be more of the same, or worse.

"This is an organic blend of vitamins, minerals, and nutrients designed to expedite your recovery. Do not worry. There is nothing in this drink that will harm you."

"How did I get here? Was I drugged?"

"You were."

"Where am I?"

"Drink, Mr. Bluford. It will help you move on to the next phase."

"Move on? Next phase? What are you talking about?"

"For the time being, you need to regain your strength. This drink will help you recover."

"Recover from what?" Dan asked, not budging.

"This is part of the Purification Process, as I said before."

"Again, with this Purification Process nonsense that no one's told me squat about."

"Drink, Mr. Bluford," Bartek said, more as a command than request.

"And if I don't?"

"Then you will remain in this hospital bed a good deal longer than necessary."

Bartek's explanation did nothing to satisfy Dan's concerns. For all Dan knew, the tumbler could be filled with poison. The only shred of reasoning Dan could generate to combat that worrisome thought was he was in what appeared to be a hospital room.

Why go through all of this trouble to poison him? Aroha could have done that in the coffeehouse. Dan and Bartek stared at each other. Dan blinked. He brought his head forward, tentatively wrapped his lips around the straw, and cautiously sucked the unknown substance into his dry mouth. The straw was made of paper, not plastic, to his surprise. The drink was cold and refreshing and had a smoothie texture that tasted of clover honey and dark chocolate.

That's good, Dan thought.

"What's in it?" Dan asked again, after having drank half of the delightful, nutritious smoothie.

"All of your questions will be answered in due course, Mr. Bluford. For now, you will need to get your physical strength back. Keep drinking," the attendant said, forcing the issue by pressing the flexible straw to Dan's lips.

By the time Dan finished drinking, both his dry mouth and hunger were gone. Bartek placed the tumbler back on the cart and lowered

Dan's bed back into the supine position; again without touching any controls.

"Do not worry, Mr. Bluford. You will be up and around in no time," the attendant said, placing the tumbler on the cart and briskly turning to leave.

"What is going on here?!" Dan yelled in frustration, summoning a strength that had escaped him since he had arrived.

"In due course, Mr. Bluford," Bartek said, unaffected by Dan's outburst. "In due course."

Bartek exited. Dan heard the hard metal click of the door locking behind him. Dan was trying to think, but he felt woozy, like he was on a mellow marijuana high. *Something besides organic nutrients was in that drink,* he thought.

Dan was still too weak to move. The questions crossed his mind of whether he was in a hospital or a sanitarium, or neither. Before Dan could formulate any answers, he was fast asleep.

CHAPTER 11

Dan awakened a few hours later from a restful sleep. He pulled back the cozy polar fleece blanket, swung his heavy legs over the side of the bed, and sat up.

He paused to wonder, for a moment, how any of this was possible—him being drugged and kidnapped. Yet, all of his creature comforts were being met; foreseen as if by some magic crystal ball.

They were most likely experienced kidnappers, Dan continued with his reasoning. Judging by their thoroughness, Dan surmised he was one of a number they had drugged and taken hostage. While he had no prior personal experience with being kidnapped, Dan believed their treatment of him was odd, for kidnappers.

A doctor and attendant in attendance? Their sincere concern—at least, Dan saw it that way—for his overall wellbeing? Who were they?

Dan speculated on possible reasons why anyone would want to abduct him. Had some ransom note been dispensed to his family or Single Organism, demanding money for his safe return? That was a real possibility in a few countries, where kidnapping was almost considered part of the national economy, but was unheard of in most of what was regarded as the civilized world.

Single Organism competitors also came to mind. That idea proved ridiculous. Single Organism competitors would resort to industrial espionage or would attempt to poach him rather than do something as crazy as kidnapping, which could possibly land people in prison and garner negative publicity.

None of his other brittle strings of speculation made any sense except for a far-reaching possibility: had he been abducted by aliens? Dan believed in intelligent extraterrestrials. But, of all of the people on planet Earth, what could they possibly want with him?

The room was pleasantly warm. Comfortable in his cotton giraffe print pajamas, Dan slipped his bare feet into a pair of fur-lined scuff slippers provided by his captures. That was how Dan viewed them, despite their hospitable treatment.

Dan stood and stretched. In the middle of his stretch, Dan realized what he was doing. He was standing and stretching. He walked around the room for a couple of minutes at different paces, feeling giddy at his muscles working again. The light scuffs of his slippers were the only sounds he heard.

Dan kicked off his slippers and did fifty pushups and jogged in place for twenty minutes to test his theory, working up a light sweat. He was barely winded. His physical strength had returned and his stamina had not been affected.

Dan slipped back into his slippers, walked over, and tried the exit door. It was locked. He examined the lock. Electromechanical.

Hospitals were installing or converting from key to electromechanical locks, the goal being to eliminate keys—a hospital fact he had learned from Toni. The automated lock was typically accessed by an employee ID, badge or access code. There was no keypad on his lock. Dan assumed that an access badge or ID was required, although he could not recall Aroha or Bartek carrying or using one.

His room was quiet. If he was in a hospital, as he believed, quiet would be expected. Dan pressed his ear to the door. Through the cold metal, he could hear faint voices fading in and out, walking up and down what Dan assumed was a corridor.

Dan repeatedly tried to force the door lever, but it barely budged. He wanted to pound on the door and scream for help, but suppressed the impulse. He reasoned it was best to wait and see what happened next, especially now that he had his strength back.

He turned to take in his antiseptic prison. The room was sparse, with a drop ceiling. The floor was a spotless, shining white linoleum with flecks of color. The smooth walls were painted a flawless light blue. His comfortable hospital bed had its side rails detracted. The ruffled blanket and sheets and head-imprinted pillows made it look slept in.

An over-the-bed wood tray table was marooned to an out-of-the way corner. A modest three-drawer cherry wood bedside cabinet was placed left to the head of the bed, a vase of fresh lavender on top, its light fragrance filling the room.

Dan was confident the perennial herbs had been placed there during his sleep, since last he remembered was the sanitary smell of disinfectant.

The scent of fresh lavender had filled his office. The deep purple plant was identical to the one in his office. Yesterday morning, was it? It was, if only a day had passed.

Five casual paces from the foot of his bed was the open door to a bathroom he had spied but not used (at least, to his conscious recollection, he had not). On the opposite wall from where Dan stood was a window. Horizontal white vinyl blinds shut tight against whatever was beyond.

Dan suppressed another impulse to clamor for his freedom by banging on the door and yelling at the top of his lungs for help. Who was on the other side of that door? Would they help, or restrain him? Best to wait until he knew more about his circumstances.

Dan drew in a deep, meditative breath. The lavender aroma filled his nostrils, and he exhaled slowly. Dan repeated the process until his impulse subsided. He looked around the room again.

The window. *Maybe?* Dan thought. He rushed over to the window, slowly raising the blinds, as if rushing the action might alert his captors. His jaw dropped and his eyes bulged with wonder at what he saw. Where in the world was he?

"Good morning, Mr. Bluford."

Dan whirled around so fast, he almost lost his balance. He had not heard them come in. Aroha and Bartek smiled as they walked toward him.

"Glad to see you are up and about," Aroha continued. "How are you feeling?"

Aroha and Bartek looked the same as when Dan last saw them, except Aroha was wearing a spring tulip-print scrub. A shiny metal food serving cart had appeared near the bed table—the same as the one Bartek had wheeled in on their first meeting.

"Much better," Dan said, in answer to Aroha's question. "I would say thanks, but since I've been kidnapped and held hostage in this room, it doesn't feel appropriate."

Aroha and Bartek laughed. "You are not being held hostage, Mr. Bluford," Aroha said.

"But I was kidnapped."

"'Exchanged' is a word we prefer to use."

"Riddles. Do you people ever give a straight answer?"

"All will become—"

"Clear in time. I know. Yet, everything keeps getting fuzzier." Dan's eyes flitted toward the door as he considered escape. Dan heard a dull thump.

"The door is locked, Mr. Bluford," Bartek said, as if reading his thoughts. Perplexed, Dan stared at Bartek and Aroha. They both had knowing grins. Neither Bartek nor Aroha had moved or even glanced at the door.

"Would you have a seat on the bed?" Aroha asked. "I would like to have a look at you."

"Do I have a choice?"

"No," Aroha said, as if demanding a child eat his unappetizing vegetables. Dan went over and plopped down on the bed.

"Quite a sight, is it not?" Aroha asked, giving a slight nod toward the window. Bartek walked over to the window as she spoke. He lowered and closed the blinds. "Not like anything you have ever seen before, is it, Mr. Bluford?"

"Where in the world am I?" Dan asked, his mind racing from what he had seen.

"Today, your questions will be answered," Aroha said. "The most important ones, anyway."

Dan believed Aroha, feeling a twinge of trepidation instead of relief from her statement. For the first time, Dan considered the possibility that maybe he did not want to know the whole truth of his circumstances.

Once again, Aroha checked Dan's vitals, adding reflexes to the list.

"Will you stand over there, please, and face me?" Dr. Ngata asked Dan, pointing to an open area of the room between his bed and the exit door. Dan did as he was asked, staring at the exit door as he made his way to the place Aroha had indicated like a prisoner desperate to make a break for it.

Dr. Ngata pulled a cube about half the size of a Rubik's cube from her right smock pocket.

"What is that?" Dan asked in awe. For some reason, seeing the device also triggered the question, "Where is my cell phone?"

"Your cell phone is at home, Mr. Bluford," Bartek said.

"This is my Portable Med Kit," Aroha replied in answer to Dan's first question. "Dr. Aroha Ngata," she said to the cube, then tapped it three times with her finger. The cube lit up before transforming into what Dan could best describe as a large notebook computer.

"You *are* aliens!"

Aroha and Bartek burst out laughing.

"How many times have we heard that one, Aroha?" Bartek said, once their laughter died.

"Too many to count, Bartek. We are not aliens, Mr. Bluford. If, by aliens, you mean extraterrestrials."

"I do."

His two caregivers laughed again.

"We are as human as you are, Mr. Bluford," Bartek said. "Maybe even more—"

Aroha cut Bartek off. "All will become clear shortly, Mr. Bluford." Bartek and Aroha made eye contact for a moment, then nodded in agreement at something unsaid.

"How does a Portable Med Kit work?" Dan asked.

"We simply call them PMKs."

The PMK had made Dan more intrigued than anxious. Aroha methodically moved the tablet from Dan's head to his toes, holding it steady, as if she were either recording or scanning him.

"Turn ninety degrees to your right, please," Aroha said. Dan did so. Aroha repeated her request and the process until Dan was once again facing her.

"Did you just take x-rays of me?" Dan asked.

"It is much more thorough than that, Mr. Bluford," Dr. Ngata said. "Come take a look."

Dan saw a virtual 3D image of his person—muscles, internal organs, skin, hair, nervous system, brain, skull, eyes, and bones. Every molecule that comprised his body appeared to have been recorded and differentiated into separate display categories.

Aroha's fingers glided over the tablet screen, manipulating the images that had been produced. Somehow, she conferred with Bartek without speaking a word, smiling as if pleased with their silent conclusions before Dr. Ngata tapped the tablet three times, returning the device to its light cube size and placing it back into her smock pocket.

"Where am I? Who are you people?" Dan asked, annoyance having replaced his fascination with the PMK.

"How about we create a one-word response for Mr. Bluford's redundant inquiries, such as 'echo.'"

"I like that, Bartek," Aroha said.

"I don't," Dan said.

"As our patient, you do not have a say in this matter," Dr. Ngata said.

"Whatever happened to patient privileges? Or don't you have such a thing, where we are?"

"Clever, Mr. Bluford, but echo," Bartek said in response to Dan's effort to ferret out information on his whereabouts.

"When am I going to get some straight answers?"

"Echo, Mr. Bluford," Aroha said, with a coy grin that Bartek matched.

Dan glared at them. He was confident that they could tell he was angry. They did not seem to care. He took a menacing stride toward his captors. Suddenly, he was frozen in his tracks like a statue with a functioning head.

"I would not attempt to overpower either of us, Mr. Bluford," Bartek said.

"You would lose, Mr. Bluford," Aroha said. "Your resistance may only delay your progress."

Dan strained to move forward. His efforts yielded no results. Aroha and Bartek looked on in silence, as if observing a lab animal exhibiting predictable behavior.

Dan whooshed out a huge breath before settling down and took in what his caretakers had said. Even if he was able to overpower them, what next? How would he get out? He had seen that he was too high up to climb out of the window. How would he unlock the door?

Neither of them had any visible access badges. Was their access linked to that light cube? Dan took deep breaths. The camphor-like smell of lavender helped calm him, and he was released from whatever force held him at bay. Dan slowly spread the fingers of his clenched fists—fists he was unaware he had made. Reason took the lead for the moment.

"Don't you want to know about my medical history?" Dan snapped. It was a strange question under the circumstances, but it was the only thing he could think of to say.

His caregivers chuckled. "We already have all of that information," Aroha replied, returning to her pleasant, matter-of-fact tone. "You have taken very good care of yourself, Mr. Bluford. You are in excellent health."

"Thanks," Dan sarcastically replied.

"Are you hungry?" Bartek asked.

His little workout had given Dan an appetite that his anger surge increased. "A little," he said.

"Good," Bartek said. "Lie down on the bed, if you will."

Dan did as asked, still battling the urge to pounce. Bartek retrieved the bed table and positioned it over Dan. After making a minor height adjustment to the table, he asked Dan, "Comfortable?"

Dan shrugged.

Bartek wheeled the food cart over. He placed wrapped plastic cutlery and a small stack of folded paper napkins on the tabletop off to Dan's right, then quickly extracted freshly prepared food items from the cart one after another, arranging them so expertly on the table that Dan need only watch.

Scrambled eggs, hash browns, spicy sausage links, fresh-squeezed orange juice, hot black tea with honey, wheat toast lathered in apple butter, and a fresh fruit cup of blueberries, strawberries, raspberries, pineapple, and kiwi.

It was Dan's favorite breakfast. How had they known? Dan managed to contain his delight. Aroha stood by, quietly observing Dan, making him feel as if his examination wasn't over.

"What's this?" Dan asked.

"Food to fatten you up for the slaughter," Bartek answered in a diabolic voice.

"Bartek!" Aroha said to the attendant, causing Bartek to laugh. Dr. Ngata moved to Dan in a fluid, swift motion, nudging Bartek out of the way, and grabbed his hand in hers. Her grip was firm and reassuring.

"Ignore Bartek, Mr. Bluford. Sometimes my colleague has a dark sense of humor. Everything is going to be fine. Right, Bartek?"

"That is correct, Doctor," Bartek said. "No harm will come to you, Mr. Bluford."

"You promise?" Dan said, startled at his willingness to play along with what he hoped was ribbing. It unnerved Dan a bit that he was starting to enjoy this banter. Bartek raised his left hand and placed his right hand over his heart. At least, Dan assumed it was his heart.

"I promise."

Dan looked deep into Aroha's eyes, trying to read whether the person he trusted most in the room was being honest. There was a gentle but powerful light radiating from her clear brown eyes, like an angelic beacon emanating from her core.

It was somewhat different from the youthful, gregarious barista upon their first meeting, or the honed, cool, confident stare of her trained medical profession.

This light was a welcoming gateway into the tunnel leading to the harbor of her... Dan's ruminations stumbled for just the right word. Soul? Dan felt a momentary quiver that yanked his breath from his chest.

"I promise, as well, Mr. Bluford." Aroha eased her hand out of his. Dan felt unstable from the loss of her connection. "Try to relax and enjoy your breakfast. When you are done, we will escort you to someone who will answer most of your questions."

"Why not *all* of my questions?" Dan felt compelled to ask.

Bartek chuckled. Aroha mused. "Some answers will only be gained from experience, Mr. Bluford," Aroha said. "We are confident you will not be disappointed, in any event."

Dan looked back and forth between Bartek and Aroha. If they were trying to lull him into a false sense of security, they had succeeded.

"Eat, Mr. Bluford," Bartek said, more as a request than command, this time. There was a compassion in Bartek's eyes that Dan had not seen before.

His caregivers exited, leaving him to decide about what to do with his breakfast. Dan could not wait to dig in once they had left. He would not give them the satisfaction of watching him enjoy this meal. The food was delicious.

Dan did not notice that they had not locked the door.

*   *   *

Dan pushed aside the bed table, now covered with empty dishes, used cutlery, and crumpled napkins. He had enjoyed his hearty breakfast, sacking his suspicions that his meal might be laced with some sort of drugs. He had to eat.

Making his way to the bathroom, he relieved himself, surprised at the size of the bathroom, but not by its sterility. Besides the toilet, counter, mirror, and sink, there was a full-size shower stall. Neatly arranged on the counter was a hairbrush, liquid hand soap, mouthwash, and hand lotion. A beige cup held a toothbrush, tongue scraper, and single-blade razor.

New and unopened toiletries. All brands Dan used. After washing his hands, he checked the medicine cabinet behind the mirror, only to discover more personal brand toiletries: toothpaste, dental floss, shaving cream, colognes, eye drops, and grooming accessories—all new and unopened, as well.

Interesting, Dan thought. He was beginning to expect this sort of thing. Dan flossed, scraped his tongue, swished with mouthwash, brushed his teeth, stripped, and took a hot shower.

He felt refreshed when he was done. Concern for his family seeped into his thoughts as Dan absent-mindedly completed his normal morning grooming ritual, snowballing from his nuclear family to his extended family and friends.

A new version of his aqua-colored luxury spa robe was hanging from the door hook. He had closed the bathroom door, more out of modesty than for any other reason. He was certain the robe had not been not there before.

Dan was beginning to wonder if he was hallucinating all of this. He did not know anything about what caused hallucinations or how they manifested. How far could a hallucination go?

Leaving his pajamas in a pile on the bathroom floor and wearing only his bathrobe and slippers, Dan stepped out of the bathroom, to be startled by another surprise.

The bed had been made and his breakfast dishes were gone, the bed table returned to its corner of the room. The lavender was still there.

Laid out on the bed was a change of business casual attire—all items that could have been plucked from Dan's closet.

Dan had not heard anyone come in. How were they doing this? These creepy surprises were becoming disconcertingly routine.

CHAPTER 12

The door opened moments after Dan finished dressing. Aroha and Bartek walked in with broad smiles on their faces.

"Time to get most of your questions answered, Mr. Bluford," Aroha said cheerfully.

"Are you ready?" Bartek asked, his enthusiasm a step below Aroha's cheerful tone.

"As ready as I'm going to be," Dan answered, allowing his nervousness to come through in his voice.

"Do not worry, Mr. Bluford," Aroha said with stern reassurance.

"We promise the next step is painless," Bartek said, his reassurance matching that of Aroha.

"That's what they say on your dentist visits," Dan remarked. "Often, those statements turn out to be misleading."

Bartek and Aroha laughed, maintaining their broad smiles. Bartek gestured for Dan to follow Aroha out of the door. Dan stepped cautiously into a wide, bright hallway to discover medical staff, patients, and visitors engaged in mobile or stationary conversations.

The smell of disinfected floors and industrial-strength deodorizes were heavy handed in their presence. The place looked like any high-end metropolitan hospital corridor anywhere in the modern world on a normal day.

No one acknowledged them as they passed, Aroha leading the way and Bartek lagging a couple of steps behind Dan, causing Dan to wonder if Bartek's role in escorting him was to assure that Dan didn't make a break for it. The thought had never crossed Dan's mind.

They walked in silence past a bank of elevators through a self-closing door leading into a stairwell. Dan's footsteps reverberated off the enclosure walls like a tap dancer. His escorts' footsteps were as quiet as mice. They entered onto a floor as wide, bright, and clean as the one they had exited, but with a different layout. There was no nurses' station. The halls were lined with regular office doors; some open, some closed. There was no activity in the corridor.

"Here we are," Aroha stopped and announced, gesturing toward an office door, her smile and behavior resembling a game show host directing a winning contestant to their next location on the set. The solid brass nameplate mounted on the door read *Indoctrination Specialist* in a bold, black, elegant cursive font.

"Where are we, exactly?" Dan asked.

"Enter, and *a number* of your questions will be answered, Mr. Bluford," Aroha said, her smile unwavering.

"What happened to *most* of my questions would be answered?" Aroha and Bartek stood in silence. Dan looked back and forth between them. Aroha maintained a look of optimism. Bartek's face was stern and resolute.

Bartek raised an eyebrow. Dan grabbed hold of the doorknob. After a couple of deep breaths, Dan found the courage to walk through a door that had no lock.

"I will be right with you." A rich baritone voice came from behind a large computer monitor on top of a large office desk—a voice that sounded oddly familiar. "Have a seat on the sofa."

Dan looked around the office. It was a nice office: spacious, tastefully decorated, comfortable—inviting, in fact. Dan spotted the sofa, walked over, and sat. It was like sitting on a cloud. Dan sank into the cushions as if they were conforming to the shape of his body. The sofa was so comfortable, Dan could imagine himself taking a nap on it.

Behind the desk was a large picture window. The drapes opened on more of the amazements Dan had witnessed earlier. Flying vehicles darted around the airways as normally as land transportation. Dan stared, still in awe.

"Sorry about that, Mr. Bluford." The voice emerged from behind the desk, and a figure rushed over to the sofa. Dan's mouth dropped open as he stood to greet his host. He could not believe his eyes, pencil-thin cornrows and a goatee being the only differences in the person. Even his style of dress was the same.

"I am Dr. Jabori Bakari." The man was smiling, clearly aware of the affect he was having on Dan. "Please have a seat."

Dan plopped back down on the sofa, the cloudlike cushions welcoming his body.

"You look just like—" Dan stammered.

"Your executive assistant Amiri Hayden. I know. He is my star-twin. You can call me Jabori."

"What is a star-twin?"

"It is like a doppelganger, but on a universal spectrum." Dr. Bakari sat in a sofa-matching armchair across from Dan while continuing to speak. "Star twins can be physically identical, such as in your case with Kwasi Gaige and mine with Amiri Hayden. Others are internal star-twins, possessing identical personalities, aptitudes, passions, likes, and dislikes. A star-twin can be of a different race or gender."

"Uh-huh," Dan said, still stunned. Dan sat there, staring as if transfixed by a startling image. "What sort of doctor are you, if you don't mind my asking?"

"Not at all. I am a psychologist who specializes in social interactions and their effects on the individual. More commonly referred to as a social psychologist."

"Really? So, am I crazy? Is this all some sort of hallucination that I will snap out of any minute, now?"

"I am afraid things are not quite that simple, Mr. Bluford."

"Simplify it for me, doctor."

"While I am a trained psychiatrist, this is not a hallucination and you are not losing your mind. Far from it. Let me start at the beginning. That should help clarify things."

"Please do. And you can call me Dan."

"Hearthlings prefer to use given names, in keeping with our tradition of respect."

"Whatever works."

"You are no longer on Earth, Daniel. You are in a parallel galaxy on a parallel planet—a parallel planet we call Hearth.

"Much is the same, within our parallel galaxies. The constellations, alignment of the planets, position of the sun, etcetera. Hearth contains the same hydrosphere land-to-water ratio of about twenty-nine percent land and seventy-one percent water, as does your Earth. Our polar regions are covered in ice, as is your Earth.

"Hearth's magnetic field is generated by its migrating outer layer of tectonic plates, solid inner iron core, and outer liquid core. One of the most interesting phenomena of our shared features is that many of the people born on Hearth have an identical twin born on Earth (or the other way around, dependent on how you choose to look at it).

"In most cases, the resemblance is physical. In some cases, the resemblance shows itself in other ways, such as having the same personality or emotional and intellectual traits. They share an aura; a spirit. In any event, we call those parallel galaxy doppelgangers 'star-twins.' Amiri Hayden is my star-twin."

"Okay, let's start at a different beginning, Amiri—I mean, Dr. Bakari."

"Jabori, please. I realize this situation will take some getting used to."

"Jabori … why am I here? On Hearth, that is."

"You have been selected to take part in our Exchange Student Program."

"What is that?"

"We choose someone from our parallel planet, Earth, and exchange them for their physically identical star-twin."

"For what purpose?"

"That will become clear during your education."

"Why me?"

"The council—of which I happen to be a member—each year reviews a short list of rigorously vetted eligible Earth candidates for our Exchange Student Program. You were chosen. We sincerely believe you will benefit from what we have to offer."

While still skeptical, Dan could not ward off his fascination. He needed to know more about … everything. "How does your vetting process work?"

"Without going into too much detail, you were observed."

"Observed where? How? Are you telling me you have people from Hearth on Earth?"

"Of course. We have people positioned in every viable segment of Earth society. Daily reports are forwarded to our various agencies on your environment, politics, science, technology ... you name it. If it is worth recording, we do so.

"If you are wondering if you are being spied on, cease that thought. We are far too busy with our own lives to be consumed with yours, although we do keep a close eye on your planet, monitoring Earthling progress (or the lack thereof) in saving yourselves.

"Only those who are to be exchanged do we study in detail. I believe it is necessary to note, here, that we are strictly on Earth to observe—not to interfere in any way."

"How are you able to do this undetected?"

"We have our ways, Daniel." Jabori smiled. This Jabori was more animated than his Amiri.

"And what exact benefits can I expect from this Exchange Student Program?"

"Ah, the benefits will become crystal clear soon enough. Be patient, Daniel. You will not want to leave when the time comes for us to kick you out of the nest."

"How did all of this happen?"

"I take it, by that question, that you mean how did you get here?"

"Yes."

"It is all based on molecular energy manipulation and wormholes. Quite simple, in theory. You excite the molecules of something to the level of light, contain that light inside a transport pod (by which you do the same), send the pod along a designated transport channel, retrieve the pod, and restore the molecules to their original forms."

"Are you talking, like, 'beam me up' stuff, here?"

"The process involved is more complex than your science fiction, Daniel, although the end result certainly is similar. We can literally transport any physical object from one place to another within our gravitational sphere without the need for a transport pod.

"Outside of our planet, a transport pod is required."

"Sounds good in theory," Dan said, staring at Jabori, unconvinced. "You're telling me you can transport people across galaxies."

"Yes, we can *and do*. Universes, as well. You are proof positive."

"I don't believe you."

"Understandable. It is only natural for you to feel that way."

"Thanks for the vote of confidence in my doubt, but that still does not address my disbelief."

"Allow me to demonstrate."

Jabori led Dan over to the nearest corner of his office to an item sitting on a wooden accent table.

"This is a portable transporter and receiving device. You will find one similar to it in every household, office, and agency throughout our territories. This device allows anyone to physically transport items from one place to another through molecular manipulation."

Dan visually examined the device. It resembled a five-gallon transparent aquarium. Four illuminated buttons poked out from its base: "Convert," "Transport," "Retrieve," and "Storage." The doctor pointed to the far corner across the room at an identical table with a similar item.

"That is the same device, different model. Pick an object."

Dan picked up a silver statue of an exact replica of a monarch butterfly feeding on a butterfly bush that was sitting on the doctor's desk and handed it to Jabori. The doctor opened the latched access door of the portable transporter and placed the statue inside. Jabori pressed the 'Convert' button. There was a faint hum.

"The 'Convert' button preps the object," Jabori said.

Dan watched as the solid statue flickered into light and then vanished, his first thought being that this was some sort of magic trick.

"This is not a magic trick, Daniel," Jabori said. "It is as real as you and I."

"I'm real. I can't vouch for you."

"Still believe you may be hallucinating all of this?"

"This all could be some sort of hallucination gone amok."

"Take a look out of that window."

Dan did so, still astonished.

"Hallucinations require a groundwork to be built upon. Has any of what you are seeing ever occurred in your wildest dreams?"

"Some yes; some no. I could be having some sort of mental breakdown."

"You are not. Believe me when I say you are one of the most stable people on your planet."

"How do I rank on *your* planet?"

"Stability is the norm on Hearth. You will fit right in, Daniel. You will come to see how real this all is, soon enough. Back to our demonstration. The statue's molecules have been transformed to pure light energy and its data digitized. We can now transport it anywhere, within reason. The greater the distance, the more dissipation may occur. Making such adjustments is not a concern, for our demonstration. You will learn more about the science of transport physics and engineering in your indoctrination classes."

"I'm going to be taking classes?"

"You are going to be acclimated to our world, Daniel. We could not have you going about ill-prepared. We can handle you. The question will be: can you handle us?

"Enough detours. Let us conclude this demonstration. In order to return this statue to its solid state, we need a converter. All transport units serve as senders and receivers. Once I press the 'Transport' button, a screen pops up."

A virtual screen about the size of a record album cover appeared with a variety of options.

"I select 'Connect,' scroll through to choose one of my pre-programmed choices, then press 'Accept' and 'Proceed.'"

The other device instantly powered up. In less than three seconds, the silver statue appeared.

Dan was momentarily stunned. He walked over, peering at the monarch statue through the glass as if it might come to life.

"You can touch it, if you like," Dr. Bakari said.

Dan removed the butterfly from the transport device. The statue was heavy enough to be a solid paperweight. Dan examined every centimeter with his critical scientific eye, turning the statue repeatedly in his hands as if attempting to verify a newly discovered historical artifact.

"Daniel, the butterfly statue that you now hold is the same one that was on my desk and in this transport device moments ago, I assure you."

"I've seen magicians perform this same sort of magic trick numerous times."

"Your skepticism is only natural. In time, you will discover that transporting, along with a number of our other advancements, is not a magic trick."

Dr. Bakari swept his hands across the window that Dan had looked through with awe.

"Do you get where I am going with this little demonstration, Daniel?"

Dan did not respond, still gazing out of the window. Dr. Bakari snapped his fingers, bringing Dan's attention back to him.

"We have touched upon how you got here. This was how it happened. You were sedated at the coffeehouse, where you stopped for a caffeine booster in two stages. An initial calming sedative was administered to you the moment you walked into the coffeehouse."

"The moment I walked in? How?"

"Through the ventilation system."

That explained to Dan why he felt a sense of tranquility while he waited for his coffee order to be filled.

"The second and final stage being administered in the coffee that you drank—which was decaf by the way. Caffeine and sedatives do not mix well."

Dan could only respond with a dumbfounded nod.

"Using equipment, we had set up in the storage room Aroha had declared as back room renovations, we converted your organic matter to light, placed it into a chamber designed specifically for the transportation of complex organic matter, converted the transportation pod to light, and transported you here in the same way that butterfly statue was transported from here to there." Dr. Bakari said, emphasizing "here to there" with his index fingers.

"Once you arrived in our retrieval area, we returned you to your natural state. I must say, a single day is a record for the Purification Process. It takes most people a minimum of four."

"This Purification Process is some sort of recovery treatment?"

"Complex organics such as us humans require a recovery period after such a long light journey, which was why you awakened in a hospital room where we could monitor you.

"Without venturing into too much detail, the Purification Process is an additional step we have added for long-distance organic transports.

We nourish our arrivals with natural nutrients to assure that every molecule is fully restored, as a precaution. There has not been a single case in over two centuries when molecular mishaps have occurred."

"Excuse me?"

"Nothing to concern yourself with, Daniel."

"You've kidnapped me from my planet and I'm supposed to accept that?"

"'Exchanged', Daniel. There is a difference."

"Incapacitated and transported to an unknown location against my will—how is that not kidnapping?"

"Kidnappers have a criminal objective, such as ransom, brainwashing or blackmail. Our goal is to educate and enlighten you."

"Cults say the same thing."

"We are not a cult," Jabori said with an amused smile.

"You couldn't have asked?"

"Once you experience our world, our society, and our people, you will understand how attempting to convince you of our existence would have been futile, even for someone who believes in intelligent extraterrestrials, like yourself."

"How do I know you're not going to experiment on me?"

"Have we mistreated you so far?"

Dan thought for a moment. He had to admit they had been treating him well. But the same could be said of lab rats before researchers proceeded with their experiments.

"No," Dan hesitantly admitted.

"You are not a lab rat, Daniel. You are a human being, and you will be treated with all of the respect and humanity befitting our species. All we ask in return is you extend to us a modicum of trust in order that we can prove our worth to you. Can you do that?"

"What about my family?"

"Your star-twin is identical to you in every aspect. As far as your family is concerned, you have never left."

"And I'm supposed to be okay with that?"

"That is our hope."

"What if I refuse to go along with your Exchange Program?"

"You do have the right of refusal. Should you do so, you will be returned home with no hard feelings on our part. After you hear what we have to say and hear our reasons for bringing you here, we are hoping you will decide to stay and accept what we have to offer."

"You're telling me that no one on my planet knows I'm gone? Not my family or friends or coworkers?"

"Not a soul."

"Suppose I do buy into all of this. How do I know that my family is safe with this star-twin?"

"You have been taken in by too much of your Earth science fiction propaganda which says that everyone or everything not of your world has some fiendish motive.

"We are human, not aliens. Do you honestly believe that a people—beings—who are capable of transporting you across galaxies would need to go to such lengths if our objective was conquest?

"Your life will proceed as if you were there. Which you are, in a manner of speaking. Toni, Wickliffe, and Mae will be protected from harm by our people as long as you are here. That's an assurance even fate cannot guarantee. You have our word on it."

"The word of kidnappers doesn't carry much weight, in my book."

"Trust does. You treasure it highly. In the end, it all comes down to trust. Think about our proposal. If, at any time, you wish to rescind our offer, we will send you home."

A soft chime sounded, followed by the sound of gentle rainfall.

"I am afraid our time is up for today, Daniel."

"I have more questions."

"Every one of which will be answered."

"This is a lot to take in, Jabori."

"We know. That is why, for the first month, we are going to spoon-feed you everything you want and need to know about Hearth."

"Hope you plan on using a baby spoon."

Jabori laughed. "Self-effacing—that is one of many qualities we like about you, Daniel—modesty. Although, we both know you do not lack confidence. We will meet again soon. Our world awaits you, Mr. Bluford. Welcome."

Jabori gave Dan a warm hug that Dan did not reciprocate. Dr. Bakari ushered Dan to the door with a polite smile, brushing aside Dan's onslaught of additional questions about his situation without further comment.

CHAPTER 13

Aroha and Bartek greeted Dan outside of the Indoctrination Specialist's office. They had been waiting for him. This time, his escorts were casually dressed in sneakers, jeans, and printed T-shirts. Aroha's T-shirt had the picture of a koala bear mother holding her joey. Bartek's had a picture of a thunderstorm spread across his chest.

"How did your first session go?" Aroha asked with genuine interest.

"Peculiar." Dan's mood was the embodiment of the word. Dan was still struggling to rectify their definition of 'exchange' for his of 'kidnapping.'

"Eye-opening. Was it not?" Bartek said.

"You could say that," said Dan.

"I just did."

A humph of a laugh escaped Dan.

"Right this way, Daniel." Aroha linked her arm in Dan's. Dan offered no resistance as they made their way down the hall, Bartek at his side rather than trailing.

"Where are we going?" Dan asked as they exited the building into a warm, bright, sunny day.

"To your room," Aroha said, in answer to his question.

"My room's back there." Dan indicated which direction he meant with a jerk of his head.

"Your new room," Bartek said. "Your living quarters."

"Dorm room," Dan said, "as in college dormitory room?"

"We prefer the term 'living quarters,' but dorm room is close enough," Bartek said.

Dan glanced back for a moment as they were walking. He saw a majestic fourteen-story white concrete textured building that had a curved glass front, high Roman-arched entrances, and which was crowned with a "Zenith Medical Center" sign that could be seen for miles.

The same types of flying vehicles Dan had seen earlier were parked at the curb near the front entrance. Their body styles ranged from mini to full size SUV, in a variety of colors from daffodil white to pitch black, "ZEC Shuttle" printed across the doors of every one.

Dan's odd feeling gave way to boyish excitement, the taut muscles of Aroha's linked arm engaging like a warm, smooth restraint, preventing Dan from bolting over to one of the vehicles.

"We'll be going in one of those?"

"Um-hmm." Aroha explained as they walked over to a gold luxury styled four door. "Shuttle service is provided for everyone on the Zenith Campus."

"Does it fly like those?" Dan pointed toward the sky. The giddy child in him needed to know the answer, despite the obvious resemblance the vehicles had to those in flight.

"Yes, it does, Daniel," Bartek said. "Built for land, air, and water."

"All of our vehicles can travel through air and water, and over any terrain," Aroha added.

"They are the only types of vehicles we manufacture," Bartek said.

"How is that possible?" Dan blurted out. "I mean—I know how in theory—but how have you mastered that capability on a production level? Are they cost-effective? Are they powered by internal combustion engines, or by some other means? What type of fuel do they use—"

"These are questions best answered by our engineers, Daniel," Aroha said, cutting him off.

"Couldn't we simply transport over?" Dan said, a note of sarcasm edged with his lingering disbelief from Dr. Bakari's demonstration. "Based upon what I've seen so far, that would seem to be the most expedient method of travel."

"We could," answered Bartek, serious in tone and manner. "Even with our ability to transport from one place to another, we prefer to travel the old-fashioned way."

Dan looked up at the vehicles jetting about. "I would not exactly call that 'the old fashioned way,'" he said softly in wonder.

Aroha and Bartek laughed. "For us, this is 'the old fashioned way,'" Aroha responded. "Shall we go?"

The doors of the gold vehicle opened like the wings of a bird preparing to take flight. Bartek stepped inside, first positioning himself behind the driver's seat. Dan sat down in the passenger seat and Aroha got in on the driver's side. Dan's seat conformed to his body, just like the sofa had in Dr. Bakari's office. The vehicle doors closed and three-point safety belts snapped into place for each of them.

"Is everyone comfortable?" The voice sounded natural, spritzed with the polite tone of an affable English butler. Aroha and Bartek answered that they were comfortable. Dan stared at the dashboard as if expecting a talking head to emerge.

"Virtual assistant?" Dan asked, sounding impressed.

"Interactive Artificial Intelligence," Bartek answered. "Standard technology for all of our vehicles. You may have noticed that your seat adapted to your body. Nanosensors are embedded in the seats that make adjustments to your body for optimal comfort."

Dan moved around in his chair, feeling squeamish, imagining nanosensors groping him.

"Are you comfortable, Mr. Bluford?" IAI asked.

Dan was comfortable. He nodded.

"Excellent."

"I didn't say anything," Dan said to the dashboard.

"Nano-cameras are also standard equipment," Aroha said. "IAI can see you. Do not worry, Mr. Bluford. You are in good hands."

"Good afternoon, Dr. Ngata. My name is Charlie. How may I assist you today?"

"How do you know my name?" Dan interjected.

"I would be happy to give you a quick overview of my functions, Mr. Bluford," Charlie said.

"Your name and detailed background information are in our database," Aroha answered. "Charlie has access to your general information. Enough to identify you, and nothing more."

"Would you like to hear more about how I operate, Mr. Bluford?" Charlie asked.

"Some other time, perhaps, Charlie," Aroha answered for Dan.

"As you wish, Dr. Ngata."

"Up for a tour of the campus, Daniel?" Aroha asked.

"Sure," Dan said feeling the opposite of the word.

"Charlie, campus tour, please."

"Extended or abbreviated, Dr. Ngata?" Charlie asked.

"Abbreviated."

"As you wish."

The engine started, quiet as a whisper. The vehicle taxied straight up until the entire campus was in full view. There were acres of development in every direction. Other vehicles zipped above, below, and around them during their ascent like bees in a hive.

The Zenith Campus layout reminded Dan of his university campus. Plenty of green space. There were varied architectural structures built of brick, metal, stone, wood and glass that announced their functions with names engraved in headstones or boldly posted on placards.

Charlie gave brief descriptions and histories of every building and green space as they flew over them. His voice altered to that of a genial expert tour guide who took pride in showing off his campus.

"That concludes our condensed tour of The Zenith Campus. I do hope you enjoyed it. Where would you like to go next, Dr. Ngata?" Charlie said, returning to his butler voice.

"Student housing."

"Right away, Dr. Ngata."

Within a minute, Charlie made a smooth vertical landing in front of a beautiful four-story, glass front building. Dan knew the name from the tour before he read it on the building headstone, "Falcon." It was named after a famous Hearthling architect, and not the bird of prey, according to Charlie.

The trio made their way inside in relative silence, stopping in front of Unit 4A on the fourth floor. "Here we are," Bartek said.

"Bartek and I will not be seeing you for a while, Daniel. Others will be helping you become acclimated. We cannot tell you how glad we are to have you with us."

Aroha and Bartek hugged Dan, who felt compelled to hug them back. Their embrace felt like family members welcoming him home. They released him.

"See you around, Daniel," Bartek said before they turned and walked away, not looking back. Dan watched them leave for a moment, oddly sad to see them go.

Dan walked through another door that had no lock, pondering the weirdness of his experiences so far and the oddity of the place in general.

*   *   *

Dan was walking toward the living room area of his new space when he heard calypso steel pan music. He froze and looked around. The music stopped after a few seconds. Dan turned in place, but he did not see anyone. The music played again. He located the sound. It was coming from what appeared to be mini speakers mounted near the ceiling.

Doorbell? Dan thought. Dan answered the door.

"Good afternoon, Mr. Bluford. May I have a moment of your time?" A woman with a Caribbean accent greeted Dan with a dazzling white smile.

The woman had a cocoa complexion and bright brown eyes. Her thick black hair was sculpted into flat twists spiraling up to the top of her head, forming a braided crown. She wore a cobalt-blue power suit with silver pumps and carried a floral shoulder bag.

Dr. Bakari had mentioned there could be physical differences between doppelgangers. This woman was shorter than Toni, with a powerful athletic figure. Could she be Toni's star-twin?

"Of course," Dan said in answer to her request, then stepped aside.

"Excellent." The woman entered as if her question had been a mere formality. Dan closed the door behind her.

"Do you like your doorbell?"

Dan thought for a moment before answering. "Love it." Which he actually did.

"I am pleased. I chose the music myself. You can change it at any time. You can even add your own sounds or melodies, if you would like. The options are quite voluminous."

"Nice to know." Dan observed that her movements were unlike Toni's. His wife moved with a seamless grace, as if her body were made of air. This woman powered her way around as if in command of her surroundings. His guest was vibrant and assertive, the opposite of Toni's cool confidence.

"I am not your wife's star-twin, Mr. Bluford. You will meet her soon enough. Allow me to introduce myself. My name is Alvita Agumanu. I am the Falcon student housing director. You can call me Al." Calling this striking woman Al seemed sacrilegious to Dan. He'd rather call her Alvita. Seemed more befitting to him.

"How charming. No one's ever said that to me before."

"*Excuse me?*" Dan said, perplexed. Al continued as if she had not heard Dan speak.

"Except my parents. You know how parents can be. They insist on calling me Alvita. 'We named you Alvita, not Al, and that is what we will call you as long as we have a voice to speak your name.'"

Alvita laughed. Her laugh thundered throughout the dormitory room. Dan could not help but smile, basking in her radiant joy. Dan knew exactly what Al meant when she spoke of her parents. The smile ran away from his face more quickly than it came and Dan froze like an animal sighting a deadly predator.

Mae marched into their home, announcing her brother with her best imitation of a procession trumpet. Wick followed his sister, showing off his second place medallion to an imaginary adoring crowd. It had been awarded to him for his class science project.

A proud and amused Dan trailed them both, closing the front door behind them, Harvey and Pearl joining in the celebration.

Dan noticed snow flurries adrift outside. Toni had to work late at the hospital. Dan had picked the children up from school. Wick and Mae were dressed in light winter wear.

"Next time, you'll get first," Dan said.

"I don't care about that, Dad," Wick responded. "I didn't do this project for a prize. I did it because I want to make a difference. Like you."

"Are you still with us, Mr. Bluford?" Al asked, snapping her fingers in front of Dan's face.

"Huh?"

"It appeared as though I lost you for a moment."

"I just had a weird flashback or memory, of a celebratory moment with my children. Except that it never happened."

"Would you like for me to call Dr. Ngata or Dr. Bakari?"

"No, no. I'll be okay, Alvita." Dan thought of his children. The joy he had only moments ago shared with Alvita spilled out of him like a burst dam into a lake of icy gloom. He missed his family. He ached for them.

"Al will do, Mr. Bluford," Alvita said, sensing the need to dial down her exuberance.

"In that case, you can call me Dan."

"I will not! I will be using your given name. It is the Hearthling way."

Dan opened his mouth to speak.

"No sense arguing the hypocrisy of my decision, Daniel. It is done."

Dan nodded his consent, but remained confused on the matter.

"Falcon is the only student housing facility on the Zenith Campus, Daniel," Al said, cranking back up her energy. "You can report directly to me any issues you may have regarding your residence."

Al opened her bag and plucked out a cube half the size of the one Aroha had produced, then snapped her bag shut.

"Alvita Agumanu," she said to the cube, then tapped it three times. The cube glowed before transforming into a 3-ring candy-apple red binder.

"Here is your welcome packet." Al handed Dan the binder with "Falcon Welcome Packet" printed on the front. Dan accepted the binder, handling it as if it might be a figment of his imagination and thus he was uncertain of its existence. "In it, you will find everything you need to know about your room and our campus. Please do not hesitate to ask if you have any questions."

"Thank you," Dan said.

"Have you had a chance to look around?"

"I just arrived."

"Allow me," Al said, abruptly walking away, fully expecting Dan to follow. He did. Al introduced Dan to his living areas and conveniences, ushering him as would a veteran real estate agent who knew every square inch of her property.

Dan had to admit that his living quarters was more like a fully furnished modern one-bedroom condominium than any college dormitory room he had ever seen.

"An Interactive Virtual Assistant is available to you 24-7. Simply say, 'Alvita, I need your help.' Try it."

"Alvita, I need your help."

"How may I be of service, Mr. Bluford?" asked Alvita's virtual double, appearing next to Al, startling Dan. She was dressed and coiffed and sounded precisely the same as the live version.

"When you no longer need assistance from your IVA, simply say, 'Thank you, Alvita, that will be all.' Try it."

Dan did as instructed. The Interactive Virtual Assistant vanished as quickly as she'd appeared.

"Why does your virtual assistant respond to Alvita and not Al?"

"Some silly quirk interactive techies have about refusing to have their creations use any name other than the proper names written on our birth certificates." Al put air quotes around the word 'creations.'

"Anyway, we strongly encourage you to remain in your room for your first day. Get to know the place a little. It is going to be home for a while. Everything you need will be delivered to you, including your meals, if you so desire. Just follow the instructions in the FWP or call upon your IVA.

"If you need additional help, feel free to personally contact me. What do you think?" Al asked after completing their circuit.

"I like it," Dan said.

"Excellent! I knew that you would."

Depression seeped in as Dan once again thought of his family. He had only been gone a couple of days, to his knowledge. How was he to know they were all right? Would he ever see them again?

"You will," Al said. "Your family is fine. Do not worry, Daniel."

"Huh." Dan stared at Al, expecting an explanation for what she had just said.

"I know you have not—"

"How do you know about my family? Why have you kidnapped me? What's going on here?"

"Aw, honey," Al said, gently cupping Dan's cheek. "Everything is alright. You simply have to trust us."

Dan snatched Al's hand away. Al was not surprised or intimidated by his action. "Enough with the riddles! Tell me what's happening!"

Al gave a slow, sympathetic shake of her head. Her eyes packed with compassion.

"It is so often the same with you exchange students. So high-strung. As I was saying," returning to her jovial hospitality voice, "I know you have not eaten anything since breakfast. I have taken the liberty of ordering you lunch. A hearty bowl of Callaloo soup, a spinach salad, and a tall glass of pineapple juice. I hope you will find my lunch choices satisfactory?" Al concluded more like a statement than a question.

Dan let out a heavy sigh. Venting his anger and frustration was getting him nowhere. Dan was beginning to accept he was going to have to ride this situation out, at least for a short while, until he could get some solid answers. "I'm sure I will," Dan muttered.

"Any questions?"

"None at the moment."

"Your room phone has been pre-programmed with the numbers of Dr. Ngata, Dr. Bakari, Bartek, room service, housekeeping, and myself. I will check in on you later." Al paused for a moment, allowing a calm seriousness to take hold.

"We realize that transitioning can be overwhelming Daniel. That is why I—and my staff—will do everything in our power to make certain you are made comfortable during your Acclimation Process."

"First it was Transformation Fatigue, then the Purification Process. Now it's the Acclamation Process. Exactly how many of these *steps* am I going to have to endure?"

Al's professional smile returned, as if fielding an amusing question by an inquisitive child. "All will be become crystal clear soon enough, Daniel." Dan half-expected Al to give his cheek a doting pinch by the way she stared at him.

"I am off," Al said briskly, striding to the front door. Dan hurried to keep up. "You know how to reach me if you need anything."

Al opened the door and stepped out. Pivoting on a dime, she turned and bear hugged Dan. "We are so glad you are here, Daniel." Her voice quavered, as pleasant as that of a lost love found. Dan was shocked. He stood stock-still, locked in her bear hug.

"Thank you," Dan finally managed to say. Al released Dan and marched down the carpeted hall toward the bank of elevators, erect and purposeful, her silver heels glinting in the hall light.

Dan stood there dazed, watching her leave and trying to get a handle on what was happening to him. He was anxious for answers to an increasing stockpile of questions. Al disappeared onto an elevator car. She never looked back.

CHAPTER 14

Dan awoke to an alarm of ringing church bells echoing throughout his living quarters. He was going to have to change his alarm, he thought.

He had taken Al's advice and stayed in yesterday. He'd spent the time getting to know his residence, familiarizing himself with the Falcon Welcome Packet information, trying to figure out what was happening to him, and missing his family, friends, and Single Organism.

There were no house rules. One could do as they pleased, whenever they wanted. All areas of Falcon were available to residents 24-7, including the commons and dining areas.

Al paid Dan an after-dinner visit, bringing her vibrant personality and Dr. Bakari, who once again insisted that Dan call him Jabori. Both guests deflected, with warm smiles, Dan's peppering of questions regarding his circumstance, repeating their run-of-the-mill answer (that by now sounded contrite and rehearsed to Dan) that he would soon come to know the answers to his questions.

Al and Jabori mostly listened as Dan vented his frustration, calming him when Dan became too agitated and forceful in his demands. They expressed their sympathetic understanding, but maintained that there was nothing they could do. His indoctrination had to proceed as outlined. It was for the best.

Dr. Bakari did shed light on Dan's earlier episode.

"Residual Connection," Jabori said.

"I had heard about that," Al said, "but never witnessed it before."

"What are we talking about?" Dan interjected.

"Residual Connection," Dr. Bakari said, "can occur between star-twins even after the mind transfer data process is severed. It's extremely rare—a phenomenon, really. One we have yet to unravel.

"It only persists between star-twins who have had a powerful celestial connection that predates their exchange. We do not know why it happens. What I *can* tell you is that the condition is often temporary and is always harmless.

"Another thing we know for certain is that your actual experience lasts only seconds, no matter how long the Residual Connection may seem to you."

"How can it be harmless when I blacked out?"

"Did he pass out?" Dr. Bakari asked Al.

"No. He simple looked dazed."

"Did you know who you were and where you were the entire time?" Dr. Bakari asked Dan.

"Yes."

"Then you did not black out. What you experienced was no more than the equivalent of a daydream."

"Let's back up a minute," Dan said. "You said something about 'predated connection.'"

"Yes. You and your star-twin already had a psychic bound before the mind data transfer."

"That's impossible! I've never heard of Kwasi Gaige, you, your world or your people before now!"

"Not on a conscious level, Daniel. The psychic connection you have exists on a subconscious level. You have probably had dreams about us without being aware they were not dreams, but visions. In all likelihood, that is the reason you have such a strong belief in the existence of intelligent extraterrestrials."

"Are you telling me that during our Residual Connection, I am seeing the world—my world—through the eyes of my star-twin?"

"Precisely. What seem like memories are actually you viewing real-time life through the eyes of Kwasi Gaige. You are seeing and hearing everything your star-twin is, at that moment."

"Can he see the world through my eyes?"

"And hear?" Al added to the question.

"Cases have varied in degrees, but in all probability, yes, although he may not be connected at the same moment as you.

"Your star-twin has been educated on this possibility. He would know what it was and would react accordingly (or, not react at all, to be more precise). Kwasi would dismiss it as a daydream or sudden distracting thought, if anyone was present."

"How is that possible, this Residual Connection—for us to have some sort of psychic bond? From what you've told me, we are millions of light years apart. Even at the speed of light, it would take years for this so-called psychic connection to travel from your galaxy to mine."

"More like quadrillions of light years, Daniel," Al said.

"It would not take that long through stable wormholes," Jabori said. "Different rules apply. Stable wormholes are galactic freeways connecting galaxies and universes—super highways throughout space, if you will.

"We map and monitor stable wormholes and know their precise locations, how to access them, and where they lead. You will learn more about stable wormholes during your studies. I hope you have better luck than I did at grasping its principals. It all seemed like scientific gymnastics to me."

"I barely made it through quantum physics," Al added. "What a nightmare." They both got a chuckle from their admissions.

"You both had classes in quantum physics?" Dan asked, astounded to hear that two people who were not physicists had studied the science.

"In high school," Al said.

"It is one of our basic requirements," Jabori said.

They were having drinks in the living room, served up by IVA Alvita. Non-alcoholic since Dan wanted to maintain a clear head. Dan had been pacing, finding it necessary to do so, given his agitated state. Jabori and Al were seated on the sofa.

Dan plopped down in the matching armchair directly across from them. The nanosensors in the chair made Dan feel cozy and he became silent, attempting to digest what he had just learned.

Al had said they were "quadrillions of light years" away from his home. One-thousand times a trillion. 'Quadrillion' had always been an abstract number to Dan: a phantom tossed about during scientific speculations.

To have been transported quadrillions of light years from home was unbelievable. It seemed that the more Dan learned, the direr his situation became. Would he ever see home again? Dan remained quiet and still for some time, staring out into space with what some might call a 'thousand yard stare,' giving Jabori concern that Dan had gone into shock.

"Would you like to go for a walk?" Jabori asked Dan after a five-minute drought of hush. "We can continue this conversation in the fresh air."

"It is a beautiful night," Al cheerfully added. "You can see the stars."

"No," Dan said, just above a whisper. "No, thank you. I'd rather be alone for a while."

Dan could not remember anything they said, after that. Jabori and Al respected his wishes. Dan did not see his guest out. He did recall Al summoning IVA Alvita and Jabori and Al having a conversation with his Interactive Virtual Assistant out of earshot before parting.

*   *   *

Dan kicked off a comforter as soft and warm as his wife's hugs, along with the memory of yesterday's Al and Jabori conversation. He felt tired; mentally rundown.

Dan had sat in that chair for over three hours, turning over in his analytical mind the probabilities of what he had been told.

By everything he knew, very little of what they were selling was possible—at least, on Earth. Yet, he was here. On Hearth (wherever Hearth was), seeing and experiencing this new world for himself.

Dan dragged himself out of a very comfortable king-size bed. Neither the bed nor comforter had nanosensors, two of the questions Dan had asked Alvita before climbing into bed.

Dan had already come to think of his IVA as simply Alvita, with little thought of her virtual assistant status.

Alvita did mention that such items were available with nanosensors if he so desired. Dan declined the offer. Alvita was unable to answer how his living quarters were stocked with so many of his things, from his clothes to his toiletries—items that made him feel right at home. Alvita stated, in response to his query, "Such information is beyond my scope, Mr. Bluford."

Dan did a morning workout of push-ups, sit-ups, pull-ups, and one of several cardio workouts he had memorized before he showered and shaved.

He choose for breakfast a vegetable goat cheese omelet with a tall glass of fresh-squeezed orange juice, hot herbal tea, and a couple of slices of brioche. Everything was delicious. Alvita appeared without being summoned, during breakfast.

"Excuse me, sir. I do not mean to disturb your meal. I was wondering if now might be an appropriate time to go over today's itinerary?"

"I have an itinerary?"

"Yes, sir. You will have daily itineraries during your Acclimation Process. Today is your first day of school!"

"*My what?*"

"Your first day of school, Mr. Bluford."

Dan sat silent for a moment, staring at Alvita for what seemed like forever as he chewed a forkful of omelet.

Alvita stood there with a pleasant smile, stoically awaiting his response. He noticed that Alvita was not breathing and chastised himself for having such a bizarre thought. Why would he expect a virtual assistant to be breathing, no matter how natural she appeared?

"Sure, why not?" he finally said. "What's on my itinerary for today, Alvita?" Dan had noticed that every time that he called her Al, she did not respond. He was fine with that.

"Your shuttle will depart at 7:45 a.m., taking you and your classmates to the Wakin Building, where you will receive your exchange student education."

"Shuttle? You mean, like a school bus?"

"We prefer to call them 'school shuttles.'"

"My classmates will also be exchange students?"

"Correct."

"Others like me, from Earth? Human beings?"

"Correct."

The prospect that Dan was not alone invigorated him. Alvita continued to give Dan a complete rundown of his day, from his class schedules to his lunch break. Dan only half listened.

He took in the weather through his picture window. Sunny, with a hazy blue sky. The sun—at least the bright yellow object radiating in the sky Dan presumed was their sun—appeared just over the horizon. Dan asked Alvita about the day's weather forecast.

"Our current temperature is fifty-two degrees with an expected high of 78," Alvita responded cheerfully, as she did to every question Dan asked her. "Humidity is expected to peek around fifty percent by early evening. Cloud cover is coming in from the south, bringing with it a twenty percent chance of afternoon rain. All in all, a typical early summer day in Atua Province."

*   *   *

Dan entered the spacious, tasteful, well-lit Falcon lobby at 7:14 a.m. It was his first venture outside of his living quarters since he had arrived. He stopped a few yards short of a clamor gathered near the front entrance, a chattering assemblage of people attempting to communicate with each other. A festival of languages was being spoken between them.

Dan had opted to go casual with an untucked plum polka dot shirt and jeans made from organic cotton and a pair of his favorite designer sneakers. He brought along a lightweight rain jacket, at the advice of IVA Alvita, in case of afternoon rain and to ward off the morning chill.

He saw the flesh-and-blood Alvita circulating amongst them. Al and four other persons, wearing sharply creased black slacks and bright red blazers with Falcon emblems sewn onto their breast pockets, were acting as translators and gracious mediators. Al bounced over to Dan and greeted him with a cheery smile, a hug, and a hearty good morning.

"Glad you could make it, Daniel."

"Did I have a choice?"

"You did—and you always will."

Dan scanned the crowd. Men and women of different ethnicities and cultures about his age were dressed in what he believed to be casual attire, some of which reflected a regional flavor. An international melody of voices filled the lobby. A United Nations conference came to mind.

"How right you are," Al said.

"Excuse me?" Dan asked, staring at Al, perplexed. Al smiled. Dan turned his attention back to the group.

"Are all of these people from Earth?"

"Yes. They are all exchange students from your planet."

"How many of them speak English?"

"One. Shall we join them?"

Al hooked Dan's arm and escorted him toward the crowd. Dan was amazed at how jovial everyone seemed. *Were they kidnapped, as I was?* he thought.

"Your classmates have been here longer than you, Daniel," Al said. "It only took you one day to complete the Purification Process. For this group, it took four to six days. In that time, they have come to understand the difference between 'exchange' and 'kidnap.' Had you not been so exceptional, perhaps you would already see this as a great opportunity as they do.

"I can promise that eventually you will be on board, Daniel," Al finished with a flirtatious flourish.

Before Dan could delve deeper into what Al said, the Falcon student-housing director introduced Dan to her assistants, then to some of the other exchange students, seamlessly translating, as needed.

By the time it became time to board the shuttle, Dan knew most of his fellow exchange students by name.

CHAPTER 15

The school shuttle parked curbside at the end of the Falcon grass-lined concrete entrance walkway. The students were herded onto the gleaming silver turtle-top vehicle that reminded Dan of a coach bus in size.

Dan was caught up in the contagion of excitement from his fellow exchange students making a ragged procession onto the shuttle. Everything on board was clean and shiny. Wall-to-wall carpeting; two rows of double-file reclining seats with a wide aisle separating the rows; adjustable plush seats offering all of the ease of a home recliner with built-in nanosensors for additional individual comfort—the shuttle climate was as cozy as his living quarters.

Above each seat were individual climate controls. The writing on his climate controls was in English. Next to him, at the window seat, sat Waqas Anwar, an industrialist from Pakistan. They had met in the lobby. Waqas was gazing out of the window, absorbing the view like a child excited with anticipation of their first road trip.

Dan glanced up at Waqas' climate controls. His indicators were written in what Dan would describe as an Arabic script. He pondered how that was possible. Only two of Falcon's five hostesses were accompanying them, serving as escorts. Al was not one of them.

The senior member of the two approached them, strolling down the aisle making certain everyone was buckled in and comfortable.

"In case you are wondering why your climate controls are in English and Mr. Waqas' are in Nastalik," the gentlewoman with a pleasant smile and voice said to Dan without prompting (Her pinned name tag read Eleonora Olsson. She had a perfect news anchor's smile, as Dan would describe it and was of average height and build with calm blue eyes), "it is because the text is actually composed of Pico-sensors that can interpret and adjust its written message into the native speaker's language."

"You're kidding," Dan said in disbelief as Waqas Anwar looked on.

"No sir, I am not."

"Interactive Artificial Intelligence?" Dan asked, remembering the correct terminology from his experience in the Zenith Campus Shuttle with Aroha and Bartok.

"In this instance, the driver controls when to release or lock the language sensors; not our onboard IAI."

"Why not use IAI?"

"You will have to ask our Interactive Artificial Intelligence developers that question, Mr. Bluford."

"Thank you," Dan said. Eleonora explained in Urdu to Waqas what she had told Dan.

"Hairat angez!" Waqas exclaimed.

"He said 'amazing'," Eleonora translated to Dan.

"Yes, it is," Dan replied to both of them. Waqas and Dan smiled at each other in mutual astonishment over this recent discovery.

"Will there be anything else, gentlemen?" Eleonora asked both in their native tongues. The two men replied, "Not at the moment." Eleonora politely moved on to check on other passengers.

The school shuttle traveled by ground to get to the Wakin Building. When one of the students asked why they were not flying, it was explained to all that it would be quicker to travel by land than to take off, fly, then land.

The drive was smooth; not as much as a single bump along the way. They passed only four other road vehicles during their short trip. Dan and his classmates were rubbernecking, noticing every bit of architecture, art work, and green space they passed, having seen very little of the Zenith Campus from ground level.

They arrived at the Wakin Building at 7:54: a large, circular building with a geometric topological spiral effect dominated by mirrored glass. They were ushered off the shuttle onto another grass-lined concrete path and into the lobby.

Despite the exotic exterior of Wakin, Dan had expected an antiquated functional interior resembling the classroom buildings of his university days. He was surprised to discover the lobby was more like that of a luxury hotel. A spacious marble-floored atrium was adorned with elegant furnishings, exquisite art, and copious green plants. His fellow exchange students were equally awed, judging by their expressions.

The lobby was bustling with activity. Humans, androids, and drones were making their way here and there. The humans who worked at Wakin stood out. They were the ones who moved with purpose, giving orders or taking them while going about their tasks, or being fixated on making their way to an appointed round.

Other people moved more leisurely, like tourists. They smiled, waved, bowed, or spoke as they passed, expressing their greetings in the languages of their cultures. They were the ones who were clearly fellow Earthlings. Seeing others like them buoyed Dan's spirits even more. He was not alone in that reaction.

Eleonora and her colleague, Enrique Pacheco, an energetic teenager with clear brown eyes and a mound of curly black hair, kept their group from wondering. Dan noticed something that struck him as odd as Eleonora and Enrique marshaled them up the stairs to Classroom 3B. No one was carrying a shoulder bag, briefcase, backpack, or anything, for that matter, that resembled the transient world he was accustomed to.

The classroom layout was the same as what Dan was used to from his university days. A penned-in space large enough to accommodate pedestrian desks was coupled with pedestrian chairs arranged in neat rows. At the front of the class was a wooden lectern. Behind the lectern appeared to be an interactive wall rather than a chalk or white board.

That was different, as was the presence of colorful perennials throughout the classroom, and the wood panel interior walls. Dan found it odd that the classroom had opaque interior walls. Why go through all of the trouble to construct a building of glass, only to obstruct the view?

On their way to the classroom, Dan could see outside from every direction. He wondered why that was not the case here. Dan sauntered over to take a closer look at the walls. A few of his equally curious classmates joined him. Eleonora and Enrique urged them to take a seat before they could unmask any clues.

Once comfortable at a desk of their own choosing, Eleonora and Enrique left, mentioning that they would see them later. Moments after their escorts' departure, a tall, thirty-something woman with apricot skin, high cheekbones, and shoulder-length lustrous black hair strode into the classroom, closing the door behind her.

She was wearing a refined desert pearl necklace with matching earrings. Her shark blue business suit looked tailored for her slender body. She anchored herself behind the polished wooden lectern, placing her long fingers firmly on either side of the lectern reading desk.

A tasteful diamond wedding band glinted on her left hand and a sterling silver gemstone bracelet did the same from her right wrist.

Shoulders back and head erect, as if standing at attention, was the most natural thing for her. She passed her steady hazel eyes over the classroom for a moment. Some students fidgeted under her gaze. Other sat in nervous silence. All attempted to anticipate what was to come next.

The elegant woman picked up what looked like a wireless earbud from the reading desk, signaling for the class to do the same. The exchange students spotted an identical device in the far corner of their desks that had somehow escaped their notice. They picked them up.

The students studied them for a moment before returning their complete attention to the elegant woman. She inserted the device into her ear. The class followed suit without instruction. Dan felt a slight tickle as the earbud shaped itself to the opening of his auditory canal.

"Good morning, everyone!" Dan heard the woman standing at the lectern say in American English. "Welcome to Hearth. We are very pleased to have you here."

Dan's jaw dropped. He looked around to see the same astonished reactions exhibited by his classmates.

"She is speaking my language!" Waqas shouted, and Dan heard him instantaneously in English. Their languages were being translated in their own voices.

"Remarkable!" Dan blurted out.

The classroom erupted in a clash of conversations as people began speaking directly to each other. Many re-introduced themselves, spouting off about where they were from and how they had gotten here.

The woman in the shark blue suit stood idly by, smiling, her smile as warm as her expression had been stern. She was undoubtedly accustomed to the reaction following this announcement.

"Settle down, please!" she said after a few minutes of allowing the class to interact. Her smile relaxed into a composed seriousness.

"You will have plenty of opportunity to get to know each other in the days ahead."

It took about another thirty seconds before her request was fully realized.

"Thank you. I am Professor Huaman," she said in a practiced, professorial voice.

The interactive wall behind her wrote in perfect cursive, "Professor Huaman," in large chalk-white letters on a black chalkboard background, even making a chalk-on-blackboard sound as it did so.

"I will be your instructor—more like your guide—into our world. The device you have placed into your ear is a miniature language translator. You may now have a conversation with anyone on Hearth, and this mini-translator," the professor pointed to her own, "will, at conversational speed, translate what that person is saying into your native tongue.

"This also works for multiple and simultaneous conversations, as you have just experienced, similar as to what is done at your international conferences, absent the headphones and electronic or human translators.

"It operates no differently than your natural hearing. The device merely provides an assist to what your mind normally does under the same circumstances. Shall we begin?"

A couple of students blurted out questions that Dan heard translated into English.

"I ask that you please reserve all questions until the end of my lecture. There is much we need to cover."

The outburst calmed.

"Thank you."

The professor took a moment to glance around the class. Some had responded verbally to her request. Most responded with gestures such as a nod or shrug. Every person, including Dan, had a look of anxious anticipation.

"Each of you has been told the story of your journey to us. Let me begin with the basics. You are now on planet Hearth, a parallel planet to your Earth, in a parallel galaxy. Our planets are identical to each other, forged in the same manner as yours, at the same precise instance. They are as indistinguishable as can occur in the natural world. Duplicate copies extend to us.

"Hearthlings and Earthlings are human beings. Approximately fifty-six percent of us have a star-twin on your planet, a phenomenon we can only speculate upon, but have formed no clear-cut answers about.

"What I can tell you is this: while you are being educated about our world and our people, your star-twin is bookmarking your lives on Earth."

Professor Huaman paused to allow the murmuring to die down as exchange students made comments to each other regarding the news.

"One of the first things every one of you should know is that your stay with us will be one year. At the end of such time, you will be returned home to your uninterrupted lives. No one will have known you were gone.

"I repeat: your star-twins have bookmarked your lives. Why are we doing this, all of you are wondering? We expect that the answer to that question and all of your questions will become clear soon.

"I realize this may be a redundant act. Since most of you have already done so, let us formalize your introductions. Please, each of you stand in turn when I point to you and tell us your name, where you are from, and a little about yourself. Include any information that you believe will help us get to know you better."

There were formal introductions as Professor Huaman asked each student, in turn, to stand. Dan and his classmates gave mini-bios about their Earth lives. What Dan learned about his Earthling comrades impressed him.

Their class was composed of an industrialist, sociologist, linguist, microbiologist, diplomat, Cardinal, musician and anthropologist, environmental physicist, historian, educator and philosopher, human rights crusader, and environmental activists.

They were all dedicated to creating a healthier planet and bringing about worldwide social and economic justice. Dan felt honored being included in what he viewed as an illustrious group.

Professor Huaman informed her students, at the conclusion of their introductions, that there were ten classrooms in the Wakin Building accommodating exchange students from every Earth nation, who were receiving the exact same education as they were. They were Class 3B (the 3B corresponding to their classroom number).

"I noticed there are twenty-three seats, but only thirteen of us," said Intan Nugraha, a human rights crusader from Indonesia. "Will there be more Earthlings joining us?"

"The number twenty-three is symbolic, Mr. Nugraha. It represents the human chromosome pairs. We were considering forty-six, but found that class size too large. We capped our class sizes at twenty-three, providing desks for maximum capacity.

"The other classrooms are filled. 3B is the only exception, giving me a welcome opportunity to grant each of you more individual attention. The short answer to your question, Mr. Nugraha, is no. There will not be more exchange students joining this class.

"You may have wondered why you were not given translation devices sooner. We have our reasons. Right or wrong, you decide. As a sidebar, did you know that there are thousands of spoken languages on your planet? All of which we have cataloged.

"Hearth has only half as many languages as Earth. We select our exchange students from a wide and varied cross-section of candidates. Many are considered. Few are chosen. You are one of the chosen few."

"I suppose we should feel honored," Dan said, not masking his sarcasm.

"Yes you should, Mr. Bluford," Professor Huaman said with a casual smile that belied her iron tone. "As should all of you. We wanted our exchange students incommunicado, without aid of an interpreter. That was a deliberate scrambling on our part.

"What knowledge any of you had of foreign languages has been stripped away. What remains is your native tongue.

"Case in point: Mrs. Chiba, you have always had a fascination with languages." Professor Huaman said to Amaya Chiba, a linguist from Japan. "You began learning foreign languages at the age of four, encouraged and supported by your parents in your efforts. As a result, you currently work as a translator and interpreter for both the United Nations and international corporations."

"How long have you people been observing me?" Amaya asked, startled by the exposé.

"Since your preschool teacher, Mrs. Sato, reported to us that you might make a good exchange student candidate."

"Sato-san is a Hearthling?"

"Sato-san *was* a Hearthling. The Mrs. Sato you are referring to is alive and well, living here on Hearth."

"Living on Hearth! I just saw Sato-san and her husband at a local market in Kagoshima where I live."

"That would have been her Earthling star-twin."

"Did Sato-san know she had been replaced?"

"Yes, she did. She accepted it for the betterment of her people, as we hope will you all. Her Hearthling star-twin's experiences and memories were transferred to her upon returning to her life, creating an uninterrupted stream of being for the person you know as a beloved pre-school teacher."

"Why didn't she say anything to anyone?"

"We asked her not to."

"And she agreed?"

"Not only are you chosen on the basis of what you can contribute to your world upon your return, but honor and integrity are also part of the selection equation."

"Will I see her? The Hearthling Sato-san?"

"I am afraid not, Mrs. Chiba. Such a reunion is forbidden. That would violate one of our strictest mandates regarding Hearthling and Earthling interaction."

Amaya's shoulders dropped in disappointment.

"Besides Japanese, you are fluent in most European languages—Mandarin, Korean, Arabic, Hausa, Hindustani, Hebrew, and Russian—are you not, Mrs. Chiba?"

"I am." Amaya said, squaring her shoulders and meeting Professor Huaman's eyes.

"With a dozen more languages of which you have a grazing knowledge."

Amaya nodded.

"Indulge me. Please compose a simple sentence in any language other than Japanese for the class. I will temporarily disable everyone's translator so that what you say will be heard truly."

Amaya struggled to do as Professor Huaman asked, frustration mounting, until she shouted in Japanese, "What did you do to me? Why would you strip me of that knowledge?"

The class voiced their sympathies with Amaya. Professor Huaman enabled their translators and waited until the uproar became a murmur.

Dan's voice was not amongst the uproar. It appeared to him that Professor Huaman had not taken pleasure in delivering this news to the class by way of Amaya Chiba, no more than Dan did when he had to terminate a Single Organism employee.

"Comparing notes and asking questions as you did moments ago would only be a distraction," Professor Huaman began. "You're doing what comes naturally for people displaced from a common environment when thrown into a unique situation. Displaced curiosities can be annoying diversions. We wanted your focus on us, as your focus is now on me in this classroom.

"Do not worry, Mrs. Chiba. All of your language skills will be reinstated upon your return to Earth."

"That is an unwarranted incursion upon her person," said Ella Claesson, a sociologist from Sweden, in what Dan assumed was Swedish (but he heard in English), "and a violation of her human rights."

"You have no rights of any kind on Hearth, Mrs. Claesson, except those afforded to you by us."

"That's absurd!" Intan blurted out.

"If you do not like our methods, Mr. Nugraha, there is the door. All of you are free to leave and return to Earth at any time."

The class fell into stunned silence.

"No one willing to take me up on my offer?"

No one responded.

"Then let us proceed. Why are you here? The short answer is that you have been chosen to participate in our exchange program. This fact has been explained to you by your Indoctrination Specialist.

"I want to emphasize that you have *not* been kidnapped. How can that be, when you have been plucked from your home? In a manner of speaking, you've been forcefully taken from your family and friends, stripped bare of the life that you have known, and placed on a foreign planet.

"It is our hope—strike that, *it is our expectation*—that you will discover our intent is neither evil nor self-serving. We have brought you here because we believe you can become the saviors of Earth."

CHAPTER 16

The professor had taken a moment to allow her words to sink in before continuing. An uneasy stillness fell over the class, like a fog blanket drifting down upon their heads. The exchange students became lost in their own thoughts, attempting to phantom the magnitude of the professor's last statement.

Professor Huaman surveyed her students with an even stare.

"Allow me to explain," she began in a slow, measured tone. "What you term as 'environment' we commonly refer to as 'biosphere.' You may hear me use those words interchangeably. It is no secret that Earthlings are abusing their biosphere, nearing a point of no return.

"We hope, from your Hearth experience and our teachings, to arm you with the knowledge and tactics to curtail what most certainly is your impending doom.

"I am not speaking of your planet when I speak of doom. The Earth will go on without human life. Your planet will miss you no more than a dog would miss fleas. I am strictly speaking of human extinction.

"Environmental abuse is not the only major challenge you face. There is also the reckless, vicious, and disturbing inhumanity you bombarded upon each other. You have weapons of mass destruction capable of obliterating life 1,000 times over. You have biological and chemical weapons designed to wipe out your fellow humans. Your contemptible mindset, driven primarily by ego and fear, might annihilate you before the environment has its turn.

"None of this is news to any of you. A large part of the reason each of you have been chosen is because, in your own ways, you are combating these issues. You cannot do it alone, as you already know. We hope to enable you with tools that will persuade a majority of your fellow Earthlings to change their ways, thereby altering your future from one of extermination to salvation.

"Let us move on, shall we?"

No one gave a verbal response. Each exchange student remained dazed, trying to comprehend what it meant to have the fate of the world on their shoulders. They had all considered what they were doing as part of the solution for the betterment of their planet, but had not seen themselves as barriers to stave off human annihilation.

To hear those realities spelled out to them in near-clinical terms from an apparent outside source was frightening.

Dan and a few others were able to give Professor Huaman a feeble nod. The students could not see it, but a cube materialized on the lectern table. Professor Huaman held it up to show to her students. The cube was small enough to fit into a shirt pocket.

"What is it?" asked Obed Addo, the educator and philosopher from Ghana.

"This is my Class 3B Education Packet, Mr. Addo. EP, for short."

The same type of cubes materialized upon each of the students' desks, to their astonishment.

"Before you are your Class 3B Education Packets. Your EPs will provide you with all of the tools you will need for your courses and to complete any assignments. *Yes*, there will be homework assignments, quizzes, and tests."

There was a collective groan amongst the class. Professor Huaman continued unperturbed. "While you will not be graded on any of your work, it will determine how long you will be required to remain on campus before you can be introduced into our society. Do not fear your EPs. Pick them up."

Some students gingerly handled their cubes. Others lifted theirs without any apprehension. Professor Huaman stepped from behind the lectern with her EP cube in hand.

"The first thing you want to do is personalize your Education Packet. Tap your EP three times. The three taps awaken the cube. A cube's normal state is dormant, to conserve power. Your EP has a power source that will last for the life of the cube, which will be longer than you will have use for. Any light source can feed your cube. Now, tell it your full name."

Professor Huaman demonstrated. "My EP has already been personalized. Give yours a try."

Dan was first. The others looked on in suspense. Dan tapped his cube three times, then said "Daniel Samuel Bluford." A spray of red light scanned him so quickly that Dan had no chance to react.

"Do not be alarmed by the light." Professor Huaman addressed the entire class. "Mr. Bluford's EP has scanned him. In that brief instant, his EP cube gained visual recognition of Mr. Bluford's identity. His EP has also taken a sample of his DNA, as has yours, from the moment you touched it. With three key elements of identification (vocal, visual, and DNA), Mr. Bluford has personalized his Education Packet. No one else can access his EP cube except him."

Dan found that to be cool. Most of his classmates felt the same, and rushed to personalize their own. A few stragglers brought up the rear.

"What, exactly, does this cube do?" Professor Huaman rhetorically asked after the exchange students had personalized their EP cubes. "As I mentioned before, this cube contains everything you will need for every course you will be taking. Let us unpack some of its goodies."

Professor Huaman tapped her cube three times. "Syllabus, lecture notes, and presentation materials," Professor Huaman said to the cube. The professor's cube glowed and hummed for a few seconds before a paper syllabus, small stack of index cards and memory stick appeared, neatly arranged on the empty desk nearest her.

"Load presentation materials onto interactive wall." The memory stick disappeared.

"Presentation materials loaded," announced audio from the interactive wall.

"Now you try," Professor Huaman said, after the student's amazement dimmed. "Instead of lecture notes and presentation materials, which your EPs do not have, let us try a student planner, notepad, smart pen, and supplies list."

Each of the students' cubes glowed and hummed to life after their jumbled requests. The items appeared before them on their desks.

"If you will take a look at your supplies list..."

Each student picked up a sheet of paper with the heading 'Class 3B Supplies List', written in their own language.

"This is a comprehensive list of all of the materials available to you in your Education Packet. Please take a moment to become acquainted with this list. In order for EP to generate these items, it is necessary for you to use the precise names on your supplies list. I recommend you keep a hard copy of your supply list handy for quick reference."

Dan read his list: Syllabus, student planner, a variety of course textbooks, stapler, sticky notes, color-coded stickers, highlighters, index cards, a memory stick, wall calendar, printing paper, glue, scissors, tape, bulletin board, smart pen, laptop, printer, scanner, dictionary, thesaurus and smartphone.

"Should you misplace your Education Packet, all you need do is call for it by name. It will recognize your voice and appear in a convenient location near you. Observe."

The professor walked over and placed her cube on the desktop of a student. She returned to her lectern.

"EP Cube Professor Huaman, return." Her cube vanished from the student's desk and reappeared on the professor's lectern. The professor held up her EP cube before the class, then set it down.

"Bear in mind that your EP cube has a 10-kilometer radius by which it can hear you. Your cube is irretrievable by such means beyond that distance.

"If you were thinking of conveniently misplacing your Education Packets when your assignments are due, think again. All of your work and my lectures are automatically backed up onto our central data base and are easily retrievable. Not that any of you brilliant exchange students would ever dream of employing such a dodge…"

Professor Huaman gave her students a mischievous smile. That brought a bemused chuckle from the class. Professor Huaman returned to the desk containing her manifested materials with her cube in hand.

"You can chose to keep your items solid by laying your hand on the item and issuing the command 'solid.'"

Professor Huaman demonstrated with her syllabus. She held it up for the class to see.

"This syllabus will remain a solid piece of paper, no longer having any connection whatsoever with my EP cube." She handed the paper syllabus to the student nearest her, Jomana Ashraf, a musician and anthropologist from Egypt, to examine and pass around to her classmates. Once each student had an opportunity to examine the syllabus and it was returned to Professor Huaman, she continued.

"To return the solid item to cube status, lay your hand upon it and command, 'cube dissolve.'"

Professor Huaman did this to her paper syllabus. Her EP cube momentarily glowed before her syllabus disappeared.

"Only an item produced by a specific cube can be returned to that specific cube."

"What if you make an item solid, then lose it, or it is damaged or destroyed?" asked Carlito Macedo, a microbiologist from Portugal.

"Then your cube can reproduce a duplicate item for you. However, anything your previous item possessed, such as files on your laptop or recorded lectures by your smartpen, will be lost in connection with your cube. You will need to recover that information from the central database.

"One other EP cube command I am going to teach you today is 'retrieve'. The retrieve command will enable you to retract whatever your cube has produced. Observe."

Professor Huaman held up her cube for all to see. "Awaken your cube." After tapping her cube three times, she gave the command, "Retrieve presentation materials."

Her cube briefly glowed. Everyone heard the interactive wall announce "presentation materials unloaded."

"Now you try. Remember: you must use the precise name of the individual item you want to retrieve."

There was a jumble of retrieve commands issued by students retracting the item of their choice. Their cubes glowed and the article they indicated returned to its source.

"To have all cube-generated materials retrieved at once, you need only issue the command 'retrieve all.'"

Professor Huaman once again demonstrated. Her syllabus and lecture notes vanished.

"Now you try."

Once her student's cube-generated items were retracted, Professor Huaman returned to her position behind the lectern, then continued.

"I know this is a lot to grasp on your first day." Her voice glided from professorial to earnest. "Trust me when I say that you will have no trouble absorbing and maintaining what you will learn here. Your student planner has your course times already noted.

"All of your classes will take place in this building in this room. I have been blessed with the privilege of being your instructor for every single one." Professor Huaman stressed the words "every, single, one" as if the prospect gave her genuine joy. The class would have taken her last comment as sarcasm, had Professor Huaman not been so sincere. "Questions?"

The students bombarded Professor Huaman with questions. Dan's was the first to be answered.

"How does this cube work?"

"The cubes are designed from a combination of Pico and Nano technology, elementary particle coding, and Interactive Artificial Intelligence," Professor Huaman answered, returning to her professorial voice, "the details of which are far too extensive to go into."

"All of that in this?" Dan responded, holding up his EP cube and peering at it as if it were a locked puzzle box he was trying to figure out how to open.

"Yes." Professor Huaman matter-of-factly answered Dan's question.

"Why must we lay our hand on an item in order to solidify it?" asked Waqas.

"The item reads your DNA signature and responds to your command. No one else can solidify an item created from your personalized EP cube."

"Does this cube technology extend to clothing, jewelry, or other personal effects?" Jomana asked.

"No. Not because we cannot create such cubes—we simply chose not to."

"Can our EP cubes produce food?" Cardinal Gregorio Jayden Ocampo from the Philippines asked.

"No, for the same reason previously mentioned about clothing, jewelry and personal effects. A word of caution: please do not attempt to dismantle your EP cube to see how it works. Your cube would literally disintegrate if you did. Should you be foolish enough to vandalize your EP cube twice in any way, then you will face immediate expulsion and be sent home."

A look of disappointment swept over some of the exchange students' faces, especially Dan's.

"Love your necklace," blurted out Nivi Lyberth, an environmental activist from Greenland.

"Thank you, but that is not a question."

Students eagerly raised their hands like pupils in urgent need to be excused to use the restroom. Professor Huaman pointed at students whose question she would answer in turn.

"Have you ever had a Hearthling die on Planet Earth while posing as an Earthling star-twin?"

"No."

"Have you ever had an Earthling exchange student die on Hearth?"

"No Earthling or Hearthling has ever died or been injured during the exchange program."

"How many Hearthlings are on Earth?"

"I am not aware of the exact number. I want to note here that Hearth has never interfered in your course of human history. That Hearthling commitment will not change."

"How is it that you are so much more advanced?" asked Russian world historian Gennady Kuznetsov. "Considering we are of parallel worlds."

"Good question, Mr. Kuznetsov. None of what we have accomplished would have been possible without the cooperation of Hearthlings. We are all human beings. What that means to Hearthlings is that we are all family.

"Why are we the way we are and you the way you are? Why are Hearthlings and Earthlings different? You will discover, during your course in Hearthling history, that human beings on our planet took different directions than those on yours. We consistently made different choices during our evolutionary development than you. We are not superior. We have applied our collective energies exclusively to the betterment of humankind and the protection of our home.

"Ecology is not merely a study, on Hearth. It is a way of life. Protecting our ecosystem and living in harmony with our biosphere is seeded into our marrow.

"Social norms are what is acceptable. We may be distinct in cultures, but we are unified as nations. The variant practices for racism and sexism on your planet never took hold on ours. They were universally rejected from the start.

"Race is an artificial construct: a fact widely known on your Earth, but ignored by enough to keep the poison of racism circulating through the veins of your societies. Prejudices are false. Culture is real."

"Does Hearth have an adoption program for Earthlings?" asked Gagandeep Acharya, a diplomat from India.

Professor Huaman laughed, along with the rest of the class, before answering. "I am sorry, Mr. Acharya. We do not."

"Why were we chosen, exactly?" asked the French Canadian environmental physicist Oliver Martin.

"To reiterate and expand, Mr. Martin: all of you, in some humane and major capacity, are working to make your world a better place socially, economically, and environmentally.

"As you are all aware, if Earthlings continue to follow the course of Earthly and human abuse they are currently on, you will become extinct. There are those who falsely believe that, no matter what, humans will adapt. In short, you will not.

"Our physiologies do not adapt easily. It took thousands of years for us to evolve to our current state. Humans will unlikely not be granted that opportunity again.

"There is still time for you to alter your fate. You are here to learn ways in which to do that. Also, based upon your psychological profiles, we knew you would not be traumatized by this event."

"When did you profile us?" Obed asked.

"On Earth, of course, Mr. Addo. The details of when and how are not important. I would like to add that you are free to leave Hearth any time you wish before your year with us is completed. We will return you to Earth disappointed, but with no hard feelings. Just say the word."

"What do our star-twins get out of this deal?" asked Cardinal Ocampo.

"Your star-twins are volunteers, Cardinal, who—"

"That's more than you can say for us," Ella said, drawing a burst of good-humored laughter from the class. Professor Huaman allowed herself a coy smile before continuing.

"Your star-twins are brave volunteers who wanted to do their part to help save Earth."

"That's it?" Waqas said.

"That is it, Mr. Anwar. You will find that Hearthlings have different motivations for taking action. Star-twins volunteer for Earth duty because we believe it is the right thing to do. We do not expect reward or praise for such actions. Those elements serve to feed vanity. We are not a vain people."

"Some Earthlings behave as Hearthlings," Dan said.

"True enough, Mr. Bluford. As examples, you have banded together in mass to protest against gross injustices, such as the fight against global warming. Your powers that be often go against the will of the majority in order to achieve their personal agendas, both legally and illegally, by exploiting rewards versus risks factors.

"The plight of your planetary or human consequences is often not a viable consideration in such decisions made by those Earthlings in control."

"Wouldn't it be easier to have our star-twins take on the task of saving our planet?" Intan asked.

"On this point, Mr. Nugraha, Hearthlings have debated whether to more aggressively intervene on behalf of Earthlings. It has been decided it would be too great a risk for Hearth, based on current human behavior on Earth—obliteration being the Earthling kneejerk reaction when faced with an unknown.

"Discovery could be catastrophic. It was decided to leave Earthlings to regulate their own fate. Hearth would do what they could to aide those who were fighting for positive change, without stepping into the fray.

"We are more advanced than you in a number of ways," Professor Huaman stated without arrogance or glee, "and more developed in others. We are not super-beings. We cannot force your people to change their ways. We would not, even if we could.

"Only you can change the minds, hearts, and souls of Earthlings in order to accomplish what must be done. We expect our education will help in your fight to achieve those goals."

"There were times when a Hearthling has answered an unspoken question or comment on something I did not mention," Amaya said. "Are Hearthlings mind readers or something?"

"Yes, Mrs. Chiba. All Hearthlings are telepaths. We are born with the ability to read minds and transmit our thoughts to others, a gift that we begin cultivating from our first few years of life. Our telepathic abilities extend to wildlife and aqualife, as well."

"You can talk to animals?" Waqas blurted out amongst the uproar, a question that silenced the din.

"We prefer the terms 'wildlife' for land creatures and 'aqualife' for those that live in water, Mr. Anwar."

"You expect us to believe that you can talk to ... non-human life forms?" asked Cardinal Ocampo.

"Yes, Cardinal. We have telepathic conversations with our wildlife and aqualife Hearthling residents, whether you chose to believe it or not."

"How?" Amaya asked. "What languages do you speak?"

"In the beginning, Mrs. Chiba, it was the same way as we communicated with our earliest ancestors. Our thoughts were composed of pictures. As we developed verbal and written skills, wildlife and aqualife did, as well. Wildlife and aqualife have even developed their own distinct languages."

"You can communicate with animals—wildlife—in the same way we are doing now?" Obed asked in disbelief. "Only with your minds?"

"Precisely, Mr. Addo." Professor's Huaman's response raised another uproar from her exchange students.

"Can you teach us to become telepaths?" Gagandeep asked after the class outburst withered from this latest Hearthling discovery.

"Telepathy is a part of our DNA, Mr. Acharya. Even still, that skill must be harvested in infancy. Otherwise, that portion of the human brain reallocates that specific region for other purposes. It is too late for any of you to become telepaths even if the possibility for each of you ever existed. I am sorry."

"Are you a democratic society?" Gagandeep asked.

"Yes, Mr. Acharya, we are. One person, one vote."

"Do Hearthlings practice capitalism, socialism, or communism?" Gennady asked.

"That is a question best answered once you leave this campus, Mr. Kuznetsov."

"Do you have a constitution?" Ella asked.

"We have two constitutions, Mrs. Claesson. One for how to treat our fellow beings. The other for how we treat the natural world."

"With all of this advanced technology and your expanded human capabilities, how is it that your world is not in utter chaos?" asked Cardinal Ocampo.

"If what we have mastered were somehow interjected into your world, Cardinal, Earthling life would be chaotic. Imagine, if you will, that you have been reared in an environment where all of this is as natural as air. None of what we do would seem out of place. It is the norm and thereby universally accepted."

"Why can't you transport our people here?" Intan asked. "You clearly have the capability."

"Move your people from your home to ours?"

"Yes."

"No."

"Why not?"

"Because this is our home. Our planet. In part, a product of our creation. We are not going to allow you to use our planet as your life rafts because you destroyed yours."

"Even by your own estimate, time is running out for us."

"Then, such will be your fate if you do not change in a hurry. We will not bail you out. Hearthlings are also human, Mr. Nugraha. We would not be saving our species by saving you.

"There is no room for you here. To introduce billions or even millions of Earthlings into our society would not only create overpopulation, but invite mayhem. We could not conform or control those of you who were determined to bring your destructive Earthling habits to our Hearth. Extermination would become our only option."

There was a collective gasp.

"I don't believe you!" exclaimed Cardinal Ocampo.

"You do not believe we will do such a thing, Cardinal? Then you are naive.

"We are not your saviors. You are. We will not sacrifice ourselves in order to save you. If you resent us for being candid on that matter, then so be it. Earthlings have made their choices, as have Hearthlings. The results speak for themselves.

"You have no one else to blame. You are literally reaping what you sow. There is still an opportunity to salvage your existence. You use the words 'Mother Nature', but you do not treat nature accordingly."

"What do *you* call nature?" asked Nivi.

"Nature, Mrs. Lyberth. The word alone holds enough reverence for us. More so than any of your self-proclaimed gods."

Cardinal Ocampo stiffened at Professor Huaman's "self-proclaimed gods" comment, but remained quiet.

"Why won't you save us?" asked Gagandeep.

"Why do you not you save yourselves, Mr. Acharya? In short, you will either save yourselves or perish. Such are the choices of responsible commonsense adults versus selfish, willfully ignorant juveniles."

There was stunned silence. Professor Huaman surveyed her class. She saw an assortment of fear, bewilderment, and anger on their faces.

She had been expecting that reaction. She wanted her students to not view what they were experiencing on Hearth as some pleasure junket. Professor Huaman needed her students to fully comprehend the magnitude of what their planet was facing. The possibility of human extinction was a matter that should slap you awake from whatever ignorant stupor you imbibed.

Professor Huaman held in check what Hearthlings intended should Earthlings fail to survive.

They were not conquerors. Her people did not seek to claim new territories or enslave their fellow mortals. Hearthlings were opportunists not by means of exploitation, but either through good fortune or by their own principled creation.

What Professor Huaman had said was true. They would not evacuate Earthlings en mass to Hearth should their best efforts fail and Earthlings became extinct. They would keep an eye on their parallel planet. They would wait until Earth settled and expunged much of the toxic heritage of its calamitous forbearers. Until it achieved a natural harmonious balance, purifying itself through the carbon of time.

How long would it take? No one knew. What Professor Huaman *did* know was that Hearthlings were patient. Should such a scenario occur, her fellow citizens would trickle in so not to disturb the delicate biosphere, making Earth a second home. They'd repopulate the sphere with their own human images, bringing a Hearthling way of life to a planet that deserved better.

"I leave you with this final thought," Professor Huaman said. "Hope." She paused. Professor Huaman never rehearsed this part of her first lecture. She required her words to resonate from the deepest recesses of her being, welling up from a place of authenticity and commitment with an honest dose of sympathy.

"Hope is one of the most powerful forces in any universe. Combine hope with belief and trust and anything is possible. Hearth believes Earth will not only curtail this impending crisis, but will thrive.

"Someday, we trust (a trust shared by a number of my fellow Hearthlings) that the locked gates now between us will be flung open, allowing Hearthlings and Earthlings to share our worlds.

"I know that you have more questions. I promise to answer every one that I can. For now, I believe you have enough to chew on.

"I will keep you no longer. Spend time getting to know your EP cube and each other. Go and enjoy the rest of your day. We will see you back here tomorrow morning at 8 a.m. sharp."

Professor Huaman picked up her cube and tapped it three times. She stared at it for a moment. The EP cube vanished.

"I have telepathically commanded my EP cube to return to my office. You will find that Hearthlings communicate predominantly telepathically. So, do not be alarmed when you observe things appearing and disappearing without a word being spoken."

Professor Huaman exited the classroom with a reassuring smile like that of a parent having delivered difficult news to her children, confident they would weather the storm.

Her students' reactions varied. Some exhibited shock. Dan was one of those. Others stared into a clear abyss with an expression of pained discouragement. A daring few glared at their professor as she strode out of the door.

CHAPTER 17

The haunting shadow of Professor Huaman's charge hung about the exchange students like an iron cloak. They pocketed their EP cubes and filed out of the classroom in a staggered line, silent but for their swirling thoughts.

Positioned on either side of the door, Eleonora and Enrique were waiting for them just outside of the classroom. Their escorts had mini-translators in their ears.

"How was your first class?" Eleonora asked with a pleasant smile. The dazed students gave disjointed responses ranging between "weird" to "frightening."

"That was Professor Huaman's pep talk," Enrique quipped. "Wait until you hear her doom and gloom lecture. That will really bum you out."

That brought out a mild chuckle from some of the exchange students. Dan was not one of them.

"We can only expect things to go downhill from here?" Obed joked, adding to the upward mood swing.

"Without question," Enrique said.

"Was Professor Huaman serious about what she said?" Dan asked, bringing the mood crashing down. "About Earth, I mean? About us?"

"Those are questions best answered by Professor Huaman," Eleonora said. "Would you like to take a tour of Wakin?"

The students responded with halfhearted nods. They sauntered down the polished curved marble stairs with handcrafted wrought iron railings from the third floor, returning to the elegant, spacious lobby.

Eleonora led the way, with Enrique bringing up the rear. They had been shepherded through the lobby, up the curved stairs to Classroom 3B, when they entered Wakin. On the way down, Eleonora educated her group about the four-story architectural marvel designed by the great Louis Falcon, a prominent Hearthling architect responsible for the creation of the Zenith Campus.

Dan closely observed everything around him. His father had taught him, through words and deeds, that you learn through the ears and not through the mouth. Dan had embraced that childhood lesson right into adulthood. At no time were his dad's words ever truer than now.

Eleonora and Enrique seemed oblivious to the androids and drones moving about, which intrigued most of the exchange students. Situated in the center of the lobby, Eleonora instructed them to look up. Natural light showered them like celestial rays.

Eleonora explained that what they were seeing was a sky roof: A roof made of tungsten glass, a special alloy that was as durable as tungsten, translucent as glass, and designed to filter out harmful ultraviolet rays. Tungsten glass constituted all of what Dan had assumed was simply structural glass.

What he wouldn't do to get his hands on that formula, Dan thought, certain he was not alone in his thinking.

"Before anyone asks," Eleonora said with a knowing smile and gazing around at what Dan was beginning to think of as her and Enrique's flock when she spoke, "you will not be given the formula for tungsten glass. It and all other advancements we have that Earth does not will not be going home with you."

The students let out a collective groan.

"Why not?" Waqas trumpeted.

"Professor Huaman will explain," Eleonora responded.

Eleonora continued the tour, ignoring minor protests from some of Dan's classmates regarding her unwillingness to clarify. The group followed Eleonora to an elevator lobby on the north side of the building. Six students accompanied Enrique on one of the glass elevators. The remaining seven boarded a second elevator with Eleonora.

Dan stayed with Eleonora. The lift was so quiet and smooth, the only indicator they were moving was the sight of passing floors. Their tour guide explained that most Hearth elevators operated on concentrated light pulses, as opposed to a mechanically assisted system. Wakin was no exception.

When asked by Dan why Eleonora continued to share such technical knowledge knowing they would not be permitted specific details, their gracious guide simply smiled and said, "Professor Huaman will explain."

Their spirits were once again buoyed as the tour progressed. Looking down from the top floor, the students could see the atrium. The marble floor gleamed. The bright green foliage was aglow.

Her flock noticed as Eleanora pointed out that floors two, three, and four had similar layouts. They were each primarily composed of a circular ring of classrooms and faculty offices. Eleonora explained that Wakin was a facility utilized for educating Earthlings about Hearth and Hearthlings. They entered Classroom 4B, a facsimile of their own 3B, with the only difference being some of the colorful array of perennials.

"Each classroom is equipped with the latest in learning technology, as found in all Hearth classrooms," Eleonora proudly announced. She placed her palm shoulder-high on a wall just inside the door. A portion of the wall about the size of a hardback novel appeared to vanish. A lighted numerical keypad was visible in the recess.

Eleonora stared at the keypad for a moment. Asterisks appeared one-by-one above the personal code underscores on the display screen. The digital lock unlocked on the display screen. All interior wood panels obstructing classroom sunlight at first appeared grainy, then seemed to dissolve right before their eyes, unveiling a clear, sunny day.

"This keypad allows you to manually, verbally, or telepathically enter the code. It's typical for most security keypads on Hearth. I telepathically punched in the code."

"Astonishing!" Carlito exclaimed. His reaction reflected how everyone felt.

"I will not explain to you what happened to those walls, although I am certain some of you have a good idea how that was possible, based on what you have seen and experienced so far."

The students rushed over to the tungsten glass walls and touched them as if to verify they were real. Eleonora mentioned that the interior panels were there so students would not be distracted from their lessons.

The students voiced their astonishment as they looked out at a world composed of everyday flying vehicles, human-like androids, and multi-functional drones operating within an environment of ample greenspace and pleasing architecture.

It was a world they were only getting to know, steeped in unlimited possibilities, as far as they were concerned. Eleonora and Enrique waited patiently by the door, as much amused by their flock as the students were impressed by the sights. It was a reaction their guides had seen a number of times in their short stint as Earthling hosts.

To say that Dan was flabbergasted would have been an understatement. Inventions he and his forward-thinking associates at Single Organism had dreamed of were happening right before their eyes.

Dan had never felt as insignificant in his innovative life as he was feeling at that moment. He was fully invested in the notion that what Single Organism was doing was pioneering, on the cutting edge of a groundbreaking science and technology bent on creating a better world, only to realize, from his few days on Hearth, that Single Organism had not even scratched the surface in technological and scientific advancements or in their effort to curtail humankind's assault on Earth's biosphere. His civilization had a long way to go to catch up to what the Hearthlings had achieved.

The tour ended at the first floor Wakin dining hall where Class 3B and their tour guides had lunch. It was a place that was called a dining hall, but more resembled a family-style restaurant.

They entered, and a waiter escorted them to a table. The waiter made brief customary small talk to place everyone at ease while they were being seated. Each cushioned chair adjusted automatically to their occupants—a pleasant feature Dan was beginning to enjoy.

The waiter handed them individual digital menus. He took everyone's drink order, which he noted on a digital pad, and left his diners to make their food choices. Enrique explained to them that they could make their selections by simply pressing the dish name, and their orders would automatically be placed.

To Dan's surprise, many of his favorites were listed on his digital menu. Dan mentioned this to his classmates, only to discover that he was not alone. The students had a good laugh about it, chalking up the coincidence as another example of Hearthlings having done their homework.

His lunch of lemon paprika chicken with steamed broccoli and long-grain jasmine rice was delicious. They had a chance to meet other exchange students from different classes during lunch.

Some had just arrived on Hearth, like them. Others had been in the exchange student program longer. Their upper classmates were friendly and encouraging, while their fellow freshmen were commensurate with their situation.

Kwasi Gaige was seated at the head of his dining room table. Dan knew this because he was seeing the world around him through his star-twin's eyes. His family was gathered there for dinner. His star-twin was wearing what his family fondly referred to as his 'Single Organism work uniform.'

Toni was in her hospital scrubs. Wick and Mae were still in their school clothes. Mae fidgeted with eager anticipation as her mother fixed her a plate of sweet peas, buttered mashed potatoes, and baked cod. Languid waves of steam rose off the peas and potatoes.

"Thanks, Mom," Mae said, digging in when Toni was done.

"You're welcome, sweetheart. Now, remember go easy. It's been a while since you've had solid food. Your tummy needs time to adjust."

"I will," Mae said, after swallowing a forkful of mashed potatoes.

"Don't forget to chew your food," Toni added. "That helps with digestion."

"In other words, don't be your usual gluttonous self," Wick said.

Mae put a forkful of cod into her mouth, then puffed out her cheeks as she chewed.

"Alright, you two," Toni said. "Behave yourselves.

Wick and Mae grinned at each other.

"Do I have to chew my mashed potatoes, too, Mom?" Mae asked in all seriousness.

"Mashed potatoes are exempt from chewing," Toni answered. "Take small servings of everything. That will make your food easier to chew and keep your tummy happy."

Mae nodded as she ate some peas.

"It's good to see you eating solid food again, Mae," Kwasi remarked.

"Thanks, Dad. Everything tastes so good."

"Huh?" Dan heard himself saying.

"How is your dessert?" Obed asked, seated to his right. Dan found himself staring down at his steady hand, which was holding a silver dessertspoon and hovering over a glass dessert bowl of half-eaten avocado chocolate mousse.

"Oh, um, delicious," Dan said, scooping out a spoonful of mousse and shoving it into his open mouth. His answer had not been honest. The avocado mousse was divine. The best he had ever tasted.

"*Mine too*," Obed said with zeal. He was having a creamy dessert Obed called Strawberry Fool that also looked delicious.

Dan glanced around the table as if reacquainting himself with his surroundings. He saw Eleonora staring at him, not glaring or fixated, but in a casual way. He must not have zoned out for very long. Eleonora was the only one who seemed to have noticed anything.

Was she aware of his star-twin connection? Had Dr. Bakari or Al shared that information with her? Could Eleonora somehow share in his experience?

From what they were learning about Hearthlings, Dan was beginning to believe anything was possible. Dan lowered his eyes to his bowl of velvety chocolate dessert. He ate his mousse in silence, pretending nothing had happened as he fought off continuous waves of homesickness.

*　　　*　　　*

The exchange students did exactly as Professor Huaman suggested with the remainder of their day: they spent time getting to know one another and their EP cubes. The students were free to go and do anything on campus. None took full advantage of their freedom, even turning down congenial upper classmates offers to escort them.

It was too soon, for Dan. He was still trying to process his first day of class, along with the world he now inhabited, as well as combating gnawing homesickness pangs.

The students were prohibited from having access to the outside world of Hearth. That access would be afforded them when the time was right—or that was the reason they were given.

Dan and his classmates hung out in the lounge back at Falcon. They energetically discussed amongst themselves what they had encountered and experienced—captivated by what they were seeing while being wary of Hearthling motives, were the prevailing attitudes.

"If this place and these people are to be believed, are Hearthlings genuine in their motives?" Cardinal Ocampo asked.

No one had a good answer to that question, primarily because no one could formulate any plausible reasons why anyone would go to such extremes to deceive them. Hearthlings were real, if they were to believe their senses.

"Are Hearthlings human?" Carlito asked.

Without performing physical examinations of their own, there was no way to determine this. They all agreed to accept, on faith, that Hearthlings were as human as they were.

"If we accept that Hearthlings are real and human, then is our Earthling paranoia coming into play regarding—for lack of a better term—extraterrestrial beings?" Dan asked. "Or are our suspicions warranted?"

Knowing he was addressing the questions to a mixed bag of believers and non-believers in otherworldly beings, everyone cited in jest their favorite examples of books they had read or movies or documentaries they had seen that villainized aliens.

The majority of sci-fi material was guilty of that sin. Dan and his classmates realized how such entertainment had influenced their views: stories told predominately through the preconceived adversarial lens of space invaders trying to take over "our" world.

No one had a decent answer to Dan's questions, in the end. Dan was glad to discover he was not the only one experiencing homesickness. All of his classmates felt the same.

Class 3B made a pact to ride out the program. Their sense of curiosity, for the time being, outweighed their longing for home. No one was to wash out. They made preliminary schedules for group study sessions and created an initial list of best-qualified tutors for areas of study based upon the course outlines listed in their syllabus, using their EP cubes to generate whatever materials they needed on the spot.

Dan was shortlisted for engineering.

As evening rolled around, Dan and a few of his classmates peeled off to hit the gym for a workout. After a shower and a delicious dinner back in his living quarters, Dan spent more time experimenting with his EP cube.

"Fascinating" and "remarkable" were the two words he used most to describe what it could do. He heeded Professor Huaman's warning about the consequences of attempting to dissect his cube to see how it worked. She'd said nothing about keeping notes based on what they had learned about Hearthling technology and what Dan had observed. Despite Eleonora's proclamation, his notes being confiscated was the worst that could happen.

Dan was toying with the idea of duplicating his EP cube (if that were possible) and dissecting the duplicate. Can a transport device duplicate objects? Would duplicating or dissecting the duplicate bring about expulsion?

Probably, Dan surmised, hashing out possibilities that would allow him to achieve his goal without punishment. He reminded himself to keep any thoughts of his plans out of his head when around Hearthlings, unaware if treasonous thoughts carried penalties, as well.

Dan was surprised at how easily he found himself accepting the Hearthlings' extraordinary technology as if it was the most natural thing in the world.

Dan fell into a deep sleep as soon as his head hit the pillow, physically and mentally exhausted, dreaming of flying vehicles and mobile androids; but not once about home.

CHAPTER 18

The next day brought what Dan and his classmates would come to know as their routine for the coming weeks. They would gather in the lobby and be transported to the Wakin Building by what the students came to refer to as their school bus.

Sometimes their school bus would go by land. Other times, their bus would travel by air. The shuttle driver liked mixing things up not only with the mode of transportation, but by taking different routes to and from Wakin. The students enjoyed the variety.

"I trust everyone had a pleasant day yesterday?" Professor Huaman asked, standing behind the Classroom 3B lectern as poised and outfitted as immaculate as the day before. All of the students vocally or with a head gesture affirmed that they had.

"I hope some of my responses during yesterday's question and answer session did not frighten any of you?" Professor Huaman asked. Her voice sounded in no way contrite.

"*It did*," blurted out Obed.

"You made us feel as though Earth is doomed no matter what we do," Ella added.

"Good!" The class was shocked by Professor Huaman's response. Her gray eyes took in her class for a moment. Every stare was riveted on her, every face anxious with concern and pinched with curiosity. Her students appeared to be breathing in unison, awaiting more.

"You are here to learn," Professor Huaman began. "What you learn in these classes and through observation can make good people like yourselves even better. We hope to arm you with an iron will to return to Earth with an unrelenting focus.

"You are literally fighting for your survival. Instilling you with certain qualities will be necessary to awaken large numbers of apathetic or despairing Earthlings into your camp of enlightenment. You can embolden your compatriots in the same way as yourselves, once there.

"Bringing a global community into the fight for survival is only the necessary first step. Those with power will resist. They will not be charmed by reason or persuaded by dire facts. They may turn to armed oppression, covert tactics, or both.

"Should those efforts against you prove ineffective or counterproductive to their cause, they may feign capitulation, typically as a front for means of manipulation, contributing to the storyline of heartfelt efforts in words for appearances sake while making few substantial concessions, if any at all.

"You want to position people of such obstinacy into the proverbial corner to where they have no choice but to comply. Once they do, then have them removed from power, because a person of such ilk cannot be changed. They can only be controlled, at best.

"Hearthlings and Earthlings have stepped from the same gene pool, but have progressed in vastly different ways. We can teach you how to be better, but not because we are better (because we do not believe for a second that we are superior to you).

"We offer you our prospective from our parallel universe: a genuine opportunity to alter your destructive course before it is too late; a chance to save yourselves from your self-imposed extinction. Any questions?"

This is creepy, Amaya thought.

"It is understandable that you would think that, Mrs. Chiba," Professor Huaman said, having read Amaya's mind. "In time, I expect, you will find all of this less creepy."

The class let out a nervous laugh.

"Shall we continue?"

"Is this a crash course on Hearth and Hearthlings?" Dan asked.

"These teachings are a series of condensed seminars on Hearth and Hearthlings, Mr. Bluford. We do not regard them as crash courses."

Gagandeep raised his hand.

"Yes, Mr. Acharya."

"How do you keep someone from reading your most personal or intimate thoughts when all Hearthlings have telepathic abilities?"

"Hearthlings have the ability to prevent others from reading their minds. Hearthlings are very disciplined. That discipline extends to our thoughts. In fact, we can mentally display a *Do Not Disturb* sign in our heads that all Hearthlings will respect."

"That's cool," Waqas said.

"What is the range of your telepathy?" Oliver asked.

"It varies from person to person. On average, our telepathic range is 50 meters."

"What about Earthlings who have telepathic powers?" Jomana asked.

"We have discreetly tested Earthlings on Earth who have claimed to have telepathy using a harmless and noninvasive brain scan. None of the claims have proven to be true.

"I am sure you have more questions about telepathy, Hearthlings, and Hearth, in general. Believe me, all of your questions will be answered in due course. I have strayed from the main topic for this class. Let us begin today's lesson."

CHAPTER 19

"You are here," Professor Huaman announced. A world map appeared on the digital wall, telescoping down to a landmass that, on Earth, would be called Peru.

"The Chavín region of the Atua Province," Professor Huaman said.

The digital map magnified an area that Dan recognized as the Andes Mountains.

"You can learn more about this region," Professor Huaman continued, "by referring to your Hearth encyclopedias that are a nested part of your EP cube's reference materials. Moving on.

"The human body," Professor Huaman said as she made her way to the back of the class. Two male and female representations of human anatomy appeared side by side on the digital board in full color, the label of 'Hearthling' or 'Earthling' stenciled beneath the feet of each.

"Earthlings and Hearthlings are anatomically identical." The digital board overlaid Hearthling male and female forms over their Earthling cousins. A perfect match.

"We are cut from the same genetic cloth. We share the same evolutionary journey fostered upon different worlds made of the same matter—what you commonly refer to as 'environment', in reference to your biophysical surroundings.

"We imply, within that definition, the inclusion of biodiversity. While it is a separate science of study, we find that by incorporating its thinking into our clinical studies of our biosphere, we nurture healthier planetary solutions. Any solution that maintains good health for the planet is obviously healthier for us.

"Biodiversity everywhere on your planet is at risk of extinction. What can you do about reversing that trend? Let us begin with the creation of Hearth.

"Our planet is a living organism. Hearthlings treat it accordingly. You will find that I will be using Hearth and Earth interchangeably. I will be using Earth familiar astrological and geographical names and historical periods that correspond to those of Hearth throughout my teachings. You will learn more about those variances once you experience our world firsthand. Hearth formed approximately 4,600 million years ago."

The digital board switched to a digital recording of Hearth as Professor Huaman spoke.

"Orbiting the Sun between what you are familiar with as Mars and Venus in your Milky Way galaxy, Hearth—like Earth—is the third planet from the Sun."

The digital recording pulled back to show Hearth's place in the universe.

"We have one natural satellite that behaves and looks precisely like your Moon."

The digital recording zoomed in on Hearth, with its moon in clear orbit.

"Hearth has a dense oxygen and nitrogen atmosphere. Our world is three-quarters ocean, and we are the only planet in our universe known to support human life.

"For those of you interested in more details regarding the creation of our universe and planet, I refer you to your own Big Bang Theory, a creation theory our scientific community supports here on Hearth."

The digital recording pulled back to display a full picture of what an Earthling would describe as the Milky Way galaxy.

"Our universe and Hearth evolved in precisely the same manner as yours. For those of you who believe a deity or deities had a hand in the creation of your universe, your world, and humankind, we have no similar teachings to share."

"Hearth has no religion?" Cardinal Ocampo asked.

"If you cogitate our steadfast conviction to our biosphere and each other a religion, then yes, we do have a religion. Otherwise, we do not practice a monotheistic faith predicated on omnipotent beings, parables, and scriptures."

"You're pagans, then?"

"We have been called worse."

"What about Armageddon?" the Cardinal pressed.

"Hearth has no apocalyptic teachings. We counsel those in need on finding purpose and focus in their lives. We have no objection if belief in a spirit or soul or God is required to achieve that goal as long as you understand that is a personal choice. You have no right to impose your beliefs upon others."

"Does that mean that Hearthlings are predominately atheists?" Cardinal Ocampo persisted.

"Most Hearthlings are what you might call atheists or agnostics. We believe you are born, you live, and then you die like everything in nature. What happens before your birth and after your passing, we prefer to leave to the realm of mystery.

"'Live a good life' is our motto. A good life involves doing for family, friends, and other Hearthlings, promoting the best of society with an unwavering eye toward a favorable legacy for future generations.

"If there are rewards for a life well lived upon death, we will embrace them. We do not mean that in the same context as Earthlings, which may involve forms of rambunctious behavior. The reward most Hearthlings would ask is to be granted the gift to watch over our planet and our fellow Hearthlings. That would be my request, if given such an opportunity."

"What happens to your soul when you die? Assuming Hearthlings have souls."

"If you are wondering whether we have any more answers to what happens to us after we leave this mortal shell, we do not. Death is an extension of life. We will cover Hearthlings' views on the topics of death and souls in science and philosophy."

Dan looked around the room. About half of his classmates were murmuring amongst themselves.

Dan was a practicing agnostic. The science of human evolution held more sway with Dan than divine conviction. Theology seemed more philosophy than hard and fast facts and rules, to him. For some of his classmates, religion was as much a part of them as their heart and lungs.

"Should this revelation be too much for some of you," Professor Huaman continued, "there is the door. Hearthlings will not begrudge you if you decide to go home. The choice remains entirely up to you.

"You will not be permitted to use this classroom as a means to promote your beliefs. Nor will you be given a platform to protest our teachings. I will say this for those who decide to leave because we do not share your faith.

"If you revered Earth as much as you do your God, then your attendance here would not be necessary. I will shut down my telepathic ability and step outside while you deliberate, leaving you to your private thoughts."

Professor Huaman stepped outside the classroom, closing the door behind her. A vocal debate sprang to life. Some were considering leaving, their feelings clear on their faces and by their agitated body language.

Dan was amongst those urging them to stay. Dan felt that Cardinal Ocampo was the key. The dissenters' eyes were upon him. The Cardinal went to the door, opened it, and asked Professor Huaman, "Can you promise me that none of your Hearthling teachings will be ungodly?"

The Professor answered loud enough for all to hear. "No. We will teach you about Hearth and Hearthlings. We will not in any way pass judgment on Earthling religious belief systems."

The Cardinal closed the door and returned to his seat, his pensive eyes cast downward as if the answer he sought would emerge from the hardwood floor. If Cardinal Ocampo left, Dan believed others of religious faith would follow. Dan focused his pleas on Cardinal Ocampo to remain.

Cardinal Ocampo settled into his chair after a prolonged silence. The dissenters followed suit. The Cardinal rose and opened the door. The Professor walked in, taking a position behind her lectern. "What have you decided?"

"Speaking for myself, I will stay," the Cardinal said. "Everyone else must decide for themselves."

Dan credited the pact they had made behind Cardinal Ocampo's decision. The man of God was also clearly a man of his word. Professor

Huaman looked around the classroom. No one moved. They stared in silence, straight ahead at their professor.

"No one?" Professor Huaman impassively asked as she surveyed the room. "Good. Word of caution: I am reinstating my telepathic abilities. Let us move on. Play 'Human Ancestors.'"

The Professor moved to the back of the classroom. The digital wall came to life. A digital recording of a primitive tribe walking across an open field on a cloudless sunny day filled the screen. They encountered another primitive tribe walking toward them.

"You are witnessing the first contact between the species Earthlings refer to as Homo erectus and Neanderthals. In your Earth history, we have no way of determining how this first meeting went.

"Judging by your history of territorialism, enslavement, dominance, and violent conflicts, we deduced that it did not go well. We also believe this first meeting of human development, based upon different bio environments, best exhibits where our human lineage took different paths.

"The first meeting of our Homo erectus and Neanderthals did not result in conflict, but in compromise and opportunity. Before our prehistoric ancestors developed written and sophisticated verbal language skills, we had telepathy. How did such primitive minds develop such a sophisticated tool?

"We do not know. We believe it came naturally to them, and they simply accepted it as their primary means of communication. We have no evidence that Earthlings possessed the same ability at that time in your prehistoric history. Only then, Hearth primitives mentally communicated with pictures, rather like hieroglyphics."

The musician/songwriter/singer from Egypt (who also possessed a doctorate in anthropology)'s hand went up.

"Yes, Mrs. Ashraf?"

"Were Hearthlings responsible for hieroglyphics and cuneiform?" Jomana asked.

"We were not. Hieroglyphics and cuneiform were created by Earthlings on your planet, just as they were developed by Hearthlings on ours.

"As I was saying, the first meeting between our Homo erectus and Neanderthals resulted in compromise and opportunity, cooperation, and respect. They shared knowledge and customs. Interbred. Formed societies that blossomed and prospered, forging the foundation for our modern Hearthling world while Neanderthals became extinct, as they did on your world.

"Their extinction on Hearth came as a result of natural selection, not due to extermination. And, as with Earthlings, Neanderthal DNA still lives on in a number of us."

"Great reenactments," Gennady said.

"These are not reenactments, Mr. Kuznetsov."

"Are you trying to tell us this is real?"

"It is."

"How is that possible?"

"We travelled back in time to record these historic events. All of our history has actual footage of the period."

"Hearthlings can time travel!" Oliver exclaimed.

"Yes. We have the technology to do so."

This news brought an uproar from the class.

"Have you ever used time travel to change history?" Gennady asked.

"Our time travel does not work that way. Whenever we go back in time, we do not exist in that period. We are like shadows on the walls of history. No one can see, hear, or sense us. We cannot make physical, verbal, or telepathic contact or interfere in any way. We can, however, record and observe."

"That's amazing!" Oliver said.

"We think so," Professor Huaman stated matter-of-factly.

"What's to stop anyone from abusing that knowledge?" Gagandeep asked. "Going back in time to alter history?"

"As I mentioned before, Mr. Acharya, we simply do not have that capability. This is not by accident. When the Council On Time Travel (or COTT) was formed, one of its strictest tenets was there would be no attempt to develop any science that would allow the alteration of an existing time line."

"You formed a committee to create time travel?" Intan asked.

"We did not, Mr. Nugraha. The committee was formed after there had been major scientific breakthroughs on time travel. Time travel is tightly controlled. There are only a handful of centers capable of time travel, and they are very secure."

"Have you ever traveled back in time, Professor?" Obed asked.

"More than once, Mr. Addo."

"What was it like?"

Professor Huaman paused for a moment before answering Obed's follow-up question. Her eyes glazed over in memory and a melancholy smile graced her face.

"Breathtaking."

"Have you—or any Hearthling—witnessed the actual formation of Earth—I mean, Hearth?" Jomana asked.

"Or your universe?" Dan added.

"No to both questions."

"Why not?" Gennady asked.

"While I don't know the particulars, Mr. Kuznetsov, what I can tell you is this: we cannot travel back in time any further than our existence."

"Why not?" Oliver asked.

"Time is irrelevant to our existence," Carlito added. "There is no connection to humans and time that I'm aware of."

"As I said, I do not know the particulars, and to my knowledge, no one does." Professor Huaman's revelations left the class both stunned and perplexed.

"Will we be permitted to time travel?" asked Ella, breaking the awkward silence.

"No," Professor Huaman responded, appearing to snap to with the disappearance of her smile, the firm set of her eyes returning.

"Why not?" Jomana asked.

"The short answer is, because we say so, Mrs. Ashraf. On some matters, you will receive no further explanation. This is one of those matters."

"Can you travel to the future?" Amaya asked.

"We cannot, Mrs. Chiba."

"Why not?" asked Nivi.

"I am not familiar enough with the science behind time travel to answer that question."

"Have Hearthlings time traveled to Earth's past?" Dan asked.

"We have not."

"Why not?" Oliver asked.

"I am told that the equipment required to be transported to Earth in order to travel to your planet's past would reveal our presence. May I continue with today's lesson?"

The class collectively conceded. The digital recording had continued to play during the classroom discussion. The Neanderthals were sharing with the Homo erectus one of their hunting strategies as they collectively stalked a herd of deer.

The students stared, transfixed, trusting that what they were seeing was real Hearth human history in the making. None of them could help but feel that, in some way, they were stepping back in time to witness their own history.

"A digital copy of this Hearthling history has been sent to your laptop. I want each of you to write a short essay, no more than a thousand words, on Hearth Homo erectus and Neanderthals during their first contact.

"I am not looking for an accurate historical summary. Simply your impressions on what you have observed about this monumental meeting."

"When will our first assignment be due?" asked Cardinal Ocampo.

"This time next week."

There was a moment of silence.

"What is it you expect us to gain from being here?" Dan asked. The question caused every student to sit bolt upright. Professor Huaman took a moment before she answered.

The greatest natural disaster in the history of the world has been the human brain. Eliminate us, and Eden will return. The thought came to Dan like a tap on the shoulder from a ghost.

Dan could not recall if he was paraphrasing, or if that were a direct quote. Professor Huaman's eyes narrowed slightly on Dan. Dan believed he detected a faint smile on her face.

"By exposing each of you to Hearthling teachings," Professor Huaman said aloud, "and sharing our experiences, it is our sincere hope we will enrich your lives. By so doing, we believe, you will in turn make it your life's mission to do so for others, with even more of a commitment than each of you already have made."

"Sort of like an Earthling domino effect," Dan said.

"More like an uplifting effect. Part of that mission will require there be changes on how Earthlings interacts with your precious planet and each other."

The class grew solemn. The exchanged students glanced at each other.

"Are there any other questions?" Professor Huaman asked. The class sat silent, as if experiencing a collective meditative state.

Professor Huaman waited. She allowed what she had said to seep in. Patience was as much a virtue to Professor Huaman as teaching. She believed they went hand and hand. The class remained silent, mesmerized by the sights and sounds of living history, viewing it more as a learning experience rather than an interesting occurrence.

Professor Huaman could sense it. She could hear it in their focused cohesive thoughts surrounding the combination of her words and the digital recording they were watching. The door to acceptance of what was at stake had opened. Earth needed them. They were gearing up to answer the call.

"None?" Professor Huaman asked, following up on her previous question. A few responded with a slow shake of their head, not taking their eyes off Hearth human history.

"Then let us continue with today's lesson."

CHAPTER 20

Escorts were no longer required, since Class 3B had translation devices. Dan and his classmates missed Eleonora and Enrique. They'd enjoyed their company and expert tour guide commentary. Al explained how the absence of escorts would aid the students in developing their independence. Class 3B came to realize Al was right in the days to come.

Hearth employed a Global Static Calendar, the same solar calendar commonly referred to as the Gregorian calendar on Earth, but with a variance.

The year was divided into thirteen months. Each month contained 28 days, with an additional day tacked onto December 28 that bears no weekday or month designation. The month of Sol was added between June and July. Every month ends on a Saturday and begins on a Sunday. Hearth employed the same solar day of 24 hours as Earth, midnight to midnight.

Monday through Friday, their school days began at eight and ended at five. Each class was forty-five minutes, with a fifteen-minute break between and an hour for lunch. Saturday and Sunday were their days to do with as they pleased.

Dan settled into the exchange student school routine. He turned in his homework assignments on time, diligently studied for quizzes and exams, and frequently socialized with other exchange students from both his class and other classes during his free time.

Aroha and Bartek would stop by once a week to chat, take in a meal together, or leisurely walk around the Zenith Campus with their "favorite exchange student." Dan developed a genuine affection for Aroha and Bartek. All indications suggested that they felt the same about him.

Dan met with Dr. Jabori Bakari once every Sunday morning at 10:00 a.m. Their meetings were informal and could take place in Dan's living quarters, the doctor's office, or some other location that the two agreed upon. Their sessions were often as informative as social.

Dr. Bakari had either the acquired or innate ability to make the direst circumstance seem almost trivial. Jabori, as the doctor insisted on being called, addressed every question Dan put to him with frankness. Even if his answer was not one Dan wanted to hear, Jabori's honesty prompted a level of trust in Dan. Dan came to see his Indoctrination Specialist as more of a friend than counselor or therapist.

The real Alvita stopped by to see Dan often. Her impromptu visits were part of what Al termed as "making her rounds" (meaning her check-in with her exchange student flock).

While IVA Alvita efficiently addressed all of Dan's hospitality needs, she did not elicit her archetype's zeal. Dan always enjoyed visits from his student housing director. They joked and laughed like two old friends, sharing hilarious memories. Al always left Dan dissolved into laughter with aching sides, wiping reflex tears from his eyes.

As the days zipped by, Dan became more and more comfortable with his circumstance. Even in the presence of other exchange students, he found himself talking and thinking less about home and more about Hearth and Hearthlings.

When Dan brought up the point during one of Class 3B group study sessions, he discovered that his classmates felt the same. They were becoming immersed in the Hearthling culture without setting foot outside of Zenith Campus.

Dan realized they were participants in a total immersion program, and it was working. When Dan shared his observation with his peers, they agreed. Instead of becoming upset about their situation, Dan and his fellow exchange students began brainstorming how they could introduce and utilize the same approach to educate and inspire people to get on board with positive environmental and social agendas.

"Congratulations, class: you are midway through your studies," Professor Huaman announced in a spirited voice. "We have covered encapsulated versions of Hearthling history, geography, government, sociology, and economics. How do you feel?"

"My head is still spinning, at times, but other than that, fine," joked Carlito. The class laughed.

"That is only natural, Mr. Macedo," Professor Huaman responded with a reassuring smile. "There is a lot being thrown at you, with little time to digest. You are all doing excellent, if my opinion matters."

Dan looked around the classroom. Prideful smiles like his own were seen everywhere.

"Do not let my reassurance go to your heads," Professor Huaman warned, still donning her smile. "You have a ways to go. In the second half of your studies, we will be covering culture, science, philosophy, technology, industry, and modern Hearthling society."

"Sometimes I feel as though Hearthlings look down on Earthlings," Gennady said. "Like Hearthlings believe they are superior."

Shock was the prevailing reaction from the students that Gennady would publicly air his grievance. Gennady had shared his feelings with Class 3B in confidence. Dan disagreed with Gennady, and said so during one of their group study sessions. Only Oliver and Cardinal Ocampo were in Gennady's camp, although Dan suspected Cardinal Ocampo's compliance centered on his persistent efforts to gather signatures from as many exchange students as possible, for his petition to include traditional religious teachings as part of future Indoctrination Programs, the good Cardinal refusing to accept the fact that Hearthlings had no conventional religion.

"What makes you say that, Mr. Kuznetsov?" Professor Huaman asked.

"There's nothing specific I can put my finger on; only a feeling."

"Can you give me an example?"

"Again, nothing specific. It's a haughty air Hearthlings have that make them behave as if they are superior, like they are catering to the less fortunate."

"How should we behave in order to appease you?" Professor Huaman asked Gennady, bearing down on Gennady with her calm, critical gaze.

"It's not a matter of ego," Gennady said trying not to sound defensive. "It is a matter of respect."

"If I may paraphrase an Earth expression, respect is not granted, but earned. What, exactly, have you done to earn our respect?"

"We didn't choose you. You chose us."

"That speaks to your potential, Mr. Kuznetsov, and you are avoiding my question."

"What have you done to earn our respect, Professor Huaman?" Gennady retorted.

"If what you have learned thus far about Hearthlings does not garner your respect, then it is not to be had. I guarantee you, Mr. Kuznetsov, that not a single Hearthling will be the least bit disturbed if you harbor such a judgment."

"What you just said," Gennady continued with his attack, "that is what I'm talking about. That haughty attitude you displayed."

"My way is direct. I do not apologize for that, for that is who I am. Most Hearthlings are candid, but not unnecessarily cruel.

"To confuse how I present an argument, opinion, or lecture with arrogance suggesting that I manifest an attitude of superiority is nonsense. It is my opinion that your criticism stems from pride, and not any Hearthling's behavior toward you."

"I have pride, I do not dispute that. I take pride in who I am and where I am from, as does every Earthling in this room."

Some of the students nodded in agreement with Gennady. Dan was not one of them. Dan did not feel the need to confirm his pride to anyone. For Dan, dignity was exhibited in deeds and conduct, not words.

"Those qualities you mentioned, Mr. Kuznetsov, are admirable. Pride can, however, be an offshoot of ego, which I firmly suspect is what is really at stake, here.

"If you expect me to conduct myself in a subservient manner, then your stay with us will prove to be of mounting disappointment.

"Hearthlings are not going to play subordinate to Earthlings in order to teach you about our way of life and how our lessons can benefit Earth. If you view our methods as arrogant, tough.

"Will my attitude be a problem, class?"

Kuznetsov looked away from Professor Huaman, sulking. No one said a word.

"Good," Professor Huaman said. Dan noticed there was no triumph in her voice, even though she had once again handed a rebellious student an inglorious defeat with only the cool, focused confidence Class 3B had come to expect from the best professor Dan had ever had.

"We are here on this pristine Zenith Campus—modestly speaking," Professor Huaman continued with a warm smile that lifted the tension from the room. Even Gennady managed a grin.

"It is a place similar to a number of your university campuses. Let me ask you this: Have you seen anyone picking up litter anywhere on the Zenith Campus?"

"No," Kuznetsov answered for the class.

"That is because Hearthlings do not litter. It is part of our normal psychology and social behavior: subconscious acts that serve the biosphere and our communities."

"Have you witnessed any unclaimed domestic pet droppings anywhere on the Zenith Campus?"

"No." This time, the answer came from Jomana. Dan looked over at Jomana, lingering, taking notice of her big brown eyes.

"Hearthlings do not have pets. We believe animals deserve their freedom as much as Hearthlings. We do have hand-raised animals that we use for labor, leisure, and food."

"Animals like cows, sheep, and goats?" Waqas asked.

"That is correct."

"You said 'raised,'" said Carlito. "Raised how?"

"All of our domesticated animals are genetically engineered."

"You can do that?" Cardinal Ocampo asked.

"We can and do."

"Even horses?" asked Lyberth.

"Yes. Our domesticated horses are all genetically engineered. We do not capture wild horses and tame them or break them—I believe that is the Earthling term for what is done."

"What about poverty and hunger?" Waqas asked.

"They do not exist on Hearth."

"Illiteracy?" Obed asked.

"Zero."

"How is that even possible?" asked Ella. "On Earth even at the best of times, there has been poverty, hunger, and illiteracy."

"On Hearth, they are facts, not possibilities. Do each of you believe those goals are obtainable on Earth?"

"Yes!" came the rousing response from Class 3B.

"Then make them happen. No excuses. Do it!"

"How?"

"Fight for them, and never, ever yield or compromise. Once they are secured, then renew the fight to assure the same will be available for generations to come."

"We *have* been fighting," Cardinal Ocampo said with a wisp of despair in his voice.

"Enlist the masses in full, Cardinal Ocampo. Making people aware of the problems are not enough. You have to convince them that what you are fighting for will directly help them."

"My battles are focused on the environment, or biosphere as you term it, Professor Huaman," Dan said.

"A healthy biosphere and healthy humanity go hand in hand, Mr. Bluford. To frame it in capitalist's terms: people who are receiving positive dividends from society have a tendency to become more fully invested in what is best for that society.

"Hence, the biosphere becomes part of that equation."

"I never thought of it like that," Dan said, considering additional ways he could convince more people to side with the environment.

"Do not get me wrong, class," Professor Huaman continued. "I know there are people on your planet who do not care about anyone but themselves. They will do anything for a buck, to coin an Earthling expression.

"There are people on your planet who delight in subjugating others. There are systems on your planet that require an impoverished exploitive population. This is nothing new. We have weeded out those people on Hearth by rendering them impudent to the point that they have become extinct.

"A few had to be exterminated. The community rules. Healthy communities are the staples of our society, trampling the individual desires for the good of the whole."

"Did you say, 'A few had to be exterminated?'" Oliver asked. "By 'exterminated,' do you mean killed?"

"We prefer the word extermination, in this case, but yes; their lives were terminated. Does that sound ruthless to you, Mr. Martin?"

"To be perfectly honest, yes," Oliver said, looking shocked, an expression shared by the entire class.

"Not in accordance with our beliefs. None of us is more valuable than our Hearth mother. If a sacrifice of the few is necessary to keep us in her good graces, then the death of a few outweighs the suffering of the many.

"It took us generations to eradicate the negative qualities of humankind to evolve to this state of harmony."

"On Earth, we make efforts to reason with such people," Dan said.

"How's that working out, Mr. Bluford?"

"Mixed results."

"In the meantime, your Mother Earth suffers, and your human brothers and sisters, as well. How far would you go to protect that which is most precious to you, Mr. Bluford?"

"I don't know."

"Imagine if the same threats levelled against your planet were levelled against your family. Would you be willing to take a life then?"

"Possibly."

"I would be willing to wager that you would, Mr. Bluford," Professor Huaman said. "In fact, I would be willing to wager that if a member of your family was in imminent danger, and the only way to save them was to terminate the source of that menace, then each of you would."

Professor Huaman surveyed the class, her expression placid, her body relaxed, and her eyes a maternal embrace. No one spoke. No one moved.

"Hearth is our most precious gift. We will go to any length to protect her from harm, including exterminating human lives."

A gasp could be heard from a few of the exchange students.

"I know most of you regard what I am saying as murder."

"You can say that again," Oliver said.

"Hearthlings consider the sacrificing of a life under such circumstances as self-defense."

"Has it ever come to that?" Amaya asked.

"In our distant history, it has."

"This Hearth utopian society you want Earthlings to emulate has been constructed upon a foundation of murder," Gennady said with a sense of satisfaction.

"Not at all, Mr. Kuznetsov.

"Throughout our earliest history, we had wars, coups, rebellions, and revolutions, as have been covered in our Hearth history courses. They were violent conflicts culminating in the tragic loss of too many human lives.

Never on the grand scale as Earth, mind you. We never had world wars, for example. Our motivations behind our fights were different. One major difference between Hearth conflicts and Earth's are that our battles erupted from our society's vehement disagreements on how to progress.

"We never killed each other over land, resources, political, or religious differences. Bloodlust is not in our nature. We never sought to enslave or oppress our fellow humans. Conquest is not in our nature. Greed is not in our nature.

"You spoke of arrogance earlier, Mr. Kuznetsov. When some of your ancestors encountered people that looked different from them and had different customs, did not your ancestors categorize them as inferior? In some cases, they classified them as barbaric, savages, and less than human. A number of your nations still struggle with that practice.

"Cardinal Ocampo, has your religion not committed the same sins? Most of you are familiar with an Earthling expression, 'Those who live in glass houses should not throw stones.' We lay our world open for full examination. Where we have been. Where we are now, and how we got here.

"When comparing Hearth's journey, thus far, to Earth, are you really attempting to charge us with crimes against humanity?

"Hearthlings have learned from our mistakes and have not repeated them. That is one of the ways we are drastically different from Earthlings, who have a depressing tendency to replicate detrimental histories.

"Our values are different. Our way of life is different. Our dreams and hopes are different from your average Earthlings. We have morphed into the people we are now at a price: closed out bills that will not come due again."

An uneasy hush fell as Professor Huaman once again ran her steady gaze over the class. Had Dan the courage to glance around at his classmates, he would have noticed they shared the same brow-beaten humiliation.

"What I am getting at?" Professor Huaman said, breaking the silence. "Hearthling and Earthling self-motivations are radically dissimilar."

"And that makes it okay?" Gennady asked. "To do what Hearthlings did?"

"It most certainly does, Mr. Kuznetsov. Our reverence for Hearth is our way of life, and I suppose you could classify it as our religion. In the same context, nature is our God.

"No, we do not sacrifice anything or practice any of the barbarous rituals that have been performed on your home world, in that regard. We simply respect and venerate our planet as we do all that we love and cherish, and treat it accordingly.

"We value Hearthling lives. Only our biosphere do we place above ourselves. Can you honestly say the same about Earthlings?"

"What about terrorism?" Gennady asked, refusing to surrender the shovel digging his grave.

"Hearthlings have never used terrorism. Terrorism springs from either oppressed people who believe they have no other recourse, or as a means of intimidation or tyranny. Neither definition applies to any Hearthling."

Gennady noticed some of his classmates glaring at him. They wanted him to shut up. Dan was one of them. They had heard enough. Gennady got the message.

"Do you consider Earthlings as members of the Hearth family?" Obed's question stunned the class. Dan felt as though they were holding their collective breaths, awaiting the answer.

"No, Mr. Addo, we do not. You are our distant cousins. And will remain in that status until Earthlings are able to prove otherwise."

Dan heard a collective exhale of disappointment.

"Are there any other issues anyone would like to discuss?" Professor Huaman calmly surveyed her students, pausing long enough to await a response.

"No? Then let us begin our lesson on the Silver River galaxy, a Hearthling twin to your Milky Way."

*   *   *

Professor Huaman had a good feeling about Class 3B. They were proving to be extraordinary. No class before had grasped the gravity of Earth's dire situation faster.

The closest Professor Huaman could remember was a class she'd had three years ago, Class 2C. That class had clutched the sense of urgency within a couple of weeks.

Coming down hard on Class 3B in her last session did not trouble the professor. She had gotten to know a good deal about the character of Class 3B. They were tough, brilliant, and resilient.

The professor had been more concerned she had lost some of her exchange students when she lectured them about Hearthling views regarding religion.

Typically, a few Earthlings would storm out, labeling her and Hearthlings as heathens or pagans, not wanting to have anything to do with their sacrilegious teachings.

She had expected Cardinal Ocampo to lead the exodus. When Cardinal Ocampo stayed, the professor was encouraged. Cardinal Ocampo's actions belied his thoughts. Cardinal Ocampo did ask his God for forgiveness, but he remained a man of his word, as Mr. Bluford had thought. The obligation Class 3B had made to each other held him fast. It was that sort of steadfast commitment that it will take to save their precious Earth.

"We are here, Professor," her Interactive Artificial Intelligence chauffer announced in a Quechua accent.

"Thank you, Khuno."

Her vehicle had landed smoothly in front of her house. Professor Huaman had been so preoccupied with her thoughts of Class 3B, she had not noticed their arrival. The engine cut off. Her seat belt automatically unfastened. Her rear passenger door unlocked. Professor Huaman sat there for a moment, glancing about her neighborhood.

It was evening. The sun was just beginning to set. Her neighborhood was alight with activity. Children were at play, some with adults joining them. Teenagers were hanging out. Working adults were coming home. A few teenagers and adults were winding down outdoor chores before heading in for their evening meal.

The professor exited her vehicle. A light rain had fallen onto the valley earlier, leaving the air smelling fresh and clean. Neighbors waved and smiled. Professor Huaman returned their greetings.

Some inquired telepathically how she was doing. She responded telepathically that she was well, and inquired in kind of them. The word 'family' came to mind during these exchanges. Family is vital to Hearthlings. When Hearthlings talk about family, they do not only mean people related by blood. Family encompasses all Hearthlings.

This was how it was throughout Hearth. The scenery may change, but not the people. Professor Huaman would make a point to share her thoughts on family with her class.

Across the street, Henrietta Rodriguez was tending her front garden. Like all Hearthlings, Henrietta had access to professional gardeners. She preferred to care for her plants herself.

The one-hundred-thirty-seven-year-old was lovingly clipping a bed of colorful perennials. Henrietta did not look a day over eighty, an age relative to forty for Earthlings.

She was a retired university professor and the eldest member of their community. Her husband had held that distinction, but Carlos Rodriguez had died last month. Henrietta lost the love of her life after over a century of marriage, nine children, twenty-two grandchildren, six great-grandchildren, and one great-great grandchild.

Henrietta had a wealth of friends in their community, but no blood relatives. Her children had answered callings that spirited them away to other provinces; some near, some far.

Distance did not dampen the endearing closeness of their family. The Rodriquez clan regularly contacted and visited their matriarch. While her friends knew friendship could not fill the void left by the departure of a lifetime companion, the community did its best.

Professor Huaman telepathically asked Henrietta if she would like to join her family for dinner. Henrietta looked up from her task, smiled, waved, and politely turned down her invitation. She had already accepted a dinner invitation from the Coppola family, for tonight.

Raincheck? Henrietta asked.

Raincheck.

They were clean, healthy, and secure in harmony with their surroundings.

Professor Huaman glanced out at the stretch of woods west of her home. The professor could see natural life (or wildlife, as Hearthlings formerly called them) going about their business in coexistence with humans.

Off to the east, near the end of her community, were fresh foundations for twenty new homes. A flock of sparrows flew by, sending Professor Huaman a picture talk greeting of 'hello.' Professor Huaman returned a picture talk greeting of 'good evening.' The sparrows were warning the neighborhood that some raccoons were planning a late night raid.

Hearth animals did not need to feed on human scraps. They had plenty to eat in their natural habitats. Mischievous creatures like raccoons enjoyed knocking over trash cans for sport.

I am home! Professor Huaman telepathically announced to her husband, who was inside their house.

I know! her husband responded in kind.

The professor passed along the information telepathically to her husband about the raccoons.

Thanks for the warning, her husband responded, sounding amused. *I will lock away our trash cans in the shed before bed. How was your day, sweetheart?*

Good, Professor Huaman responded. *I will tell you all about my day over dinner. How was your day, honey?*

I will tell you all about my day over dinner. They shared a mental chuckle.

I am making a Mediterranean casserole," her husband said.

Vegetarian?

Of course. Do we ever eat anything else?

Sounds delicious!

I thought I would try something new. I hope you and the children enjoy it.

I am sure we will. You are a chef.

I am a good cook, but 'chef' may be stretching the truth a bit.

You always say that, darling. This meal will turn out as all of your meals do. Delicious.

As do yours, honey.

Now who is stretching the truth?

Mental laugh.

See you in a minute, dear.

Love you.

Love you more.

"Will you need me for the remainder of the day, Professor?" Khuno asked.

"I will not."

"Very well, madam. Have a good evening."

"Thank you, Khuno."

Two energetic young children charged at their mother as soon as she stepped through the front door. At the same time, Khuno settled Professor Huaman's vehicle into the charging bay of their two-car garage.

CHAPTER 21

The sun was shining on a clear, bright Sunday morning. Dan was writing essays, 'The Constitution of Humanity' and 'The Constitution of Nature.' Professor Huaman had asked her class to step back, clear their minds of any preconceptions, and write essays on what Hearth's International Constitutions meant to them, in twenty-five hundred words or less.

The Constitution of Humanity expounded on the preamble "All humans are created equal no matter their race, gender, or sexual orientation." The Constitution of Nature enriched the concept: "Our natural world is our greatest gift. Hearthlings will forever cherish and respect Hearth in all we do."

Dan had come to understand that these engrained precepts were the bedrocks of Hearthlings' philosophy and worldview. Dan was having no trouble writing about the two intrinsic documents to Hearthlings' way of life. Whittling his essays down to twenty-five hundred words or less was proving to be a challenge, however.

Dan had accomplished his goal on The Constitution of Humanity after seven drafts, using all twenty-five hundred words to do so. He was on his fifth condensing of his essay on The Constitution of Nature when he heard the soothing sounds of gentle rain and distant thunder.

Dan had changed his door alert only last night. He had become fond of changing his door alert and found himself doing so almost daily. Dan had become like a child in a candy store: there was such a wide range of delicious audio choices. He seemed to fluctuate the most between music and nature. Dan returned to his writing.

Gentle rain and distant thunder sounded again.

Dan pressed the peephole app on his EP-generated cell phone. Dr. Jabori Bakari appeared on the screen, casually dressed, relaxed, confident, and neat and tidy as always. Dan had lost track of time. It was time for their usual meeting, this one to take place in his room.

Dan hated to break his creative flow. He had been writing since four in the morning, and considered asking Dr. Bakari to come back later.

IVA Alvita appeared. "Shall I answer the door, sir?"

"That's alright, Alvita" Dan said. "I'll get it."

IVA Alvita vanished with the same smile on her face as when she'd appeared. Dan had learned in class how Interactive Virtual Assistants worked.

Beings like IVA Alvita consisted of brain-like functioning, with a shell composed of dense lighting that behaved like solid matter. IVAs did not have a nervous system or internal organs or biological functions. They could alter their light matter to fluctuate between solid and light.

Dan answered the door, his thoughts focused on his essay.

"I hope I am not disturbing you, Daniel?" Dr. Bakari asked with an ingratiating smile, something that came as natural to the doctor as blinking.

"Not at all," Dan lied. "Come in and have a seat."

"Thank you."

Dr. Bakari sat on one end of the short living room sofa. Dan sat across from him in the matching chair. Conformed seating was a feature Dan had become accustomed, and was a source of pleasure.

"How are things?"

"Things are going well," Dan said in answer to Dr. Bakari's question.

"I trust Professor Huaman is not being too hard on you?" Dr. Bakari said with a bemused smile.

"Does Professor Huaman know of any other way?"

They both laughed. "Not from what I have heard," Dr. Bakari said.

Dr. Bakari had read Dan's mind when he asked if he were disturbing him. He knew Dan was being polite. The doctor had caught sight of Dan's office as he walked to his seat on the sofa. He could see

Dan's open laptop and memo pad, the penholder filled with pens, pencils, and color highlighters neatly arranged on his desk.

The doctor knew it would have taken Dan only a moment to clear them away and return all of his tools to the EP cube. It was his charge's passive-aggressive hint for Dr. Bakari to cut short his visit. Dr. Bakari was not going to oblige.

"What are you working on, Daniel?" Dr. Bakari asked. Dan explained.

"The International Constitutions, the backbone of Hearthling society," Dr. Bakari said with pride.

"Care to read over what I've written? I could use your Hearthling insights."

"This is not about us, but about you, Daniel. We do not want you to regurgitate our teachings, but absorb them. Make use of them as you see fit when you return to Earth."

"Which brings to mind a question. When we return to Earth, what is to stop any Earthling from telling the world about Hearth?"

"In part, trust. In part, validity."

"I don't follow."

"We trust that you will keep Hearth a secret as we ask, Daniel."

"And if we don't?"

"That is where validity comes into play. There is no way you can prove we exist with your limited Earthling technology. Not our galaxy, not our planet, not our people.

"You would be labeled as another UFO or extraterrestrial believer with no hard evidence to back up your claims. To use a crude Earthling term, you would be dismissed as a crackpot. A person of your standing would be diagnosed as having broken under the strain of your high-pressure position at Single Organism."

"Hearthlings have it all figured out, don't you?"

"We try. Now, let me ask you something, Daniel."

"Ask away, Dr. Bakari."

"Jabori, please."

"Forgive me, Jabori. I will do my best to remember from here on out."

"Do I still remind you of your personal assistant, Amiri Hayden?"

It had been weeks into his crash course on Hearth and Hearthlings. Still, Dan's first thought when he saw his Indoctrination Specialist was of his personal assistant. "Very much," Dan answered.

"I am afraid your Amiri and I share many traits, but a number of our life choices have been different. One day, you will come to see Amiri and me as individuals, as I see you and your star-twin."

"One day," Dan said. He believed Jabori. He did not know when that day would come. "Have you met my star-twin?"

"Of course. Star-twin volunteers are made to go through rigorous psychological testing before we permit them to take on an Earth assignment. I am a member of the evaluation team."

"Is he like me—as close as he can being a Hearthling and all, I mean?"

"I know what you mean, Daniel. Without going into too much detail, he is your physical identical twin. You two share many personality traits. Both of you are brilliant, natural leaders with analytical minds."

"Will I meet him one day?"

"No. It is against Hearthling policy for star-twins to meet."

Dan remembered the reason Professor Huaman gave Amaya for why she would not meet her star-twin teacher, but thought it was worth a try. Dan was quiet in thought when Jabori spoke.

"Back to your question regarding how we know our secret will be kept. Have you ever heard of Hearth or Hearthlings before now?"

"No."

"We have been operating on your planet for centuries, as you now know. You have even come in personal contact with a few of our exchange students, three of which are your friends."

"Who?"

"That information will become available to you once you return to Earth."

"Hearthlings and your secrets..."

"We are guarded as to when we parcel out information to Earthlings. We want to make certain you are open and ready to receive it."

"I'll pretty much believe anything at this point."

"I hope not. We did not choose you because you were gullible, Daniel. Quite the opposite, in fact. We chose people who are strong-willed, intelligent, and circumspect. We want you to question everything."

"We have."

"Great!"

"I'm going to take a meal break," Dan said. "Care to join me?"

"I would love to."

"Would you prefer we eat out or in?"

"You chose, Daniel."

"In it is. Alvita, I need your help."

"How may I be of service, Mr. Bluford?" IVA Alvita said before acknowledging Dan's guest. "Good day, Dr. Bakari."

"Good day, Alvita."

"How are you today, Dr. Bakari?"

"Well, thank you."

"Alvita," Dan said. "We would like to order—what time is it?"

"Ten twenty-three a.m.," Alvita answered.

"We would like to order brunch," Dan said.

"Here are today's in-house brunch menus," IVA Alvita said. With a wave of her hand, two digital tablets appeared. Alvita handed one to Dan and the other to Jabori. An in-house brunch menu was displayed on each tablet. "If you would like to order elsewhere, I can provide you with menus from any of the Zenith Campus restaurants."

Dan and Jabori viewed the available dishes for a few moments.

"In-house will do for me," Dan said.

"Suits me," Jabori added.

IVA Alvita nodded and stood by patiently as Dan and Jabori made their food and beverage choices.

"Very good, gentleman," IVA Alvita said. Dan's virtual assistant stood rigid and silent as if her battery had died for a few seconds. "Your orders have been placed. They will be delivered in approximately twenty minutes."

"Thank you, Alvita," Dan said. IVA Alvita smiled, nodded, and then moved to set the dining table.

"Do you still think about Earth, Daniel?" Jabori asked over brunch.

"Sometimes."

"Your family?"

"Family, friends, home, Single Organism—you name it."

"Pollution, war, racism, poverty, global warming."

"Maybe not everything, Doctor."

"If it puts your mind at ease, everyone and everything within your Earth circle are doing well."

"I would be more reassured if I were on Earth to verify that for myself."

"You are free to leave at any time, Daniel."

"I and the rest of Class 3B are determined to see this through."

"Is that the only reason you are staying? Out of loyalty to your mates?"

"I'm curious, to be honest, Doctor. We've learned a lot in our short time here."

"About Hearth."

"About Hearth, Hearthlings, and about ourselves. Earthlings, I mean."

"Good or bad?"

"Good, as far as Hearthlings are concerned. Bad, for Earthlings. Your people are more advanced than we are. I don't simply mean in a scientific and technological sense—I mean overall, as a people, if what we are learning at Wakin is true."

"It is. Have you had another Residual Connection with your star-twin?" Jabori said, seamlessly switching subjects as easily as a breeze.

"Not since the incident in the Wakin dining hall that I told you about."

Jabori nodded.

"Does that mean it's over?" Dan asked.

"Doubtful."

"Is that good or bad?"

"A Residual Connection is in no way harmful to either of you. It is merely a unique umbilical cord phenomenon that only occurs between a miniscule percentage of exchange students and their star-twins."

"I'm a laboratory specimen by which you hope to gain further knowledge about this phenomenon?"

"Nothing so devious. We simply want to keep a close eye on you to make certain you are okay."

"I'm fine, thank you. You will be the first to know if I do have another Residual Connection."

"Being first is not necessary, but I do insist on being kept in the loop."

"Will do, Doctor."

"Jabori, remember?"

Dan nodded. "Do you have any children, Jabori?"

"My wife and I have two children, Kali and Ayar, ages ten and six."

"Then you know what I'm going through; how I feel about being separated from my family."

"I can promise you, Daniel, it will all be worth it. What we are teaching you here will help your fellow Earthlings and your planet build a better world for future generations."

"Now you sound like one of Single Organism's marketing slogans."

Jabori laughed. "Those are wise words to live by. The fundamental philosophy that we are the caretakers of our planet is centrally infused in every Hearthling. We function with the forthcoming generations in mind. Their futures are our constant consideration."

"Why does that sound familiar?"

"The 7th Generation Principal, perhaps?"

"Yes, yes! The 7th Generation Principle, as practiced by the First Nations."

"That is correct. Do you remember what it is?"

"To paraphrase: no matter the source of the issue, how our decisions affect descendants seven generations into the future must be taken into account, in order that they will enjoy the same natural gifts that we do now."

"A loose interpretation, but you get the gist. Hearthlings developed the same philosophy. The difference between Hearth and Earth is that the 7th Generation Principle is encased in our way of life. We have stretched that philosophy out to ten generations."

"I used to believe in the 7th Generation Principle."

"What changed, Daniel?"

"Obdurate reality sunk in. Compromises became necessary, especially in my line of work. Some of our decisions that we term as 'best possible scenarios' may prove costly to future generations."

"Perhaps it is time to bring your line of work in line with your philosophies, Daniel?"

"A lot easier said than done, Jabori."

"Is that not often the case?"

Dan pondered how he could more fully apply the 7th Generation Principle while chewing a mouthful of his Rajma vegetable salad.

"I didn't know you were married, Jabori."

"I am."

"You're not wearing a wedding band," Dan said, glancing at Jabori's ring finger and noticing a tan line left by what Dan assumed was a ring. Dan held up his ringed finger to further demonstrate what he meant. "Is marriage without jewelry not a Hearthling custom?"

"Our wedding customs are similar to yours, as you well know from your Hearthling sociology course."

Dan nodded. Jabori was right. They had covered Hearth's basic social customs in class. That still didn't explain why Jabori had chosen to hide the fact that he was married.

"Wearing a wedding ring is a custom that Hearthlings and Earthlings share," Jabori continued. "I do not wear my ring while on campus. It's a way of separating my professional life from my home life.

"And, yes, Hearthlings do wear wedding bands and have nuptials and practice many of the same ceremonial rituals Earthlings cherish in—as you say—tying the knot."

Jabori had obviously read Dan's mind regarding his curiosity, judging by Jabori's volunteering of unwarranted information, latched onto his answer. Dan was becoming accustomed to Hearthlings reading his thoughts, something he had been initially guarded about.

He found that the harder he tried to shield his thoughts, the more jumbled his thinking became. Now he was at the point where he relaxed. Whatever thoughts came his way, he let them be. In doing so, he found he had more control over his thinking. His thoughts became less random and sporadic and more focused, disciplined, and constructive.

"What's she like, Jabori?" Dan asked. "Your wife?"

"Powerful, intelligent, beautiful, independent, and loving. A lot like your Toni."

"What's her name?"

"Doba."

"How long have you two been together?"

"We have been married going on ten years. We have been together for much longer. You are familiar with the term 'high school sweethearts'?"

"Of course."

"We were middle school sweethearts. I saw Doba before first class of a new year. I, along with my best friends and classmates, were filing into middle school. We were in our final year. Doba was one grade below us.

"Our middle schools are the same as yours, Daniel, spanning seventh, eighth, and ninth grades. It was a beautiful day, a warm, clear, still summer with no hint of autumn.

"There she was. Alone, wearing a flower print dress and powder blue sneakers, appearing a little lost amongst the chattering mayhem of young people rushing about."

"By chattering," Dan interrupted, "do you mean verbal?"

"Telepathic chattering, which is no different to us as verbal chattering is to Earthlings. Doba looked radiant to me. I stood frozen in place, unable to take my eyes off her.

"A few of her classmates noticed Doba's confusion and took her under their wings. The first bell sounded before I could offer my assistance. I sought out Doba at lunch and introduced myself. We talked.

"Her family had moved to our province only a couple of weeks earlier. I would be dishonest to omit that our first meeting bolstered my infatuation with Doba. Love came later. I have only fallen deeper in love ever since. From the moment I realized I had found my life mate, I employed all of my romantic energy to convince Doba to feel the same about me."

"Did you go back in time for that recollection?" Dan half-jokingly asked.

"Only in my memory," Jabori replied with a pleasant smile.

"How much do you know about my wife?" Dan asked, circling back to Bakari's statement regarding his Toni's resemblance to Doba.

"Everything. We are very thorough in our research."

"My star-twin..." Dan began, finding the courage to ask one of the questions he dreaded learning the answer to. "Does my star-twin replace me in every aspect of my Earth life?"

"You want to know if your star-twin is having sex with Toni."

"Yes," Dan said, after swallowing hard.

"Yes, he is, Daniel. You must remember that your star-twin is, in every aspect, you. If you have this impression that Toni senses something in him that is different or out of place, than you would be mistaken. Your star-twin *is* you, as far as Toni is concerned. I am sorry if that fact upsets you."

"Wouldn't you be upset if you discovered Doba was having sex with another man?"

"Hearthlings do not practice monogamy. Doba has had other sexual partners, as have I. Hearthlings do not place the same restrictions on sexual relationships as Earthlings. We are an open society in a number of things, sex being one of them.

"Sex is a physical pleasure. Making love is when that physical pleasure is accompanied by love. Hearthlings do not believe that falling in love is restricted to one person. You can fall in love as many times as you want. Marriage is, however, that bond that precludes all other personal adult relationships. Does that make sense, Daniel?"

Dan recalled Professor Huaman's brief homily on Hearthlings' views on sexuality. The open sex part was omitted from the professor's lecture. Dan wondered if her omission was deliberate, or not regarded as important.

"Let me know if I can help clarify the Hearthling philosophy on sexuality further, Daniel," Jabori added. The doctor finished eating, wiped his mouth clean with a cloth napkin, drank the last of his fresh squeezed papaya juice, and leaned back in his chair, appearing satisfied with his meal.

"Will do," Dan said, thinking it was clear what Jabori was saying, Yet accepting it was where Dan had a problem. He believed in there being one love of your life. Toni was his.

"What about unwanted pregnancies or sexually transmitted diseases? If for no other reason, remaining monogamous will limit those occurrences."

"Hearthlings have full control over our reproductive process. I mean that literally. No couple can have children unless the man and woman are in complete agreement."

"Are you telling me you can control pregnancy with your minds?"

"Precisely. Men tell their bodies to produce infertile sperm. Women tell their bodies to produce infertile eggs. It is actually quite simple once you get the hang of it.

"Reproductive regulation is taught to our children well before they reach puberty. By the time Hearthlings reach childbearing years, they have already mastered the techniques, which explains why few children are born out of wedlock on Hearth.

"Although, children born out of wedlock are no big deal to us. All children are loved and cherished equally. As for sexually transmitted diseases, we eliminated those centuries ago."

"Amazing," Dan said, spellbound by what he was hearing. He tried to imagine what Earthlings would be like, if they could mentally control their capacity to reproduce. In addition, the eradication of sexually transmitted diseases would be a dream come true. Would it promote a liberated carnal paradise, or feed into debauchery on Earth?

"Can you deny that you have not been physically attracted to other women?" Jabori asked.

Dan knew exactly where Jabori was going with that question. Being human, how could he not? What had always stopped Dan from acting on those charged impulses was his love for Toni and their children. His marriage vows were another devotion lock that kept that door closed.

There was, however, a hacksaw being applied to those hardened impediments against infidelity.

One of Dan's classmates, Jomana Ashraf, the musician/songwriter/singer from Egypt who also possessed a doctorate in anthropology, was in her early thirties with large smoky brown eyes, silky pecan skin, an unbridled laugh, and a smile that would shame the sun.

Jomana was happily married to a television producer. They had a four-year-old son. Dan tutored Jomana in engineering and physics. Jomana tutored Dan in ancient human societies and cultures.

Their tutoring sessions always concluded with talk about their families: how much they missed their children and how much they missed their spouses. Dan found Jomana charming intellectually, and physically beautiful. His desire to kiss Jomana when they were alone in close quarters crossed his mind more than once. Dan believed he read in Jomana's eyes the same wish.

"When the moment of longing neared magnetism, the two would-be adulterers found a way to break their trance. Dan was weakening. He did not trust he could stop himself for much longer. The dam would break if they ever kissed. Knowing that Toni was having sex with his star-twin complicated matters even further.

"Of course," Dan said in response to Jabori's question. "That doesn't mean I should act on it."

"Even if the attraction is mutual?"

"It does not matter. Marriage is an exclusive contract—an eternal promise to a single person for a lifetime bond. To cheat on your partner is a violation of her trust and makes an abomination of your marriage."

"Our marriage contracts have no such restrictions, written or implied, within them. We are human beings who are unashamed of our natural desires. Sex is a pleasure Hearthlings enjoy to the fullest."

"I would like for you to leave, now," Dan said, uncomfortable with the direction the conversation had taken.

"As you wish," Jabori said, not appearing the least bit taken aback by Dan's sudden request. "I am sorry if I have offended you, Daniel. Should you want to talk, or need someone to listen, I am always available."

"Please leave."

Jabori left without another word. IVA Alvita showed the doctor out. Had she been listening the entire time? Dan briefly wondered as he sat staring at his empty salad bowl, trying to vanquish from his mind the image of his star-twin having sex with Toni.

CHAPTER 22

"'Imagination is more important than knowledge. Knowledge is limited. Imagination encircles the world.' Your Einstein said that approximately a thousand years after our Runako Phiri, with one caveat.

"Mr. Phiri said, 'Imagination embraces the universe and beyond.' They were not star-twins, but twin scientific geniuses and amateur philosophers. And both were correct in their assertions," the President of the Exchange Student Program, Professor Huaman, said in her commencement speech from the stage of the Wakin auditorium.

The graduation ceremony was being held on a Friday, one week after their program completion. The Wakin auditorium had been transformed from a large lecture and entertainment hall into an intimate venue with continental seating and all of the traditional college graduation décor, props, and colorful flora that seemed a Hearthling staple in almost everything they did.

A floating gold banner spanning center stage read, in sparkling letters, "Congratulations, Exchange Students!"

There was little of the pomp and circumstance of your typical Earthling college or university ceremony. There was no processional and no national anthem or graduation song or greetings from the President or Board of Trustees. There were no student or guest speakers.

As exchange students entered the auditorium, they were ushered to their assigned seats. They listened to an inspirational commencement speech from Professor Huaman, scripted to send them out into Hearth with gleeful hearts. When they received their Certificate of Completion scroll (which was made of real parchment), the back digital wall of the stage posted an array of photos from each student's homeland.

Instead of making students sad or melancholy, the photos of home bolstered their spirits and made them cheer even louder for each other.

Another Earthling graduation tradition Hearthlings did not indulge in was the wearing of caps and gowns. Earthlings were encouraged to wear clothing that made a show of their ethnic heritage. Experienced Hearthling fashion designers were available to help Earthlings create something special for the occasion, if what they sought was not currently in their closets.

Most of Dan's classmates dressed in something traditional. Ella wore a blue and yellow Swedish folk costume with daisy pattern embroidery. Obed wore a hand-woven colorful Ghanaian kente cloth (like a Greek toga, with cultural symbolic patterns). Lyberth wore a beaded amauti with trousers and boots, all made of synthesized animal fur and skins, that celebrated her Inuit heritage. Waqas wore a purple brocade sherwani with gold churidar, black wool Jinnah cap, and decorative leather khussa shoes.

"Conservative," Waqas told Dan, which was the way he preferred to dress.

Cardinal Ocampo was a big hit in his bright red Roman Catholic cassock, chasuble, and liturgical vestments, waving to the audience from the stage as would the father of the Roman Catholic Church greeting his flock.

The most striking outfit (agreed upon by all) was Amaya's *jūni-hitoe*. Amaya had explained to Class 3B that she would be wearing a Japanese court costume that had been worn by empresses during important ceremonies (which she regarded her graduation to be). Amaya had shown Class 3B her handmade sketches of what she intended to wear, explaining to them in detail how her costume would be made.

As Amaya made her way up to the stage, a wave of awe-struck recognition moved through the crowd. The wave collected into a swell of applause that became deafening once Amaya surfaced on stage.

The designs and colors of her clothing were so intricate and captivating that Amaya was, in Dan's opinion, a living work of art. An elaborate hairstyle known as *suberakashi*, along with special hair ornaments, completed her look.

Being true to her modest self, Amaya attempted to rush off stage after accepting her certificate and hug from Professor Huaman. Her professor refused to allow Amaya a speedy exit.

Professor Huaman grabbed Amaya by the hand and stood her a few steps clear of the lectern near center stage for all to see. People rose to their feet, adding cheers to their rousing support of her custom choice.

So overwhelming was their appreciation that tears of joy filled the eyes of her flushed face. After taking several bows and issuing a stream of heartfelt, humble thanks, Amaya could stand it no more. The beauty of the ball made her graceful exit, waving her certificate hand to her adoring crowd.

Dan had felt left out of the ethnic heritage suggestion, in a sense. He was American born and bred. If he were to embrace ethnic wear, he would prefer it be of his ancestral Africa (Ghana and Mali, as his DNA test had revealed).

Dan dismissed his initial intention of representing urban African-America, regarding it as a cultural choice rather than ethnic. If he were on Earth, Dan would not dress so casually on such an auspicious occasion. To be true to his origins, Dan would need to reach back to his ancestral roots, of which he had little knowledge.

Pressed for time, Dan decided against exploring that option. Few people knew that the men's tuxedo originated in the United States. A Hearthling designer created for Dan an elegant black tuxedo with a formal pleated front white shirt for his cultural heritage ensemble. His designer coupled Dan's tailor-made outfit with silver cufflinks engraved with Dan's initials, a handmade matching silk black bowtie, and shimmering black leather shoes. Dan loved the ensemble, and so did everyone who saw him wearing it.

Dan's star-twin had been announced. Kwasi strolled out onto a well-lit stage with microphone in hand to a warm round of applause. His imposing figure stopped center stage. He looked poised and confident in a tailor-made classic black tuxedo, crisp white shirt, shimmering black leather shoes, and a specially designed silk bowtie with the company logo.

It was the Single Organism Leadership Conference. Kwasi was this year's keynote speaker. The large, posh conference hall was packed, straying from the typical auditorium-style seating for a more comfortable dining room arrangement.

Anyone who was anyone at Single Organism was in attendance. At Kwasi's table sat Toni, fellow board members Seo-yeon Hong and Russell Davis, and their spouses. Amiri Hayden, with his live-in fiancé Gianna Lastra, were Dan's special guests.

Everyone was elegantly dressed and coiffed for the occasion. Dan's star-twin raised his hand. The applause died down, then ceased.

"We are human beings," Kwasi began in a silky bass voice that resonated throughout the room. It was Dan's voice, "born of this planet we call Earth. No matter your faith or belief, those facts are indisputable. What does it all mean?

"To be a human being, in accordance to one modern English dictionary, is to be 'a man, woman, or child of the species Homo sapiens, distinguished from other animals by superior mental development, the power of articulate speech, and an upright stance.' This is a definition that explains our individual mortal existence. Humankind.

"Then there is humanity: generous, compassionate, sympathetic—offshoots of being human. We contain humane virtues possessed by everyone in this room—traits abounding within most people in the world, in my opinion, despite what detractors would have us believe.

"To embrace our humanity requires that we take responsibility for ourselves, each other, and this planet we call home. We are a Single Organism whose health and welfare are predicated upon the actions of all.

"Our company was founded on that principle, to answer the calling of our Mother Earth. Each of us contributes to sustaining and maintaining this natural balance of Earth in our own way, using science and technology to promote, reverse, or restrain destructive environmental practices wherever we find them, when given the opportunity."

The crowd rose in unison, giving Kwasi a brief but genuine ovation. Dan felt the standing ovation was as much self-congratulatory by the conference attendees as a kudos to the speaker.

Dan understood and saw nothing wrong with feeling good about their accomplishments. He remembered when, asked to be this year's conference keynote speaker, he'd wanted to stress refocusing on the big picture; one that branched beyond what they had achieved with science and technology.

His star-twin humbly waited for the applause to cease and people to retake their seats before moving on.

"We can do more," Kwasi said, as if they were of one mind, stepping forward to downstage center. "I know that is not what you want to hear. I didn't want to say it, to be honest."

That brought rolling laughter from the audience.

"I harken back to our mission statement—one that we founding members drafted in an overcrowded office. It was an office that lacked just about adequate everything except for the belief, determination, and devotion by its tenants, to wholly contribute to making a better world not only for human beings, but for all of its inhabitants. In so doing, we care for the birth mother of life as we know it.

"We are now a multi-billion dollar global corporation racing toward becoming a trillion dollar one. Business is great! Better than we ever imagined. Let's not forget our core commitment in each and every thing that we do.

"In fact, let us redouble our efforts in each and every choice that we make. No decision is too small or large to not germinate from our vow to a healthy environment; a healthy society; a healthy world. We are the leaders on the path for each step forward Single Organism takes. Let not our bottom line ever take precedence over our core values."

"Go forth and do great things," Dan heard Professor Huaman proclaim. "Go forth and do small things. Go forth and make a lasting, positive difference for all humankind." Professor Huaman concluded her commencement speech to a standing ovation. Dan was amongst them, wondering how much he had missed during his most recent Residual Connection episode.

The celebration went off without a hitch, with graduating Earthlings from all of the Indoctrination Programs being cheered as they took the stage to accept their scrolls.

Graduating an entire indoctrination class had never occurred throughout the history of the program. This class was no exception. Twelve percent of this indoctrination class had washed out or elected to return to Earth, for a variety of reasons. This was information Dan had gathered through the exchange student grapevine. Of the ones who elected to return home, the reasons were homesickness, religious conflict, fear, or simply feeling overwhelmed.

All thirteen members of Class 3B paraded across the stage, some with stilted gaits; others with exuberant dance celebrations; but most with strides of pride.

Dan did not understand why he should feel satisfaction for such an accomplishment. After all, they had been kidnapped and more or less forced into this situation. However, he did feel a rush of pride, with his biggest regret being that his Earth family and friends were not there to witness the event.

Class 3B was astonished when, after presenting the first exchange student with their certificate, Professor Huaman elected to hug him rather than shake his hand, repeating her act with every Earthling who crossed the stage. That simple act of affection was, for Dan, the first time he regarded Professor Huaman as simply human rather than a Hearthling.

The exchange students were free to make their way at their leisure to their graduation party at the Wakin dining hall. The dining hall had been transformed into a grand ballroom. Exchange students filled it with the graduation buzz still resonating, congratulating each other and talking with their professors.

Dan, Amaya, Oliver, Ella, Nivi, Waqas, and Gennady were recapping their experiences with Professor Huaman when Dr. Jabori Bakari joined them. Every one of Dan's classmates in the gathering knew Dr. Bakari. He was their Indoctrination Counselor, as well.

"Professor Huaman," Dan began, "allow me to introduce Dr. Jabori Bakari."

Professor Huaman and Dr. Bakari kissed. The two stood next to each other, arms wrapped affectionately around the other's waist.

"We have met," Professor Huaman said. "Jabori is my husband."

Dan's jaw dropped, along with his classmates.

"You're Doba?" Dan exclaimed.

"I am," answered Professor Huaman with an affectionate smile, kissing Jabori again.

"Why did you not tell us?" Amaya asked, looking to either of them for an answer.

"We prefer to keep that knowledge to ourselves," Jabori said, "so as not to interfere with a student's openness and trust in either of us."

"All of the times I was talking to you about Professor Huaman … about your wife…" Gennady trailed off before he could finish.

"Remain confidential, Mr. Kuznetsov," Jabori said. "Client/patient confidentiality. Besides Gennady, not much of what you shared with me, Doba did not already know. We are telepathic, remember?"

"I keep forgetting," Gennady said, with mounting discomfort.

"If my husband told me all of the mean things my students said about me, I would be a nervous wreck."

"Somehow, I doubt that," Oliver said.

"True," Professor Huaman said, "but it would not make your lives any easier."

Everyone laughed but Gennady, who scurried away in embarrassment. Class 3B had come to realize that Gennady had developed a major crush on Professor Huaman. Dan could only imagine what Gennady might have said or thought about the professor that caused him such shame.

All of the exchange students were seated at dining tables according to their graduating class. Faculty members and their guests had their own tables in a separate section. After a delicious three-course meal from an eclectic menu prepared by the Wakin chefs, the ballroom was filled with the ebullient sounds of people letting loose. There was music and dancing and animated conversations.

The DJ played every Earth song that the exchange students requested and then some. Even Cardinal Ocampo joined in on the celebration, exhibiting some good dance moves and putting aside his determination to bring Catholicism to this pagan society. No alcohol was served. Those who were initially disappointed got over it rather quickly. Dan could have cared less about the absence of spirits.

Jomana Ashraf had opted for modern Egyptian fashion, inspired by the pharaohs. She wore an elegant black silk tulle haute couture gown embroidered with ancient Egyptian symbolism and gold open-toed heels. Her shoulder-length brown hair fell upon a delicately bejeweled collar, her only jewelry being her wedding ring.

Jomana looked stunning. Dan had fallen in lust with Jomana, and she with him. They confessed their longing for each other during a study session a few days before graduation, culminating in a steamy kiss. Their kissing was becoming more passionate, with no limitations in sight, when they were interrupted by the sound of Grover Washington's saxophone classic, "Mister Magic." It was one of Dan's dad's favorites, and his door alert selection for the day. IVA Alvita appeared.

"Would you like for me to answer the door, Mr. Bluford?"

"Who is it, Alvita?"

"Mr. Obed Addo and Mr. Waqas Anwar."

"That's okay, I'll get it," Dan said. "Thank you."

"Very good, sir," Alvita said before she vanished.

Dan looked into Jomana's beseeching brown eyes. They were a reflection of how he felt. With silent agreement and severe disappointment mixed with guilt, the two indigent lovers uncoiled their bodies, regained their composure, and answered the door together after the third alert.

Obed and Waqas burst in and invited them to join the rest of Class 3B to an art exhibit on campus that was supposed to be epic. Neither of them appeared surprised to find Jomana in his room.

Classmates had kidded Dan and Jomana about something going on between them, in the beginning—a charge they could honestly rebuff. Over time, the kidding ceased, but not their observance.

Professor Huaman never placed Dan and Jomana together, when dividing the class into groups. Dan and Jomana believed Professor Huaman had intercepted their thoughts regarding each other— thoughts Dan knew he was unable to control. While Hearthlings had no problem with copulation between consenting adults in wedlock, Professor Huaman was fully aware of how many Earthlings viewed the matter.

Dan and Jomana accepted the invitation with jittery smiles. Obed and Waqas could not stop talking about the exhibit. Dan and Jomana responded at appropriate times during their exuberance to show their interest, though they comprehended little of what Waqas and Obed were saying.

Their friends—and they had become friends—either did not notice, or ignored Dan and Jomana's original unease. Dan had no doubt that he and Jomana would have consummated their friendship, if not for the intrusion.

Jomana and Dan agreed to meet only with a group or in public places after reprimanding themselves about their near-infidelity the next day. The two also made it a point to not sit or stand next to each other, whenever possible. Their mutual attraction had become too strong, and they did not want to risk doing anything they would later regret.

Their stipulated conditions for meeting did not work. Denying their attraction for each other only made matters worse. The tempted couple avoided each other completely outside of class for the final days leading up to graduation.

Jomana and Dan managed to enjoy the party, along with all in attendance, dancing with each other, joking, laughing, and having carefree fun. The sexual tension between them seemed to be waning. Dan enjoyed Jomana's company and found her even more beautiful than ever.

Professor Huaman had mentioned, during her commencement speech, that the exchange students should relish tonight, because soon they would not see each other again until they returned to Earth.

Knowing this would be their final temptation seemed to give the heated couple a sense of relief, rejuvenating their exclusive contractual relationship to their Earth partners like shelters in the storm. Dan knew he would never forget Jomana. He secretly hoped she would not forget him.

CHAPTER 23

A special brunch was held in honor of the graduating exchange students in the Falcon dining hall the day following graduation.

Alvita Agumanu, Eleonora Olsson, Enrique Pacheco, along with the other members of Al's host staff, also attended. Al chimed for attention by tapping her water glass with a metal spoon midway through the meal, and rose to her feet, poised and powerful, wearing the Falcon cobalt blue uniform and silver pumps and braided crown of thick black hair that exchange students had come to know as her trademark hairstyle.

"May I have everyone's attention, please?" Al announced in what still sounded to Dan like a Caribbean accent. Her bright brown eyes scanned the room. Everyone gave Al their full attention.

"As some of you already know, all graduating students will be vacating Falcon on Monday. Each of you will meet your new host this weekend.

"Do not concern yourself with packing. We will make certain all of your belongings arrive safely at your new homes.

"I am afraid we are kicking you out of the nest, my darlings. You will not be permitted to return to Zenith Campus once you leave, until time for your departure to Earth."

Al delivered the announcement with as much regret as a mother conveying difficult news to her children. There was a murmuring amongst the students. Al raised a calming hand.

"I know, I know: this is a bittersweet occasion for all of us. Saying goodbye is never easy. It seems as though my staff and I were just getting to know you, and it is time for you to leave. I want to take this moment on behalf of all of us to thank you for giving Hearthlings, such as myself, an opportunity to make your acquaintance."

Every Hearthling present gave the exchange students a rousing round of applause. A few of the students stood and bowed. Every student exhibited an appreciative smile.

"We hope your stay with us has been a pleasant one," Al continued after the applause ceased. "It has been both a pleasure and a privilege to serve you in this capacity. If the graduating classes will please raise a glass..."

Al waited until each of her staff and the graduating class did so.

"May your journey from this day forward be one of good fortune and ceaseless wonder."

A somber mood floated through the room at the conclusion of the toast. Students who had, moments earlier, been filled with good cheer were picking at their food, attempting to avoid eye contact with each other. The moment had come for Class 3B and other exchange students to part company. No one was ready to say goodbye.

Al tapped her glass and rose again. "Come now, students! If I knew you were going to take the news so badly, I would have had you sedated and shipped off instead!"

That brought a chuckle from the crowd. It was a clear reference on how they had come to be on Hearth.

"This is not a wake," Al continued in her vibrant manner, displaying her dazzling smile, "but a time for celebration! Think of all you have accomplished, the friendships you have forged, and the wonderful memories you have created. Those times will always be with you. You will carry them wherever you go. Look at you, all gathered together in triumph. Celebrate!"

Al's speech lifted the somber mood like sunlight dispersing fog. The atmosphere returned to a positive flow of energetic chatter and laughter. Al took her seat, looking on with the modest pride of someone who had once again did her job well. It was her life calling; a blessing she never grew tired of fulfilling.

Class 3B gathered in the Falcon public space for a final group goodbye after brunch. Cardinal Ocampo said a prayer to protect and guide them moving forward. The Falcon hosts made their final best wishes to Class 3B before darting off to greet a new class of exchange students who were gathered in the lobby.

All around, there were wishes of good luck and playful admonishments amongst the graduates to behave so not to embarrass Earthlings, coupled with hugs, kisses, and solemn promises of reunions when they returned to Earth.

Back in his room, Dan could not ward off his sense of loss. He walked around, looking here and touching there. There was artwork and knickknacks he had accumulated. Houseplants he had nurtured. Dan assumed they would travel with him to his new residence. He was not certain he wanted to bring them along.

It was early Saturday afternoon. The day was overcast, with intermittent sunlight eclipsing the gray. By Monday morning, Dan would be leaving. He was going to miss his classmates, Professor Huaman, Jabori, Alvita, Eleonora, Enrique, Aroha, Bartek, and a host of other Hearthlings Dan had gotten to know in passing. In seven short weeks, Unit 4A, Falcon, Wakin, and the Zenith Campus had become his home away from home.

"Alvita, I need your help," Dan said. IVA Alvita appeared.

"How may I be of service, Mr. Bluford?"

"I wanted to thank you for all you have done to make my stay at Falcon comfortable."

"That is very kind of you to say, sir, but serving you is what I am programmed to do."

"Nevertheless, you do it well, and it is greatly appreciated."

"Thank you, sir. Will there be anything else?"

Dan stared at IVA Alvita, seeing the physical likeness of Al without the substance. Nonetheless, Dan wanted to hug her or at least shake her hand, but felt that either was inappropriate. They would somehow amount to the equivalent of embracing an android or drone or air.

"There will be nothing else, Alvita. I hereby formally relieve you of your duties."

"Thank you, sir. Moreover, might I say it has been an honor serving you, Mr. Daniel Samuel Bluford. I have no doubt you will serve your planet well."

To Dan's shock, IVA Alvita turned on her silver heels, just like the real Al, and marched away, vanishing through the front door as if walking off into the sunset.

No sooner had IVA Alvita left then Dan's door alert sounded with the tolling of church bells. Dan felt it an appropriate choice. Dan answered without checking to see who was there, opening the door.

Jomana stood before him, dressed causally in jeans, a blouse, sneakers, and what appeared, to Dan, to be a full complement of jewelry. Her hair was pulled back in a ponytail. Her beautiful eyes were red as if she had been crying. Without a word, Jomana threw her arms around Dan and kissed him. The passion of her kiss staggered Dan.

"I will miss you most of all, Daniel Bluford," Jomana said in a quavering voice, her smile as sad as her eyes. Jomana rushed off before Dan could respond. Dumbfounded, Dan watched her dash down the hall and burst through the exit door leading to the stairwell, her lovely image a pleasing ghost floating through his mind.

Dan eased shut the door. He touched his lips with his fingers, replaying the kiss. "Same here, Jomana Ashraf," Dan said to himself.

A text message alert snapped Dan out of his trance. It was from Jabori, asking Dan to meet him in his office at his earliest convenience. When Dan walked into Jabori's office a few minutes later, there was Aroha and Bartek. Dan had been disappointed they were not at the graduation ceremony or after-party.

"I will leave you three alone," Jabori said, stepping out and closing the door behind him. Aroha was wearing her barista outfit, complete with nametag. Seeing her dressed that way made Dan laugh.

"Are you making another trip to Earth?" Dan asked Aroha.

Aroha answered with a smile, "Not any time soon. I thought I would wear this for you. A little something to remember me by."

"How could I ever forget you, Aroha?"

"Sorry we missed the festivities, Daniel," Bartok said, "but that is not really our thing."

"We are not much into ceremonies or parties," Aroha added.

"Not a problem, I'm glad to see you."

"We wanted to wish you well," Bartok said.

"And to tell you how proud we are of you," Aroha said, tearing up.

"Thank you for all that you've done for me. Waking up in a strange place under peculiar circumstances is difficult. You calmed my fears and helped alleviate my doubts. I don't know how I would have made it this far without you two."

"Promise me you will not try any rough stuff with our Hearthling brothers and sisters," Bartok said. "They might decide to teach you a hard lesson you will not forget."

The three of them laughed.

"I'll remember that," Dan said to Bartok. Their amused smiles were mixed with sorrow. *How brief the time together. How great the attachment*, Dan thought. Aroha and Bartok nodded as if they had read his thoughts. "You were my first contacts," Dan said.

"You are a good person, Daniel," Bartok said. "That was a big reason why you were selected."

"Be yourself, Daniel, and you will be fine," Aroha said.

"Good point," Bartok added.

"I guess this is goodbye," Dan said after a prolonged uneasy silence.

"Yes, it is," Bartok said.

Tears spilled from Aroha's bright brown eyes. "We will miss you, Daniel."

"Not as much as I'm going to miss you two. I know I'm not permitted to return to Zenith Campus. Is there any reason you can't visit me on the outside?" Dan smiled, amused at the thought of him referring to himself as a released inmate. Aroha and Bartok got the inference and smiled with him.

"There are strict rules prohibiting contact with any exchange student once they have left an indoctrination campus," Bartok said.

"Even for exceptions like you," Aroha added. "It is for your own good."

Bartok moved in for a hug. Bartok patted Dan on the back after they released, then Bartok walked to the door. Aroha and Dan stared at each other like good friends working up the courage for a final farewell.

Dan reflected on the time he was considering poaching the barista for Single Organism, and his sad smile broadened. The thought occurred to him: had Aroha been reading his mind the entire time they were in the coffee shop?

"Yes, I was," Aroha said, answering his unspoken question.

"I will miss you most of all, Aroha, my Hearthling undercover agent."

Aroha laughed, the joy lighting up her tear-stained face.

"That was fun, I have to admit," Aroha said, wiping away her tears. Aroha started to say something more, but lunged forward instead, hugging Dan so hard, he felt as though his ribs would break. Dan hugged her back, as he would his own daughter. Aroha rushed toward the door when they broke. Bartok opened the door as Aroha approached and she bolted through the open door, not looking back. Bartok left with a sad wave. Jabori returned with a comforting smile, closing the door behind him.

"How did it go, Daniel?" Jabori asked.

"Sweet sorrow, like most of what I'm feeling today."

Jabori nodded. "I have a surprise for you."

"Another one?"

"Yes."

"Must you?"

"I must."

Jabori walked over and placed his hand on the doorknob. "Allow me to introduce you to the matriarch of the household where you will be staying. Are you ready?" Jabori asked, his voice sounding more like a command than a question.

"There's no time like the present." Dan straightened and attempted to steel himself.

Jabori looked at Dan as if he were unconvinced. After a sharp nod from Dan, Jabori opened the door. In walked Toni. She walked over to Dan and said, "Hello." Dan was dumbstruck. He felt the room spinning. Jabori and Toni grabbed an arm and helped Dan, on wobbly legs, over to the sofa. The sofa embraced Dan. Then everything went black.

CHAPTER 24

When Dan came to, he found himself seated on the sofa between Bartok and Toni's star-twin.

Seeing his wife's star-twin had overwhelmed him. Aroha had returned, hovering over Dan like a hummingbird examining a flower. Jabori stood next to Aroha. Toni's star-twin was gently holding his hand, her hand smooth and warm in his. It was a natural fit, as if they had been doing so for a lifetime. The sofa embraced Dan. He looked around at a room full of concerned faces.

"How are you feeling?" Aroha asked, removing a cool, damp cloth from his forehead.

Dan heard himself saying he was fine, but he was still feeling dizzy. "What happened?" Dan sounded groggy.

"You fainted," Jabori said. "Not to worry. It happens sometimes, when first meeting a significant other's star-twin."

"That's reassuring," Dan said, managing a faint smile.

"Drink this," Bartok said. Dan took the tall glass of water offered him. It tasted cool, clean, and refreshing. His head cleared almost instantly.

"I thought you two had left," Dan said to Aroha and Bartok, attempting to stand.

"Sit," Aroha commanded, gently placing her hands on Dan's shoulders and forcing him down, "until you regain your strength."

"Dr. Bakari called us back to make certain you were okay," Bartok said.

"I find it best to leave physical consultations up to the professionals," Jabori said.

"I'm fine," Dan said. "Thanks for your concerns."

"I agree," Aroha said. "All of his vitals are stable. Give him a minute to get his bearings."

"You examined me while I was passed out?" Dan asked Aroha.

"Yes. This surprises you, Daniel?" Aroha added with a smile as if to say 'we have been here before.'

"We have never lost an Earthling' and we are determined that you not be our first," Bartok said.

Dan sighed. "Are you sure I can't take you back to Earth with me?" He addressed all but his wife's star-twin.

"Positive," Jabori said after the chuckling ceased.

"We will be off," Aroha said.

"Again," Bartok added. "Try not to have any more medical emergencies during the rest of your stay on Hearth, Daniel."

"As much as we love seeing you," Aroha added, "we would prefer it be under more pleasant circumstances."

"Gotcha," Dan said.

Thanks for your assistance, Jabori telepathically said to Aroha and Bartok. The medical team nodded before leaving.

Dan turned his attention to the woman holding his hand. Her resemblance to Toni was uncanny. Same radiant espresso skin, thick shoulder-length black curls, high cheekbones, and mesmerizing brown eyes.

"Can you give us a minute?" Jabori said to Toni's star-twin.

"Certainly, Doctor," Toni's star-twin said, patting Dan's hand before letting go and standing tall and sturdy, spine straight as rebar. "You are going to be fine, dear," she added with a reassuring voice and dimpled smile, her tone the same one Toni would use on her patients to ease their fears. She exited the office and softly closed the door behind her.

"Sorry about the shock, Daniel. We find it is best to dive right in in matters such as these."

"I certainly took the plunge."

"Daniel, you are going to discover that Toni's star-twin has a number of the same qualities as your Toni," Jabori began, ignoring

Dan's sarcasm. "I once again want to caution you. Take your time and get to know her as an individual."

"Understood."

Dr. Bakari eyed Dan warily. "I believe you believe what you are saying, Daniel. My hope is that your belief takes hold in your mind."

"I can do this Jabori."

"You will be living with her."

"As husband and wife?"

"Not in the formal sense, as on your Earth, but in a manner of speaking, yes, if you wish."

"I don't wish. She's not Toni."

"Either way, it will not matter to her or any Hearthling." Jabori abruptly stood and walked over to the door. "I will give you two a chance to get better acquainted."

"What is with you leaving when the going gets tough, Jabori?" Dan half-jokingly asked.

"This is your journey, Daniel, not mine. I will be right outside if you need me. Take your time."

Jabori opened the door. Dan noticed, as he hadn't before, that Toni's star-twin was wearing a tiered, graphic floral print, maxi dress and laced black sandals. The multicolor mixed-stone necklace and matching coil bracelet were perfect compliments to her outfit, making Toni's star-twin appear both casual and regal in Dan's eyes, as Toni appeared when wearing a similar ensemble.

"We will be fine," Toni's star-twin said, sounding exactly like his wife. Toni's star-twin sat next to Dan. "I promise to take good care of him, Doctor. I did not mean to startle you, Daniel. Are you alright?"

Dan nodded.

"Allow me to introduce myself. My name is Abiona Gaige. I am Toni Wilma Bluford's star-twin, as you have noticed, and the wife of your star-twin, Kwasi Gaige."

"Daniel Bluford. Most people call me Dan."

"I know who you are," Abiona said with the same smile Toni exhibited when she believed Dan was being silly. Dan wondered if his star-twin's Abiona behaved the same under similar circumstances. "I would prefer to call you Daniel, if that is all right with you?"

"Daniel it is."

"You are an Earthling," Abiona said, more as a statement than a question.

"I'm not the only one on your planet."

"You certainly look human."

"Thanks," Dan said sarcastically. "What were you expecting, horns and a tail?"

"No insult intended. It is one thing to learn about something in the abstract than come face to face with its reality."

"I suppose."

"You are my first Earthling."

"Notice any differences?"

"Some. Your mind is undisciplined, for instance."

"I thought I had improved my mental discipline since I've been on Hearth."

"You still have a ways to go in that department."

"Anything else?"

"Your aura."

"You can see my aura?" Dan asked in disbelief.

"All Hearthlings can, when we chose."

"What else can Hearthlings do that Earthlings don't know about?"

"You will discover our full capabilities in due course."

"What about my aura?"

"It is diminishing. Most Hearthling auras are brilliant. Some so much, so they can be blinding."

"Mine is diminishing?"

"Yes. Your colors lack vibrancy, as if you are in constant turmoil, draining your strength."

"Being kidnapped and held hostage on a strange planet in a strange universe might have something to do with that."

"It is not that, Daniel," Toni's star-twin said as she studied Dan's aura more closely. "For an aura to fluctuate as is yours would require continual gnawing conflicts that mean a great deal to you."

Dan thought about Single Organism. The company had been founded on the principle of placing Earth first. They had built an industry on products that delivered on their mandate.

A majority of the founding principles who now composed the board of directors were now willing to renege on that promise. Greed had set in. They had become eager to shave costs by replacing some expensive Earth-friendly materials with cheaper, environmentally harmful ones in order to fatten profits.

The board had gradually gone from a majority in dissent of such design changes to a majority in favor, with Dan remaining one of the few holdouts.

Dan was witnessing Single Organism transform into one of the businesses that he and his colleagues had railed against during their inception, a mindset he was beginning to see filtering down through the ranks. It was a ghastly change that Dan was feeling more and more powerless to curtail.

Was the uphill battle to restore the Single Organism mission draining him? Was the pressure really taking that great of a toll? Abiona chose to remain silent, if she had read his thoughts.

"You're telling me all Hearthlings can see my aura?" Dan asked, still in disbelief.

"Not only yours, but everyone's. Human, animal, plants—all living matter. We can chose to see their aura or turn them off like a light switch."

"Thank you for clarifying. It must be nice to have that ability."

"I suppose," Abiona said. "Since Hearthlings are born with that ability and are trained from childhood to read auras, who are we to say?"

"You are married to the man who is sleeping with my wife."

"Yes," Abiona answered matter-of-factly. "As well as standing in for any other functions you would normally perform when you are at home."

"Doesn't that bother you, to know your husband is sleeping with another woman?"

"Should it?"

"Yes!"

"It does not. We both have other sexual partners." Abiona briefly explained the differences between Hearth customs and Earth customs regarding monogamy, essentially repeating what Jabori had told him earlier on the same subject.

"Are there any areas that you would like for me to clarify or elaborate on that might help you better understand our conjugal rights?"

Dan was not a Hearthling, but an Earthling. Whatever other failings his people may have on this matter, he vehemently disagreed.

"No, I understand," Dan said. "What you call 'conjugal rights', most Earthlings would term as an 'open marriage.' What I don't get is how Hearthlings are able to disassociate their feelings to permit another to have sex with a person that they love?"

Dan thought of Jomana making him feel guilty and hypocritical. He noticed Abiona's eyes widen slightly, as if she had intercepted his reflection but would not give it voice.

I see," Abiona said, giving Dan a sympathetic smile. "You and I will not be having sex, Daniel, despite your strong physical resemblance to my handsome husband.

"Unless we connect on a personal and intellectual level, then I will be off limits to you. That could change once we get to know each other better, in which case we can revisit the possibility."

"Gee, thanks."

"You are welcome."

"Are you getting when I'm being sarcastic, Abiona?"

"Yes. I simply choose to ignore your sarcasm, in most instances. You will discover that Hearthlings are, by and large, not a sarcastic people."

"That's not been my experience here on the Zenith Campus."

"Zenith Hearthlings are unique, in that regard. It's an acquired trait from being in the company of Earthlings, I suppose. I'm doubtful any of them carry sarcasm with them off campus."

There was a moment of quiet before Abiona spoke. "Who is Spock? What are Vulcans, and why do I remind you of them?" Abiona asked, having read Dan's mind.

"Spock is a fictional extraterrestrial character on an Earth sci-fi television show. He comes from the planet Vulcan—a planet where the people live by logic and reasoning and are virtually devoid of emotions."

"Sci-fi?"

"Science fiction."

"I do not recall a planet Vulcan in your universe."

"As I said, science fiction."

"And you believe I have no emotions, Daniel?"

"I drew that conclusion from our exchange."

"Because I did not respond favorably to your sarcasm."

Dan thought for a moment. He realized Abiona was correct. That was precisely how he had drawn his conclusion. "I apologize. I should not have thought such a thing."

"No need to apologize. My feelings—and I do have feelings—are not hurt. Also, never apologize for what you are thinking. It is one of the truest expressions of our individual natures. You will find that Hearthlings are not easily offended because we have access to each other's deepest thoughts when the subject permits."

"Still, I feel bad, and it would make me feel better if you accepted my apology, Abiona."

"Apology accepted, Daniel. Allow me to apologize if I have hurt your feelings in any way, and if I come across as cold and uncaring."

"No need for you to apologize, but thank you just the same."

"It could have been worse," Abiona said.

"How?"

"You could have called me an ice queen, if I am using that Earth term correctly."

"You are properly using that offensive term," Dan said, sounding relieved.

"Shall we try again?" Abiona asked with a smile that so strongly resembled Toni's, it almost made Dan hyperventilate. Abiona once again enfolded Dan's hand in hers, an affectionate action that Dan had already become too comfortable with.

"It would be my pleasure, Abiona Gaige," Dan said in response to Abiona's question.

Abiona perked up as if struck by a novel revelation. "I must say, you look exactly like my Kwasi."

"You look exactly like my Toni."

"I cannot wait to hear all about your wife. You will forgive me if I, from time to time, mistakenly call you Kwasi while you are in my care."

"If you'll grant me the same latitude regarding Toni."

"Then it is agreed. We offer each other pre-emptive forgiveness for our foibles regarding mistaken identities."

"Can I have my hand back, Abiona?"

"I am going to hold onto your hand awhile longer, Daniel."

"As you wish."

Abiona smiled a smile he adored on Toni. It was a smile that made him uneasy about Abiona.

Toni took Kwasi's hand. They were seated in the back of a limousine, casually dressed and comfortable, on the way to the airport after the conclusion of the Single Organism Leadership Conference.

Holding hands was a constant between he and Toni; a subconscious act; a physical connection that occurred like aligned magnets. Witnessing Kwasi holding his wife's hand in the same affectionate manner made Dan wince.

"Your keynote address was brilliant, Dan," Toni said. "It set the proper tone for the remainder of the conference."

"Thank you, honey. I did my best."

"Take it from me, your best was good enough."

"Do you think it will make a difference? Change the course the company is taking placing profit over planet and people?"

"Seo-yeon was already on your side."

"Seo-yeon's loyalty has never waivered. Based on our conversation afterwards, Russell will be giving his full support to our founding principles. The rest of the board members, I'm not so sure about. Most of them were on the fence. Which is something, considering they had been steadfast about shaving costs."

"Economic success can alter people's motivations."

"I don't believe my fellow founders have sold out—only momentarily lost their way.

The CEO has had a powerful influence over our Board of Directors since we brought him in to manage our overwhelmingly expanding financial duties. At that, he has done a great job. In so doing, he has also corrupted our original vision in order to fatten profits."

"From what I observed, the CEO wasn't happy. His bottom-line message was losing traction with the leadership."

"My hope is that the board will find their way back before it's too late."

"I believe they will, sweetheart." Toni kissed Kwasi. "You Single Organism people are a stubborn lot."

"That stubbornness—as you put it, my darling—played a big role in why we are the success we are today. No compromises; staying true to our beliefs…"

"Be patient, Dan. The ship will right itself."

"And if it doesn't?"

Dan had been gone for only seconds. He and Abiona had sat in silence during that time.

"You connected with my husband?" Abiona said more like a statement than a question.

"How did you know?"

"Dr. Bakari explained to me about your Residual Connection to Kwasi."

"Yes, I connected with Kwasi. Did you see what I saw?"

"No. Your mind went blank. Kwasi is doing well?"

"He is doing quite well as me."

"That is good."

"I suppose."

"You keep forgetting one thing, Daniel."

"What's that?"

"You will be home, this time next year. This condition is temporary. Try to live in the moment, as I am doing, and you will find our precious time together will fly. You will once again hold your Toni in your arms before you know it, hug your children, and return to the life that is yours."

"I will try to do as you say and live more in the moment. These Residual Connections don't help."

"I would think the opposite."

"How so?"

"I would think they would give you comfort to know your family is fine. It certainly gives me comfort knowing my Kwasi is well."

"When you view it through your optimistic lens, it is comforting to know."

"You are agreeing with me to put me at ease. That is not how you really think or feel. Please share your true thoughts with me."

Dan took in a deep breath before speaking. "The truth is, I don't like being replaced. I suppose we all would like to believe we are unique; one of a kind. Then something like this happens and shatters that belief.

"I've been replaced by a physical duplicate of me, and my family, the people closest to me in the entire world, don't know he's an imposter. Discovering something like that strikes at the heart of your necessity."

Abiona said nothing for a moment. Dan was curious if Abiona was not only reading his mind but his body language, facial tics, aura, or something more about him that was part of Hearthling normal perception sets.

"Self-pity does not become you, Daniel." Abiona said in the same tone that Toni used to warrant his full attention and press hard a point.

"Excuse me," Dan said.

"You are feeling sorrow for yourself. You have been thrust into a situation that you cannot control. For a person accustomed to being in a position of authority, you are feeling powerless, right now."

"I thought Dr. Bakari was the psychiatrist," Dan quipped.

"It does not take a psychiatric degree to diagnose what you are feeling. I might feel quite the same way if I were in your position."

Dan thought about what Abiona said about self-pity, for a moment.

"Part of what you say is true. That does not dismiss my feelings regarding how much I miss my family and being a part of their unit."

"As any loving husband and father would. Try to take comfort in knowing they are being cared for precisely the same as if you were with them."

"I am going to need more time to accept that thinking. If I ever do."

Abiona patted Dan's hand. "We will do our best to make your stay with us as comfortable as possible. It is my personal hope that, somewhere along the line, you'll find peace with your circumstances."

Peace, Dan thought. *What an amazing word. What an incredible concept, that is so challenging to achieve.* Abiona read Dan's thoughts and smiled her agreement.

*   *   *

Dan remained dazed from his time with Abiona when they parted after their two-hour meeting.

That seemed to be the general condition of Class 3B and the other exchange student graduates. They all reported on their astonishment at meeting Hearthling duplicates of their Earthling spouses, friends, or relations.

Jomana caught up with Dan, Obed, Ella, Amaya, Cardinal Ocampo and Waqas in the lobby. They were on their way to meet the rest of Class 3B for a farewell dinner at a campus veggie restaurant called Demeter.

Jomana pulled Dan aside and asked if she could speak with him alone for a moment. The rest understood and went on ahead.

Jomana apologized to Dan for her earlier behavior. She had been feeling conflicted. Between her longing for her absent husband and her attraction to Dan, her desires had "boiled over."

Dan not only understood, but also told Jomana that he had felt the same way. Seeing their star-twin spouses brought them back to their senses. Jomana offered her hand. They shook on it, a lingering handshake as they were drawn deeper into each other's gaze.

Dan wanted to pull Jomana near and hold her like a man long separated from his love. Dan knew that, at that moment, they were kidding themselves. The feelings they had for one another were genuine.

Jomana slipped her hand from his. They gave each other a friendly hug. The forbidden couple rushed off to catch up with their former classmates after taking a couple of deep breaths to calm themselves.

Neither dared asked the other the intimate question that was lurking on the tips of their tongues: how were they going to respond when—not if—those same desires erupted toward their spouses' body doubles?

Neither was aware that Al had secretly observed the whole scene between Dan and Jomana with an approving smile.

*　　*　　*

Dr. Jabori Bakari dropped by Dan's room for a late Sunday afternoon final visit. He handed Dan a pillbox containing white tablets that looked like aspirin.

"Those are Occlumency pills, developed specifically for Earthlings. They will prevent Hearthlings from patrolling your mind. Your private thoughts will once again remain private. You only need take one pill every thirty days."

"How do they work?"

"They allow your body to create an electromagnetic field that prevents us from accessing your brain activity, something Hearthlings can do naturally—the difference being that we can turn our barrier off and on at will. The Occlumency pill does not give you the capability of choice."

"These pills are completely harmless?"

"One-hundred percent. If you should accidentally take more than one pill a month, do not worry. Once a single dose is in your system, any additional dosages are harmless.

That should not happen, anyway. The pill box has a built-in reminder to alert you when it is time for your next dose."

Dan swallowed a pill as fast as he could. It dissolved quickly and tasted like peppermint. Dan waited to feel something.

"You will not feel any different. It will take a couple of minutes to work its way into your bloodstream before the barrier will be in place."

"Why didn't you give us these pills before?"

"Because we wanted access to your thoughts. Today is when we part company, my friend. It is time for you to enter our world; time for you to get to know the real Hearth. Do you have any lingering questions for me?"

Dan felt as though he should, but he couldn't think of one.

"Your personal belongings, including your Education Packet cube, will be transported to your new residence. Your EP is a parting gift from us at the Zenith Campus. It has been an honor and a privilege knowing you, Daniel Samuel Bluford. You will be missed."

Jabori hugged Dan. Dan returned the hug. Brothers in a farewell embrace.

"Be well," Jabori said.

"You too," Dan said before they parted.

"He is all yours," Jabori said to Abiona, who had been waiting outside his dormitory room door. She wore a pair of black ballet flats, an ombre ethnic tunic top, and sapphire jeans.

Again: casual and regal came to Dan's mind. Abiona extended her hand with an inviting smile. Since their prolonged conversation in Jabori's office, Dan had become comfortable around Abiona. Dan took one last look around Unit 4A, strolled over to Abiona, and cordially took the hand proffered him.

Abiona escorted Dan from the building to her vehicle parked by the curbside in front of Falcon. Jomana, Obed, and Waqas were being escorted to similar vehicles by those that Dan assumed were Hearthling star-twins from their Earth lives.

The exchange students gave each other sad waves before getting into their awaiting transports. Dan stared out the front passenger window at Falcon, allowing the mixed emotions of melancholy and enthusiasm to rush through him without restraint. Dan heard Abiona give the vehicle one command once she was strapped in behind the steering wheel: "Home."

CHAPTER 25

The vehicle was set on automatic pilot. Abiona's hands rested comfortably atop the steering wheel, her body nestled into her form-fitting seat, the cabin as quiet as light as they cruised through the air of a clear blue sky.

"My children are anxious to meet the man who so closely resembles their father," Abiona said.

Abiona's voice was the same as Toni's: a pacifying tone that placated Dan and made him feel at ease. A taste of home, as his mother would say.

"Did you show your children a picture of me?" Dan asked, curious to know of their reaction.

"If, by picture, you mean photograph, no. That would spoil the surprise."

"I wish someone would had shown me a picture of you before we met."

"Why?" Abiona said, sounding puzzled.

"It would have prepared me. Seeing you for the first time came as quite a shock."

"I noticed," Abiona said with a bemused smile. "What about the photographs you have of your wife?"

"I don't have any, Abiona."

"You do not have any photographs of your wife or family on your phone?" Abiona said, her tone peppered with disbelief.

"Nope."

"You were not allowed such things?"

"I don't know about that. All I know is, I don't have any. None of my wife or children, family or friends. They live only in my memories, for the time being."

"Was your phone confiscated?"

"More like it was left behind."

"I am sorry, Daniel. I did not know."

"It's not your fault, Abiona. I guess the Exchange Student Program Committee didn't think of everything."

Abiona nodded. "You could be right, or maybe they did have forethought on this matter."

Dan looked quizzically at Abiona. "What do you mean?"

"It could have been their way of compelling you to relinquish your past in order to embrace new experiences."

Dan nodded, turning to stare back at the Zenith Campus. Dan had to admit that Abiona's reasoning made sense. After what felt to Dan like an eternity of awkward silence, Dan said, "I can't wait to meet your children."

He emphasized *your children*, a distinction Dan was making more for himself than Abiona.

Dan turned his gaze forward. He realized, as he watched the Zenith Campus disappear from view, that the campus had been perched atop a plateau. Ahead of them was a stretch of mountain systems Dan knew on Earth as the Andes Mountains of western South America.

"Where does Kwasi work? What does he do?"

"My husband is the Director of the Pequannock Energy Program."

"Impressive."

"Kwasi would describe his work as 'fulfilling.'"

"That too, I would imagine."

"Would you like to see photographs of my children?" Abiona asked.

Dan considered Abiona's question for a long moment, wondering, as Abiona had suggested, if seeing a picture of her children might spoil the surprise. One thing was certain: Dan was ready for what might be, in an odd sort of way, a family reunion.

"I'll wait to meet your children in the flesh."

Abiona affirmed Dan's response with a sympathetic nod. "Tell me about Toni?" Abiona asked.

Dan did so after a heavy sigh, speaking of Toni with pride, respect, and longing.

"Toni sounds amazing," Abiona said when Dan concluded.

"She is," Dan said. *Much like you,* Dan thought, immediately chastising himself for thinking such a thing.

Dan needed to cap the welling sadness inside of him for what he was leaving behind on Earth and at the Zenith Campus and embrace the adventure of what lie ahead, as Abiona suggested.

He took a few deep, cleansing breaths, a meditation technique Dan had learned from a yoga instructor he'd once dated. Abiona said nothing, if she noticed.

"Where do you live?" Dan asked.

"Pequannock Province. It is in the northeastern portion of a place called the United States of America, on your planet."

Dan remembered where the Pequannock Province was located from his Hearth education. He was, nonetheless, grateful for the geographical reminder. Dan had studied the Hearth map in detail, in relationship to Earth.

About three-quarters of his studies had stuck. Dan had total recall of the Zenith Campus province, continents, and countries as well as some capital cities, bodies of water, mountain ranges, and large forests.

From all intents and purposes, Dan knew they were headed to the Hearth equivalent of where his Earth home was located, Pequannock Province, better known to Dan as Golden Meadows.

Dan sat quietly, endeavoring to imagine what to expect. Abiona appeared to be enjoying the view, occasioning a glance his way. Dan assumed the Occlumency pills were working. Neither his silence nor his mind barrier seemed to trouble Abiona.

"I do not get out this way very often," Abiona said. "I forget how beautiful Atua Province is."

Dan nodded in agreement with Abiona's evaluation of Atua Province. Dan noticed they had only encountered a few air vehicles, so far, on their trip once they'd cleared the Zenith Campus. He looked down at the terrain.

Not much ground traffic, Dan thought, reflecting on how bustling Zenith Campus was at this time of day, with a constant vitality of dynamic energy.

"This region of Atua Province is what you would consider country or rustic. Mostly farms and uninhabited land are out this way. Human habitation, that is. Traffic will pick up as we enter more heavily populated areas."

"Can you read my mind, Abiona?" Dan blurted out.

"No, Daniel, I cannot."

Dan was oddly saddened by the news. He had become accustomed to Hearthlings reading his thoughts. The ability had made communication easier rather than more challenging, as one would expect.

"Then how did you know what I was thinking, just now?" Dan asked. "About the lack of traffic?"

"I observed what you were looking at and made a presumption."

Dan was beginning to wonder how well Abiona might already know him; how much information had been provided to her and how much intrinsic knowledge she might possess about him due to his resemblance to Kwasi.

"Can you still see my aura?" Dan asked.

"Yes. The Occlumency pills do not inhibit your body's energy flow."

"Are you reading my aura now?"

"No. Would you like me to?"

"Not really, I was just curious."

Dan looked down at the terrain. He saw large swaths of cultivated earth. From what Dan could make out from the air, there were crops of corn, potatoes, pumpkins, and sunflowers. Dan could not be certain without a closer examination of the other companion crops.

Their trip moved along at a smooth, steady pace. Dan had grown accustomed to traveling in flying vehicles while he still marveled at the engineering. For the first time, a question came to mind regarding the crafts—one he was surprised he had not thought of before.

"Why aren't we experiencing any turbulence?" Dan asked. Being out in the open making him fully aware they were flying no differently than if they were in a passenger jet.

"I do not know much about how these vehicles operate, Daniel," Abiona said. "I can put you in touch with an automotive engineer who can answer your question."

"I would like that."

"No problem. We are having good weather, so that helps for a smooth ride. During storms, we would be experiencing turbulence."

"Humph," Dan said, adding Abiona's statement to his growing list of mental notes. Dan had started compiling data on everything he was learning that was not covered in their studies, making extensive notes about his Hearth experience in what Dan was calling his Hearth Journal that he had set up on his EP.

Until Dan could reconnect to his EP, Dan trusted no other way other than his memory to keep track of any new information.

"When storms occur," Abiona continued, "you will predominately find terrain travelers."

"It being easier to navigate on the ground than in the air during a storm," Dan added. "Not to mention, less likelihood of being struck by lightning."

"Precisely," Abiona said with a proud grin, one that reminded Dan of Professor Huaman when a student correctly answered one of her more challenging questions.

Dan realized, at that moment, that he was still very much a student. Zenith Campus had only been the beginning. Hearth was going to be an inexhaustible teacher. The question for Dan was how much knowledge he would be able to retain.

They passed over farmlands, fields, cities, towns, forests, ocean, rivers, and streams. Vultures, cranes, geese, storks, and condors soared alongside them, on occasion.

Abiona had a telepathic conversation with some of them, filling the birds in on the stranger accompanying her, as Abiona later informed Dan. The high-flying birds were very much aware that Dan was not a Hearthling. They had also been educated about Earthlings from other Hearthlings.

Abiona informed them that this Earthling, Daniel, would cause them no harm. The birds warned that Daniel had better not try anything or they would see to it that he not live to return to his accursed Earth.

"You're kidding?" Dan responded, feeling indignant as she informed Dan about her conversations. "Why are you even discussing me with those ... birds?"

"It is their planet too, Daniel. They have a right to know what is going on."

"You're telling me that Hearthlings have dialogs with wildlife regarding Hearthling matters?"

"Yes, if they are in any way affected by them. That is only fair, do you not think?"

"That must slow progress to a crawl when it comes to any new construction."

Now it was Abiona's turn to become indignant, her words slicing the air as sharp as razors.

"Look around you, Daniel. Take into account what you have seen and experienced on Hearth so far. Modestly speaking, we are more advanced than you in every sense of the word. Yet, you have the audacity, the bold-faced arrogance, to make such a ridiculous claim. Human progress without addressing all factors that vision of progress affects is idiotic."

Dan was embarrassed. He muttered an apology that appeared to have no effect on Abiona.

"If you are going to get along with Hearthlings, you are going to have to demonstrate more discipline and restraint in what you do and say.

"Hearthlings will tolerate much of your Earthly ignorance of our ways and our people. We will give you a wide berth to digest what we have to offer.

But we will show little patience with a representative from a planet whose humans are spiraling toward extinction making disparaging remarks about Hearth. It only makes you sound like a fool. Do you understand?"

"I'm sorry, Abiona. I didn't mean anything by it."

"That is something I am going to have to become accustomed to from you."

"I don't follow."

"Hearthlings say what they mean and mean what they say. That is clearly not always the way of Earthlings."

"True. We can be evasive."

Abiona said nothing in response, as if analyzing what Dan had confessed and constructing a means of how to address it.

Dan realized that Abiona's conversation with the birds was not what had irritated him. It was the combination of being kidnapped from Earth, being forced from his Zenith Campus comfort zone, and being replaced by a body double on Earth with no one recognizing the difference.

At Zenith, Dan had begun to see this experience as a voyage. He had the company of other Earthlings to help bolster that perception. Now he was heading toward another unknown, alone.

Dan was afraid. He was also too stubborn to confess his fear—not even to himself. Dan had made it this far without washing out. Pride and an aching curiosity would not allow him to quit now.

Abiona pointed out more geographical information during their journey, as if their recent exchange had not occurred. Much of the geography was familiar to Dan, in a sense. Dan had seen enough of Earth to recognize certain coastlines, mountains, peninsulas, forests, deserts, savannahs, lakes, and rivers.

They passed over a luxuriant tropical green region of landscapes embodying a myriad of lakes and streams, bounded by table-top mountains, wetlands, and savannahs known as the Pachamama Forest on Hearth. It was an area familiar to Dan as the Amazon Rainforest on Earth.

"Is the Pachamama Forest as unspoiled as it appears, Abiona?"

"Of course. We would no more do harm to the Pachamama Forest than ourselves. It is a major part of our planet's ecosystem. We would be reckless to willfully damage something so precious. There are plenty of places on Hearth to cultivate all of our needs without disturbing the planet's natural environment."

Dan reflected on the ongoing decimation of the Amazon Rainforest that was occurring on Earth. He felt embarrassed and ashamed. There was no higher reasoning at work, here. Abiona spoke commonsense.

Random high-flying birds soared past, only engaging in conversation with Abiona to say hello, and to ask how she was. None asked about Dan. Dan surmised they already knew what they needed to know about the Earthling.

Dan and Abiona stopped for occasional bio breaks, doing the same for meals and refreshment and taking advantage of the opportunities to stretch their legs rather than utilizing the onboard portable transporter to order in. Their solar-powered vehicle had no need to refuel.

Dan's seat was as comfortable as his dormitory sofa, form fitted to his body. Somewhere over the Yazoo Province, an area on earth known as the Mississippi Delta, Dan dozed off.

CHAPTER 26

Dan awoke as their vehicle touched down on a paved road wide enough to land a passenger jet in the midst of a pristine neighborhood, the vehicle having fluently transitioned from aerial to terrain.

The yellowish glow of streetlights lined their path like runway edge lights. Faint white stars flickered against a clear velvet sky of encroaching darkness. The last glimmer of a bright red sun descended behind some not too distant forested mountain ranges. The place they were taxiing through, Dan would describe as a high-end suburb.

The stark similarities between his Golden Meadows neighborhood and this place were striking. Yet, there was something dissimilar about them, not only in structures, but in feel, as if the homes were shells of the familiar, but their contents were different.

Dan let the feeling slide as he continued to take in the sights. The homes appeared modern. Each home had a generous front yard divided by mosaic stone walkways centered on wide patches of manicured grass bordered by hedges. The road they traveled was the only road Dan saw, extending through both ends of the community with no end in sight either way.

"We are almost home, Daniel," Abiona said in a near whisper.

There was sparse ground and air traffic. A few people were out, doing last-minute chores, as far as Dan could tell. It looked very much the same as his Earth neighborhood. They were taking out the trash, compost and recycling, or inspecting something about the house or front yard.

Most homes appeared settled in for the night. Not only was Dan struck by the elegance of the neighborhood, but the calmness of everything, as if he had entered an unoccupied cathedral or church. 'Serenity' was the word that sprang to mind. The whole community felt as though it were at peace.

"Golden Eagle?" Dan asked.

"Yes," Abiona answered.

"Reminds me of Golden Meadows."

"Is that your Earth home?"

"Yes."

"Then it must be nice."

"We think so."

"We, meaning you and your family?"

Dan thought for a moment before he answered. He hadn't realized he'd used the pronoun "we" instead of "I."

"Yes," he answered, feeling a sharp tug of homesickness in his heart.

The vehicle glided onto a paved driveway and parked, not turning off the whispering engine.

"We are here," Abiona said.

"Will you need me anymore, Mrs. Gaige?" a pleasant tenor male voice from the vehicle asked.

"No, Duke. That will be all for today."

"Then I will retire to the garage, ma'am. Goodnight."

The doors unlocked and the seatbelts disengaged. Abiona got out and stretched. Dan got out, stretched, and yawned. The right door of the attached three-car garage opened. Duke pulled in, parked, and shut down, hunkering down like some slumbering beast closing the garage door behind him.

"Your vehicle referred to you by name, the same as vehicles did at the Zenith Campus for anyone who got in. Are they preprogrammed with all of that information?" Dan asked as they walked along the curved herringbone brick walkway toward the front entrance. It was a two-story luxury brick Colonial with a two-story foyer, as Dan's real estate cousin Omari would have described it.

"Vehicles are preprogrammed, as you said, to a point," Abiona began in response to Dan's question. "The Zenith Campus vehicles were most likely reprogrammed after arrival to respond to anyone associated with the Zenith Campus or their guests.

"Public domain vehicle programming, as it is called, as you will find with all public transportation. Once you take possession of a vehicle, then it becomes yours. You reset the programming so that it only responds to you or other members you give license.

"Duke and every citizen vehicle contain private domain vehicle programming and are responsive only to specific persons. Does that make sense?"

"Perfect. Thank you."

"Anytime, Daniel."

The same feeling of peace embraced Dan when they entered the house.

"Allow me to give you a brief tour before you settle in," Abiona said. Dan answered with a nod. Abiona opened her unlocked front door and Dan took notice.

Doors are rarely locked at the Zenith Campus, Dan thought. *Security must not be an issue in the real world on Hearth, unlike Earth.* His supposition nourished his tranquil feeling.

Spacious, but not cavernous, the house appeared modern, to Dan. Not Earth modern, but Hearth modern, from the beautiful and tasteful décor to items Dan could only speculate on as to their function, as Abiona described their "state-of-the-art kitchen."

Abiona informed Dan, "If you are at any time in need of food or drink, help yourself. Whether guest or resident, the same rule applies in this house. Everyone cleans up after themselves."

"Sounds familiar," Dan said, thinking of Toni repeatedly laying down the same household law.

"Pardon?" Abiona said, looking quizzically at Dan.

"Nothing. Where are the children who can't wait to meet me?" Dan asked as they climbed the living room stairs to the upper floor.

"At a friend's house," Abiona said. "I misled my darlings to believe you would not be arriving until next week."

"You lied to them."

"Yes," Abiona said matter-of-factly. "For their own good. They would have been restless with excitement if I had not."

Dan laughed. "Be it Hearth or Earth, parents' reasoning in regards to their children is the same."

Abiona laughed. "I suppose that is true. Mayowa and Ifelayo will return in the morning. I suggest you enjoy the peace and quiet while you can."

"Really?"

"Yes, really," Abiona said with a knowing grin. "They may be darlings, but they have the energy of giant hummingbirds, and ceaseless curiosities to match."

Dan thought of the hectic environment of his own household and knew what Abiona meant.

"Be prepared to be bombarded with nonstop questions," Abiona added as she led Dan through an open door.

"That's only natural," Dan said. "I can handle it. You have a lovely home."

"Thank you, Daniel. This place is our shelter. Hearth is our home."

Abiona stopped outside of the open doorway of a room they were about to enter and stared at Dan, her steady gaze firm upon his face only inches away.

When his wife wanted to get a clear read of Dan, she would gently cup his face in her hands. Toni would do the same to Wick and Mae, for the same purpose. Dan always felt spellbound when Toni handled him that way.

The way Abiona was staring at him made Dan feel the same. Dan wondered what Abiona saw, trusting the Occlumency pills were still working. Was she reading his eyes, micro-expressions, or his aura?

"I believe you can handle it, Daniel Samuel Bluford." A sparkle gleamed in her brown eyes.

"This is one of our guest rooms," Abiona said as she led Dan into the room. "I felt you might be most comfortable with a room of your own, at least until you become acclimated to our Hearth way of life."

Dan wondered what Abiona meant by that last statement, but didn't pursue the point out of concern of where it might lead. Dan looked around.

The room easily accommodated a king-size bed. A hand carved wooden headboard matched the two elegant nightstands. All of Dan's requested dorm room items were in place. His knickknacks, art pieces, and plants looked out of place amongst the elegance. His Education Packet was centered on a modern writing desk set in front of the east window.

Dan allowed his glance to continue past the desk, not wanting to give Abiona any indication of how anxious he was to access his EP cube.

"This will be satisfactory," Dan said with mock nobility and an approving nod. He truly was pleased and impressed.

"Good," Abiona said, Dan's sarcasm lost on her. "Should you need anything at all, do not hesitate to ask."

You, Dan thought. *I need you.* Dan immediately stomped on the idea and drop kicked it out of the window of his mind.

"Thank you," he said to Abiona with a pleasing smile he seemed unable to control.

"There will be time enough for such things," Abiona said as if having read his mind, accenting her statement with a gracious smile. "Sleep well, Daniel."

Dan watched Abiona leave, quietly closing the door behind her. Abiona and Toni were becoming interchangeable in his mind, the very thing that Jabori had warned Dan about. They would have made love if Abiona had been Toni, christening the bed with a feverish passion and not stopping until Dan had exhausted every ounce of mounting sexual hunger—a hunger Dan had been experiencing since his forced separation from Toni.

Dan had believed himself in control of his carnal desires as result of his maturity and being a happily married man. His Hearth experience was teaching him that he was wrong. His carnal desires had not disappeared. They were being fulfilled by Toni.

Was that also a lesson he was supposed to learn during this exchange program? How could he be so gullible? He was a human being; a man laden with all of the biological needs of every man.

The thought of Toni making love to another man only gave him angry ammunition to give in to his impulse and increased his desire for Abiona, if she would have him. He had been saved, by forced separation, from fulfilling his lust with Jomana. Dan had a strong feeling that his time with Abiona would hold no such reprieves.

Dan walked around, taking in the luxurious room while making his way over to the desk. He turned on the desk lamp, circling back to turn off the bedroom lights, then picked up his EP cube.

The EP cube came to life from his touch, glowing even brighter than before (or, at least, Dan imagined it was). Dan felt as though he were holding an old friend; a severed appendage reattached.

Dan requested his latest Hearth Journal, along with his favorite writing pen. A suede leather-bound journal embossed with a detailed color image of the planet Hearth and a number 7 instantly appeared upon his desk. The image the national symbol of Hearth.

Beside it was a chunky ballpoint pen with a comfortable grip. While the journal could take dictation from Dan and record it in his own handwriting, Dan most often preferred the personal touch. There was something about writing in longhand that allowed Dan to process his thoughts more efficiently. It kept him connected to the knowledge and experience in a way that dictation sometimes lacked.

Dan sat in an ergonomic chair that welcomed him with embedded nanosensors conforming to his shape. The desk faced the window on the front side of the house.

The cordless woven wooden blind was raised. The stars were more pronounced, now. Their twinkling lights spackled the cloth of a moonless silken night sky, the verdant mountains diamond-shaped silhouettes to the east.

Dan recorded everything he could remember since his last entry, writing well into the night and filling Hearth Journal 7, then midway through Hearth Journal 8.

CHAPTER 27

Dan opened his eyes fresh from a dream he could not remember to find two young children standing by his bedside, eyeing him. Their curious brown faces belonged to Wick and Mae, to his groggy mind. Had Dan been dreaming? Was Hearth a subconscious fantasy? Had Dan awakened to his Earth reality?

A quick glance about the guest bedroom alleviated Dan of such a notion. Hearth was no dream. This was not his Golden Meadows bedroom. The Hearth children confirmed Dan's new reality when they spoke.

"Good morning," Dan said.

"It is morning," Mayowa, Wick's star-twin said.

"Good or otherwise," Ifelayo, Mae's star-twin, added.

"Is that a common Earth expression?" Mayowa asked.

"Yes, it is."

"How do you know?" Ifelayo asked.

"How do I know what?"

"Whether it is a good morning or not?" Mayowa asked. "You have only just awakened."

"I am happy to be alive. That makes it a good morning for me."

"Makes sense," Ifelayo said.

"Why not say, 'happy to be alive'?" Mayowa said.

"You have a point there," Dan said.

"I have a point anywhere," Mayowa said. The children smiled at Dan in triumph.

"I will change my good morning to happy to be alive for you two."

"We concur," Ifelayo said.

"You must be Mayowa and Ifelayo?" Dan pointed at each of them as he said their names.

"That is correct," Mayowa said.

"What should we call you?" Ifelayo asked.

"Mr. Bluford will be fine children."

"How did you know our names?" Ifelayo asked.

"Your mom told me."

Mayowa and Ifelayo looked at each other. Such a look when passed between Wick and Mae meant that they were drawing a joint conclusion in a silent communication between close siblings. Mind reading, of a sort.

Dan knew it was different with Mayowa and Ifelayo. They literally could read each other's minds and carry on a telepathic conversation.

"Remarkable," Dan said. "Absolutely remarkable. If I didn't know any better, I would swear you were my children."

"We will take that as a compliment," Mayowa said.

"You should," Dan said.

"We cannot read your mind," Mayowa said.

"I have taken a pill that blocks you from reading my mind."

"Why would you do such a thing?" Ifelayo asked, puzzled.

"Because Earthlings can't read each other's minds. Their thoughts are private. Having our minds read makes us uncomfortable." Dan left out the part about having become accustomed to having his mind read, and how he missed the experience.

"Then how can Earthlings tell what the other is thinking?" Ifelayo asked.

"We communicate our thoughts through written, verbal, sign, or picture language."

"Picture language like we do with wildlife and aqualife," Ifelayo said.

"Except we draw the pictures by hand."

"Interesting," Mayowa added. "We, too, have sign language, but have few occasions when its use is necessary."

"How do you communicate with people who cannot hear?"

"Deafness is only temporary, in our society," Ifelayo said.

"Conditions such as deafness and blindness, along with most other human frailties, can be corrected," Mayowa said.

"Even during the brief time when a person may be blind or deaf, we can still communicate," Ifelayo said.

"By telepathy."

"Yes," Mayowa said. "Unless there is serious brain damage prohibiting a mental link, but that is rare."

"Remarkable," Dan said, more to himself than the children. Mayowa and Ifelayo looked at each other before returning their gaze to Dan.

"Back to the subject of mind reading," Mayowa said.

"Sometimes Earthlings can read what a person is thinking by their behavior, body language, or facial expressions."

"Like now," Mayowa said.

"I'm sorry?"

"You appear to be uncomfortable," Mayowa added.

"There is tension in your face," Ifelayo said.

"And wariness, like you are unnerved by something," Mayowa said.

"Do we make you uncomfortable?" Ifelayo asked.

"I had no idea," Dan said, holding up his hands as a sign to ask for a moment. Dan closed his eyes, took in three deep, calming breaths, then opened his eyes. "How's that?"

"Better," Ifelayo said.

"Much better," Mayowa said. "Now you appear relaxed."

"You look a lot like our dad," Ifelayo said. Both children leaned in closer to scrutinize Dan's face. While Dan understood their curiosity, he felt like an unidentified specimen being examined for the first time.

"So I've been told," Dan said after the children leaned back. "Or maybe, it's your dad who looks a lot like me."

The children laughed. "That would be something Dad would say," Ifelayo said.

"Six of one and a half-dozen of another," Mayowa said.

"Is that a common Hearthling expression?"

"Yes," Ifelayo said.

"Earthlings use it, too."

"Really?" Mayowa said. "What else do Hearthlings and Earthlings have in common? Besides sharing the same DNA?"

"You know about Earthlings and DNA?"

"Of course," Mayowa said.

"We study those subjects in school," Ifelayo added. "We learn a good deal more about DNA than we do about Earthlings."

"Our Earth studies are a general overview," Mayowa added. "If we desire to learn more on the topic, then we can pursue the subject further at the university level."

"How old are you?" Dan asked.

Mayowa said, "I am ten."

Ifelayo said, "I am six."

"I knew I would find you two here." Abiona burst into the room, dressed casually in jeans, a tie-dye sweatshirt, and low-cut sneakers, her dark curls flowing over her shoulders framing her clean smooth face. "I thought I told you not to bother Mr. Bluford."

"We were not bothering Mr. Bluford, Mom," Mayowa said.

"We were staring at Mr. Bluford while he slept," Ifelayo added.

"Then Mr. Bluford woke up," Mayowa tacked on.

"It's true," Dan confirmed.

"Come away, children." Abiona waved her children toward the doorway. The children ran from the room, giggling. Abiona turned to Dan with a proud and amused smile. "I am sorry they ambushed you. Are you okay?"

Dan thought for a moment. He was more than okay. He felt as though he were home, in an odd sort of way. Home with his family. It all seemed so natural. Dan answered Abiona with a nod.

"They were supposed to be retrieving their EP cubes that they had conveniently forgotten while I waited for them outside."

Dan chuckled at the thought, imagining his own children executing the same ruse, if they were in Mayowa and Ifelayo's position.

"What?" Abiona asked, wanting to share in Dan's amusement.

Dan wondered briefly if Jabori's warning to Dan not to confuse Abiona with Toni extended to her children, as well. Dan was certain that it did.

"Nothing," Dan said.

Abiona did not believe Dan, but let the matter drop. "I had planned for a formal introduction. I suppose the children have already taken care of such?"

Dan laughed. "They have, in a manner of speaking."

The pronounced and pleasant sound of harp music came from outside.

"The school shuttles are here," Abiona said. "Do you need anything before I go?"

"Go! Don't worry about me."

"I will not be long. Would you like some breakfast?"

"I can make my own breakfast."

"I would not hear of it, Daniel Bluford. You are a guest in our home," Abiona said in an admonishing tone before rushing off.

Dan walked over to the desk window and looked out. His star-twin's cotton pajamas and slippers fitted him as if they were his own. Dan saw two shuttles resembling passenger bullet trains, parallel parked in the middle of the street.

Parents were ushering their children aboard. Abiona, Mayowa, and Ifelayo were amongst them. The mixture of men and women acted no different from Earth parents and children under the same circumstances. The children appeared between the ages of five through twelve.

There were hugs, kisses, and cheerful waves of goodbyes. Dan noticed that none of the children had backpacks or lunch boxes or anything to indicate they were being shipped off to school.

Dan could not be sure, but he saw no clue that a word was spoken by anyone. Greetings, good day wishes, and reminders or gentle admonishments to behave, from parents, as well as their children's responses, appeared to be telepathically communicated; common interactions Dan preferred done in the chattering Earthling way.

Parents stood back and watched the transports take off vertically once the shuttle doors closed before jettisoning forward. Not a single parent left before the shuttles were out of sight.

Dan stepped away from the window immediately, noting in his Hearth Journal what he had seen and experienced this morning.

CHAPTER 28

Dan glanced up from his journal, deep in thought. An odd feeling swept over him; an inclination he was being watched. His first thought was that somehow wildlife was the source of his uneasiness.

Dan turned in his chair, startled when he discovered two people standing close enough to reach out and touch him. A tall, slender, golden-skinned man with thick salt and pepper hair and intense medium brown eyes glared at him. Beside him stood a smooth dark-skinned woman, two heads shorter, with natural corkscrew curls and dark brown eyes that matched the man's intensity. They were holding hands.

Dan attempted to cover his journal with his upper body by leaning forward. They ignored his action. They must have noticed what Dan was doing well before he'd detected their presence. They did not seem to care. They simply stared at him as if awestruck.

"Your resemblance to our son is extraordinary!" the woman said.

"I would have mistook you for Kwasi had I not known better," the man added, sounding equally mystified, his voice as deep as the ocean.

Dan sat still, allowing them to stare at him as if he were some exotic creature and stunned that Kwasi's parents looked nothing like his own.

"Please stand up," the man said.

Dan rose and stood in front of them. Kwasi's parents touched his face, shoulders, and arms, confirming his existence.

"Remarkable!" the man said.

"He wears his hair shorter than our Kwasi, but aside from that…" The woman could not seem to find the words to complete her thought. Dan wondered if she had done so telepathically.

"Regardless," the man said, his deep voice now commanding. "You are Daniel Bluford," he stated rather than asked.

"I am."

"The Earthling," the woman said, her voice firm and authoritative.

"One of them."

"I am Achak Gaige," the man said.

"I am Patricia Gaige," the woman added. "We are Kwasi's parents."

"I gathered as much," Dan said.

The couple stared unblinkingly at Dan, their expressions stoic. Dan extended his hand. "Nice to meet you."

They glanced at his suspended hand, perplexed by what the gesture meant, neither accepting his offering.

"Thank you," Achak said. "Is that some sort of greeting gesture?" Abiona's parents glanced back at Dan's hand.

"It's a means of greeting on Earth. You grasp my hand with one of yours. It is called a handshake."

"I see," Patricia said. "Hearthlings do not 'handshake.'"

Dan dropped his hand and glanced away, not knowing what to say or do.

"We have come to tell you," Achak said, "that we are not in favor of you staying in our son's home."

"Or being around our grandchildren," Patricia added.

"We know next to nothing about Earth or Earthlings," Achak said.

"We care little about you or your Earth issues, to be frank," Patricia added.

"Earthlings made their bed and should be made to lie in it, as far as we are concerned," Achak continued.

"Is that understood?" Patricia said, sounding more like a threat than a question.

Dan nodded, still not knowing how to respond. His first instinct was to apologize for being an intrusion, as his star-twin's parents were making him feel, and for being an Earthling, resisting the added impulse to apologize for all of the humans who contributed to destroying the ecosystem of a planet no different from their own.

"Ready for breakfast?" Abiona asked, having slipped into the room without Dan noticing. "I see you have met my in-laws."

"In-laws? What is that?" Achak asked.

"It is an Earth term, Father, used to describe a relative by marriage," Abiona explained. Turning to Dan, Abiona continued, "Hearthlings refer to their spouse's parents as 'mother' and 'father.' We refer to our own parents as 'mom' and 'dad.'"

"How do you know about this term 'in-laws,' Abiona?" Achak asked. "Did this Earthling teach you?"

"Kwasi taught me," Abiona answered, cutting Dan off before he could respond. "My husband shared some of his Earthling teachings with me from time to time."

Dan had the feeling Achak had more to say on the subject, but completed his comment telepathically.

"Is there an Earthling Exchange School for Hearthlings?" Dan asked Abiona, surprised he hadn't thought to ask the question before.

"No," Abiona answered. "All Earthling Exchange education is done online."

"In answer to your question, dear," Patricia said with a warm smile directed at Abiona, "we have met the Earthling,"

"My in-laws decided to pay us a surprise visit," Abiona said.

"Abiona, to be honest," Achak said his eyes softened at the sight of his daughter-in-law, "we see no reason why you should be made to invite Kwasi's star-twin into your home."

"I was not made to do anything of the sort, Father. I had a choice. I gladly welcome Daniel into my home."

"Like you welcomed that bobcat kitten," Patricia said. "Your parents told us all about your little experiment and how that kitten shredded your living room furniture."

"Not to mention, he was not potty-trained," said Achak. "No creature of the wild ever is, or should be."

"Your parents could not convince you *not* to keep him," Patricia said. "You were determined to domesticate that kitten."

"It did not work out that way, now, did it?" Achak said. "You had to let him go free; back to nature where he belonged."

"Mother, Father, I was eight years old at the time," Abiona said with an amused grin. "The whole experiment only lasted a few hours.

That was how long it took for me to realize the truth of what you are saying.

"Besides, that is not the whole story. The kitten followed me home from a hike I had taken in the woods. I had seen where he lived. He was curious about where I lived. We were playing in the living room. He became over excited, which explains his lack of potty-training.

"My brother and sister were out and about with friends. Dad was helping a neighbor with some woodwork. Mom called me into her studio to show me her latest painting. When I returned to the living room, the kitten had shredded some of our stuffed furniture in order to see what was inside. Something, I might add, that Mom and Dad found hilarious.

"I am still grateful to my parents for allowing me to discover that lesson on my own. I do not know exactly how that story equates to Daniel being in my home, but Daniel is not an animal. He is a human being who is already potty-trained. You are potty-trained, are you not, Daniel?"

"I am," Dan said, uncertain if Abiona's question was sarcastic or sincere.

"There, you see. One issue resolved."

Achak and Patricia gently shook their heads. Patricia placed a hand upon Abiona's cheek much in the same manner Abiona had laid hands on Dan.

"Our clever, clever, daughter," Patricia said. "We love you."

"We respect you," Achak said. "We are simply concerned."

"For you, Mayowa, and Ifelayo," Patricia said. "Who knows what sorts of problems this Earthling brings?"

"None that we cannot handle," Abiona said.

"He is human," Patricia said.

"That much is clear," Achak added.

"We are trying to help them save themselves," Abiona said.

"We know all of that, dear," Patricia said.

"I still do not know why we should get involved," Achak added.

"If they chose to destroy themselves, that is their prerogative, I say," Patricia said. Achak nodded in agreement.

Dan assumed they were having their conversation verbally rather than telepathically for his benefit. He decided to speak up. "I am standing right here, you know."

"We can see that," Achak said, and his glare returned.

"Does he think we are blind?" Patricia said to Abiona.

"Again, right here. Anything you want to know about me, simply ask."

"Do you think we are blind?" Patricia repeated, this time directing her question to Dan.

"No, I don't. Where I'm from, when you're having a candid discussion about someone in their presence, it is considered rude."

"What better time to have a candid discussion about someone but in their presence?" Achak asked. "How else could they respond?"

"On Hearth, it is considered rude to have a candid discussion about someone behind their back, as the expression goes," Patricia said.

Dan had to admit that their logic was sound.

"I'd like to take a shower and shave before breakfast," Dan said, flustered, making a vague attempt to clear the room.

"We will wait to serve breakfast until you are ready, Daniel" Abiona said. "Mother, Father, let us give Daniel some privacy."

"He is already using Occlumency pills to prevent us from reading his mind," Achak said.

"How much more privacy does an Earthling need?" Patricia asked.

"Father, Mother, please—we discussed this. Daniel is staying here during the duration of his exchange."

"Your mother said you were a stubborn child," Achak said.

"A characteristic I share with you, Father," Abiona said.

"That is true, Achak," Patricia said with a nod. Achak chuckled.

"Alright, Mother and Father, you have both had your say on the matter. Let us go."

"We hope with all of our hearts, darling," Patricia said, "that allowing this Earthling into your home does not prove to be a hard lesson we could not prevent you from learning."

Achak and Patricia glowered at Dan as their daughter-in-law ushered them from the room, Achak and Patricia still holding hands as if joined at the palms. Dan recognized that look.

Even though Mia and Wick were young, Dan had encountered a few incidents that brought out the lethal parent in him. They were always instances that involved an adult posing a threat to his children. Dan had sent threatening looks toward the offenders, making them aware that if any attempt at harm came to his Mia or Wick, he would not hesitate to resort to violence to protect them.

Dan sat back down at his desk. He was able to document what happened almost verbatim and felt better when he was done, as if writing about the incident was therapeutic, releasing him from the tension he was experiencing.

Dan had wanted to keep his journal secret. He wondered, now that his journaling was out, how the rest of his stay with the Gaige family might go. Dan made a mental note not to leave any of his journals lying about.

He was not concerned about Abiona's in-laws peeking. Clearly, their only interest in Dan was to see him gone from their daughter's home. While Abiona may respect his privacy, curious children like Mayowa and Ifelayo might not.

CHAPTER 29

Abiona had pointed out a closet full of men's clothes and dresser drawers filled with men's accessories and undergarments during her guest bedroom tour. She had moved some of her husband's belongings from their master bedroom to the guest room for Dan's convenience.

While Kwasi's style was more casual than Dan's, both men had good tastes. Dan had asked Abiona if she thought Kwasi would mind Dan wearing her husband's clothes.

"I doubt it," Abiona replied to Dan's question. "Kwasi can simply replace them when he returns, should he have a problem with another man wearing his clothes."

Dan wondered if he would be nuking his wardrobe when he returned to Earth. Dan had tried on some of Kwasi's things after completing his journal entries for the night. He and Kwasi wore the same sizes in everything.

Dan showered, shaved, and dressed in no time. He was nervous about leaving his guest quarters, although he was not sure why. He was not looking forward to seeing Abiona's in-laws again.

Dan had overcome greater adversaries in both his personal and professional life. Something else had him on edge. Dan had believed he had gotten past his doubt and gathered the courage to see this journey through. Maybe Hearth reality had become too tangible for him.

Dan had felt this way before, but this time he firmly believed that if he left his room, there was no turning back.

"There are times in every person's life when they must make the hard choices," his father would say. "All or nothing; you are either going to do it or not." It took Dan a minute to embrace his moment.

"Where are your in-laws?" Dan asked when he walked into the kitchen, having looked for them on the way.

"They decided not to join us."

"Too bad."

"Why?"

"I would have liked to continue our discussion." To Dan's surprise, he meant what he said.

"You will have your chance soon enough. I asked them not to stay. I thought it best for the time being, until you are acclimated."

"If you think that's best."

"I do. You look handsome," Abiona said with a smile. Dan returned her smile, feeling uneasy at the compliment. "Everyone in the neighborhood wants to meet you," Abiona continued.

"Everyone?"

"Almost everyone."

"I suppose that makes me some sort of celebrity."

"Why is that?"

"People who are considered popular on Earth can achieve celebrity status."

"Because of their accomplishments. Like our noteworthy scientists, politicians, educators, philosophers, artists, activists, and such, who contribute to our humanity and help make Hearth a better and stronger society."

Dan thought for a moment before he answered. He was no expert on the celebrity subject. From his observation, Earthling luminary status had been ransacked by popular culture. He was uncertain he was not confusing momentary fame with celebrity. Fame was often acquired by far less noble endeavors, since star status was oftentimes utilized as a means for economic gain.

"Something like that," Dan said. "Your neighbors probably want to get a firsthand look at the Earth specimen."

"Why are you being so negative, Daniel?"

"I'm not being negative. I was being sarcastic."

"You were hiding behind your sarcasm in order to mask how you really feel or what you really think. Why not be plain-spoken?"

Dan regarded Abiona's evaluation of him for a moment. He knew that sarcasm was often used by Earthlings in a variety of ways for a variety of reasons to bridle or mask a direct truth that may—for at least at the moment—be a challenge to face. Dan primarily believed he used sarcasm as a source of amusement. Did it make it less honest than plain talk, especially if so many others employed the same mockery?

"It's my way," Dan said.

Abiona observed Dan for a moment. "So be it," she finally said, as if the matter was closed to her.

A thought suddenly occurred to Dan. "Abiona, do you think your husband Kwasi is using sarcasm in his role as me?"

"I suppose he would if he were to remain in character." Abiona laughed.

"What's so funny?"

"I was imagining my Kwasi bringing home your sarcasm. The children would be dumbfounded at their father's behavior."

"Once they've been around me for a while, they'll get used to it."

"Not to use it, I hope." Abiona laughed again.

"You do realize you were just being sarcastic," Dan said.

"I am." Abiona looked quizzically at Dan. That look told Dan that Abiona had meant what she said about Kwasi, sarcasm, and the children. That realization stung a little.

"What's for breakfast?" Dan asked, to change the subject.

"I apologize," Abiona said.

"For what?"

"For hurting your feelings."

"You didn't."

"There was a flash of pain in your eyes that says differently."

"It was just a touch of gas. It comes and goes."

"Sarcasm. A tool to protect one from discomfort. I see more clearly, now."

"Abiona, breakfast?"

Abiona touched Dan's arm. She held his gaze for an uncomfortably long time, making him feel vulnerable.

"Breakfast is ready," Abiona said. "Make yourself comfortable."

Dan turned to the breakfast nook. A round blonde-wood table was set for two. The chairs were made of the same wood as the dining table. Dan took a seat in front of one of the place settings. The chair did not conform to his body.

Dan was disappointed. He had become accustomed to that cozy accommodation. Abiona brought over a bowl of steaming scrambled eggs, plates of sausage links, and hash browns and set them on the table.

"Help yourself," Abiona said.

"I'll wait for you," Dan said. Abiona smiled and then turned away. Dan always preferred everyone be seated at the table before eating. Abiona returned with a pitcher of fresh squeezed orange juice and a plate of hot buttered toast. Abiona made a final trip for the teakettle before she sat down across from Dan.

"Everything looks and smells delicious," Dan said.

"Thank you, Daniel," Abiona said. "I must warn you that the links are vegan. We do not have meat in this house."

"That's okay," Dan said. "The Zenith Campus was vegan, too."

The mention of Zenith Campus brought on a wave of sadness. Dan missed his 3B classmates, Professor Huaman, Jabori, Alvita (both human and IVA), Aroha, and Bartek.

"Try one," Abiona said, sensing something was wrong.

"Try what?"

"One of the sausages."

"Oh! Sure."

Dan took a bite from one of the two sausage links he had placed on his plate. The texture was different from meat, as he had come to expect. These links were spicy. They reminded Dan of hot link meat sausages on Earth.

"This is really good," Dan said.

"I am glad you like it," Abiona said before eating a forkful of eggs.

Everything was delicious, and just the way Dan liked it. The eggs were light and fluffy. Toast evenly buttered. Hash browns perfectly cooked, orange juice room temperature rather than chilled, and black tea flavored with a variety of spices—a tea his family would sweeten with honey. Dan always drank his straight.

Dan did not believe this perfect breakfast was a coincidence. He was convinced Abiona knew things about him; more than she had let on so far. Dan resisted the urge to confront Abiona about what he suspected, for the moment.

"Again, I want to apologize for my children," Abiona said as they ate. "Sometimes they are whirling dervishes that refuse to be controlled."

"I'm not a child expert, but they're doing what all normal children do, in my limited experience. They're simply looking to satisfy their curiosities."

"I am not a child expert either, but I believe that philosophy applies to human beings in general."

"No need to apologize for your in-laws either."

"Why would I?" Abiona asked matter-of-factly.

"For some of the things they said to me. They were rude, to be honest."

"My in-laws spoke their straightforward truths. I see no need for them or me to apologize for that."

Dan nodded. He did not agree with Abiona's reasoning, but accepted it as a Hearthling characteristic he had repeatedly encountered, something Dan was going to have to become accustomed to. "Thick skin, son," his dad would say. "Thick skin."

"I can't get over how much Mayowa and Ifelayo look like Wick and Mae," Dan said with good humor.

"Is Wick your son's actual name?" Abiona asked.

"It's his nickname. Short for Wickliffe. Do you have nicknames for Mayowa, Ifelayo, or Kwasi?"

"Hearthlings do not have sobriquets. What is the reason for doing so?"

Dan had to think for a moment. He had been in the practice of nicknaming people all of his life and he had never been asked why before. "I suppose it helps to create a sense of familiarity with another person."

"That cannot be accomplished when using one's full name?" Abiona asked.

"I suppose it could."

"There were no photographs included in your information packet," Abiona said.

"Information packet? You mean, like a bio?"

"If by bio you mean biography, then yes."

"When were you given this information packet about me?"

"When it was established you would remain with us for the duration of your stay on Hearth."

"How well were you briefed on me?"

"General background information. Your date of birth, some facts about your personal and professional life, whether or not you had any health issues, your likes and dislikes. Nothing intimate or embarrassing, and practically nothing about your family except for the fact that you have one."

"My life, in a nutshell."

"Not your entire life, but relevant facts, as I inferred."

"Nothing concerning my childhood?"

"Nothing. Not much before you and your friends founded Single Organism."

"Is that when Hearthlings first took notice of me?"

"I do not know."

"Who would?"

"The Exchange Student Program Committee handles Earthling matters. They would know the answer to your question."

"Who sits on the committee?"

"I do not know."

"I would like to know who these Earth managers are."

"Exchange Student Program Committee information is available online. If I were you, I would focus on what I could learn that could help my people and my planet rather than doing detective work on your current circumstance."

"You're not me. I need more answers."

"Why?"

"It's important to me."

"More important than saving Earth or Earthlings?"

"Meaning, exactly, what?"

"If Hearthlings and Hearth were headed down the same path as Earth and there was an opportunity to save my people and planet, as is being offered to you now, for me, that would supersede any personal quest for answers."

Dan was conflicted. His logical mind knew that what Abiona was saying was right. He should not lose sight of what his purpose was for being on Hearth. But his curious self needed to know more about who was behind the curtain pulling the strings.

"You look perplexed," Abiona said.

"I am more upset than perplexed that someone gave you private information without bothering to mention that fact to me."

Abiona laughed. "Why?"

"Because it would have been nice to know."

"Why?"

"It's a common courtesy to let people know when you are shelling out their personal information."

"Really?"

"Yes, really."

"Is that an Earth custom?" Abiona asked, as if she already knew the answer.

"For the most part," Dan shakily answered, knowing that businesses, governments, and criminals often mined citizens' personal information without their knowledge.

Single Organism had a policy to do deep background checks on potential employees who would be exposed to any sensitive or classified information. While they notified applicants they would be doing so before having them sign an agreement stipulating such, they never revealed to the candidate what they'd uncovered.

Dan felt like a hypocrite for protesting. That did not dampen the sense of betrayal Dan felt for his invasion of privacy.

"They should have told me," he said.

"I can show you the information packet they gave me, if you like."

"I'd very much like."

"After breakfast. Now, eat your food before it gets cold."

"Was Toni informed that your husband, Kwasi, would be moving in with her and our children?" Dan asked.

"No," Abiona said. "Your wife was not informed." Dan expected Abiona to say more, but it never came.

"Do you think that is fair?" he asked.

"I do," Abiona said. "In the interest of keeping Hearth a secret from Earthlings, it is most certainly fair."

"It doesn't seem fair to me."

"Your response only has merit if our circumstances were equal. They are not. To be candid, we hold all of the cards—are you familiar with that expression?"

"Yes."

"Secondly, we do not have to intervene at all. We could simply sit back and observe Earthlings spiral down into the whirlpool of their own demise."

Dan ate in silence in a momentary stupor, thinking and staring off into space.

"Now that you have been made aware of the information packet," Abiona said after an extended period of quiet consumption, "will that change your behavior toward me?"

Dan thought before he answered. "I honestly don't know."

"Sometimes you are funny, Daniel Bluford."

"Then why do I feel like you are laughing more at me than with me?"

"Sometimes you are correct in that assumption, but not always. Finished?"

Dan looked down at his setting. His plate was clean. His glass of orange juice was empty and there was only a sip of tea left in his cup. He drank the last of the tea, then said, "Finished."

They had finished the eggs, toast, and links, between the two of them. Most of the hash browns and tea were gone, and half the pitcher of orange juice. It was a hearty meal, and Dan felt it right down to his toes.

"What would you like to do today, Daniel? Besides review your information packet."

Dan had not given the matter any thought. "I would like to go for a walk," Dan said, surprised at how easily the answer came to him.

"Around my neighborhood?"

"If it's not too much trouble."

"No trouble at all," Abiona said. "Walter." An Interactive Virtual Assistant appeared, wearing a housekeeping uniform. "Please take care of the breakfast dishes and clean up the kitchen."

"Right away, ma'am."

"Thank you," Abiona said to Walter. "Shall we?" Abiona asked as she stood to a stunned Dan, who was staring at her IVA servant, who set to work with a smile.

CHAPTER 30

Dan reviewed a digital copy of the information packet given Abiona in the privacy of his room. It turned out to be precisely what Abiona had summarized: general background information, with a few personal and professional facts thrown in.

Dan was disappointed. Reading the packet made him feel conventional. While he wasn't a braggart, 'ordinary' was never how Dan had viewed himself. Dan saw himself as exceptional in both intellect and accomplishments. The bland reporting on his life reflected none of those qualities. It could have been the bio of billions of nondescript Earthlings except for the specifics regarding his association with Single Organism.

"Ready?" Abiona asked' popping her head into his doorway and pulling Dan out of his thoughts.

"Sure," Dan said, rising from his desk.

They made their way outside, Abiona not bothering to lock the front door. Abiona surprised Dan by taking his hand, more as an offering of direction and protection, as with a youngster, rather than that of a lover or a friend.

The neighborhood was relatively quiet except for the occasional ground and air vehicles and Hearthlings working outside. The day had turned overcast, with gray clouds that threatened rain. A young couple jogged past them, smiling without saying a word. Abiona smiled back. Dan looked on with a blank expression.

"They said hello," Abiona said. "Telepathically, of course."

"I see," Dan said. "Not many people out."

"We have a handful of retirees. About half of my neighbors work from home. Some will pop out for a visit as word gets around that you are here. The rest are at work elsewhere.

"There is no mandatory retirement age on Hearth. Since retirement brings with it no additional benefits, and most Hearthlings are doing work they love, it is typical for Hearthlings to work up to the point they can no longer do the job or perish. Our society cherishes experience as well as youth, Daniel."

A credo Single Organism attempted to employ, Dan thought.

"See the laborers working the grounds?" Abiona asked.

Dan nodded, acknowledging men and women at different locations, dressed in forest green overalls. Dan and Abiona stopped to watch them work.

"They are our professional landscaping crews."

"What exactly do you mean by *ours*?"

"They live and work in our community. This is their contribution to our neighborhood; to our society. They nurture the natural beauty you see all around," Abiona finished with a wave of her free arm across the community.

Dan had noticed the landscaping crews at Zenith. He had regarded them no differently than contracted services that worked for Single Organism.

Most Earthling homeowners, Dan knew, did their own yard work, be it out of necessity from an affordability standpoint or preference. The idea of having a dedicated landscaping and gardening workforce as part of the community never occurred to him. Dan wondered if anyone on Earth had considered the idea. Were they, by chance, influenced by a Hearthling if they had?

"You don't do your own yard work?" Dan asked, incredulous at the idea.

"We do not. Do you find that peculiar?"

"A little."

"Hearthling neighborhoods have specialists residing in each community. Plumbers, electricians, technicians, carpenters, etcetera, who attend to the community's needs. They are well trained and educated in their fields and love their work.

"Each Hearthling is free to do as they please, within community guidelines to maintain their residence. Most take advantage of the community services provided.

"Most Hearthlings are not consumed with the do-it-yourself concept. Why not have someone who loves the work and is best at it do it for you?"

"For me, part of the joy of being a homeowner is doing the work myself. I enjoy gardening and landscaping."

"Are you good at it?"

"I'm not bad. It is an ongoing learning experience."

"Do you have the time to give your grounds all of the attention they need?"

"I wouldn't call them 'grounds.' They're much too small for that. But, no, I don't have the time to give them all of the attention they need."

"Our landscaping crews are the best. Why would I want to tinker around with something when I have at my disposal people who are great at it, and have ample time to do it right?"

"Personal fulfillment, a sense of accomplishment, communing with nature."

"I commune with nature every day. I get a sense of accomplishment and fulfillment from life, my work being part of that equation. My family and friends are another piece, as well as my planet and people. Do you not feel the same sense of fulfillment in those areas?"

"I'm talking about creating something with your own two hands. There is something..." Dan struggled to complete the thought.

"Gratifying," Abiona said.

"Exactly! Gratifying about the whole experience, when you can look at something you've made and say 'I did that.'"

"Are you a hands-on worker at Single Organism?"

"In a way, I am."

"You assemble the products Single Organism manufactures?"

"Not literally."

"Figuratively is not hands-on, Daniel."

Dan could not think of an immediate response.

"You still feel a sense of accomplishment, do you not?"

"Yes."

"Our combined visions of the neighborhood we want exist because we made it so. I do my part with my home and my family, as does everyone in the Golden Eagle community. I directly contribute with community service, and as an organizer.

"We all have roles to fill, Daniel; our parts contributing to the whole. When I see the amazing work our landscaping and gardening crews do to keep Golden Eagle beautiful, I, too, feel a sense of accomplishment, for their achievement is no different from my own.

"Am I making myself clear?"

"I believe so. I feel that way every time I see a product roll out of our factory, as if we all contributed to that accomplishment."

"Which do you enjoy more? Your personal accomplishments, or—if I may label them as such—your professional ones?"

"I would have to say, my professional accomplishments."

"Why?"

"Personal accomplishments, you have more control over. Professional ones typically require teamwork."

"You are a team player," Abiona said with a teasing smile.

Dan laughed. "I suppose I am."

"Welcome to team Hearth, Daniel Bluford."

A pair of ravens landed on Abiona's shoulders. Abiona greeted them with nods, diminishing her smile. Dan looked on, not knowing what to do. The ravens kept their black eyes trained on Dan, then flew away about a minute after they'd landed.

"What was that all about?" Dan asked.

"That was Nodin and Vaclava. They are president and vice-president of the Pequannock Wildlife Liaison Council. Once a month, our human council meets with the Wildlife Liaison Council to discuss any new and ongoing issues and future projects."

"You're kidding?" Dan said. Abiona stared blankly at Dan. He took her expression to mean that she was not. "What did they want?"

"They wanted to know what your story was. They can tell you are not a Hearthling."

"What else is new?"

"I told them you were visiting from Earth. They wanted to know how long you were going to stay. I explained to them you were an exchange student and that you would be leaving in a few months.

"They wanted to know if more like you would be coming. I told them no—not to our community, but there are a few Earthling Exchange Students sprinkled throughout Hearth. They seemed satisfied with my explanation."

"I don't see why it's any of their business."

"Do we really have to go over that again, Daniel?"

"I suppose not."

The visit from the ravens caused Dan to realize something: that the Hearthling birds they had encountered en route to Golden Eagle from the Zenith Campus had taken notice of Dan. They sensed he was different, and it made them wary.

"The wildlife of Hearth has heard of Earthlings through us," Abiona explained, sensing Dan's uneasiness. "You may be surprised to learn they know as much about your planet as we do. They do not hold Earthlings in a positive light, as you might imagine, possessing that knowledge.

"You will be closely watched by the wildlife of our world, Daniel. You will not even know they are there most of the time. Get used to it."

Abiona's warning gave Dan the creeps, frightening him in a way he had not felt since becoming aware of his circumstances; making him feel more like a prisoner than a guest.

"Do they believe I may bring the worst of Earthling ways, in regards to nature, here to Hearth?" Dan asked.

"They are aware that is possible. They also know that Hearthlings would not allow it. They are curious. Curious to know how beings who look so much like us could behave so differently. In the wild, being so far out of character could be a lethal enigma."

"I'm an enigma for them to be puzzled out."

"You are more like a case study to determine, should the need ever arise, how they would destroy you."

Dan was shocked. "Are you telling me that animals can and would plot to kill humans?"

"Earthlings, Daniel, not Hearthlings. They know they have nothing to fear from us. Earthlings have proven to be quite a different matter. Your people pose a direct threat to their existence."

"Couldn't the same methods they would use to annihilate Earthlings be employed against Hearthlings?"

"We have no concern that such an event will occur."

"You can't be serious."

Abiona's steadfast gaze told Dan that she was. "Imagine, if you will, that wildlife posed a threat of extinguishing Earthlings. How would you react?"

"My survival instincts would kick in, Abiona. I would defend myself and my family."

"You would, in all likelihood, do more than that. You would move to eliminate the threat."

"I suppose I would."

"Wildlife on Hearth feels the same about Earthlings. They would seek to eliminate a potential threat to protect themselves and their own. They are only following the natural instinct for survival that we all possess."

"Doesn't that concern you?"

"Why should it?"

"That they may come to see Hearthlings the same as Earthlings, and seek to eliminate the threat?"

"Not at all."

"How can you be so confident?"

"Trust."

"Trust!"

"Hearthlings, wildlife, and aqualife have developed a longstanding trust, over the centuries. We have worked together to build a granite-solid coexistence through coalitions and communication. We trust each other without fault, no differently than one Hearthling knows they can trust another Hearthling. Can the same be said about Earthlings, about each other?"

"No."

"Then, perhaps that is where Earthlings need to start."

Dan nodded, in surrender more so than in agreement. Every time he thought he'd discovered solid similarities between Earthlings and Hearthlings, something like this would happen to sabotage that bridge.

"No harm will come to you," Abiona said. "Hearthlings will see to that."

"Good to know," Dan said, meaning every shred of sarcasm his tone intended.

"Shall we continue our walk?" Abiona asked with a pleasant smile, giving his hand a gentle squeeze. Her smile was becoming an effective means of consoling Dan.

Dan trusted Abiona, just as he had grown to trust so many Hearthlings at the Zenith Campus. Dan nodded his consent and they were on their way.

CHAPTER 31

There were mixed reactions to Dan as he met some of Abiona's neighbors, including the landscaping and gardening crews.

Dan took notice of the melting pot of Abiona's neighborhood. Every race of person he could imagine lived there. Colonization and conquest never occurred on Hearth. Dan had learned that from his Hearth history classes. Races and cultures had come together and learned from each other. They grew and coalesced into a global society with room and respect for all. People migrated to areas that suited them. That was how Hearth neighborhoods were formed.

Each Hearthling had to be informed that Dan was not telepathic, and that they would have to voice their communications. None asked Dan why they could not read his mind. Abiona had telepathically explained to them about the Occlumency pills Dan was taking, that blocked access.

They were perplexed at why Dan would do such a thing, but accepted her explanation. Some were excited, and welcomed the Earthling to Hearth. Others simply looked at Dan, shrugged as if to say they saw nothing special about him, and politely moved the conversation along. Their reactions disappointed Dan.

The idea of being a celebrity had more appeal to Dan than he had realized. Abiona kept their visits short, so not to disturb her neighbors for long. She issued an open invitation to stop by her house, when they had a chance, to get to know Dan better.

Dan and Abiona were enjoying vegan salads in the kitchen and some interesting conversation when a thought occurred to Dan.

"I noticed the houses are of different styles and sizes, like in my Earth neighborhood, Abiona. Custom-built. Not like the cookie-cutter homes found in many of our suburbs or large developments. Is this the norm, or is Golden Eagle an exception?"

"It is typical for every Hearth neighborhood, Daniel. Each resident is assigned a certain amount of land. A single person receives fewer square meters than a couple. A couple with one child gets more. A couple with two children receive yet more, and so on and so forth. The style of your residence is of your own choosing."

"The community doesn't have a say in your style of home?"

"None whatsoever. You can only go as high as three stories, and basements are only permitted where zoning allows."

"All of these things are free?"

"You use the word 'free' as if they are gifts. They are not. As citizens of Hearth, the provisions of food, clothing, and shelter are rights."

"Rights given to people who do not contribute equally to your society, Abiona."

"Who is to judge the value of one's contribution to society, Daniel? You?"

Dan felt stumped on that one. He believed maladies such as poverty could be eliminated under capitalist democracy, yet, each year, the problem only grew worse. Every answer to Abiona's question that crossed his mind made him feel arrogant and foolish.

"You are the acting Director of Polar City Single Organism Research Lab Facilities, Daniel, are you not?"

"Correct."

"Can anyone else do your job as well as you?"

"Clearly, it is believed someone else can, since your husband has stepped into my role. Time will tell if he is successful. Other than my star-twin, I can't think of anyone, offhand."

"Can anyone else do your job better than you?"

"My same answer applies, Abiona."

"Oftentimes Hearthlings—those of us who are interested in Earth matters, as I have become—believe that many on your planet are in their positions based upon who they know rather than skills and education."

"Are you saying that nepotism is a common practice on our planet?"

"I am. You are a director because you are one of the founding members of Single Organism."

"As it should be."

"Your strengths are engineering and science, not organization and business."

"I learned the other aspects of my position—and let me add, in my defense, that my becoming director did not happen overnight. I put a lot of hard work into obtaining that position."

"As did your colleagues on Earth. None of you would have been permitted to become an organization leader. A person educated, skilled and experienced in that area would have been placed in your position."

"Leaving me to do what?"

"Explore your passions for engineering and science without limits."

At first, Dan was insulted by Abiona's comments. But the more he thought about it, the more he rather liked the idea.

Dan loved engineering and science. He loved being a member of a hands-on team that made concepts and designs come to life. As much as he liked people, Dan had never enjoyed the bureaucracy and mountain of paperwork involved with his position.

"The trick is finding someone who would be as passionate about what we do at Single Organism as are our founding board members."

"Not so much a trick as desire, Daniel. You may not need to look any further than your own front office, in your case."

"Are you referring to Amiri Hayden?"

Abiona nodded.

"What makes you say that?"

"Summarize, in your own mind, what he does for you. Not in terms of his job requirements, but what he does beyond the call of duty."

Dan gave Abiona's comment serious thought. His conclusion was that, on the organization and bureaucratic side, Amiri was his right-hand man.

"Exactly!" Abiona said, as if she had read Dan's mind. "You two make a great team."

"Agreed; but how does that alter the organization's ruling class? Every member of the board has an Amiri."

"I do not need to answer that question for you. You will discover a way if you possess the will."

"How would you go about making such a change?"

"On Hearth, there is no such need, since we operate in that manner."

"I'm getting fed up with you and other Hearthlings' sense of superiority over Earthlings," Dan said, sounding annoyed, having finished his delicious meal, he dropped his salad fork in his empty bowl and pushed them aside, sipping on his half-finished glass of lemonade and wiping his mouth with his cloth napkin.

Abiona grabbed his discarded dish and utensil, having finished her salad just before Dan. She took their dishes over to the kitchen sink to rinse them for placing in the dishwasher. Dan followed her, carrying his lemonade and napkin.

"We harbor no sense of superiority over Earthlings, Daniel." Abiona said while rinsing the items. "We are simply acknowledging how we are different, and our disagreement with how Earthlings do things."

Abiona placed the rinsed items in the dishwasher. Dan finished his lemonade and placed the empty glass in the dishwasher himself.

"If you do not like it, tough," Abiona said as she closed the dishwasher. "We will not adapt to coddle your insecurities. This is our planet, populated with my people, and you can always leave."

There was no trace of animosity or anger in Abiona's tone, simply the resuscitation of cold, hard facts. Abiona grabbed Dan's hands, peering into his eyes.

"We have spoken our truths as we see things. Hearthlings do this constantly. It is how we live and grow together. It is my hope that you will come to feel the same."

Abiona released his hands and cupped his face in her hands. Her reassuring smile dissolved his anger. Abiona's phone vibrated. She checked her caller ID.

"Excuse me," Abiona said, stepping away from Dan. "I have to take this call." Dan nodded his understanding as Abiona answered "Yes" to the caller, using her voice rather than telepathic connection.

Abiona listened for a moment, her face calm, her eyes focused on some point in the distance.

"I see. I will be right there. I have to go," Abiona said after hanging up.

"Are the children okay?" Dan asked with as much concern in his voice as if they were his own.

"Mayowa and Ifelayo are fine, thanks for asking. An emergency meeting has been called by the Golden Eagle Council. There is a wildlife/Hearthling issue requiring our immediate attention."

"Can I come?" Dan asked, anxious to witness how a meeting between animals and humans worked. "I promise I'll stay out of the way."

"Not this time, Daniel," Abiona answered unapologetically. "Are you going to be all right on your own?"

"I'll be fine," Dan said, managing to keep the note of regret out of his voice.

"Some of the neighbors would be glad to have you over."

"Don't worry about me."

"I should only be an hour, two at the most. Duke and Walter will be at your disposal. If you decide to take a trip, simply order Duke 'home' and he will return you to us."

"Go, already, Abiona!"

"I will leave you with your thoughts."

Abiona surprised Dan with a quick peck on the cheek before she was off.

*   *   *

Dan had watched Abiona leave, his irritation subsiding with each step she took. He was falling in love with Toni's star twin. He was falling in love with a Hearthling.

As much as he hated admitting it to himself, he was becoming attached to Hearth. He wished he could bring his family here to experience what he was experiencing; the founding board members, too, so they could see that their dreams were possible beyond their wildest imaginations.

Dan would never be a Hearthling, not only because he did not possess their gifts of telepathy or abilities to communicate with animals or detect and read auras, but because to be a Hearthling was the same as being an Earthling. You had to be born and bred into their society. This was a conclusion that, for the moment, made his heart ache.

Alone, Dan felt a sudden chill. He realized he was isolated on a planet where he had few friends and no real family. His self-pity only lasted a moment. Dan was in the midst of an adventure like none he would ever know again. He loved escapades. He would be embracing these moments like a child holding tight to a beloved gift if he were on Earth.

Dan roamed about the house, dispensing with the siren song of defeat and retracing Abiona's house tour from the night of his arrival.

The house seemed even larger in the daylight. While not a mansion, the residence was bigger than his Golden Meadows home. The downstairs was an eloquent dwelling with living room and study fireplaces, vaulted ceilings, tasteful furniture, and fine art. It was a cozy and inviting residence where any weary traveler would feel safe to lay their head.

The study was adorned with a wall of wooden bookshelves lined with hardcover books. Dan perused the titles. Subjects from science to religion, history, art and literature, physics and philosophy, and more caught his eye.

Dan knew from his exchange student teachings that hard copies of books were print-on-demand, since all Hearth reading materials were digitized. Hard copies were considered an extravagance and were permitted primarily for libraries, museums, universities, and specified organizations such as the Exchange Student Program.

Citizens had to request a hard copy edition and state their reason for needing one. The Gaines family had delivered good reasons to be granted such luxuries, judging by the wall of books Dan saw before him.

All upstairs doors were wide open. Dan peeked inside Mayowa and Ifelayo's rooms. The children's rooms were decorated in much the same style as his own offspring with what Dan assumed were their current Hearth heroes, crushes, and personal interests (assumed, because Dan did not recognize any of the people in the posters the children had framed and mounted, and he had no idea what Mayowa and Ifelayo's interests were).

Dan noticed one big difference between his children and their star-twins: Ifelayo was the messy one, while Mayowa was neat. The opposite was true in his home. Wick was the messy one, while Mae was neat.

Dan passed the connected guest room that shared his Jack and Jill bathroom. His companion bedroom was unoccupied. Both guest rooms were fully furnished, with mirrored layouts. The other guest room was rustic, with cinnamon pine, hardwood floors, and brass lamps in contrast to Dan's guest room, which exhibited a sophisticated style despite his dormitory room infusion.

A king-size bed atop a zebra-stripped area rug stood out the most. A cinnamon pine writing desk set was placed in front of a window facing in the same direction as his own.

The primary bedroom was contemporary and luxurious. Dan stepped inside. It was double the size of the guest rooms, with a crystal chandelier, private bath, entertainment center, fireplace, and a bed larger than his own.

Dan was in awe of how seamlessly the décor fit together. He wondered if Abiona and Kwasi had done the decorating themselves, or if they'd had an interior designer conjure up this dream.

He did not touch anything. Dan already felt as though he was violating some unwritten code of trespass. Dan wondered if Abiona missed having her husband beside her as much as he missed Toni. Dan lingered until guilt forced him to move on.

He returned to his room after his tour. Gray light poured through his windows. He saw birds riding the winds and vehicles knife the air beneath an overcast sky. Dan wondered if he was being watched by the animal kingdom at this moment. If so, how?

Dan plopped down on his bed and stretched out on his back, knees bent, feet remaining flat on the floor. He placed his hands on his stomach, twiddling his thumbs.

The chill of loneliness returned. He missed his Earthling compatriots. He could commiserate with them. He could not get this annoying feeling out of his system and move on.

Dan stared up at the cloud white ceiling, wondering how he had gotten himself into this predicament but knowing—or believing, at least—that he could return to Earth at any time.

CHAPTER 32

Dan's star-twin was at his desk in his office. Kwasi was in the middle of writing a damning report on Single Organism's participation (or lack thereof) in corporate social responsibility programs when he received an instant message from Logan Asher.

The CEO of Single Organism wanted to know if Kwasi had a moment for a video conference call. Kwasi answered that he did. Within seconds, the call from the CEO came through.

"Good morning, Dan," Logan said in a self-assured voiced. A smooth-shaven, chiseled face with perfect silver-blonde hair and confident blue eyes filled Kwasi's 27" color monitor. Kwasi placed the CEO on speaker rather than using his headset, leaving Amiri or anyone else in close proximity to his office access to their open-door conversation.

"Good morning, Logan."

"First off, I would like to say how impressed I was with your coordination of the leadership conference. Everything was first rate."

"Thanks, but the credit belongs to the conference committee. They did all of the heavy lifting."

"Under your direction, but you're being modest. That's one of the things I like about you, Dan."

Kwasi was being honest. Modesty was a quality he and Dan shared. This was not one of those moments either would have chosen to concede to that trait. The CEO for Single Organism did not issue compliments lightly. Logan was up to something.

"Great keynote address at the conference, Dan. I agree with what you said one hundred percent. What I wanted to talk to you about was highlighting some of the business realities that your keynote address neglected."

"Anything specific?"

"Your emphasis that Single Organism was veering away from the company's mission statement by being fiscally responsible."

"I said no such thing."

"I believe you did."

"What I emphasized was that we should never chose cost over our ongoing commitment to the welfare of the planet and its inhabitants."

"From a business prospective, the two go hand in hand."

"If I may be blunt, Logan..."

"Please do."

"The bottom line should always take a back seat to our planet and its future."

"That's not sound business practice, Dan. Which is why I was brought on board, if you recall: to shore up the financial side of Single Organism."

"You were brought on board, Logan, because our business was growing so rapidly that we were no longer able to keep up."

"You're saying I've gone overboard in my efforts to cut costs?"

"The onus is not on you, Logan. I'm not making you out to be the bad guy."

"Sure sounds like it to me."

"A part of your job is to help trim the fat. No one is disputing that, especially me. The responsibility falls on us—the founding board members—to decide what effect those cost-cutting measures will have on our products and our people, both of which have a larger responsibility to the planet."

"You believe I have gained undue influence over the board?"

"I know you have, without them ever realizing it."

"I think that's absurd."

"Now who's being modest? You are a very persuasive person, Logan. We both know that. Profits are high, and our people are living better material lives than most ever imagined."

"Then, what's the problem?"

"Too many board members have become blinded by the bling. We've lost sight of who we are and what we stand for."

"I'll fight you on this, Dan."

"I'd expect nothing less from someone committed to their business principles. You should know I'm not only ready to fight, but to win. This is not some power struggle for me, Logan. I'm fighting to save the soul of my company."

"This may surprise you, Dan, but I'm a strong proponent of what Single Organism stands for outside of the numbers-crunching. That was what drew me to take this job over a half-dozen lucrative offers."

"The more areas in which you can cut costs, the more customers you will attract; not to mention repeat customers. Our competition is not obsessed with as many details as what you propose.

"Like it or not, Dan, we *do* have competition. Major competition. Competitors who have won contracts by simply underbidding us. Cost is a business reality we cannot escape."

"I agree. Cost is a significant driving force in gaining new contracts, but so is quality."

"But—"

"Please allow me to finish, Logan."

"Go ahead."

"Quality is what generates more return business than any other— customer satisfaction. If I'm not mistaken, we have more repeat business than all of our competitors combined." Kwasi knew it to be true because he had done his homework.

"You're correct."

"We are also the number one company people turn to when they are dissatisfied with products our competitors have delivered."

"Correct again."

"We are constantly receiving new business by word of mouth about the superiority of our products and services. Those factors stem more from commitment to quality than costs."

"I can't argue that point."

"Suppose we use some of the less expensive design elements in our products in order to shave costs, with full knowledge they do not meet our environmental criteria, as some of our competitors have done?

Design elements that are not only environmentally unsound, but failed in their basic field functions?"

"Then we avoid those specific products."

"Trail and error is not an option for us, Logan. Especially not in the field. That's why Single Organism does such extensive testing before releasing a product for production. Expense is already instituted into that process. We know what works before it ever hits the market with streamlined budgets already sewn into their creation."

Logan's hard-line stare filled the screen.

"Logan, don't get me wrong. You're doing an amazing job on the financials," Kwasi managed to say without sounding conciliatory or condescending. "We wouldn't be in this position without you. It's your job to keep us focused on the bottom line. And you do your job extraordinarily well."

"Thank you."

"It's our job—I'm speaking of myself, the founding board members, and leadership—to remain vigilant on why we started this company. To me, that means saying no to any cost-cutting measures that have an adverse effect on our mission statement.

"That goes for people, as well as products. It's also why we remain a private rather than a publicly traded company, as you have been trying to influence us to become."

"Making Single Organism a publicly traded company would considerably increase company profits."

"It would also open the door for us to be forced into implementing cost-cutting measures at every turn in order to keep shareholders happy."

"Board members would still be the primary shareholders, and thereby have the final say."

"A public stink by disgruntled shareholders who disagreed with our approach would, in likelihood, have an adverse effect on our business and reputation."

"I don't think it would come to that."

"I, for one, am unwilling to take that chance. The rest of the board agrees with me on this matter."

For the first time, Logan glanced away from the camera.

"This is not personal, Logan. I hope you understand."

"I hope *you* understand that I will always be placing profit first."

"I do."

"I can see I won't be winning you over to my way of thinking any time soon, Dan."

"You are correct, sir."

"Hopefully, we can meet in the middle on some of these business decisions."

"There's always hope."

"See you at the next board meeting, Dan," Logan finished with a surprising smile that warmed his hard face. It was a smile that Kwasi recognized as sincere.

"I'll be there, Logan."

CHAPTER 33

Abiona returned shortly after Dan snapped out of his Residual Connection to find Dan still resting on his bed, recapping what he had witnessed.

"Are you all right?" Abiona asked.

"Fine, thanks," Dan said, standing. "Taking a little afternoon siesta." Dan decided not to share his latest star-twin episode with Abiona. "How was your council meeting?"

"We came up with a solution that pleased everyone."

"What was the problem?"

"Some beavers wanted to build a new dam a few kilometers downstream from our agreed-upon location. Their new location would cause flooding, siltation, and create a barrier to migrating fish. Their experts—"

"Their experts?" Dan interrupted, giving Abiona his full attention.

"Yes."

"The beavers have their own experts on such matters."

"They know what is best for them, which makes them experts in their field."

"Of dam building."

"Beaver dam building." While Dan was trying to digest what Abiona had just told him, Abiona continued. "Their experts had scouted the new location and found it offered better protection against predators."

"Predators? There are predators around here?"

"We live in a community of humans, *wildlife* and aqualife. Hearth wildlife is not confined or controlled, like in one of your zoos or game parks."

"What are your zoos like?"

"We do not have any. We do not have any institutions that imprison aqualife or wildlife for the sake of our amusement or education. We go to where they live. May I continue?" Abiona asked, appearing more amused than annoyed.

"Sorry," Dan said.

"We reminded their council that they had unanimously approved our final plans."

"The beavers have their own council?"

"Yes, the beavers have their own council. We saw no valid reason why the previously approved decision should be altered."

Abiona stopped as if there were nothing more to say on the subject.

"What happened next?" Dan asked, anxious for more details.

"We debated their pros and our cons of what the new location would do to the environment and came to a compromise. The beavers could move their dam half-a-kilometer further downstream. That would improve their protection with no effect on the environment."

Dan took a moment trying to imagine what a human/beaver debate would look like. All he could envision were animated versions.

"Are your meetings always held at your community center?"

"We alternate our local meetings between the Golden Eagle Community Center and nearby forest clearings, dependent on who called the meeting, and its purpose."

"Do you have these sorts of meetings often?" Dan asked.

"Often as need be. For example, when we want to clear land for human habitation, we have meetings with the affected wildlife and aqualife to determine what would be best for all concerned."

"Seriously?"

Abiona stared at Dan. She did not look amused.

"It is our duty," Abiona continued, "since aqualife and wildlife will be uprooted by our move. We come to agreements about how to proceed; what we can do to help them transition and relocate. We move forward once those details are ironed out. We take care of the local aqualife and wildlife's needs first, before preparing the territory for our habitation."

"What if the wildlife or aqualife (or both) disagree with humans moving in at all?"

"Then we find another location, with their help."

"You make it sound so simple."

"The process is anything but simple. It is simply best for all involved. On your planet, humankind operates with a different mindset. You seek to control your environment. On our planet, we seek to work in concert with our environment. We operate on a principle of harmony. Our way takes more energy, effort, and planning."

The pleasant sound of harp music filled the air. Abiona started. "Is it that time already?" Abiona said before rushing off.

Dan went over and looked out at the sight from his desk window. He witnessed a similar scene as that morning. The school shuttles were returning. Only, this time, eager parents were welcoming their children home.

Dan made out Abiona. Mayowa and Ifelayo ran into their mother's arms as if they were returning from a long absence. The joy on their faces was like that of Christmas morning, in his house, when presents were being opened.

Everywhere he looked, there were hugs and kisses between parents and children, as if their experiences had been the same.

Dan did not treat Wick and Mae that way. When seeing his children off to school, "Be good, learn much," was his usual brusque send-off. "How was school today?" was his common refrain when he first saw them after school.

To the former statement, his children replied something in the neighborhood of "Will do" or "Sure thing, Dad." Trite reflex responses without a hint of sincerity and minted with a splash of sarcasm. To the latter, they might have an interesting tale to relate that may or may not have anything to do with their classroom education.

That was the way of working two-parent households across his nation. Some were immersed in their careers. Others struggled to survive, having to schedule quality time (if that option were even available).

Nurturing a child to maturity was becoming an untenable challenge in modern society. The balance between economic imperative and parental nurturing had become lopsided.

Why was that? Dan asked himself. When did the sheer joy of being a parent diminish in his life? Dan would have to do something about that when he returned to Earth. Prioritize his family. Give Wick and Mae more unwarranted attention and affection, even if that meant taking a step back in his career. Dan began jotting down his recent experiences and feelings in his Hearth Journal, not wanting to lose the spark of his revelation.

Mayowa and Ifelayo burst into his room in the middle of his notations.

"What are you doing, Mr. Bluford?" Mayowa asked.

"Making notes in my journal."

"You keep a journal?" Ifelayo asked.

"Yes."

"Can we read it?" Mayowa asked.

"No."

"Why not?" Ifelayo asked.

Dan wondered if their seesaw approach to speaking was something formulated, or intrinsic between the two siblings.

"Because it is personal. Do either of you keep personal journals?"

"No," Ifelayo answered.

"Why not?"

"We have not thought to do so," Mayowa replied.

"A journal is a great way to recount your life experiences. As you get older, memories can fade, disappear, or become distorted. A journal can help bring them back into focus."

"Even bad memories?" Ifelayo asked.

"If you choose to record them, then yes. Even bad memories. I prefer to record good memories, myself."

"Are you having good memories with us, Mr. Bluford?" Mayowa asked.

"The best."

Mayowa and Ifelayo smiled at each other.

"We have no need for journals," Ifelayo said.

"Why not?"

"We have memory cubes," Mayowa said.

"What are memory cubes?"

Mayowa and Ifelayo looked at each other and their faces lit up. Dan assumed they were having a telepathic conversation and had arrived at an agreeable conclusion.

"We will be right back," Ifelayo said, before they rushed from the room, brushing past their mother. Dan could hear the children stop running.

"I told them to slow down," Abiona said. "They are not disturbing you, are they?"

"Not in the least."

"What is their hurry?"

"I was explaining to them why I keep a personal journal, and they mentioned something about memory cubes."

Abiona nodded. "I see."

"What are they?"

Mayowa and Ifelayo brushed past their mother in a hurried walk, saying, "Excuse me, Mom," as they did so. They held crystal-like objects no larger than a sugar cube.

"I will let them explain," Abiona said, exiting with an amused smile. The children walked up to Dan and presented the crystal cubes to him. Dan was afraid to touch them. They appeared so fragile.

"Do not be afraid, Mr. Bluford," Ifelayo said, as if sensing his discomfort.

"They will not break," Mayowa said, dropping his cube on the floor and repeatedly stomping on it.

Dan received their gifts with mild trepidation. Dan could not make out the material. The cubes reflected the light in the room like polished glass. Dan felt he could toss it into the air and it would float like a dandelion seed, the object was so light—despite Mayowa's recent demonstration of its durability, when it had fallen like a stone.

"These are memory cubes," Mayowa said.

"These contain our memories," Ifelayo added.

"I suppose you could say they are the Hearthling version of a personal journal," Mayowa said.

"How do they work?"

"The same as EP cubes," Mayowa said.

"They are personalized," Ifelayo added.

"Allow us to demonstrate," Mayowa said.

The children presented their hands, palms up, for Dan to return their cubes. He did so. Mayowa and Ifelayo walked to the open area near the center of his guest room and looked at each other, then nodded.

Mayowa stepped back out of the way. Ifelayo gave a mental command to her memory cube. What Dan would describe as a holographic scene came to life, complete with sight and sound, and in full color.

Ifelayo was walking along, holding a man's hand. She looked up. Kwasi's smiling face came into view. Words were not spoken. Judging by the expressions on Kwasi's face, he and Ifelayo were having a playful telepathic conversation not unlike the verbal ones Dan had with his daughter when they were kidding around.

Ifelayo gave the memory cube a mental command to cease. The scene vanished as quickly as it had appeared. Ifelayo was beaming, appearing bright and cheerful, just like in the memory.

"My turn," Mayowa said. Ifelayo stepped back. Mayowa moved forward. Mayowa did as his sister had done with his cube.

Mayowa is flying a colorful three dimensional tubular kite, a box kite Dan recognized as a Spintube, on Earth. Mayowa is looking up at a clear blue sky. The kite is dipping and soaring and spinning high in the air. The kite string handle in his hands occasioned into view as Mayowa made adjustments. A man's hand was placed on his shoulder. Mayowa looked up into the proud face of his father.

Mayowa ceased the memory in the same manner as his sister. Dan was flabbergasted.

"Those were your actual real-life memories?" Dan asked.

"Yes," Ifelayo said.

"Right down to the smallest detail," Mayowa added.

"That is not all," Ifelayo said. Dan waited while Mayowa and Ifelayo finished their mental conversation. Mayowa reenergized his memory cube.

The memory was of Mayowa and his family at a festival. The day was clear and sunny. Mid-afternoon, Dan would guess. The Gaige family was strolling along at a leisurely gait, enjoying the sites.

To Dan's shock, Mayowa stepped into his memory. He smiled and waved at Dan and Ifelayo. His presence appeared not to have any effect on what was happening.

"My brother is now able to taste, smell, and touch everything in his memory."

On cue, Mayowa walked over and plucked a wad of pink cotton candy from the cotton candy stick of a passerby. The teenager did not react. Mayowa walked over to a popcorn vendor. He picked up a bag of popcorn with steam rising from it. "Smells delicious," he said, taking a couple of appetizing whiffs before popping a couple of kernels into his mouth. "Lightly salted, just the way I like it."

Mayowa exited his memory. The memory continued to play.

"Amazing," Dan could only say. The children stared at him, smiling and looking pleased. "Where's the popcorn?" Dan finally asked.

"Still in the memory," Ifelayo said.

"While you can visit a memory," Mayowa said, "you can no more alter it than you can the past."

Ifelayo nodded her agreement. Mayowa gave his memory cube a mental command. The scene vanished. His sister stepped to his side. Dan would not have been surprised if they were mentally holding hands. They seemed, to him, to be that close.

"How many memories can one cube hold?"

"One year," Mayowa said.

Dan eyed the remarkable crystal-like cubes the children held between their thumbs and forefingers.

"Can I get a memory cube for myself?"

"You will have to ask Mom," Mayowa said.

"Our parents get our memory cubes for us," Ifelayo said.

"How do they work?"

Mayowa and Ifelayo looked at each other and shrugged.

"We do not know," Ifelayo said.

"Does your mom know?"

"Maybe," Ifelayo said. "Dad knows, for certain."

"Engineering and science are Dad's specialties," Mayowa said.

"Are you not the same as our dad, in that regard, Mr. Bluford?" Ifelayo asked.

"Yes and no. Hearthling engineering and science is far beyond anything we have on Earth."

Mayowa and Ifelayo held a mental conversation, then looked back at Dan with no response.

"How do the memory cubes record your memories?" Dan asked.

"Like this." Ifelayo held her memory cube about two inches from her eye. A fine bluish light emitted from the cube and appeared to penetrate her pupil. The light switched off after a few seconds. Ifelayo smiled when it was done, pleased with her demonstration.

"That's it?"

Mayowa and Ifelayo nodded.

"Did that hurt?"

"I did not feel anything," Ifelayo answered.

"It never hurts," Mayowa added. "Once the light switches off, that means your memories are all up to date."

"Fascinating."

Mayowa and Ifelayo looked at each other in silent conversation.

"What are you two thinking?"

"Private stuff," Mayowa said.

"Mom is calling us," Ifelayo said.

Dan did not hear anything. "Telepathically?"

"Yes," Mayowa said.

"We have to go," said Ifelayo.

"See you later, Mr. Bluford," they said in chorus before dashing from the room.

CHAPTER 34

The next time Dan saw Mayowa and Ifelayo was at dinner. They ate to the clink of utensils on dishes, food compliments, and energetic conversation, the Gaige family agreeing to verbalize their thoughts for Dan's benefit.

The children seemed less interested in Dan than commenting on their day. They mentioned how great it was to see Grandma Patricia and Grandpa Achak, who had popped by school to surprise them. Mayowa and Ifelayo exuberantly talked about what happened at school and with their friends. Abiona listened, questioned, and commented when appropriate.

Dan sat in silence unless called upon, enjoying the spirit of the gathering, missing his Earth family, but trying not to show it.

The dishes were cleared after dinner by Walter. The children were made to do their homework. Dan and Abiona enjoyed a conversation that consisted mainly of Abiona filling Dan in on the details of what and who the children had been referring to at the dinner table.

Abiona checked Mayowa and Ifelayo's homework. The children prepared for bed. The family sat in what they called a meditation circle on the floor in Ifelayo's room, employing twenty minutes of quiet meditation to shut down their minds and tune into their bodies before sleep.

Dan was asked to join, but declined. He was never good at meditating or shutting down his active mind. Then the children were off to bed, tucked in by their mom with a warm hug and a goodnight kiss.

Dan retired to his room, made entries to his daily journal, and reviewed some of his technical notes on past and new discoveries.

The remainder of the week was uneventful. Dan fell into the normal Gaige family routine, surprised at how similar it was to his own and helping when he could.

Abiona had taken a temporary leave of absence from her position as Regional Director of Astronomy. Dan had objected when he discovered what she had done, but Abiona would not hear of it. She believed it her duty to make Dan's stay as pleasant and informative as possible.

The children became more interested in teaching Dan about Hearth than learning about Earth and Earthlings, although having an Earthling staying in their home had made them popular amongst their peers.

Mayowa and Ifelayo were spending the weekend at a friend's house in another neighborhood, leaving Abiona and Dan alone, a situation that made Dan uncomfortable. Abiona's resemblance to Toni notwithstanding, his attraction to Abiona was growing stronger.

The physical attraction had been there from the start. That was one concern. His feelings for Abiona were extending beyond friendship. Dan began thinking of Abiona as his wife every moment he was with her.

A number of times, he caught himself on the cusp of calling Abiona 'honey,' 'sweetheart,' 'darling,' 'dear,' or some other term of endearment reserved for the beloved women in his life. Dan wondered if Abiona knew what was going on with him.

Dan was grateful for Occlumency pills. Had Abiona—or anyone—been able to read his thoughts, embarrassment would not begin to describe how he would feel.

Abiona escorted Dan to the Golden Eagle Community Center after Friday's dinner. She informed Dan that a birthday party was being thrown for one of their neighbors at the center, and Dan had been invited. The main hall of the center was a large rectangular room with bright overhead lighting and basketball court tiles. The décor for the evening was an elegant dining room, with space reserved in the center for dancing. Dan wondered if the décor was normal for a Golden Eagle birthday party, but considered it impolite to ask.

Abiona took Dan's arm as if they were a couple. Dan did not hide his pride in her action. The place was filled. It appeared as if the entire neighborhood was there. Dan recognized the landscapers, neighbors he had met and seen in passing, and, to his shock, Achak and Patricia Gaige. Abiona led Dan to the center of the room. The crowd gathered around. The entire room erupted with "SURPRISE!" before Dan could ask what was going on.

A large virtual banner appeared near the ceiling that read "WELCOME TO HEARTH, MR. DANIEL SAMUEL BLUFORD." Dan was dumbfounded as Hearthlings rushed to him to pat him on the shoulder or back or give him a firm hug. Even the ones who had shunned him earlier were now all smiles and warmth.

"We had you going, did we not?" one Hearthling said, who had told Dan he saw nothing special about him

"You were putting me on this whole time?" Dan said in disbelief.

"I believe he has got it!" said a neighbor Dan knew as Raphael. The room exploded with laughter.

"Forgive us, Daniel," one of the landscapers said, whom Dan had met on his first walk with Abiona. "We could not resist putting you on a bit."

"It was Abiona's idea!" yelled a Hearthling from the back.

"It was not!" Abiona said in her defense. "Do not believe him, Daniel. It was Dr. Bakari's idea. I will admit that the standoffish ruse was to throw you off, and for our own amusement."

"Dr. Jabori Bakari?" Dan said surprised. "My Indoctrination Specialist?"

"One and the same," Abiona said. "We have been planning this party since the time I agreed to be your host. Dr. Bakari thought the ploy of being disenchanted about having an Earthling on Hearth, followed by a surprise welcoming party, might help loosen you up in order for you to relax and enjoy your Hearth experience more."

Dan thought for a moment. He realized Jabori was right. The star-twins seemed to serve equal measure in his life, albeit in different capacities on different planets. Achak and Patricia embraced Dan, to his amazement.

"Quite a performance, would you not say?" said a beaming Patricia.

"Worthy of the stage," Achak added with a smile, patting Dan on the shoulder.

"My in-laws—as you called them—are professional actors," Abiona said.

"You must view some of our stage, film, and broadcast performances," Achak said.

"We will give you a list later," Patricia said with a wink as she and Achak graciously stepped away to allow other Hearthlings their time with Dan.

Hearthlings welcomed Dan with hearty enthusiasm. The ones Dan had previously met hung back, giving others an opportunity to introduce themselves. Dan heard familiar ethnic terms when Hearthlings described themselves, such as Cuban, Wangunk, Finnish, Cambodian, Sudanese, or Liberian—terms they used with pride. He was astonished to learn that, while the people of Hearth saw themselves as one, they maintained individual cultural identities.

Abiona broke away from Dan for a moment. Dan noticed her excitement as she hugged a handsome couple who seemed to appear out of nowhere. They were wearing colorful Yoruba aso oki-style clothing. The woman, Abiona's height, was fit, with radiant espresso skin, high cheekbones, and cascading, lustrous black curls.

The man, a head taller than the woman, was broad-shouldered with mocha skin, a smooth baby face, and braided long dreadlocks. Positioned between the couple, Abiona led them by the hand over to Dan with all the giddiness of a child. Other Hearthlings stepped aside and let them through.

"This is Daniel Bluford," Abiona said with all the exuberance and pride of a ten-year-old. "Kwasi's star-twin. Daniel, this is my mom and dad." Dan could not miss the strong resemblance Abiona shared with both of her parents.

Abiona had her mother's lovely face and her father's enchanting brown eyes. Yet, Dan could not help but wonder why her parents did not more strongly resemble his Earth in-laws, given that their daughter was the exact likeness of Toni.

"Remarkable," the woman said, her voice matching the stunned expression on her face. Dan noted how Abiona's velvety soprano sounded like her mom, and therefore both sounded like Toni.

"Pleased to meet you," Dan said, extending his hand without thinking. To Dan's shock, the man gave him a firm handshake.

"An Earth custom, so I am told. Pleased to meet you as well, Daniel. My name is Daivika Jaheem." His voice reminded Dan of a healthy heartbeat, for some reason: rich, steady, and strong.

"Mine is Funmilayo Jaheem," Abiona's mom added, her dimples showing as she smiled. "It is very nice to meet you, Daniel."

Daniel resisted the urge to extend his hand again, instead, exhibiting the curt nod that Hearthlings used in place of a handshake.

"I should have introduced my parents properly." Abiona flashed an embarrassed smile. *Even flustered, she is beautiful,* Dan thought.

"No worries," Dan said.

"Honey, it is fine." Daivika hugged his daughter. Abiona appeared as a child in her father's powerful arms.

"It is not a big deal," Funmilayo said. "We are sorry your brother and sister could not make this unique occasion."

"Sohalia, Abiona's sister, is a geologist," Daivika said to Dan. "Off world on Mirihi, on a geological dig. Mars, is it not?" Daivika asked Abiona.

"That is correct, Dad," answered Abiona. "Mars would be the planet equivalent in your Milky Way galaxy, Daniel. My brother, Kaab, is the governor of the Yoruba Province. Our homeland province; the place where we grew up."

"We talked to Kaab just before we arrived," Funmilayo said.

"He is guest speaker at a mayor's conference being hosted in the Yoruba Province," Daivika said, "and could not break away."

"They both send their love," Funmilayo said to Abiona.

"You will have an opportunity to meet everyone soon enough, Daniel," Abiona said.

"At our yearly family gathering," Daivika said, "to which you are formerly invited."

"I'm looking forward to it," Dan said.

"As well you should," Daivika said without a hint of arrogance. "How do you like our planet so far?"

"To be honest, I'm intimidated by Hearthlings and your accomplishments."

"Understandable," Funmilayo said. "You will become acclimated to us in no time."

"I hope you're right," Dan said.

"I know I am, Daniel."

"I actually prefer to be called Dan."

"As opposed to 'Earthling,'" Daivika said with a chuckle.

"As opposed to Daniel."

"Daniel is your name, is it not?" Funmilayo asked.

"Yes, but Dan is my familiar name; my Earthling-abbreviated name."

"Yes, yes," Daivika said. "Abiona told us all about that Earthling custom."

"We have been over this before, Daniel," Abiona said. "Hearthlings prefer to use given names. You would not want to insult us, would you?" she finished with a knowing smile; a smile her parents shared. Every Hearthling within earshot nodded in agreement.

"Daniel, it is," Dan conceded, not feeling as though he had lost anything from his concession. The room exploded with laughter, followed by a chant of "Daniel! Daniel! Daniel! Daniel!"

Dan was overwhelmed. His macho male conditioning was the only thing that prevented him from shedding tears of joy.

"It appears you are a celebrity, after all," Abiona said after the chanting ceased. "How does it feel?"

Dan considered the question for a moment before answering, "Awkward."

The evening proceeded like any well-catered, festive celebration with great food, wine and spirits, music and dance, and an abundance of laughter. Hearthlings flooded the dance floor as the evening wore on, resembling their Earthling cousins. There were good to moderate dancers and others who did their own thing.

To Dan's surprise, the music consisted of Dan's favorite Earth artists, selections Dan was queried about by curious Hearthlings. When Dan asked Abiona how they knew what music he liked, she explained it was simple.

"Kwasi had passed on your favorite music playlists to the Exchange Student Program Committee. The committee, in turn, relayed digital copies of your music to us. We put together our own playlists from what was sent. Do you like our arrangements?"

"Very much," Dan said while dancing with Abiona to "Shining Star" by Earth, Wind & Fire.

Dan was informed that the wait staff were all Interactive Virtual Assistants. He was not surprised. Dan had discovered what IVAs were capable of from his time at the Zenith Campus. He was impressed when he learned IVAs had done all of the catering.

The only close contact Dan had with any virtual life form was Falcon student housing director Alvita Agumanu's IVA. IVAs were not utilized in such a capacity at the Zenith Campus, to his knowledge.

Dan took a close look at each waitperson whenever they passed near. He recognized Walter, Abiona's house servant. He could not tell they were not human. *Remarkable*, Dan thought. *Such technology would revolutionize Single Organism. Change the world, for that matter.* Dan made a mental note to learn all he could about the creation of IVAs.

The intimacy Abiona displayed at the party and the smooth bourbon Dan was drinking found him treating Abiona as he would Toni. Midway through the festivities, the dignified, middle-aged lieutenant governor stood proud and regally stated, "In honor of our special guest, Mr. Daniel Bluford, we will continue our efforts to vocalize our thoughts, as we are doing here tonight.

"I realize that, for many of us, this will not be easy. I have not spoken this much in months. As good hosts, I feel it is our duty to make our exchange student as comfortable as possible. I would like to make a toast to our honored guest. If you will raise your glasses..."

Hearthlings raised their glasses in unison as Dan looked on.

"To Mr. Daniel Samuel Bluford. May your life be long and fulfilling, may your journeys always lead you home, and may love be there to greet you."

In chorus came the Hearthling response, "Well said!"

Whether he kissed Abiona or she kissed him after the toast did not seem to matter. Dan was in trouble, and he knew it. He found Abiona irresistible. The crowd cheered them on. Even Achak and Patricia joined in. They did not seem bothered by the fact that their son's wife was kissing another man.

Abiona managed to settle everyone down, deflecting their jubilant encouragement with the ease of a champion fencer. Dan became flustered and speechless for a bit before easing back into party mode.

The party ended at precisely 2:30 a.m. No one had left. Everyone gathered their belongings in an orderly fashion. Dan said goodnight to Abiona's parents and in-laws, the magistrate, and a number of other Hearthlings whose names he struggled to remember. The tireless IVAs were left to clean and straighten up. The IVAs would return to their assigned homes once done.

People were still buoyant on their way out, but no one appeared intoxicated. Dan asked Abiona about why that was as he helped Abiona on with her coat, still enjoying the warm buzz from the smooth 80-proof bourbons he had sipped for much of the evening.

Abiona explained that the IVAs monitored everyone's alcohol intake. You were cut off before you become inebriated, after which, you were only permitted water or non-alcoholic beverages.

Dan and Abiona strolled home arm-in-arm on a clear night of stars and half-Mwezi-light ('Mwezi' the Hearth name equivalent for 'moon'). Moments like this reminded Dan of Earth at its best.

"Something just occurred to me, Abiona."

"What?"

"I have not once heard a Hearthling use a contraction."

"We do not. Anything we have worth saying deserves full voice."

"Why? Contractions work just as well."

"Clarity and brevity can be obtained without contractions. In fact, we believe that, by not using contractions, we have built a stronger discipline in thought and expression. By expression, I mean in both speech and writing."

"I got that. Does it trouble Hearthlings that I use contractions?"

"Not at all. It is a part of who you are. It distinguishes you from Hearthlings."

"You mean, it helps Hearthlings recognize me as an Earthling."

"There are a number of factors identifying you as an Earthling, Daniel. Any Hearthling you meet will know you are an Earthling before you say a word. For instance, your inability to read minds or see auras or communicate with nature."

"I get the picture."

"Do not begin sulking or feeling self-pity. I will not have it."

"I'm not doing either. I'm just trying to get the lay of the land."

"You appear to be sulking and feeling sorry for yourself, to me."

"How's that?"

"Slumping shoulders, a wayward tone of voice, avoiding eye contact."

She is good, Dan thought. He *was* slipping into a self-pitying mode, only he had not realized it until Abiona pointed it out.

"How would you have me behave?"

"Be yourself, Daniel. If you feel angry, resentful, or frustrated then let it out. Whatever you feel or think, express it. There will be no judgment or reprisals on my part."

"What about other Hearthlings? Will they be as sympathetic?"

"I cannot speak for all Hearthlings. As for myself, I understand some of what you are going through. We have both been separated from people we love."

"You still have your family and friends and home, Abiona—people and planet, for goodness sake. You have not been uprooted from your life."

"That makes you angry."

"You're damn right, it does! Hearthlings plucked me out of my happy life without giving me a say!"

"For the greater good."

"I know, I know—for the survival of our planet."

"Not the survival of your planet, but of your species."

"What are you saying?"

"We are but an organism on this living planet. The better we treat Hearth, the better our lives are for doing so.

"Humbling ourselves in such a manner keeps us vigilante as to what our host requires. We determine whether it is something we can provide, or if we should step aside and let nature take its course. Hearthlings understand that we need Hearth. Hearth does not need Hearthlings."

"Earthlings understand that."

"Then you most certainly do not practice what you preach, if that is the case, judging by the deteriorating condition of your planet; much of it due to human actions."

Dan could not think of a response or defense. Abiona had made her argument without any malice behind her words, no differently as if she were reciting from a textbook on the subject.

Abiona identified, for Dan, the Hearthling names of some of the stars and constellations they viewed, changing the subject as deftly as a soaring bird, much like the distant silhouettes of birds in flight against the night sky.

Dan sensed a presence. More than one, in fact. When he could pry his attention from Abiona or the heavens, Dan casually glanced around the neighborhood as they strolled.

The night was quiet. There were no stray animals rummaging about. Dan hadn't noticed if Golden Eagle had a rodent problem. An odd thought settled upon Dan.

There had been no wildlife representatives at his surprise party. Did that mean they didn't welcome him? Did Hearth wildlife still distrust him? Would they continue to watch? Were they spying on him now?

CHAPTER 35

Nothing happened between Dan and Abiona. They made it home, talked a little more about the party and the beautiful starlit night, gave each other a friendly goodnight kiss on the lips and a hug, Then went to their separate bedrooms where they slept alone.

Walter made breakfast, allowing Abiona to sleep in. Breakfast conversation was light and cheery. The couple talked about how much fun they'd had at the party, citing comical events that made them laugh and touching moments that made them sigh.

Abiona asked Dan if he was up for a road trip. Dan said, "Absolutely!"

Dan and Abiona hopped into Duke after breakfast and headed for Mattatuck, a city 52 kilometers by land and 40 kilometers by air, southwest of Pequannock Province. The sky was clear along their flight path. Gray clouds loomed overhead. The couple encountered a smattering of other Hearthling air travelers and birds in flight along the way.

"Sorry about the kiss, Abiona," Dan said a couple of kilometers into their trip. "I kind of got swept up in the moment."

"You mean, the kiss at the party."

"Yes."

"We kissed each other, Daniel. I wanted that kiss as much as you did."

"I shouldn't have."

"Are you feeling guilty?"

"Yes." Dan felt a need to say more. "It's complex, Abiona."

"Not to me."

"I don't expect you to understand. Hearthlings think differently about these matters."

"I admit I do not understand Earthling guilt built on monogamy. We are human. Humans require companionship. Sometimes companionship presents itself in people other than our spouses.

"That in no way diminishes the love I have for my husband, as I know that nothing we do will undermine the love you have for your wife."

"It's not that simple. When I look at you, I see Toni. Having an affair is traumatic enough. Having an affair with a woman who reminds me so much of my wife .. well, it's … emotionally debilitating."

"I am not Toni. I am Abiona."

"Not to me. Spending time with you is the same for me as being with Toni."

"Are you falling in love with me, Daniel?"

"I believe I am."

Abiona let out a hearty laugh. It was not an evil or biting laugh—more like one of warm amusement. "You are not falling in love with me, Daniel."

"Excuse me?"

"I am your Toni substitute. You love your wife. I love my husband. I do not love you, Daniel. I care about you, and am attracted to you not because of your remarkable physical resemblance to Kwasi. You are not Kwasi. I know that. I am clear on the distinction.

"Daniel, you are a brilliant, sensitive, courageous and insightful man. Those qualities draw me to you. Can you describe me separately from Toni?"

Dan thought for a moment. He could not, and told Abiona so.

"I could tell after our kiss at your surprise party. You were not ready. I did not have to read your mind to know that."

"You were."

"I was open to the possibility."

"To be clear, Abiona, we are talking about sex."

"I am talking about intimacy, which sex may be a part of, Daniel."

For some reason, getting this out in the open made Daniel feel better. It removed the elephant from the vehicle, as far as Dan was concerned. He was grateful to Abiona for not bringing up the fact that Kwasi was having sex with his wife, the difference, in his mind, being that Toni thought she was sleeping with her husband.

Dan believed that if circumstances were reversed and Abiona had been exchanged for Toni, then he would have been doing the same with Abiona. There was still something diabolically unfair about the situation, as far as Dan was concerned.

If Toni were in his position, selected as an exchange student living on Hearth under similar circumstances, would she succumb? Would her need for adult intimacy overwhelm her Earthly marital vows? That was the basic desire he was combating within himself. Dan did not know the answers to those questions. Only Toni did, and that conjecture ate at him.

A few kilometers outside of Mattatuck, Dan saw a flurry of activity. Vehicles darted, hovered, and glided above Mattatuck like a bee colony around its nest. Buildings of varied heights, composed of glass, steel, brick, and stone, formed an impressive skyline.

Before they became part of the bee colony, Abiona switched Duke over to automatic pilot. Dan looked down at a city teeming with life. The level of human activity dwarfed Pequannock Province and even eclipsed that of Zenith Campus.

The sight gave Dan an electric thrill, as if the Hearthling energy from below rippled up and infested him. They descended toward the roof of a twelve-story, circular, concrete structure, vehicle traffic whipping around them, making Dan a bit nervous about how fast some were traveling, and how close a few came to Duke.

Abiona remained at ease, not appearing to notice the speedy air traffic. Even the flying birds dismissed the darting vehicles.

"This entire city is solar powered," Abiona said as Duke continued his descent. "Most above-ground urban areas are solar powered, on Hearth. We take advantage of wind or hydroelectric in open regions. We also have power plants that produce energy from solid waste."

"You mean, garbage."

"Precisely. For underwater provinces, we utilize hydroelectric exclusively, for obvious reasons. Mattatuck is a typical example of an Hearth terra city. On occasion, we employ coal or nuclear power plants."

"I'm surprised you use coal or nuclear power at all. Both are environmentally controversial on Earth."

"We took the time to discover how to recycle and neutralize nuclear waste for safe disposal before implementing our first nuclear power plant. We also perfected clean-burning coal. We synthesize our own uranium, coal, gas and oil. We do not extract them from the planet. They are much too valuable for maintaining the natural order and evolution of Hearth."

"Sounds amazing."

"It is not. It is the norm for Hearth. The environment is our first priority, not an afterthought."

A roof panel slid open, allowing Duke ample space to continue his descent. They landed in a parking area. Duke switched over from flight to ground transport. His display panel showed a grid with alphanumeric choices. "N34," Abiona said. Duke perfectly parked in a spot marked "N34."

Dan looked up when they got out. The roof had appeared opaque from the outside. Looking up, Dan could see through the roof as if it were made of clear glass.

"The roof is made of solar panel collectors," Abiona said, having noticed Dan staring up at the view of a misty sky.

"Similar to the ones I saw at Wakin."

"You would have to ask the architect for specifics. What I can tell you is that the material allows sunlight to pour through to charge our solar-powered vehicles while protecting those same vehicles from the harmful natural elements."

Dan nodded, making another mental note to learn the specifics about Hearth's solar panels. "Why make the roof appear opaque?"

"I asked that same question of an architect I met at a luncheon not long ago. They made it appear that way to prevent birds from crashing into the panels (in the same way birds will occasionally crash into clear glass)."

As they walked to the elevator, Dan noticed an enclave to the right of the elevator banks. It was a vehicle service area. Dan couldn't imagine it was a filling or rechargeable station. All of the vehicles he had seen were solar-powered.

As they drew closer, Dan saw vehicles being serviced by men and women in spruce green (what would be called, back on Earth, 'automotive uniforms').

"What a great idea," Dan said, more to himself than Abiona.

"What?"

"Do you need an appointment to have your vehicle serviced there?" Dan pointed at the vehicle service area.

"That would help, but it is not necessary. They will squeeze you in if they can."

"What sort of maintenance do they do?"

"Whatever is necessary. Those VTs—Vehicle Technicians—can do it all."

Dan noticed a few androids. They were not in uniform, and appeared to be assistants to the VTs. Dan restrained himself from asking the question of whether the VTs were Hearthlings or IVAs.

"Do Hearthlings typically come to parking garages to have their vehicles serviced?"

"Every province has their own vehicle maintenance stations. Most people have their vehicles serviced there." Abiona pointed to the banner across the service area entrance that read 'Stellar Vehicle Center.'

"Centers like these are typically used for emergency repairs. As a footnote, Daniel, we do not determine what and when our vehicles need maintenance. The vehicles do."

"Duke decides when he needs a tune-up?"

"Precisely. Should something happen to Duke's ability to self-assess, then human intervention may be required."

Dan's electric energy became tinged with a touch of eerie, at street level. The weather was cool and crisp. Fall weather, as it would be called back on Earth. Hearthlings were dressed appropriately, in windcheaters and coats. Hearthlings hurried about no differently from Earthlings in large, overcrowded cities.

Being in the company of telepaths was like experiencing the soundless world of the deaf, in a manner of speaking. People were talking, but Dan was unable to hear a word. There were not even moving lips to read. In this way, the Zenith Campus proved, to Dan, to be a microcosm of Hearth.

Dan had first experienced this phenomenon at the Zenith Campus. *Disconcerting*, was his initial impression. He thought he had become accustomed to the telepathic Hearthling way of life, but the combination of being amongst this throng of Hearthlings and living in a place where Hearthlings voiced their thoughts for his benefit made him realize he was wrong.

He also realized that the influx of verbal communication he heard at the Zenith Campus must have been done for the benefit of Earthlings. He still found Hearthlings' silence en mass to be disturbing.

Dan missed being able to eavesdrop on strangers' conversations. He felt alien, having to voice his thoughts and having others forced to do the same for his sake.

Abiona was acting as a tour guide when Dan noticed something. Hearthlings were staring at them as they passed. Dan asked Abiona about it.

"They can tell you are not a Hearthling."

"Is it because we are speaking?"

"That is what draws their initial attention."

"Is it because they can't read my mind?"

"That, too. Your aura also gives you away. My fellow Hearthlings were speculating if you were one of the Earthlings they had heard about. I mentioned that you were—telepathically, of course."

Dan nodded, not at all surprised by Abiona's answer. Being viewed as a curiosity was becoming the norm for him. "I'm surprised they didn't want a closer look at me," Dan wondered aloud.

"Hearthlings would not be so rude. They would only introduce themselves under these circumstances, if invited. I did not extend that invitation. Unless you wanted me to, Mr. Celebrity," Abiona said with a smile.

"No!" Hearthlings passing nearby looked their way. "No thanks," Dan said, having lowered his voice.

Abiona was giving Dan a brief history of Mattatuck as they stood on the corner of a busy intersection near the entrance of a high-rise office tower. Dan took in the modern architecture, admiring the efficient city planning that managed to include a number of well-placed urban parks.

As was the case at the Zenith Campus, there was a bustling of humans, androids, drones, and IVAs. More Hearthlings were smiling and nodding at Dan as they passed. Dan asked Abiona what was going on.

"Your aura is changing, Daniel. I noticed a change at your surprise party. It is becoming stronger; exhibiting a more positive glow. More like that of a Hearthling aura."

Dan could not help but smile at the news. Dan could feel himself becoming a part of the Hearthling energy surrounding him. It was a warm, echoing reverb that seemed to fill him to overflowing.

Out of embarrassment and modesty, Dan detoured the conversation to traffic. Abiona explained to Dan why there were no personal vehicles on the roads. They were unnecessary. There were ample shuttles to take anyone anywhere they wanted to go within Mattatuck if they choose not to walk. That was a practical idea that continued to meet with resistance in his own country on Earth.

"Free of charge?" Dan asked about the shuttles.

"No cost, if that is what you mean by that expression."

Dan froze. His face exhibited shock. "Look at those people over there!" he said in a loud whisper.

Abiona glanced in the direction Dan was staring. She saw what appeared to be a family of five. Two adults, two teenagers, and a preteen.

"What about them?"

"They're nude."

"I can see that."

"Aren't there laws against public nudity on Hearth?"

"No. Should there be?"

"Of course!"

"Why?"

"Because … they're nude! Don't you find their nudity obscene?"

"You say that as if the human body is some sort of abomination, Daniel. Do you find the human body obscene?"

"I don't feel that way at all. It doesn't mean I want to see anyone's body who chooses to put his or hers on display."

"Do not look."

"How can I not look? They're nude—in pubic!"

"Turn your eyes away from them, if their bodies offend you that much. You would think Earthlings would have more to concern themselves with than whether or not people are wearing clothes."

"What about the children?" Dan turned in place, seeing children everywhere.

"What about them?"

"They shouldn't be exposed to this."

"Exposed to what, Daniel?"

"Public nudity."

"Why not?"

"Because … it may be harmful to their development."

"There have been Earth studies to confirm your assertion?"

"None that I'm aware of."

"Look around you, Daniel." Dan did as Abiona asked. "Do you see anyone, including children, showing any concern (aside from you) about that nude family?"

Dan took a moment before he answered honestly. "No, I can't say I do."

"Your logic escapes me, Daniel. We have entire communities who are naturalist. They are tribal, in that respect. You have tribes who wear little or no clothing on Earth."

"That's different. All industrialized and civilized nations, by and large, do not practice nudism."

"Who decided that naturism was indecent, on your planet?"

"Society in general accepted nudism to be improper."

"Earthlings, as did Hearthlings (if you believe in evolution as we do), evolved from tribes who existed as tribes. Clothing came about not out of shame regarding our bodies, but as a means of protection against some of the harsher elements. Since Earthlings progressed in the same manner, then at some point in your history, decisions were made by certain Earthlings to demonize naturism."

"You have beautiful clothes."

"Yes, but they do not define me. They are simply things."

Dan knew nudists—people who celebrated the natural human body in all of its stages, from young to old. He had always found the subject taboo. He respected and believed that the human body was an amazing biological achievement.

When it came to putting it on display, Dan much preferred baring it all in private. His wife had no such hang-up. Toni had constantly paraded around the house nude before the children were born.

Dan could only answer to the current parties involved in perpetuating that notion. Historically, he could not say.

"Wearing clothing is like being in a package, Daniel. People may become curious about what is underneath. When the clothing—or packaging—is removed, the mystery is gone. Strip away that wrapping long enough and we naturally move past the physical and seek other means by which to connect—if we choose to do so at all."

"It is relative. Would you not agree?"

Dan had heard similar arguments from Earth nudists. "I agree in theory, but not in practice, Abiona. Public nudity is taboo, to me."

"You are free to make that choice for yourself, Daniel. You are not free to force your views upon others. Look away, if public nudity troubles you. Do you equate nudity with sex?"

Dan shrugged his shoulders. "I suppose I do."

"You do realize there is no correlation. To do so is mental conditioning. If four physically identical women stood before you nude, right now, you would be attracted to one over the other three."

"Assuming I found the women attractive, what you say is true."

"Why one and not the others?"

"Something about one of them would stand out. Something distinctive."

"Which says more about you than the women."

"True again."

"Need I remind you of what drives pure sexual arousal, Daniel?"

"Apparently you do, Abiona, because I'm not getting the point."

"Inherited sexual response patterns and societal influences."

"Okay?"

"My point being: nudity in and of itself is not a sexual trigger."

"What about our natural drive to procreate? That is genetic; not mental conditioning."

"There are no better examples than teenagers going through puberty. The instinct to procreate may culminate in nudity, but does not begin there. Pubescence through adolescence earmark a lot more developments than sexual feelings.

"If nudity was the primary means of physical attraction, then why does one female or male chose another male or female over another in societies were nudity is the norm?"

"Aren't they cold?" Dan said, refusing to give in to Abiona's argument.

"Clearly not." Abiona paused for a moment. Her expression was a mixture of curiosity and confusion. She looked deep into Dan's mystified eyes. "Perhaps it is because we are born and bred telepaths. Thoughts—even of a sexual nature—are laid bare to us. They seem more of a curiosity we explore mentally without taking a physical step unless we chose.

"We are educated about our bodies and those of the opposite gender. We are taught the biological lessons of what it is to be human. I suppose that being indoctrinated in such a manner constitutes our views—and those of my fellow Hearthlings—on human nudity, as your upbringing has done for you."

Abiona was correct and Dan knew it. It boiled down to indoctrination. He had been taught that public nudity was wrong from as far back as he could remember. It was a sin in the eyes of religion and indecent in the eyes of the law.

Dan could not find the words to express his irritation. "If public nudity is permitted, then why do most Hearthlings wear clothes?"

"Because we chose to, as that family has chosen to be nude."

"Are you telling me that anybody can go about nude at any time of their choosing?"

"Except on special occasions or events that require clothing, such as formal affairs often do, then the answer is yes. Anyone is permitted to go about naked if they wish."

"Wow!" Dan said, watching the nude couple disappear into a department store after having done some window-shopping without drawing a single accusatory glance. "Have you ever ventured out into public nude, Abiona?"

"I have, as has every member of my family."

"And you didn't fill self-conscious?"

"About what?"

"Being nude in public."

"Nudity in public or private—what difference does it make?"

"It makes a world of difference."

"How so?"

"Well ... because ... it's indecent."

"We are back to calling the human body indecent. You were not born with such a stigma. I am curious as to what manner of teachings precipitated such views."

"I don't know. It is a general precept of our society."

"American society."

"Yes."

"Do the rest of the humans of your world share the same anti-nudity belief system?"

"I can't say for certain, but I would say most."

"Just when I think I have Earthlings figured out, you prove me wrong, Daniel Bluford."

"Thanks ... I think."

"I promise that, during your stay, I will not have any display of public nudity. I will even refrain from my typical nude sunbathing."

"I appreciate it," Dan said. "And the rest of your family?"

"You mean Mayowa and Ifelayo?"

"Yes."

"I will ask them to do the same. They do have free will. If they chose to parade around au-natural, then that is their choice."

Dan felt uncomfortable at the thought of Mayowa and Ifelayo parading around in the nude. He thought of Wick and Mae, and how he had not seen his own children without clothes since they started bathing themselves. He could not imagine being in a house filled with nudists, let alone public nudity.

"We have dedicated events and days to naturism. It reminds us of our most basic selves. It is quite liberating. You should try it sometime."

The most shocking thought came to Dan.

Maybe he would.

CHAPTER 36

Abiona and Dan spent the entire day walking around the city. Abiona educated Dan about the rich and cultured history of Mattatuck. Dan drank in the sights, sounds, and smells like an elixir; a heady concoction that made him dizzy on Hearthling energy, beautiful architecture, and remarkable engineering encompassed within efficient urban design.

Dan asked Abiona why there were no high-rise buildings. Abiona explained that international law forbid any structure to be more than twenty stories high. She did not know the reasoning behind such a limitation.

Dan speculated that, since Hearthlings had flying vehicles, any time they wanted a view from up high, access was available. Dan asked Abiona to confirm his speculation. Abiona agreed that it might be a possibility, but believed there was more behind the law than that. She advised they ask a city or urban planner to learn more. Dan liked the idea.

Abiona mentioned that one of each happened to live in their neighborhood, reminding Dan that they had met at his surprise party. Abiona was certain that both of them would be happy to answer any questions Dan might have on the subject, over dinner.

They stopped for lunch at Vegano, a restaurant Abiona was fond of when she was in the city. The staff knew Abiona by name. For Dan's sake, they spoke aloud to Abiona and Dan while still engaging telepathically with each other.

Abiona placed their orders with Dan's permission. The service was gold-star. Dan had what he self-ordained as an international palate. Due to his world travels for business, and their family's constant cravings for overseas vacations, he had tasted food from many regions.

The meal turned out to be what Dan would describe as the best Portuguese food of his life. Hearthlings had no such ethnic distinctions in their cuisine, despite dish names defining their origins.

After a lunch that had Dan ready for a siesta, they continued their walking tour, exploring the southern portion of Mattatuck. The sky had cleared, bringing with it a deeper chill still a few Celsius shy of cold.

Abiona had taken Dan's arm during much of their tour, making them appear as a contented couple enjoying a stroll. Dan was uneasy walking arm-in-arm with Abiona, at first, but did not have the courage to speak up.

After their talk in Duke, Dan believed that Abiona had come to respect his position. Dan was acquiescent to the situation.

A few minutes into the second leg of their city tour, Dan found himself holding Abiona's hand, feeling at ease with her soft, firm, warm fingers entwined in his while imagining it was Toni's hand.

He enjoyed Abiona's personal attention as much as the tour. Dan even managed to stop gawking at or commenting on the occasional nudists they encountered along the way.

Dinner was at another of Abiona's favorite restaurants, Gentle Shores, where they once again received excellent service. Dan was given the same thoughtful consideration there that he had enjoyed at Vegano, a form of treatment he was now calling 'Earthling Protocol'—a term he would further define in one of his journals as Hearthlings' deliberate showing of respect for their Earthling exchange students; a part of which is verbal communication.

Gentle Shores was an elegant, romantic restaurant filled with soft lighting and soothing instrumental music that surrounded diners like a cozy blanket. The menu was French.

Hearthling French fare was little different from that of Earth, in its dishes. Dan felt comfortable ordering for himself, French food being one of his favorites back on Earth. The bouillabaisse was the best Dan had ever tasted.

"Delicious!" was Dan's repeated refrain as he savored his meal between stimulating conversation with Abiona. He concluded that he'd had never had better French food on Earth.

"I thought we would spend the night in the city," Abiona said, after they had roamed the city for another hour, upon leaving Gentle Shores. She led Dan into the spacious lobby of the Himmel Hotel, a place that, by all appearances, Dan would refer to as a "luxury hotel."

"Sure," Dan said, feeling awkward and curious at the same time. He gazed about the palatial lobby as they approached the front desk. It reminded Dan of some of the opulent places he had been to on Earth.

They entered a magnificent room on the top floor of the hotel. Dan would call the room the Presidential Suite, but Hearthlings had no such designation. The room had a panoramic view of the illustrious city skyline and beyond. Vehicle taillights glowing like mechanical fireflies in the silken, blue night sky.

"How did you manage to swing this?" Dan asked, standing beside Abiona, both of them admiring the view. Abiona reclaimed Dan's hand. Dan had no objection. He would have taken her hand had she not done so.

"I mentioned to the hotel manager that I would be bringing a special guest into town."

"You didn't happen to mention I was an Earthling, by chance?"

"I did. I asked her if I could show you the best view of the city. She was happy to oblige."

"How do hotel reservations work on Hearth? With no need for payment and the like."

"You contact the place you would like to stay, tell them how many people will need a room and for how long, and they reserve it."

"Sounds like a regular reservation—absent any payment."

"Most Hearthlings stay with family, friends, or even acquaintances when they travel. Hearthlings stay at hotels more for the experience rather than out of necessity."

"Then, why have hotels at all, Abiona?"

"Why not, Daniel? I have found hotels to come in handy, on occasion—if you do not want to put someone out for whatever reason, for instance. Staying at a hotel resolves that concern."

"Do you have motels?"

"What are motels, Daniel?"

Dan loved the way his name rolled off Abiona's tongue, like ice-cold lemonade into his thirsty ear.

"Roadside accommodations for motorists," Dan answered.

"We have something similar. We call them 'motor courts.' They are established in areas that are scarcely populated for stops between long trips or places to stay nearer regions that are natural and only permitted minimal human disturbance." Abiona slipped her hand from Dan's. She put her arms around his waist as they continued to admire the view.

"Why do I get the feeling you've been here before, Abiona?" Dan said, wrapping his arms around her.

"Kwasi and I have, on occasion, occupied this room," Abiona whispered into his ear. Dan's breathing quickened and his heart raced. "A little getaway, if you know what I mean, Daniel."

Abiona gave Dan a sly wink and a smile. Dan knew exactly what she meant. He would have to be a simpleton not to.

Dan wanted Abiona. He'd ached for her during his most private moments. Dan had fallen in love with Abiona. Whether it was due to her eerie star-twin resemblance to Toni or Abiona herself, he desired her just the same.

"Only you and Kwasi?" Dan asked, playing along and bearing in mind Hearthling views on monogamy.

Abiona ran a lithe finger along Dan's cheek and along his chin, circling his mouth and soul gazing, her enchanting brown eyes finding connection with his spirit. "Until now," Abiona said in a seductive whisper that made Dan's breathing deepen.

Dan felt as though he were on a dizzying cliff when Abiona kissed him. Abiona paused, soul gazing again. One step forward and he would fall into the abyss of her desires. There would be no moral salvation; no virtuous arguments to justify his actions.

"Say my name again, baby." Dan had meant to say Abiona, but the affectionate reference slipped from him like the voice of longing. Abiona kissed Dan again. She moved her lips close enough to brush his ear.

"Daniel, Hearthlings have a saying," Abiona crooned, her voice a perfect match to Toni's. "Do not hate your body for telling you the truth."

Abiona's full, soft lips pressed firmly against his. Her hand rested behind his head with a gentle grip that would not allow Dan escape from her hunger. Dan's lips parted with a pleasurable sigh and Abiona's tongue invaded his mouth, exploring every area of Dan's cavity for pleasure zones.

Dan placed his hands on Abiona's waist with the intention of pushing her away. Instead, he found himself pulling her closer, pressing their bodies tight. Their tongues and lips synchronized in a lustful modern dance and the last resolve of his resistance was burned away by the heat of their passionate kissing.

The rest was a blur, for Dan, of undressing and mutual oral stimulation that culminated in amazing ... what Dan would later call lovemaking and Abiona would refer to as sex.

Abiona's body was exquisitely fit from regular exercise and genetic blessings. Her brown skin was soft and silky-smooth. She had a birthmark on her inner right thigh in the same place as Toni's, the difference being that Toni's was in the silhouette of a small bird while Abiona's was in the shape of a fig leaf.

Kwasi was in the shower at the end of the day.

"Mind if I join you?" Toni asked.

"Not at all."

Dan witnessed their passionate embrace; the mounting fever of their kisses; the water flowing over their nude undulating bodies. This time, the experience felt more like a dream than a Residual Connection.

Abiona and Dan bathed together in the large bathtub Dan jokingly referred to as a wading pool: lovers having playful fun after their hot embers of passion had cooled. Then they fell into a blissful sleep in the warmth of each other's arms.

CHAPTER 37

Abiona and Dan's return trip home the next day in Duke was cheerful. Dan awoke that morning contented, as he did after the best nights of love-making to Toni. Dan had no doubt that his recent Residual Connection with Kwasi had everything to do with his lack of nuptial guilt.

What Dan found most interesting was that Abiona appeared to be no different. She had the same glow she always had. Her personality was as pleasant as ever, her candor notwithstanding. Abiona exhibited no more or less affection toward Dan. It was as if nothing had changed between them; as if their night of passion was as normal to her as sharing a laugh about an amusing story.

"Did you take me to Mattatuck to seduce me?" Dan asked, the question coming to him like a sudden STOP sign around a blind curve.

"Of course not, Daniel. I could have seduced you at home, if that were my intent."

"Feeling that confident in your seductive powers, are you?"

"Yes. Although I will admit, as I have gotten to know you better, my physical attraction to you has increased. Being alone with you in Mattatuck aroused my attraction into action."

Again, Abiona spoke in that matter-of-fact tone that intrigued and sometimes annoyed Dan, leaving him speechless on the subject for the remainder of the trip.

Monday was routine, for the most part, in the Gaige household. Mayowa and Ifelayo were escorted to their school shuttle by their mom. Dan updated his journal on his latest events and discoveries, including their night of passion. Dan and Abiona had a delicious breakfast together, prepared by Abiona, Abiona's IVA house servant Walter being tasked with his usual breakfast clean-up.

The doorbell chimed and Abiona answered.

"Daniel," Abiona said to Dan from the doorway of the study. Dan had wondered into the study, only to find himself leafing through a fascinating book on the rudiments of Virtual Engineering that was light years ahead of anything on Earth. Dan halted his reading, returned the book to its place on the shelf, and joined Abiona.

Standing next to her was Mehdi Abadi, a well-groomed, handsome man with laughing brown eyes and a pleasant demeanor. Mehdi had attended Dan's surprise party.

He was one of four physical trainers available to the Golden Eagle community (physical trainers were a government requirement for every Hearthling community). The two men greeted each other as Hearthlings with a curt nod.

"Nice to see you again," Dan said to Mehdi. Mehdi stared back at Dan with a faint smile.

"Please voice your thoughts around Daniel, Mehdi," Abiona said. "Remember, he cannot read our minds."

"My apologies, Daniel," Mehdi said, his voice deeper than Dan remembered. "Nice to see you again, as well. A group of us are taking a hike. We would like to know if you and Abiona would like to join us."

"Sounds like fun," Dan said. "Does Kwasi have hiking gear I can borrow?" Dan asked Abiona.

"My husband had planned on replacing his old hiking gear but never got around to it before he left."

Dan and Mehdi followed Abiona into her home office. From her computer, Abiona ordered everything Dan needed for hiking. The items were teleported to them within minutes. Dan was geared up and ready to go in no time.

Another example of how Hearthlings have surpassed Earthlings in the convenience of modern living, Dan mentally noted, contemplating how he was going to incorporate some of this marvelous technology back on Earth for Single Organism.

Mehdi and Dan met up with the rest of their hiking party, Gessica, Sahan, Madison, Seguin, and Aleja, at the Golden Eagle Recreation

Center. It was a healthy group of men and women of different sizes, shapes, and colors. Neighbors. A melting pot of Hearthlings.

It was a blend Dan was becoming pleasantly accustomed to seeing everywhere he went on Hearth. Everyone was glad to see him. Abiona was unable to join. She had a round of conference calls with members of her department that required her input.

"Do not worry," Mehdi had informed Abiona. "We will take very good care of Daniel."

"I have no doubt of that," Abiona had replied. Dan felt equally confident in his Hearthling hosts, for reasons he could not explain.

They were going to nearby Naugatuck Forest for their hike. Dan had admired the Naugatuck Forest from his bedroom window from afar. He had wondered how much it resembled the Connecticut, Naugatuck Forest that he was familiar with back on Earth.

His initial impression as their shuttle flew over the forest was it appeared richer and fuller than did its Earth namesake. More pristine than what Dan could remember.

Their shuttle landed in a northern clearing. A wildlife greeting party was awaiting their arrival. All types of animals and birds, from an enormous black bear to tiny brown sparrows, populated the group. Dan found himself both fascinated and unnerved by the gathering, not knowing what to expect.

"This is a surprise," Dan said to Mehdi about the wildlife reception, as they disembarked.

"They knew we were coming," Mehdi replied. "We cleared our hiking permit with the Wildlife Committee a week ago."

The wildlife assemblage calmly pressed forward, led in flight by two ravens. Dan recognized their leaders, Nodin and Vaclava. Dan was beginning to accept his communication limitation. He needed to be patient when telepathy was in play. Those involved would eventually include him in the conversation.

Nodin and Vaclava verified that the agreed-upon trails were still acceptable. The telepathic conversation turned to the real reason the wildlife reception was assembled.

A number of the forest inhabitants wanted to get a firsthand look at a fabled Earthling, Dan was told by Mehdi, who had been informed by Nodin.

"They want to know if they can examine you. Nothing clinical; simply a closer look."

Dan looked around at the gathering of beasts, fascinated, more than anything, at seeing such a varied group of creatures in peaceful coexistence. How could he refuse? Dan nodded his consent.

The wildlife studied, touched, and sniffed at Dan. Like a willing lab specimen, Dan stood still. There was constant chatter coming from the animals. Dan asked his fellow hikers, "Do they understand each other?"

"Yes," Mehdi answered.

"In the wild," Seguin continued, "they are what we humans would call multi-lingual. All wildlife understands each other."

"Why we do not speak their languages," Gessica added. "Their thoughts are coming through quite clearly."

"They are commenting on the differences between you and Hearthlings, Daniel," Madison said.

"Such as?" Dan asked.

"How you smell, feel, and even look," Mehdi said.

"Some have commented that your skin and hair feel the same, but are not as radiant as Hearthlings," Aleja said.

"Your body is strong, like most Hearthlings," Seguin said. "However, there is a faint stench about you they cannot seem to place. Like that of a decaying corpse."

"Gee, thanks," Dan said.

"I am only repeating what some of the wildlife is thinking, Daniel."

"Overall, Daniel," Mehdi said, "they are unimpressed."

"They were expecting more drastic differences between you and us," Gessica said.

"Like a third eye, or an extra appendage," Dan said jokingly.

"Actually, yes."

The Wildlife collective backed away from Dan like a crowd disappointed by a carnival exhibit that did not deliver on its promise.

"Nodin and Vaclava thanked Dan for his tolerance," Mehdi relayed. "They hope we enjoy our hike."

Before Dan could respond, the contingency dispersed into the wilderness. "What happens next?" Dan asked.

"They will spread the word about you," Mehdi said. "What they have learned. Their impressions. Before you know it, news of Daniel the Earthling will have dispersed through Naugatuck Forest like mist in a dream."

"I've heard that Hearthlings can communicate with reptiles and fish. Is that true?"

"It is true, Daniel," Madison answered.

"Can animals communicate to fish and reptiles, as well?"

"Reptiles directly communicate with wildlife and are regarded as part of their family," Seguin responded. "Aqualife and wildlife have translators amongst themselves."

"There are animal and fish translators."

"That is correct," Gessica said.

"How does that work? Do fish and animals go to some kind of academy to learn how to communicate with each other? Is that also done telepathically?"

"We do not know the specifics on how aqualife and wildlife translation works," Aleja said. "We do know it is verbal, not telepathic."

"We can connect you with Hearthlings who are well versed on the subject of wildlife and aqualife communication, Daniel," Mehdi said, "if you are interested."

"That's alright. I was just curious."

Dan was dumbfounded. He was having trouble accepting that what they were saying was possible. He still had not gotten past humans and animals communicating telepathically.

To discover that animals talked to each other and that fish and reptiles communicate with animals. Dan could understand these things in theory, but to bear witness to the actual process was beyond his Earthling comprehension. "Wow," was all Dan could say.

"'Wow' as in you are amazed, Daniel?" Sahan asked.

"Definitely amazed." The Hearthlings looked at Dan with blank stares. "You're not amazed by any of this?"

"We have lived our entire lives with 'this', as you put it," Mehdi said. "For us, this is normal."

"I'm envious of your normal." Again, with the blank stares. Dan's hiking companions remained silent. Dan knew they were having telepathic conversations. Were their conversations centered on his admission of envy, or something more? He was curious, but exercised his newfound patience.

"We consider envy a negative characteristic, Daniel," Mehdi said.

"We prefer the term 'respect,'" Madison added.

"Respect, it is," Dan said. "I respect your normal."

"Good, and thank you, Daniel," Gessica said. All of the Hearthlings smiled and approvingly nodded at Dan. Seguin and Aleja patted Dan on the back.

"Ready for that hike?" Mehdi said with the gracious smile of a seasoned diplomat.

"I suppose," Dan said with derision. Everyone stared at Dan, not comprehending his sarcasm. *Mental note to self,* Dan thought. *Tone down the sarcasm. Think, but don't speak.* "I'm ready."

"Great!" Mehdi said enthusiastically.

The group surrounded Dan, giving him plenty of space to see and maneuver within their ragged circle.

"What are you doing?" Dan asked.

"As we have said before, no harm will come to you on Hearth," Mehdi said. "You are under our protection."

"I thought there was nothing to fear."

"There is nothing to fear from us, Daniel," Aleja said.

"Wildlife is not under our control," Gessica said.

"They make their own decisions for their own reasons," Seguin said.

"Should they collectively, or individually, decide you are a threat..." Sahan said.

"They might mean you harm," Madison concluded, as if the whole conversation was one uninterrupted thought.

"I see," Dan said. Again, with the blank stares. This time, they made Dan uneasy. He glanced around the forest, attempting to spot possible threats to his life.

"Do not worry, Daniel," Mehdi said. "We will protect you. Let us be off!"

The group moved as one, allowing Dan to set the pace. Dan found his edginess dissipating as the sights and sounds of the glorious forest soothed him.

Dan always experienced peace when he was out in nature. He felt connected to life in the wild, as if he was linked to the womb of his genesis birth.

Dan felt as though he were home. Not in the familiar sense, like the home, he had made with Toni, but something less complex and much more chi-oriented. Dan found himself speaking less and observing more as calmness settled in. His companions had no problem following in his footprints of verbal silence.

A family of pumas crossed their path about 10 meters ahead. A male, female, and four cubs. The family halted.

"Are those mountain lions?" Dan asked, breaking their silence and staring at them in disbelief. Mountain lions had not been a part of the wildlife group that examined him.

"That is another name for them, but yes, Daniel, they are," Mehdi answered, not the least bit disturbed by their sudden appearance.

"Do you have mountain lions on Earth, Daniel?" Seguin asked.

Dan thought for a moment. He had never seen a mountain lion except in a zoo. There were no nearby mountains or forest for them to prey, where he lived.

"Yes," Dan finally answered, mesmerized by how ferocious the family of big cats appeared in the wild.

Like Mehdi, none of the other Hearthlings appeared concerned by their sudden appearance. Their large, wide-set eyes observed the hikers. The female and cubs continued on a few moments later, as if they had no interest in humans. The male approached. Mehdi stepped forward to meet him.

The male was huge—about 3 meters long and over 100 kilograms, Dan would have guessed. The male sat down on his haunches in front of Mehdi, appearing proud and majestic, his solid grayish-red fur coat pristine. Mehdi did not seem the least bit intimidated by the massive carnivore. Together, they walked back to Dan. The beast's predatory eyes fixed on Dan.

One of the Hearthling credos is "nature is balance." The group kept emphasizing that mantra to Dan at every opportunity during their hike.

Everything done within the natural world is to maintain a sense of harmony and balance. Nature is not concerned with individual organisms on Hearth or throughout the universe. Nature only seeks harmony and balance over the length and breadth of its domain.

"He is asking about you, Daniel," Mehdi said of the male puma. "He wants to know if you are the Earthling he has heard about. I told him that you are."

He let out a deafening roar that would have sent Dan scampering, if not for Seguin and Aleja holding him in place.

"What was that all about?" Dan yelped.

"It is his way of saying hello," Seguin said.

"Hello," Dan said in a quavering voice he did not recognize.

"He is wondering how Earthlings taste," Gessica said. The Hearthlings guffawed.

"I told him that he would no more taste an Earthling than he would a Hearthling," Mehdi said.

Nice to know humans can joke with carnivores about being devoured, Dan thought but did not say, holding fast to his commitment to eradicate sarcastic comments.

The big cat let out another thunderous roar, then got up and strutted away.

"What was that last roar about?" Dan managed to ask after an audible swallow.

"That was his version of a laugh, Daniel," Gessica said.

"Nice fellow, once you get to know him," Seguin said.

"You know him?"

"We have had some interesting conversations."

"We not only hike in the wild to commune with the forest, Daniel..." Aleja said.

"But we commune with wildlife, as well," Sahan added.

"So the mountain lion is not going to eat me?"

"Of course not," Mehdi said with a chuckle. "No harm will come to you by human or beast, here on Hearth."

"You didn't include fish and reptiles in your declaration." Dan was not being sarcastic.

"Fish nor reptile, either."

"How can you protect me?" Dan asked, ashamed at the quiver remaining in his voice.

"We have our ways," Madison said. "Do not fear."

Seguin and Aleja waited for Dan's shaking to subside before they released him.

"Shall we continue?" Aleja asked Dan.

All eyes were on Dan. His first thought was to ask them to take him home. Abiona's home; the safe comfortable place he now considered home. Dan tamped down his fear. He trusted these Hearthlings.

Before that moment, Dan had not fully realized he was willing to trust them with his life. Dan did not know if he could walk, but nodded. They resumed their hike. Dan was unable to reconnect to his earlier peace. The roar of the mountain lion and the joke about how he would taste kept replaying in his mind.

Dan was grateful for Occlumency pills. Had his companions had access to his thoughts, there would be no telling what opinions of him they might draw.

Back on the shuttle, everyone had buckled in when Sahan asked, "Tell us more about our Earthling cousins."

Dan's first thought was, *maybe you should ask wildlife*. He recalled his self-promise to eliminate spoken sarcasm from his mindset and instead simply asked, "What would you like to know?"

Dan was peppered with queries about Earth and Earthlings on the trip back. Some of the questions had become old hat. "Why do Earthlings pollute their planet? Why is your Earth rife with poverty and homelessness? Why do Earthlings possess weapons of mass destruction? Why do Earthlings abuse your scientific knowledge to produce chemical weapons? Why is there illiteracy? Why are Earthlings destroying their natural environment? Why does racism exist amongst your people? Why does race exist? Why do Earthlings murder each other? Why do Earthlings have wars? Why do Earthlings torture each other?"

Other questions were personal or innocuous.

"What is your Earth family like? What do Earthlings do for entertainment? What sort of sports do Earthlings play? Do you have any hobbies? What sort of work do you do? Do you enjoy it?" It was after the question "Do Earthlings like broccoli?" that Dan had an idea. He would have to run it by Abiona first, to see if his idea was feasible.

CHAPTER 38

By the time Dan returned from his hike, the children were home from school. Mayowa and Ifelayo were in their rooms, with friends. Dan headed for Abiona's office, anxious to tell her about his idea.

She was on a virtual call with multiple persons. Dan did not want to disturb Abiona, so he continued walking. The moment reminded him of his Earth home, as he passed by Abiona's office; the differences being that Dan would be on a video call and Toni would be looking in on him.

A pang of homesickness gnawed at Dan. He headed straight for his room. His thoughts were on Wick, Mae, and Toni. He wondered how everyone was doing and longed to be back in his Golden Meadows home, if only for a day, to check in on his family. He wished he could do the star-twin Residual Connection at will.

Dan made it to his room without having to speak to anyone, which turned out to be fine with him.

Abiona looked in on Dan about an hour later, to find him seated at his desk. Dan had showered and changed into a pair of baggy jeans, designer low-cut sneakers, and an oversized cotton sweatshirt: comfortable items that had accompanied him from Earth.

Dan had conjured up a laptop from his EP cube and was immersed in his writing. Abiona slipped in behind Dan, unnoticed until she rested her hands upon his shoulders.

"What are you working on, Daniel?" Abiona asked, staring at the laptop screen.

"I have this idea, Abiona." Dan said with the same enthusiasm that he had when he and his friends started Single Organism. Dan stopped what he was doing and turned his full attention to Abiona. Her hands slipped from his shoulders, falling gracefully to her sides, forced to do so by Dan's sudden movements of turning and standing. Her presence made him pause.

The night before, they had been lovers. In those moments, Dan felt as close to Abiona as he felt with Toni. There was love in his heart. Whether that love beat for Abiona or Toni or congealed into one did not matter at that moment.

His touch, his lust, and his passion were fueled by love, manifested in a boiling hunger that overflowed from him. He prodded himself. *Abiona is not Toni.* Still, Dan wanted to take her hands, as he would Toni's under these circumstances, but dismissed the notion.

"Now, hear me out," Dan said preemptively. "While Hearthlings are teaching me about your way of life and your planet, what is preventing me from doing the same for Hearthlings, about mine? But, on a broader platform.

"Most Hearthlings only know that Earth exists. They don't know about Earthlings or our history. It's from my interaction with the hiking party that I've decided to move forward with this idea. It's an idea I began considering at my welcoming surprise party—a means by which to educate ordinary Hearthlings about Earth.

"It could also serve as an opportunity to answer questions about Earth and Earthlings, correcting Earth and Earthling misconceptions."

"How do you propose to do that?"

"I want to start a forum."

"A forum?"

"A personal website."

Abiona's face lit up with hungry curiosity. "Tell me more, Daniel."

"I want to create an Earth Forum. A website designed to teach Hearthlings about Earthlings. A place where I can answer questions from Hearthlings about my world and my people. I may even be able to connect with other exchange students and add their perspectives and experiences, both on Earth and here on Hearth.

"I can also use this forum to help dispel misinformation about Earth and Earthlings that may be floating around." Dan smiled inwardly as he reflected on how disappointed the wildlife who had examined him had been to discover Dan was just another human, his flesh not living up to their myths.

"What do you think, Abiona?"

"I think it is a wonderful idea, Daniel!"

"I'm still hashing out the details."

"I am sure there is a lot for you to work out. Can I help?"

"Not at the moment, but thank you."

"My pleasure, Daniel. I do not mind saying that your idea is exciting!"

"We'll keep this between us for now."

"Of course. I will leave you to it." Before exiting, Abiona said, "Dinner will be ready soon. The children's friends will be going home, which means my darlings will eventually return their attention to you. Keeping this a secret from them will not be easy."

"You mean, they might read your mind?"

"I can compartmentalize our secret in a place you might regard as a mental lockbox. I am concerned about you. Once they get wind that you are up to something, they will not relent until they have answers."

"Good point. Any ideas?"

"Leave them to me. I will keep them at bay, for now. I cannot say for how long, Daniel. They have their father's tenacity."

"The tenacity you speak of comes from both of their parents, as far as I can see."

Abiona smiled as if she agreed. "I will do what I can."

"Thank you."

"Do not thank me yet."

Abiona left an ebullient Dan with that thought and he returned to feverishly jotting down details for his proposed Earth Forum.

*　　　*　　　*

Dan blurted out his Earth Forum idea to Mayowa and Ifelayo over dinner. Abiona was stunned.

"What happened to keeping this between us?" Abiona asked Dan. Dan shrugged, making a face as if he had been caught in a harmless lie.

"A what?" Ifelayo asked.

"An Earth Forum," Dan said.

"What is an Earth Forum, Mr. Bluford?" Mayowa asked. Dan explained what he had in mind. Mayowa and Ifelayo became even more excited about his plan than Abiona. Mayowa and Ifelayo offered Dan ideas about how to set up his Earth Forum website, spouting off web design terms that Dan only half followed.

The children seemed to notice Dan's confusion and offered to help Dan build his Earth Forum. Dan happily accepted their offer, proposing to compensate them for their efforts. Abiona, Mayowa, and Ifelayo looked at Dan, perplexed.

"What do you mean by 'compensate?'" Abiona asked.

"Repay Mayowa and Ifelayo, in some way, for helping me."

"It is our pleasure to help you, Mr. Bluford," Ifelayo said.

"We do not require compensation for lending assistance to a fellow human being," Mayowa added.

Abiona looked at her children with pride. "I could not have said it better myself, my darlings."

Dan was embarrassed. He had defaulted to what could be defined as a generous Earthling custom. Before Dan could apologize and explain that rewarding voluntary assistance was an Earthling tradition, Mayowa spoke.

"Even if he is an Earthling." Everyone exploded in laughter.

"I believe you have infected one of my children with your sarcasm, Daniel." Abiona said, in the wake of their laughter.

"It appears I have," Dan said.

"Sorry, Mom," Mayowa said.

"No need to apologize, son. Only, make certain you break yourself of the habit before your father returns."

"Do I have to?"

"You most certainly do. We are Hearthlings. We speak straight and true. We do not deal in sarcasm."

"Well, at least I will have until Dad returns. Can you teach me more about Earthling sarcasm?" Mayowa asked Dan.

"Me too," Ifelayo said, both children pressing forward with excited expressions.

Dan looked at Abiona. He had come to know Abiona well enough to read her, despite his inability to read minds. Her eyes said no.

Apparently, her thoughts were the same, since Ifelayo voiced, "Why not, Mom?"

"Sarcasm can be entertaining," Dan said. "Amongst Earthlings, it often is. We use irony to mask our true intentions or feelings.

"Have either of you looked up the word 'sarcasm'?" Dan asked the children.

They shook their heads.

"Do so, when you have the chance. I can recall an Earth dictionary definition of sarcasm: 'The use of irony to mock or convey contempt.' It would be nice to know if your dictionary defines sarcasm in the same way."

"You can teach us how to use it responsibly."

"I can't teach you something I have not taught myself, Mayowa. I have been indoctrinated with that way of thinking. In the same way, you have been indoctrinated into respecting your planet and fellow Hearthlings. Your mother's right. Sarcasm can become a bad habit. It's one I am trying to control in myself."

The children nodded at Dan as if they understood better than he did.

"No more sarcasm," Mayowa said.

"I agree," Ifelayo said.

"Me too," Dan said. Abiona, Mayowa, and Ifelayo erupted in laughter. Dan looked on with feigned shock. "What?"

"You were serious," Abiona said.

"Because we do not believe you, Mr. Bluford." Ifelayo said.

"Maybe," Dan said. Everyone laughed. For a few moments afterwards, the Gaige family and their Earthling guest ate in amused silence.

"There is still the matter of presenting your plan to the Exchange Student Program Committee, Daniel," Abiona interjected, breaking the mood.

"What do they have to do with this?" Dan asked.

"Everything," Abiona said. "This will have to be cleared by them before you can proceed."

"Do you think there'll be a problem?"

"I have no idea, Daniel. This is my first dealings with the Exchange Student Program Committee on such a matter."

"Perhaps I should write a proposal."

"That would help."

Dan appeared disheartened. Abiona read his mood. "I am sure we will be able to work something out. They seem very reasonable, to me. Do not worry."

Dan nodded. While he agreed with Abiona's assessment of the Exchange Student Program Committee, there was a twinge of doubt that nettled him regarding his Earth Forum idea.

What if they said no? Dan had known more successes than failures in his life, but he was no stranger to rejection. Dan began considering contingency plans.

"In the meantime," Dan said to Mayowa and Ifelayo, feeling rejuvenated by his own reasoning, "what do you say we get started on the Earth Forum website this weekend?"

"Why not after dinner?" Mayowa asked.

"There is the matter of homework which I know neither of you have done," Abiona said.

"After we have done our homework, Mom." Ifelayo said.

"Then you will shower. We will meditate and you will go to bed."

"Yes, Mom," Mayowa and Ifelayo said in unison. What surprised Dan was they did not pout or sound disappointed, as his children would have been. Instead, they seemed pleased, as if Abiona's decree was a gift instead of a command.

"Your mother's right," Dan chimed in, as he would to support Toni in the same situation. "There's no need to stray from your routine. I still have a number of details to work out before we'll be ready to build a website."

"First thing in the morning," Abiona said, "I will contact the Exchange Student Program Committee and issue your request, Daniel."

"I'll finish the proposal tonight."

"I hope they say yes," Ifelayo said.

"Me too," Mayowa added.

"Let us finish our dinner and go on with the rest of our day."

Dan, Mayowa, and Ifelayo nodded their agreement with Abiona.

CHAPTER 39

Abiona had a closed-door meeting with the Exchange Student Program Committee shortly after Mayowa and Ifelayo were off to school. Dan was not permitted to attend.

Abiona informed Dan that the committee was impressed by his proposal. However, they had stipulations they were going to impose before Dan would be allowed to move forward. The committee demanded complete control over the Earth Forum content. Everything Dan posted had to meet with a committee appointed representative's approval. Dan would be permitted a maximum of one hour per day of his choosing—excluding weekends—to answer Hearthling questions. Dan would be allowed another hour to post additional Earth and Earthling facts, with the same weekend restriction for content posting to apply.

Social media was different on Hearth than on Earth. Since Hearthlings were more technologically advanced, they often virtually connected through their cubes or other devices in the same way Earthlings connected on their smartphones. A personal website containing a blog was more what Dan had in mind.

A personal website like the one Dan was considering would be archaic, by Hearthling standards. He did not want it to be virtual. Dan felt that would distract him from addressing whatever issue was placed before him.

The committee concurred. Virtual connect was out. There would be no postings of digital recordings, photographs, or likenesses of any kind of Daniel Samuel Bluford or any Hearthling; most especially the Gaige family.

The committee emphasized "That the purpose for the Exchange Student Program is to give Earthlings an extensive overview of our beloved Hearth and our Hearthling way of life. We do this in order for Earthlings to return to Earth with an invigorated enthusiasm to battle for the salvation of their people and their planet.

"Spending time on a website, no matter how well intentioned, will not accomplish that goal. The committee wants Dan to be engaged with Hearthlings in the flesh and not cyberspace."

Dan's contingency plan for Earth Forum had been to use his EP cube to set up lectures and presentations that he would give at the community center. He asked Abiona if he could do so.

Abiona refused to help. She agreed with the committee's ideology regarding the Exchange Student Program. Immersion in their culture was imperative, if Dan was to learn and grow.

Dan was disappointed and surprised by Abiona's decision, considering how supportive she had been about Earth Forum.

Dan would be permitted to do local presentations and have in-person meetings with Hearthlings and wildlife on a limited basis. These meetings and presentations would be recorded and not shared with the general public.

In regards to having contact with fellow Earthling exchange students, the answer was a hard and fast no. Abiona went on to explain that the program separates Earthlings so they do not congregate, which would be the natural thing to do under the circumstances.

The committee wished Earthlings to be immersed in Hearthling culture, and Hearthling culture alone. If the committee felt in any way that Earth Forum interfered with the prime directive for him being here then the committee would terminate his website.

Should Daniel Samuel Bluford agree to these conditions, then he would be permitted to create and launch Earth Forum, provided each province granted their approval.

Dan was so excited when Abiona gave him the news that he hugged and kissed the messenger of glad tidings. Abiona was neither shocked nor embarrassed by his reaction. Dan was both. Dan darted from

Abiona's office to his room before he made the situation even more awkward for himself.

Provincial consents were granted within days of committee approval to proceed. Dan refined and narrowed his vision for his Earth Forum website in time for the weekend. While Abiona had a professional website, the children had helped her set it up. Abiona had no interest in social media.

Dan shared her attitude. Mayowa and Ifelayo had generated social websites for their personal use. Like many Earth children, young Hearthlings knew the software like the back of their hand.

Unlike Earth, Hearth did not have competing software or operating systems. Hearthlings had developed one for each function, that was continually updated and improved.

Holding fast to his clear vision, Dan was able to guide Mayowa and Ifelayo. Dan possessed marginal knowledge about computer programming. He discovered, by watching Mayowa and Ifelayo, that setting up his website was even easier than doing so on Earth.

Prepackaged software that was readily available on the Net was simple and efficient to use. The children generated the Earth Forum website based on Dan's instructions with ease.

Abiona notified the Exchange Student Program Committee that Dan wanted to test his website locally before launching it globally. The committee agreed. Abiona arranged for Dan to give a presentation about his Earth Forum in the Golden Eagle Community Center, a presentation Abiona and Dan billed as a surprise. Only Golden Eagle residents were invited.

The weekday meeting was scheduled to occur mid-morning, at a time that would accommodate most Hearthling schedules, and when the children were away at school.

Dan had given dozens of Single Organism presentations over the years. He always felt a nervous edge of excitement about them; the proverbial butterflies in his stomach. The kickoff meeting for his Earth Forum website held no exception.

There was the usual spread of hot and cold beverages and, in this case, fresh fruit and baked goods were provided to attendees. Dan did what he typically did when given the opportunity before a presentation: he mingled with the packed house of Hearthlings and wildlife representatives with Abiona by his side, something that could be referred to on Earth as schmoozing.

Dan always enjoyed the pre-game personal interaction most. Those moments gave him a chance to take the pulse of the audience. They granted him an opportunity to meter their expectations without giving away what was to come, allowing him to tweak his presentation to lean in a certain direction, if need be.

His pre-game interaction with Hearthlings and wildlife representatives provided Dan with no such indicators. The gathering was there to satisfy their curiosity about what the Earthling had to say, and nothing more.

"Thank you all for coming," Dan began. "I know you're busy. I appreciate your taking the time to attend this presentation. I won't keep you long.

"Welcome to Earth Forum," Dan concluded his opening after a dramatic pause.

Dan stood behind a wooden lectern stage to the right of a huge, wall-size virtual screen. An immense digital recording of a revolving Earth that Mayowa and Ifelayo had found online filled the space. Imposed over the image in big bold letters was the heading "Earth Forum." Beneath the heading, in smaller text, was the mission statement.

Dan pointed to the text with a laser pointer that also functioned as a wireless computer mouse and read the mission statement aloud. His wireless microphone was working perfectly.

"It is the hope by the creator of this forum to enlighten and educate Hearthlings about their genetic cousins from a distant galaxy.'

"Click anywhere on the homepage to enter the site," Dan went on to say. He demonstrated. A new webpage appeared, one with a digital fireworks display and rectangular rainbow-colored tabs across the top. A bit ostentatious, but that was what Dan was going for.

"Notice the tabs at the top of the page. Dan pointed to each prominent tab as he rattled them off. "'Questions, Answers, Earth, Earthlings' and 'Comments.' The 'Questions' tab is for any questions that Hearthlings, wildlife, and aqualife may have about Earth and Earthlings."

Dan selected the 'Questions' tab. A plain beige dialogue box appeared. The box had a 'Name' line with an empty box section beneath it. Centered beneath the box section was a 'Submit' button.

"Simply fill in your name and your question in the box section and press the 'Submit' button when you are ready to submit your question. The questioner will receive a personal response to their question. No one else besides myself and an Exchange Student Program Committee representative will have access to our communications. All types of Earth or Earthling questions are welcomed."

Dan demonstrated. He typed in his name from the wireless keyboard on the podium, then filled in the box with the question, "Do Earthlings like broccoli?"

There was an outburst of laughter and wildlife sounds as the audience read the question. Dan waited for their amusement to dissipate before continuing. He pressed the "Submit" button.

A default response resulted: "Thank you for your question. The Earthling, Daniel Bluford, will answer as soon as possible. Please be patient."

"No question is considered taboo or minor. I will do my best to give you direct and honest answers. If I don't know the answer, I will simply say I don't know, and direct you to Hearthling experts who can answer your question.

"The 'Answers' tab is next to the 'Questions' tab at the top." Dan clicked on the Answer tab. The sample question appeared, followed by the answer. Dan read the content aloud.

"'Question: Do Earthlings like broccoli?

"Answer: 'Earthlings are not homogeneous—not in our thoughts, beliefs, behavior, desires, or tastes in food. Some Earthlings like broccoli, while others do not. To eat or not eat broccoli is a matter of personal taste; unlike Hearthlings who, I am told, all enjoy vegetables.'

"In the 'Answers' section," Dan continued, "you will find a complete history of what has come before. All questions are anonymously posted. This would be a good place to check before submitting your question, to see if it has already been answered.

"Are there any questions about the Earth Forum site so far?"

Dan looked around the room. Since Hearthlings normally did not speak, there was no audible indicators on how his presentation was going. He could sense Hearthling interest by their rapt attention. Dan could not tell how the wildlife representatives were responding. He continued.

"Next to 'Answers' is the 'Earthling' tab. Here, I will post facts about Earthlings." Dan clicked on the Earthling tab. An Earthling fact appeared. Dan read it aloud.

"'Earthlings are the human inhabitants of the planet Earth.' Some of the facts may expand upon your questions. Others will be items I believe may be of general interests to Hearthlings, wildlife and aqualife."

Dan paused again. The room had not changed.

"Next to 'Earthling' is the 'Earth' tab. Here, I will post facts about my planet, both geographical and the effects of human activity." Dan clicked on the Earth tab and again read aloud what appeared.

"'Earth is the third planet from the sun in our solar system, orbiting between planets Mars and Venus within the Milky Way galaxy many light years from Hearth. Earth is identical, geographically and atmospherically, to Hearth.'

"Lastly, the 'Comments' tab." Dan clicked on said tab and a blank, milky-white page appeared. "As you can see, the 'Comments' section is currently empty. I don't expect that to be the case for long. This is a place where you can comment on anything from the answer to a question, Earth or Earthling facts or opinions, or share ideas about improving the website as long as your comments are centered on Earth, Earthlings, or the Earth Forum.

"Sidebar comments will be purged beforehand, assuring those comments will never appear on the website. The commentator will be notified directly as to the specific reason or reasons their comment was rejected.

"All of the web pages have a 'Search' box feature." Dan pointed to the magnifying glass icon in the upper right hand corner with his laser pointer. "This will aide in your quest to discover if any questions or topics you are curious about have been covered." Dan demonstrated. He said "Milky Way" and the words appeared in the search box.

After hitting 'return' on his laser pointer, the words *Milky Way* were highlighted within the displayed text.

"All input can be typed in or telepathically or verbally dictated. A 'Search' box has been placed on the homepage that will allow you to find text data throughout the entire site. Navigating your way around the Earth Forum website is as simple as that. Are there any questions?"

After a prolonged pause, Mehdi stood and asked, "When will your Earth Forum become available, Daniel?"

"I expect the Earth Forum site to launch within a couple of days upon approval from the Exchange Student Program Committee of my initial content."

Mehdi nodded then retook his seat, a precursor to the procedure that other Hearthlings would follow.

"What can we learn from you that we cannot learn from our Hearthling experts on Earth and Earthlings?" Aleja was the next to stand and ask.

"Firsthand insights. The type of knowledge that comes only from experience and can't be gained or duplicated from mere observation and study."

There were smiles and nodding all around the room. Nodin took flight, landing on Abiona's shoulder. "What can the wildlife and aqualife communities expect to gain from your Earth Forum?" Abiona asked on behalf of Nodin.

"You can learn of our shortcomings in dealing with our natural world. What mistakes we have made and some we continue to make, and what we are trying to do to rectify them."

Nodin bobbed twice, then flew back to rejoin Vaclava. There was silence, but Dan believed the wildlife representatives were pleased by his answer.

Madison asked, "Are we only permitted to ask you questions through your Earth Forum website about Earth and Earthlings, now?"

"No, of course not. You can ask me anything you'd like whenever we see each other."

"Why are you the first Earthling to come up with this idea?" Sahan asked.

Dan shrugged, wondering the same thing. "I don't know."

The audience burst into laughter, wildlife joining in their own ways. Dan knew the laughter was a result of what he had said earlier about how he would answer a question for which he did not have the answer.

"Are there any other questions?" Dan asked, sharing in their amusement. There was none.

"Each of you will receive hyperlinks that will allow you to link to the Earth Forum site," Dan said once the laughter ceased. "I would appreciate your honest feedback on your user experience. Any suggestions you might have to improve your user experience are welcome.

"Let me conclude by saying that I am only permitted to answer your questions for one hour per day, Monday through Friday. I will do my best to address your questions and comments in a conscientious and speedy manner.

"All answers, comments, and opinions stated on Earth Forum are my own. Should any of you discover mistakes in my reporting, please feel free to share them with me. I will update them on Earth Forum once they have been vetted and verified and then will send out a notification of the corrections."

Dan had written an official acknowledgement on the homepage, containing much of what he had said regarding his level of responsibility. The committee representative removed the disclaimer, deeming it unnecessary. When Dan asked about the possibility of lawsuits, he was reminded that civil lawsuits did not exist on Hearth—a fact he had forgotten from his teachings.

"If there are no more questions, this presentation is concluded. Thank you for coming. Enjoy the rest of your day."

Dan was shocked when he received a standing ovation. He looked over at Abiona, who was standing a few meters away. She was applauding along with everyone else, beaming with pride. Dan was ill prepared for the level of enthusiasm his Earth Forum website received. Everyone was clearly anxious to participate in the trial run.

"You're too kind," Dan said, raising a modest hand, visibly embarrassed. He gave up trying to quell the outpouring of praise after a couple of unsuccessful efforts. Dan waited patiently, giving intermittent thanks for the audience appreciation and feeling more like a part of the Hearthling community than ever before.

Afterward, he mingled with Hearthlings and wildlife that, for the moment, he felt more at home with than his own kin.

CHAPTER 40

The inaugural day for Dan's Earth Forum had arrived. Dan was excited and anxious. He hadn't felt this level of eagerness since he and his friends launched Single Organism. Abiona allowed Dan to use her husband's office. It was an impressive study that Dan was considering duplicating once he returned home.

Dan did not have to concern himself with watching the clock while he was on the website. He was automatically kicked off Earth Forum after one hour and was only granted access again after a twenty-four-hour period. Another hour of access was permitted Dan to post Earth and Earthling information, with the same limitations being enforced.

In the weeks to come, Dan discovered how serious the council was about maintaining complete control of the Earth Forum. Dan was permitted to see only one question at a time—a question of their choosing. Once Dan answered that question and hit enter, the question and answer dissolved from his screen. Then the next question would pop up.

Dan surmised that the council had determined if Dan had only one question to address. Then he would spend less time off-line, preparing answers for questions that he would later enter live onto the website. If the council had foreseen that possibility, then they were correct in their thinking.

Dan was notified by the council representative about a library dedicated to Earth and Earthling information that was digitally accessible. He was granted access, for the purpose of vetting his own Earth and Earthling site information.

Dan thanked the council representative and asked their name. The representative declined to give it, saying that it was not necessary for Daniel to know them by name. If he needed a moniker to refer to in their communications, CR (for Council Representative) would do fine.

Dan was amazed at the extent of Hearthling's Earth Library. It was chock full of Earth and Earthling information, from science to literature to history to philosophy and industry to news publications. Every area of study and interest was covered.

Associated with the Earth Library was an Earth Museum, a museum filled with Earth items that Hearthlings had brought back during their exchange, studies, or vacations.

Dan was surprised to discover a detailed biography about his involvement with Single Organism in the industry library section—one that had been penned by a Hearthling writer that Dan had never met (at least, not to his knowledge).

Mayowa and Ifelayo dominated the dinner conversation with accounts of their day, as usual. Their boundless energy matched that of his own Wick and Mae.

Dan marveled at their fresh view of the world. He had found himself wishing to be able to reconnect with such youthful optimism in the days before his exchange, to tune in to their positive perspectives for a recharge of what he had deemed possible. It was a commitment he'd felt oozing from his grasp, on Earth, despite his best efforts to improve planetary and human circumstances.

When the children finished, Dan asked the family gathering a question that had been nagging at him about the Earth and Earthlings digital library. The Gaige family admitted they were familiar with the Earth archives, as they called it.

Abiona said she had used the archives. She had written a couple of research papers juxtaposing Earth and Hearth histories during the same timelines.

The children confessed they only used the Earth archives when assigned a project that required information about Earth or Earthlings.

"Did you read about me in the Earth archives?" Dan asked.

"Yes," Abiona answered. The children nodded in agreement.

"What did you think?"

Abiona, Mayowa, and Ifelayo looked confused by the question. "We do not understand," Abiona said.

"Did you find my biography interesting?"

"Ah," Abiona said. "We were debating whether your question was centered on ego or vanity."

"Telepathically debating."

"Yes," Abiona answered.

"Both, if I were to be honest."

"Forgive us, Daniel," Abiona continued. "Hearthlings understand egotistical motivations, although we do not bow to them. We do not comprehend vanity. Hearthlings find it a wasted emotion."

"Yes," Mayowa answered. "We were impressed by your biography."

Ifelayo nodded, chewing a mouth full of vegetarian taco that she was obviously enjoying.

"You share similar backgrounds in science and engineering with their dad."

"Not only that, Mom," Ifelayo said, now able to speak having swallowed. "Mr. Bluford and Dad are trailblazers in their fields."

"They are creating inventions for the betterment of society," Mayowa said. "That is what impressed us."

Dan nodded, waiting for more to be said. No one at the table accommodated him. He looked around the table to discover everyone enjoying their meal. It didn't appear that their recent conversation was anything special.

"All we needed to know was contained in your information packet," Abiona said, breaking the verbal silence. Dan was certain they had been having another telepathic conversation about him.

"There is more information about me in the archives than in my information packet."

"True, in a professional sense," Abiona said. "The archives do not enlighten us on what kind of human being you are. That can only be discovered by personal interaction, as you eluded to in your Earth Forum presentation the other day. That person is who most interested us. Am I right, children?"

"You are correct, Mom," Mayowa and Ifelayo said in unison.

Dan thought about what Abiona said. It was true. Dan had read his online biography. His rise with Single Organism was covered. So were his professional and academic accomplishments. His awards and collaborative and independent inventions were listed. There was no mention of his personal life; not even a simple note about him being married, with children. It was sterile, factual reporting on deeds.

"Why have you not answered any of my questions on your website?" Ifelayo asked.

"Mine, either," Mayowa chimed in.

Dan looked at the children, amused. "You don't have to ask me questions through Earth Forum. I'm right here. You can ask me anything you like."

"Right," Ifelayo said, as if the idea had just occurred to her.

"Fill me in on what I've missed," Dan said.

*　　　*　　　*

Dan asked his CR if other exchange students had access to Earth Forum. He was told they did not. Other exchange students had been made aware Earth Forum existed and were permitted to view the website's content, but were not allowed to participate in any fashion.

The Exchange Student Program Committee believed that allowing other exchange students to do so would result in the tribal effect they were attempting to avoid, not to mention the strong possibility of mixed messaging.

Trolling, antagonism, and negativity were not Hearthling characteristics; although Dan could not be certain, since all Hearthling input was screened by the appointed CR. Dan had been prepared to weed out such questions and comments, as would have been a constant chore on free-speech Earth.

Dan was given pre-approval by his CR to front load the website with answers to some of the questions he had been asked in person. The broccoli question and his response were at the top of the list.

Question: "Do Earthlings like broccoli?"

Answer: "Earthlings are not homogeneous. Not in our thoughts, beliefs, behavior, desires, or tastes in food. Some Earthlings like broccoli. Others do not. To eat or not to eat broccoli is a matter of personal taste, unlike Hearthlings, who, I am told, all enjoy the vegetables."

Question: "Why is your planet rife with poverty?"

Answer: "The definition of poverty can vary from country to country. In the United States, where I am from, I believe it is safe to define physical poverty as having little to no income and few material possessions.

"Worldwide cheap, forced, and exploited labor is the norm. Many jobs are not paying what is referred to in my country as a living wage, or provide decent benefits, if any at all. People are abused in this manner to serve the wealthiest and most powerful of their nations, no matter what economic structure is in place.

It's a brutal reality that stretches from farmlands to industry, leaving remedying mass poverty on the shoulders of philanthropists or government agencies endemic with greed.

"It will take more than an unrelenting worldwide economic and government commitment to absolve poverty: it will take a change of Earthling hearts and minds to expel poverty from my planet."

Question: "How can Earthlings call themselves human when you commit inhumane atrocities against each other? Forced labor, slavery, and human trafficking ... these are but a few instances of the brutality of your world. Please explain."

Answer: "To my shame, I have no acceptable defense for these atrocities. There are a number of reasons given for these despicable practices. None of them are valid, in my opinion.

"The horrible crimes of slavery and forced labor have their roots in avarice, exploitation, and subjugation. They have been with Earthlings since before recorded history—cruel systems that reward only a few, in most instances.

They are granted license by the many who are willing to disregard or placidly accept the suffering of their fellow humans."

Question: "Why have Earthlings not done more to stop global warming on your planet?"

Answer: "Aside from the complex challenges posed in implementing strategies to curb global warming on our planet, there are resistant factors driven by politics, commerce, contrasting scientific data, and denial; to name a few that erect barriers to change.

"Since, at the root of limiting our human-caused climate crisis is modifying how Earthlings live, substantial global actions require global responsibility ranging from the individual to governments and businesses fully committed to acting in a cohesive manner to stem our critical situation.

"Some efforts are being made in some quarters to address this mounting crisis. In other quarters, little to nothing is being done. Time will tell if we are too late."

Question: "Why do Earthlings murder each other?"

Answer: "That is a very difficult question to answer. If, by murder, you mean homicide, then Earthlings have a variety of excuses for the intentional and unintentional unlawful taking of human life.

"Power, self defense, sexual attraction, revenge, intoxication, drugs, money, superego ... the list goes on.

"There are those who contend that we are predisposed killers, genetically encoded predominately in our males by our history of violence as an innate evolutionary curse. Others believe the obsession to kill is a mental defect or disease, born in some and bred in others, fostering an irresistible impulse to take a human life. This is the basis of most legal insanity pleas.

"Why so many senseless killings occur amongst Earthlings can be debated, although I can state with certainty, from what I have witnessed in our Earthling news reports on the grisly subject, that no one explanation fits all."

Question: "Why is there not more being done to stop pollution on your planet?"

Answer: "Stopping or minimizing pollution on our planet will be a never-ending battle, in my opinion.

"Unlike Hearthlings, Earthlings pollute whatever environment we inhabit. Raising our consciousness on this matter and taking actions to stop it is the only way that I foresee changing our course.

"I have extensively studied this subject back on Earth. We sometimes unfortunately detect some pollutions after the fact due to shortsightedness from not doing our homework or ignoring warnings for economic or convenience sake.

"This places us in the critical position of backtracking in order to remedy dangerous conditions (if such efforts are taken at all).

"Governments, businesses, and the public all contribute to the problems. Efforts are being made by each to change that trend.

"Single Organism is the company that I helped found. Our mission is to provide conscientious solutions for a wide variety of uses, with the environment at the forefront of our designs.

"More and more companies are thinking as we do, as are more people and governments. We are hopeful that, in time, we will be able to get a handle on these issues before it is too late."

Question: "Why do Earthlings have wars?"

Answer: "My father has a belief: that it is impossible to make peace with people who are not at peace with themselves. While I concur with his outlook, there are a wide range of reasons why Earthlings have gone to war.

"They include political, religious, ideological and economic differences, land, resources, power, prejudice and racism (from a grand sense of superiority), and perhaps the only reasonable motives for such violent conflicts, as efforts for freedom or liberation or to uphold peace and regain or maintain stability.

"All world wars were initiated by governments, for some of the reasons I have previously listed. Many civil wars can be traced back to those roots, as well.

"Wars, on my planet, can bind one nation against another, creating a sense of unity against a collective threat. I, am of course, simplifying why Earthlings persist in violent combat against each other, excluding personal issues by leadership with the authority to institute armed conflicts."

Question: "Why does racism exist amongst your people?"

Answer: "The psychology of racism is an ongoing worldwide debate. Self-interest, science, governments, and media have all contributed to legitimizing the persistence of this degenerate belief, justifying inequalities.

"Racism has been a malady of most Earthling civilizations. Why does this illness persist? I honestly do not know. It would require the reeducation of practically every person on my planet in order to purge this disease from our societies, in my opinion, since most of us have been infected in one form or another."

The first new Earth Forum question Dan received was, "Why are Earthlings destroying their natural environment?"

Answer: "In many cases, Earthlings are not aware of, or are dismissive about how their actions may have a negative effect on Earth's natural environment, in my opinion.

"Consumption behavior, agricultural and air pollution, water degradation, waste production, mining, plastic pollution, overpopulation, deforestation, landfills, and the depletion of resources are some of the contributing factors to the demolition of that which gives us life.

"Education is key. We must teach all to live in harmony with our planet, raising Earthling consciousness to a mindful level when it comes to our natural world and accepting responsibility for what we have sown, taking immediate, concerted action to globally resolve these issues as opposed to continuingly raping and looting our planet to fulfill our rapacious demands."

CHAPTER 41

Earth Forum. Question: "I have heard Earthlings have something called an economy. What is that?"

Dan recalled, from Professor Huaman's teachings on politics at the Zenith Campus, that Hearthlings regarded Earth as having no genuine democratic nations, citing the United States as an example.

"Free-market capitalism is dead in the United States. Monopolies and oligopolies have taken over, having in their pockets either financially or philosophically (and, in some cases, both) a majority of policymakers and law enforcement entities.

"As a result, the United States is a capitalist democracy. I emphasize 'capitalist' because private owners govern policy, permitting democracy when it either benefits or does not interfere with industry, trade, or personal fortunes."

Dan chose to draw upon his Earth teachings on the subject, responding from a purist's point of view.

Answer: "Simply put, an economy is the state of a nation in regards to its wealth in terms of its resources, production, consumption of goods and services, and currency. An economic system is an ordered way of fulfilling the needs and desires of the people. The manner in which these provisions are provided defines the type of economic system.

"Two predominate economic systems are currently utilized by Earthlings. They are: capitalism and socialism. In the United States, the region in which I live, modern capitalism is the reigning economic system.

"In theory, capitalism promotes private ownership, free market competition, and minimal government intervention. Nestled within this ideology are the expectations that, through incentives for the pursuit of personal profit and free market competition, society as a whole will prosper.

"Modern socialism takes the opposite approach for fulfilling the needs and desires of the people. Socialism is an economic system in which the government controls ownership and the means of production for the good of the collective.

"Cooperation, rather than competition, is encouraged. Personal profit is not a consideration under a socialist system. The needs of society transcend those of the individual.

"Some nations combine socialism and capitalism into social democracies, combining government-controlled industries with private property ownership.

"If you would like to learn more about the Earthling economic systems touched upon in Mr. Bluford's answer, there are volumes of Earthling texts written on the subject and its history. Please check with the Earth Resource Center for more detailed information."

The last paragraph was appended to Dan's answer by his CR. Information that would become a common refrain to a number of Dan's Earth Forum answers.

There were also comments that Dan found interesting. Amongst them:

"Something I find disturbing about Earthlings is what you are forced to fight for or against. The environment, poverty, illiteracy, and overall equality, to name a few. Qualities you should covet are means for combat. That is not a healthy mindset for a dominate species."

"Nothing moves forward in our society until their environmental impacts have been accessed and fully evaluated and deemed safe. How can Earthlings not think the same way?"

"Mr. Bluford, I read your answer to the question regarding an economy. I took a couple of courses on Earth studies at university and could not comprehend Earthling economics. 'An economic system is an ordered way of fulfilling the needs and desires of their people' helped clarify that for me in a way my studies never did.

"I will not delve into what I learned regarding the inadequacy of any of your Earthling systems to provide for the needs of the many. That fault seemed to lie more with selfish Earthling proclivities rather than economic theory.

"Hearthlings track the production and consumption of goods and services for resource purposes. They are not linked in any way to what you call 'profit.'

"There is no necessity for commerce in our society. There is no bartering system on Hearth, as well. Whatever your needs, they are met because you are a citizen of Hearth.

"One of my professors summarized Earthling gluttony this way: 'Where there is desperate need, there is a nurturing ground for greed.' I agree.

"Hearthlings are not a selfish or egocentric people. At no time do our needs venture into the excessive. We do not understand those motivations in Earthlings; nor do we care to.

"If you do not mind my saying, Mr. Bluford, the more I learn about Earth, the more blessed I feel to be a Hearthling."

"I am an Earth Studies major. Many things trouble me about the people of your planet. My studies have convinced me that, in order for Earthlings to survive, they will have to make drastic changes in how they treat each other and the planet.

"I was not convinced Earthlings were capable of doing so. You give me hope."

∗   ∗   ∗

At first, Dan found the five days a week, two hours a day limitation frustrating. Dan gradually accepted the stipulations and made the most of his web time.

Within a few weeks, Earth Forum became the most popular website on Hearthling internet, sparking an interest in Earthlings and Earth like never before. All questions and answers were in English, Dan's dominate language. Translations were handled by his CR.

Dan decided not to respond to any personal questions online. The few he had received, Dan declined to answer. He passed his decision regarding personal questions on to his CR; after which, he no longer received personal queries.

Between the Earth Forum and spending more time socializing with Hearthlings, Dan felt more and more at ease; more a part of the community.

Aside from the Gaines family, Dan developed other friendships. Dan became the adopted Earthling of the Golden Eagle community. Everyone looked out for him. There was no place in Abiona's community that Dan could go without receiving a friendly greeting and becoming engaged in a stimulating conversation (much of it more concerned about Dan's welfare, and if there was anything he needed from them).

He became friends with his regular hiking party of Mehdi, Gessica, Madison, Seguin, Sahan, and Aleja. So much so, that Dan suggested their hiking club—as he called it—take on a name, citing it as an Earthling tradition. None of his hiking mates was thrilled about the idea. Dan kept pressing until they finally conceded.

Dan started with the obvious one: The Pequannock Hiking Club. The party informed Dan that there were numerous Hearthlings in Pequannock Province that gathered and hiked in surrounding forests on a regular basis.

"What would distinguish us from them?" Mehdi asked. Dan agreed. Dan threw out other suggestions: Falcon, Naugatuck, Zenith, and Golden Eagle. None of them resonated with his hiking mates. They passed when he asked for input, making it clear it was Dan's idea. He should be the one to come up with a name.

Dan was about to give up when it came to him like a revelation. The Golden Gardens Hiking Club, Dan explaining to them that Golden Gardens was where he lived on Earth. It was the Earth equivalent, of sorts, to their Golden Eagle. They politely accepted the hiking club title, conceding to their Earthling guest if for no other reason, than to move Dan off the topic.

Dan also developed a kinship with local wildlife, Nodin and Vaclava being his continual connection (although none was as close to him as the Gaige family).

When Dan thought of home, these days, he thought of family, friends, and Hearth, and seldom about Single Organism or Earth.

Dan was not immune to Abiona's charms, no more than he was from Toni's. Dan needed a woman. He needed a lover. One thing Dan knew about himself is that he was never a one night stand type of guy. 'Love 'em and leave 'em' was not in his makeup, either.

Dan was turned off by women he disliked, no matter how physically attractive they were. He needed a connection with his lover; an emotional connection. That meant taking the time to get to know them.

Dan had gotten to know Abiona. Aside from Abiona's strong resemblance to Toni, Dan liked his wife's star-twin very much.

Being with Abiona was like experiencing the sweet beginnings of his romance with Toni. Dan wondered if he had fallen in love with Abiona. So, what if he had? Their relationship would be over in a matter of months. He would be back on Earth with Toni and Abiona would have Kwasi back.

Dan knew that Abiona would have no trouble adapting to the switch. How would he fare knowing his wife had been party to a spouse swap that she knew nothing about? How would Dan tell Toni about Abiona? Star-twins or not, Dan was not certain how Toni would react to such news.

It helped Dan to remember that he was supposed to keep Hearth a secret. Dan had already worked out how he would incorporate the engineering and scientific discoveries he had encountered on Hearth. He would simply credit them from having come from his own imagination, his biggest obstacle being that he was no good at keeping secrets from Toni.

Dan succumbed. Abiona and Dan became lovers, his matrimonial guilt fading until it vanished. His star-twin Residual Connection ceased, as well.

At first, the loss worried Dan. He was unable to engage with his Hearthling counterpart and felt as if he had lost touch with an intimate informant. He felt bad not just for his sake, but for that of his Earth family.

Dan contacted Dr. Bakari to discuss the matter. It was wonderful to virtually connect with his friend. After catching up on what had transpired in their lives since last they spoke, Jabori assured Dan that it was normal for the Residual Connection to cease, once the parties had settled into their new lives.

"Congratulations, Daniel!" Jabori exclaimed. "You are embracing your situation. That is wonderful! Welcome to Hearth!"

"How are my fellow exchange student graduates doing?" Dan felt compelled to ask.

"You will know soon enough. You arrived together, and you will be returning to Earth together."

Dan felt an unexpected wave of sadness ripple through him at the thought of leaving Hearth. Dan heard a voice he didn't recognize, informing Jabori that his next appointment had arrived. Dan wondered if the person Jabori was about to see was another Earthling.

"Take care, Daniel," Jabori said in haste. "I have to run. Feel free to contact me at any time for any reason."

Dan nodded in response, with an appreciative smile, before their connection was terminated.

CHAPTER 42

Earth Forum. Question: "Is there any real natural wildlife remaining on your planet? From what we have seen, much of Earthlings' view of nature is their facsimile of such."

Answer: "You make a good point. Much of what remains as wildlife on Earth is sparse in comparison to Hearth. Earthlings have a tendency to destroy whatever wildlife we encounter, be it intentional or unintentional.

"Modern habitat devastation on our planet occurs due to urban sprawl, manufacturing, mining, deforestation, agricultural methods, and livestock farming. All these often have adverse effects on wildlife and the environment.

"One gross example of direct Earthling catastrophic impacts on wildlife that readily comes to mind arises from the history of my own country.

"Throughout the 18th and 19th centuries, American bison were shamelessly slaughtered, reducing herds that totaled in the tens of millions to an estimated 1,000 by Earth's 1900s. The reasons for such butchery varied between sustenance, commercial sale, and sport.

"Another diabolical objective pinned to this wanton carnage was to deprive Native Americans—the indigenous people of the Earth country in which I live—of a vital means for their physical and spiritual survival, in an effort to force them onto reservations and into an agricultural way of life.

"Legal means to limit the problems humankind has forced upon wildlife and the environment are typically understaffed and underfunded, permitting offenders to continue with their practices knowing that the worst they will receive if caught, will be an insignificant punishment.

"Such legal impotence creates a forced reliance upon voluntary ethical practices of businesses and citizens to prevent such atrocities from occurring. That would work if every Earthling bore a personal sense of responsibility for Earth, as Hearthlings have for Hearth.

"Whether due to willful ignorance, apathy, or disbelief, most Earthlings do not."

*   *   *

"The Jaheem family gathering is next week, in keeping with semester break for the children," Abiona said as she and Dan strolled arm in arm around her neighborhood on a pleasant day. With no landscaping, construction or other noisy activities, the neighborhood was quiet. Serene. Peaceful. The sky was clear. Birds could be heard singing. A warm, steady breeze brushed their skins. "My parents invited you to join us, Daniel. Remember?"

Dan was slow to answer. He had been entranced by Abiona's company and the serenity of the day. It took a moment for him to remember that Abiona's maiden name was Jaheem. "I would love to," Dan finally responded.

"Good. The rest of the family cannot wait to meet you."

Dan had wondered—outside of Abiona's parents and in-laws—why none of the Jaheem or Gaige family had taken an interest in him. Abiona's parents made it a point to greet Dan and enquire about his wellbeing when they talked to Abiona and their grandchildren. Kwasi's parents did the same. None of the other relatives bothered.

Dan was never introduced to them or invited to join their conversations. Were they not curious about him? He certainly was about them. Dan found that behavior peculiar, given the amicable nature of Hearthlings. At the same time, Dan did not believe it was his place to ask about whether or not he was being snubbed.

*   *   *

The pristine and comfortable public transit shuttle from Mattatuck arrived at May Haven Station one hour and sixteen minutes after departure. The land/air vehicle spent most of its time in the air, where passengers encountered little turbulence on a partially cloudy day.

Aboard the half-filled transport were Dan, Abiona, Mayowa, and Ifelayo. Dan and Abiona were seated next to each other. The children sat across from them, facing the adults. Dan and the Gaige family had garnered attention by being the only passengers speaking aloud. Dan and his star-twin family had grown accustomed to being noticed for their vocal peculiarity outside of Pequannock Province.

The question was asked telepathically of Abiona if Dan was an Earthling. Abiona responded telepathically "yes" to the middle-aged man across the aisle. Next came the question from his traveling companion if Dan was the Earthling responsible for the Earth Forum website. Abiona again answered, "Yes."

News of the Earth Forum Earthling being aboard spread through their section like a supersonic wave. Some passengers gathered around Dan and the Gaige family, audibly peppering Dan with questions and comments about Earthlings and Earth.

The shuttle attendants corralled the rambunctious Hearthlings back to their seats. Dan found the experience more amusing than threatening. Abiona and the children informed Dan of some commuters attempting to speak to Dan through them.

"I explained to my fellow Hearthlings," Abiona said, "that we are on holiday and the Earthling would only be addressing the populace through his Earth Forum."

"Well put," Dan said, planting a kiss on Abiona's cheek. The children giggled. "What's so funny?" Dan asked.

"Our dad kisses Mom like that all of the time," Ifelayo said with a grin.

"We find the resemblance amusing," Mayowa added, with a smile of his own.

"Like what? Like this?" Dan gave Abiona another peck on the cheek, creating another round of giggles from the children. They heard a few soft laughs from fellow passengers.

Some Hearthlings were obviously eavesdropping. Dan wondered if it was all of the Hearthlings on the shuttle or simply the ones within earshot. Everyone on the shuttle knew that Dan was the Earthling responsible for the Earth Forum website by the time the shuttle landed, although no one approached Dan or the Gaige family.

May Haven Station was located on the coast of Kitahikàn Utènay, Lenape, at what would be considered Ocean City, Delaware on Earth. The structure had two dominate shapes: a large circle made of tungsten glass that served as the passenger station and a tangential line connected at the east quadrant of the circle that served as the boarding area.

All in all, May Haven Station reminded Dan of the Greek capital letter omega. The glass walls exhibited colorful virtual aquatic scenes, giving one a sense of being submerged in a glass submarine. The station was tidy, well-lit, and organized.

May Haven Station was busy, reminding Dan of Shinjuku or Grand Central train stations back on Earth. People were going about as you would find in any hectic train station—with two major differences, Dan noticed.

While some Hearthlings moved quickly, none seemed to be in a rush, as if time or their shuttle would wait no matter when they arrived.

The other was: there was no commotion, as was normal in an Earth station. Dan had not realized before how much the sound of human voices filled his busy travel places. He missed that din, sparking in him a surprising pang of homesickness.

Dan and the Gaines family boarded the Blue Marlin Ferry, walking across a connecting bridge into the gaping mouth of the floating vessel. Once all passengers were seated and strapped in, the ferry submerged. Dan was astonished at what he saw during their steep, steady descent into the depths of the Atlantic Ocean (an ocean name shared by Earth and Hearth).

The abundance of natural sea life seemed to ignore them, as one might ignore any common sight. Hearth vehicles darted about like frightened sailfish. Dan made out an underwater structure in the shape of a starfish near the ocean floor.

They were approaching the city of Taíno. When they were within docking range, Dan saw that the starfish was made up of adjoining structures in a honeycomb pattern about two-thirds the size of Mattatuck.

"While the vast majority of Hearthlings prefer living on land," an article Dan remembered reading online said, "There is a small minority who chose life under the seas. These Hearthlings feel a greater sense of serenity living in the ocean. Why that is, no one knows. Even the ocean dwellers cannot definitively explain their motivation."

"This is your captain speaking." The confident voice came over the cabin speakers, interrupting Dan's train of thought. "We will be docking at Taíno Station shortly. We expect your trip was pleasant. Should you have any comments or questions regarding our service, please feel free to note them in our onboard log. All input is welcomed. Thank you."

Their comfortable voyage dry-docked just over an hour from departure. No one had queried or approached Dan or the Gaige family since the Mattatuck shuttle incident, although Dan detected a few furtive glances his way.

Dan conjectured that word had been passed on to leave the Earthling and his traveling companions alone. Like good Hearthlings, they obeyed.

Abiona's parents greeted them at the arrival area. They had no luggage. Everything they needed had been transported ahead. The children rushed into the waiting arms of their grandparents, who scooped them up like rag dolls with bear hug embraces, planting yummy kisses all over their grandchildren's beaming faces. When done with one grandchild, the grandparents switched to do the same to the other.

Abiona and Dan walked up to the happy gathering, enjoying the excited exchanges of affection between grandparents and grandchildren.

Abiona was filled with warmth and joy, exhibited in her unbridled smile. Dan held an awkward grin, feeling like a third wheel and trying not to show it. Reality crashed down on Dan in the presence of such happiness.

This was not his family, no matter how welcome they made him feel. Abiona's parents bear-hugged their daughter, in turn, who bear-hugged them back. Each parent planted an adoring kiss on Abiona's forehead, as you would a beloved toddler.

"Good to see you again, Daniel," Abiona's father said to Dan, who'd found himself standing off to the side of the reunion. Dan shook the proffered hand. Not a word had been spoken until that moment, making Dan all the more uneasy.

"Good to see you again, too, sir."

"Call me Daivika."

Dan almost let slip for Daivika to call him Dan before he remembered the Hearthling preference for the use of given names. "Thank you, Daivika," he said instead.

"Daniel," Funmilayo said with a genial smile. Abiona's mother gave Dan a polite hug, gently cupping his face in the same fashion Abiona so often did when she wanted to peer into the recesses of his being. Dan welcomed her touch. Her gesture put him at ease.

They made their way down a connecting tunnel with the rest of the arriving crowd toward the concourse. Dan kept stopping every couple of steps, gawking, awestruck, at the spectacle.

The tunnel was made of a clear material, including the walkway. Dan speculated that it was some glass composite similar to, if not the same as, the tungsten glass used at the Zenith Campus.

They were on the ocean floor. Sunlight did not penetrate to this depth. Dark waters were all around. Yet, Dan could see as well as if he were in shallow water.

The ocean was teeming with life. How was that possible, with no distinguishable exterior lighting? Somehow, the interior lighting must have made it possible, Dan guessed. Again: the question of how? Working in combination with the clear material in composite, it was possible to see outside without light extending beyond the tunnel. Dan speculated that the tunnel material was tinted, camouflaged, or both. Then it dawned on him.

Hearthlings had worked in conjunction with the sea creatures in this area to build this underwater city. Everything Hearthlings had done, Dan was confident, had met with aqualife approval or compromise. It was an interesting thought that left Dan no closer to solving his engineering conundrum.

Dan was seeing the ocean in a way he never had before. It was like walking through the world's largest natural aquarium without having any effect on the sea life around them. Dan was mesmerized by a large school of fish doing an erratic water dance to a rhythm only they understood.

"Amazing, is it not?" Abiona said, settling in beside him.

"Yes, it is," was all Dan could convey.

"Do you have anything like this on Earth?"

"Not even close."

Abiona took Dan's hand. "Come along, Daniel. You will see more captivating sites such as this one during our stay."

Abiona led Dan away like a rapt child too spellbound to will his body to move. Dan turned to see the rest of the family staring at him, amused by his reaction. Dan was tickled at himself rather than feeling embarrassed.

Hearth was awakening something in him; an emergence he had not realized until that moment. He felt invigorated and alive, like a child discovering the world anew.

Which, he was. Hearth was not Earth, despite its clone resemblance. When had he developed blinders to the world around him? His world? His planet?

Dan had believed himself to be Earth-conscious. Didn't his family recycle, compost, and maintain an environmental diligence? Didn't he work for a company whose business it was to be ecologically mindful in everything they did?

But, when was the last time his family had communed with nature? Gone camping or hiking, or even taken a leisurely walk around their own neighborhood?

Not in years. The world he was focused on saving had become background imagery in his global tapestry of salvation. Dan equated the revelation with doing everything one could to provide for a child without spending quality time with them.

He thought of his children Wick and Mae, the family he would be returning to in due course, and how he treated Mayowa and Ifelayo as his own. He knew that neglecting any of them had not and would not happen. They were always his first priority.

Earth was no longer his top priority. Single Organism was. He reflected on the battles he had been losing to keep Single Organism true to its mission statement. The board had been making more choices based on profitability rather than ecological effects.

The fight was going out of him. Single Organism was edging toward becoming one of those companies that talked a good game, but did not deliver on their promises; the type of company they had railed against when he and his colleagues began Single Organism.

Dan would need to sound the alarm if he could not dissuade his once-like-minded associates to return wholeheartedly to their original mission statement without compromise.

As they boarded a monorail car, Dan was glad no one could read his mind. He had gone off on a mental tangent and no one seemed to notice. Ifelayo had gleefully claimed the hand of her grandfather. Mayowa had done the same of his grandmother, albeit in a calmer fashion.

His Hearthling family was obviously having lively telepathic conversations amongst themselves, ones their outward expressions and body language did not hide.

No sooner did the monorail train start than they arrived at Zemi Station. The journey as quick as if they had been aboard a vacuum tube. Dan noticed that the monorail track was glowing when they disembarked.

"Our monorail systems run on light tubes," Daivika said to Dan as if reading his thoughts.

"How's that possible?" Dan asked, still staring at the rail.

"I do not know, Daniel. I can connect you with Taíno's lead transportation engineer who could answer that question for you, if you would like?"

"I'd like that very much."

"Consider it done."

"Come along, Daniel," Abiona said, tugging Dan by the hand as Dan continued speculating on the monorail's engineering.

The monorail had dropped them off in the middle of town. All was bright and busy with Hearthlings on the move. Downtown Taíno contained the same varieties of stores, markets, restaurants, shops, living quarters, and office complexes that you would find in Mattatuck, except on a smaller scale. Daivika hailed a shuttle that took them to the Jaheem home.

There was a neighborhood in the Atabey Province half the size of Pequannock, but with a similar layout; one of the major differences being that none of the houses had front lawns. A large oval green space centered in the province was across the street from the front of each house: Heketi Park.

The Jaheem home was a bright, white, open, two-story Mediterranean-style home that seemed to glow as if sitting in the Florida sunshine, with sloping tiled roofs, wooden shutters, and a wealth of windows. It sported an interior that Dan was delighted to discover, held hardwood floors and light-colored walls, was tropical-themed, and was as spacious and free-flowing as the exterior suggested.

Dan could see people inside through the uncovered windows. He was surprised to discover how many when they walked in. They were people he recognized from photographs about Abiona's home; Hearthlings whose names Dan knew, as told to him by his hosts.

Abiona's older brother was the spitting image of his father, right down to his long braided dreadlocks and strong, rich, steady voice. His wife, Dia, was stately and firmly built, with twinkling eyes and an enchanting smile that elevated her dignified bearing, which was accentuated even more by her African head wrap, with matching earrings and choker.

Sohalia, Abiona's younger sister, the geologist, possessed the same physical features as her mom and sister on a shorter and thinner body. Next to her stood her husband, Olufemi Chukwu, a distinguished man with warm, peaceful eyes and a pleasant demeanor.

Abiona, Mayowa, and Ifelayo were met with exuberant greetings all around. Abiona's family expressed themselves the same as any close-knit Earth family ecstatic at seeing each other. Dan stood back, relishing the spectacle.

It was a handsome group, well versed in the art of non-verbal expressions of happiness. It was like watching a silent film, only the characters did not exaggerate their actions, and there were no captions. Dan could use his imagination as to what was being said, based on

Hearthling body language and facial expressions that were no different from Earthlings under similar circumstances.

In turn, the gathering introduced themselves to Dan as if he were the guest of honor.

The first to do so was Kaab. Dan was impressed with how seamlessly Hearthlings switched from telepathy to vocalizing, as if they were one in the same, as Dan met the rest of Abiona's blood relations and their spouses and kin.

He scanned their faces for star-twin connections to his family, friends, and acquaintances back home. There were resemblances, in some instances, but no one who was a dead ringer to any Earthling he knew.

Abiona, Mayowa, Ifelayo, Bartek, Kwasi's parents, and Jabori remained the only ones Dan had seen so far. Dan was disappointed.

"Forgive us for not taking the initiative, Daniel," Kaab said during his polished introduction. "We wanted to greet you in person. There's nothing like a face-to-face meeting to get to know someone. Did you feel you were being snubbed?"

The question surprised Dan and made him wonder if his Occlumency pills were working. While he denied feeling any such way, Dan was certain his reaction gave him away.

"Again, I apologize for our inconsideration," Kaab said with a sincere smile, a quality Dan had not known many Earthling politicians to possess.

Next to be introduced was Kaab's wife, Dia.

"My, my, you are the spitting image of Kwasi," Dia said to Dan. "How does that make you feel, Abiona?"

"Like Kwasi never left home."

"I can see why."

Sohalia and her husband Olufemi and the adult cousins on Abiona's side of the family joined the introduction procession, all with firm handshakes and smiles. A bevy of nieces and nephews, ranging from ages five to fifteen, gathered around Dan, staring more than talking.

Mayowa and Ifelayo were not amongst them, having disappeared somewhere inside the house. The children were polite and respectful after their introductions. Dan speculated that they were expecting him to be like a freak show exhibit, although they had no such thing on

Hearth. When the children discovered the Earthling was physically no different from any other adult Hearthling at the gathering, they became bored and drifted away.

Dan made it known about his Residual Connection with Kwasi while talking to Achak and Patricia Gaige, news he had only shared with Abiona since his relocation from the Zenith Campus and perhaps in an effort to reignite the phenomenon that had appeared to cease.

The room fell quiet and still from the news, even for a Hearthling gathering that consisted primarily of telepathic conversations. Kwasi's parents stepped up to him, their kind and loving eyes gazing at him as if they were seeing their son.

An Earthling term crossed Dan's mind; one that living amongst Hearthlings had taught him to be true. "Sometimes, silence speaks louder than words."

Everyone in the room except Abiona stood back and observed. She remained at Dan's side. Her in-laws stepped closer, examining Dan as a racehorse trainer might examine a thoroughbred horse. Achak was first to speak in a natural bass tone that seemed to hum with words.

"Patricia, no matter how many times I see Daniel, I remained stunned by his resemblance to our Kwasi."

Patricia smiled. "I cannot read your mind, Daniel." Her voice possessed a mesmerizing lilt.

"No, ma'am. Remember, I'm taking pills that prevent Hearthlings from doing so."

Patricia smiled and nodded. "Now I recall. No matter. Is our son alright, Daniel?"

"He's doing well."

"You know this how?"

Dan thought for a moment before speaking. Peering into the faces of Kwasi's parents, he imagined how his own parents would be hurting under the same circumstances, in need of encouraging answers. Dan wondered for a moment if his parents had sensed a difference in Dan; if they somehow knew Kwasi was not their son.

"The Exchange Student Program wouldn't allow any harm to come to your son."

"I trust Hearthling institutions completely," Patricia said.

"It is Earthlings that concern us," Achak added.

Dan was hurt by the comment, but understood their concern.

"What is this Residual Connection with our son that you speak of?" Achak asked. Dan could sense other people in the room moving closer upon hearing Achak's question, making Dan a bit uneasy.

"We do not understand," Patricia said, her steady gaze calming Dan.

"According to my Indoctrination Specialist, Dr. Jabori Bakari, Kwasi and I have a star-twin connection that extends beyond our physical resemblance. We share a cosmic symbiotic joining, as well.

"It's rare, but happens between star-twins, at times, even without an exchange. When it happens without the exchange, each person interprets their experiences as dreams or daydreams."

"You can communicate with Kwasi?" Achak asked, clearly stunned by the news. Dan saw similar reactions from the rest of the people in the room. Although there were no audible outbursts of astonishment, their expressions gave them away. Dan could imagine what they were thinking. Patricia and Abiona appeared to be the only ones comforted by Dan's confession.

"No, sir. During our connection, I experience what Kwasi is experiencing through his eyes. I can't intervene or communicate with him in any way."

"Does Kwasi know the two of you are connected at the time?" Abiona asked.

"Not according to Dr. Bakari. Our connections are one-sided, like a vision or viewing a broadcast event. You can observe, but nothing more."

"Interesting," Achak said. "Can Kwasi do the same? Have these visions through your eyes?"

"According to Dr. Bakari, yes. For all I know, Kwasi could be sharing our experience right now."

Patricia lovingly cupped Dan's face in her hands, searching his eyes for signs of Kwasi.

"You more than look like my son. You *feel* like my son. Am I making myself clear, Daniel?" Tears traced her cheeks.

"Yes, ma'am," Dan said, his eyes misting, fighting back tears of his own. They stood there as statues for what seemed to Dan like time standing still. Achak gently placed his hands on his wife's shoulders.

"He is not our son, Patricia, no matter the resemblance. He is *not our son*. You must forgive my wife. Kwasi and his mother are very, very close. She misses him terribly. So do I."

"Try not to worry," Dan said to Patricia and Achak, as if speaking to his own parents. "You will see Kwasi soon."

"I know," Patricia said, affirming Dan's statement with a nod. "But I still miss him."

Patricia patted Dan on the cheek. "Enjoy your stay, Daniel. I hope you find what you need amongst our people."

Patricia turned and walked away. Achak followed her, one arm draped over his wife's slumping shoulders, her arms squeezing her husband tight around his waist. The crowd parted, allowing them ample room to leave gracefully and giving them a consolation touch as they passed.

Dan watched Kwasi's parents disappear up the flight of handcrafted wooden stairs, Abiona, Mayowa, and Ifelayo trailing them. For Dan, it was like watching a funeral march—parents mourning the loss of their child, his widow and their children in tow.

It was the first time Dan had been made aware of the toll their exchange had taken on those who loved Kwasi. Everyone had been so accommodating of his situation. It never dawned on Dan that some Hearthlings might be suffering from the switch.

Dan was considering ending the exchange, not for his sake, but for the sake of Kwasi's parents. Dan knew he had the authority. Achak and Patricia Gaige left the gathering shortly after Dan's confession, never to be seen by Dan again.

*   *   *

The pall of guilt created by Dan's Residual Connection news to Achak and Patricia Gaige remained with Dan for the remainder of the day. Everyone did their best to help Dan move on from the experience and feel at home.

Dan was shocked to discover, when it came time to settle in, that he and Abiona would be sharing the same bed. Not that he minded. For whatever Earthly reason, he had expected them to have separate rooms, under the circumstances. Separate beds, at the least; not to be treated as if they were a married couple.

While they snuggled, Abiona asked Dan about his Residual Connection with Kwasi. Dan explained the process in more detail. He went on to give Abiona condensed accounts of the events, in chronological order, beginning with his first experience during lunch at the Wakin dining hall on Zenith Campus.

The big question never came—the one Dan was expecting from Abiona. Did he ever have a Residual Connection with Kwasi when they were having sex? The answer was no. Perhaps Abiona already knew the answer to that question. Dan did not have the courage to pursue whether Abiona did or not.

"Do you plan on writing about Residual Connection on your blog, Daniel?" Abiona asked in a dreamy voice, teetering on the cusp of sleep.

"I hadn't. Do you think I should?" Dan asked with a yawn.

"I would not if I were in your position. If one of your followers were to broach the subject. I would refer them to the Exchange Student Program for answers."

"If the question of Residual Connection were to come my way via the Earth Forum, it would not surprise me if it were redirected to Dr. Bakari."

"Is he not the expert on that matter?"

"As far as I know."

"In my opinion, best not to get caught up in something you do not completely understand."

Dan thought for a moment. While Jabori understood Residual Connection much better than he did, the good doctor had described it as a phenomenon.

Dan agreed with Abiona, not because he was worried about getting in over his head, as Abiona had been hinting, but he agreed with Abiona in having someone more expert tackle the issue.

Abiona rested her head on Dan's chest as she often did when they slept together. He thought about Abiona's advice. It was wise counsel, driven by logic and concern. Abiona was behaving like a wife attempting to protect someone she cared for.

Her husband? Had Abiona fallen in love with him as he had fallen in love with her, or was he reading too much into her consideration? Was Abiona somehow protecting Kwasi until his return? The possibility that Abiona had fallen in love with him was more to his liking. It was a possibility that rocked Dan into a restful sleep.

CHAPTER 43

Earth Forum. Question: "What is religion?"

Dan thought about the question for a moment. He had only been asked *about* his religion on Earth; never to define the practice. He recalled a definition given in a lecture by a university philosophy professor.

Answer: "'Religion unto itself is a belief system coupled to a doctrine of life.'"

Question: "What religion do you practice?"

Answer: "To paraphrase an Earthling spiritual leader on my planet, "My religion is very simple. My religion is kindness."

Question: "It appears to Hearthlings that some Earthlings on your planet practice what we term as Religious Arrogance. Believing that one belief system is superior to all others thereby places them in an exultant position to enter some fabled spiritual kingdom beyond our bound of flesh.

"This behavior has been the source of multitudes of conflicts and oppression. Why is it that those elements, that should bind your people most, serve, too often, as sources of conflict or oppression?"

Answer: "I wish I knew the answer to that question, but I don't."

*　　*　　*

Dan awoke to an acapella chorus. He looked out of the second story window of Abiona's bedroom to discover hundreds of Hearthlings gathered in Heketi Park; young, old, and in-between, lifting their voices to a song Dan did not know, in an unfamiliar language.

The chorus was both unified and ragged, like a carved piece of furniture still being refined. Good singers could be heard alongside the tone deaf.

Dan saw Abiona, Mayowa, Ifelayo, Daivika, Funmilayo, and the rest of the family joyfully lifting their voices with their neighbors. Dan had heard a good deal of music while on Hearth, most of it polished and professional. This was the first time Dan had heard what he would classify as an amateur offering of such magnitude.

The assembly cheered and applauded at the song's end. There were hugs and gleeful waves as they parted. Dan quickly dressed and rushed downstairs. Clusters of family were spread throughout the first floor, spilling into the backyard.

Adults were in the company of adults. Children, in the company of other children. All were telepathically chatting amongst themselves.

Everyone was in high spirits. There was no mention of the occurrence between Dan and Kwasi's parents (at least, not in Dan's presence) for the remainder of his stay.

Dan approached Abiona, Kaab, Sohalia, Dia, Olufemi, and Funmilayo, who were gathered in a loose circle. Kaab and Sohalia opened the circle to allow Dan a place.

"Good morning, Daniel," Kaab said, breaking the verbal silence of the festive gathering. "I take it you heard us singing?"

"I did. What's the occasion, if you don't mind my asking?"

"Not at all," Funmilayo said. "What you witnessed was the Taíno Canticle, or a Hearth praise and worship song. Once a month, we congregate in each province to sing a song of thanks for the blessings we have received.

"It is an ocean dweller tradition: one that makes us remain connected to our planet and each other. We send out good vibrations."

Dan chuckled.

"Did I say something amusing?"

"No, Funmilayo. I'm just reminded of an Earth song." The group, clearly not making the connection, stared unflinching at Dan. "There was a popular song, 'Good Vibrations', that was released on Earth in the sixties. Before my time, but I've heard it. Your use of the phrase 'good vibrations' reminded me of it."

"I see," Funmilayo said, still not comprehending. "How is that amusing?"

"Earthling inside joke, I'm afraid. I'll pull up the song from the Earth archives so you can have a listen."

"We would like that, Daniel." Dan was uncertain whether Funmilayo was sincere, or just being polite.

"I've never noticed anything like your Hearth praise song on land."

"Land dwellers like myself, Daniel," Dia responded, "offer our thanks more in what you might call silent prayers."

"Although we do sing and hum," Olufemi said, "more as a means of exercising our vocal chords."

"Which we normally do in small groups, and in private," Kaab added, "so not to disturb other Hearthlings. Some provinces have choirs fashioned for the sole purpose of vocal exercises."

"I never heard any such choirs at the Zenith Campus."

"Because most Hearthlings only work at the Zenith Campus. The majority live in the surrounding areas."

"How did this ocean dweller tradition come about?"

"You mean, what is its origin, Daniel?" Funmilayo asked.

"Yes."

"I can answer that," Abiona said. "Correct me if I am wrong, Mom."

Funmilayo gave her daughter a confident nod to proceed. Abiona went on to explain the origin of ocean dweller praise and worship songs. They dated back to the construction of the first Hearthling underwater city.

While working with local aqualife, Hearthlings discovered that most aqualife gave thanks to the ocean for all of its blessings, just as Hearthlings and wildlife do for their habitats.

The ocean dweller canticles are blessing songs composed by Hearthlings and local aqualife in the native Hearthling language of the area. Hearthlings remind each other every month of how fortunate they are, with song—a song that resonates good vibrations to the ocean life around them.

"Did I miss anything, Mom?"

"Perfect, my dear," Funmilayo said with a proud smile.

"Each underwater city has its own Hearth praise and worship song." Kaab added. "An anthem, if you will, composed in the same manner as the original."

Funmilayo lovingly touched the shoulder of her son and Kaab patted his mother's hand in response.

"I didn't recognize the language," Dan said.

"Garifuna," Funmilayo said. "Do Earthlings speak Garifuna?"

"I imagine some do. I'm not one of them." The Garifuna language did not ring a bell with Dan. He would learn more about Garifuna when he had the chance.

"Allow me to translate into English," Daivika said, before singing the Taíno Canticle in a silky, baritone voice that reminded Dan of the Earthling singer Lou Rawls.

We gather here to praise our beloved planet.
To honor her blessings for beings large and small.
To give thanks for the air, water, soil and sky,
and all of the grandeur and splendor that is Hearth.
We humbly accept our place
in this vast and glorious universe.
We are neither the beginning
nor end of creation amongst its stars.
Let each deed I undertake be
as much benefit to our planet as to
wildlife, aqualife, and my fellow Hearthlings.
Let each word I speak
serve them in equal measure.
We love Hearth!
We respect Hearth!
We cherish Hearth!
Forever thanks be, to our sacred Hearth!

The room erupted in applause and cheers. Daivika took several bows before the room settled down. A long yawn of a moment passed before anything more was said.

"Hearthlings consider it their personal responsibility to nurture this hallowed planet we call Hearth," Sohalia said, "respecting all Hearthlings, wildlife and aqualife. Do Earthlings feel the same about Earth?"

Dan had already answered that question numerous times, in person and on his Earth Forum website. Perhaps Sohalia was not a fan.

"In theory, yes."

"Not in practice?"

"Too often, not in practice."

"To see a World in a grain of sand..." Sohalia said.

Dan recognized the line. It was a quote from an Earthling poet. He added, "And a heaven in a wild flower/Hold infinity in the palm of your hand/and eternity in an hour."

"You know the poetry of Sebastian Calbert, Daniel?"

"I don't, Sohalia. An Earthling poet, William Blake, wrote a poem that begins with that same line."

"*Auguries of Innocence?*"

"Yes. How did you know?"

"More like coincidence than knowledge. *Auguries of Innocence* was written by our Sebastian Calbert."

"Do you remember the rest of *Auguries of Innocence*, Daniel?" Dia asked.

Dan went on to recite the entire poem without a hiccup, startled that he remembered the prose so clearly.

"It obviously left quite an impression on you," Kaab said once Dan finished. Dan nodded in agreement.

"How long ago did your Blake write *Auguries of Innocence?*"

"Sometime in our 1800s. I'll need to research it, to be more accurate."

"About four centuries ago, Earth time," Abiona said.

"Yes."

"That would correspond to around the same time Calbert published *Auguries of Innocence* here. Sebastian Calbert and your William Blake may have been star-twins."

"They very well could've been. Did the Exchange Student Program exist back then?"

"Yes, Daniel," Daivika answered. "I have become curious about such things as star-twins and the Exchange Student Program, since our Abiona is living with a man who is embroiled in both. No offense, Daniel."

"None taken."

"Our Galaxy Program—I believe Earthlings call it 'Space Program'—is centuries old. Our Intergalactic Travel Program is an infant, by comparison.

"When we discovered our human cousins on Earth, within your Milky Way galaxy, we observed you from afar and within. We lived amongst you—as we still do today—without ever being discovered, gathering information to determine whether or not to make contact.

"After learning as much as we could about your fellow Earthlings and your cultures, we decided it best to maintain our distance and remain hidden."

"In other words, you spied on us."

"Yes," Daivika answered without the slightest guilt. "'While Earthlings resemble us in many ways,' to quote a Hearthling scholar on the subject, 'they have much to learn about humanity and the well-being of their planet.'

"It was decided that Hearthlings would fashion a program to educate Earthlings in matters where Hearthlings have had success.

"Not to create Hearthling clones, but to guide Earthlings in hopes of making your people and your world as healthy and happy as ours. Hence, the Exchange Student Program was born."

"Dad, I am impressed," Abiona beamed. "You have done your homework."

"Thank you, dear."

"Star-twin connections between Hearthlings and Earthlings were occurring long before there was an Intergalactic Travel Program."

"That would be accurate, Daniel," Funmilayo said. "Like Daivika, I became curious about the man living with our daughter, who was the spitting image of our Kwasi. While I am no expert, I did take the time to learn more about star-twins."

"It was a topic well covered on your Earth Forum," Kaab added.

"Earth Forum proved to me that star-twin connections are real," Olufemi said, "and not a myth, as I'd believed before. I hope to meet my Earthling star-twin, one day." All of the Hearthlings gathered nodded in agreement.

"I can't take credit for most of the star-twin information posted on Earth Forum. My Indoctrination Specialist, Dr. Jabori Bakari, wrote most of the informative pieces. I only added a few touches from personal experiences."

"Nonetheless, it is a marvel," Funmilayo concluded with a smile. Dan smiled back at his Hearthling mother-in-law.

"Thank you, but it's a team effort. I am permitted access to any information that I need, as well as input from numerous Hearthling experts who contribute mightily to the content."

"Can you elaborate on the Residual Connection phenomenon you mentioned to Kwasi's parents?" Funmilayo asked. "I saw nothing about it on Earth Forum."

Dan went over in his mind what he had previously stated about Residual Connection. He thought it best to start from the top.

"As I've learned, star-twin connections between Hearthlings and Earthlings are plentiful. Then there are Residual Connections like the one I have with Kwasi, which is rare."

"How would you describe the experience?"

Dan was about to respond when he felt as though time stopped. The people in the room appeared frozen. His vision turned inward. A flicker of Kwasi's presence materialized, then another and another, linking together images like a film reel gaining momentum until the scene came into sharp focus.

Kwasi had an arm around Toni. His other hand rested on Wick's shoulder, who was standing in front of him. Toni had both arms draped over Mia. They were in hiking gear, their backpacks placed near their feet.

The day was young; the sky a hazy blue. The sun had started to peak over distant mountain ranges. They stood atop a mountain ridge, staring down at a rich green forest canopy, wispy strands of faint gray morning mist still evaporating like angel hair being plucked from the valley.

"It's been years since we've been here," Toni dreamily said to Kwasi. "Why did we wait so long to return?"

Toni was right. Dan and Toni hadn't been there since Wick was born. Dan recognized the view. Its splendor made him feel inconsequential and serene, at the same time.

"I don't know," Kwasi answered. "Life had us too busy, I guess."

"Thank you for showing us this place," Wick said with a tremor in his voice.

Mae nodded in agreement with her brother, a faint smile on her face and warm tears rolling down her cheeks. "It's so beautiful."

Through Kwasi, Dan could hear the faint roar of a distant waterfall and felt the cool, crisp mountain air on his skin.

"What do you say that we make moments like this a priority in our lives?" Kwasi asked. The Bluford family nodded. Toni brushed away her daughter's tears, kissing her cheeks. Kwasi pulled Wick close into a firm hug. The family continued to gaze in awe at the splendor of a natural world, in silence. Dan joined them in spirit.

"Ethereal," Dan heard himself say, glancing around to see if anyone had observed his momentary blackout. No one appeared to have noticed.

That wasn't uncommon. Dan had come to know that, while a Residual Connection could last for minutes, only seconds had passed.

"Ethereal," Dan repeated, "is how I would describe it. A conscious out-of-body experience; literally seeing the world through another's eyes."

"Sounds fascinating."

"Not to me, Dia."

"Why not?"

Dan reflected on his recent Residual Connection. The word came to him with honest ease. "'Disturbing' is closer to what's it like for me."

"You do not enjoy having Residual Connections with Kwasi?" Kaab asked.

The question threw Dan. Not only had he never been asked about his enjoyment regarding his Residual Connections, but the idea of pleasure never crossed his mind.

"I do draw comfort from our connection. Knowing Kwasi is taking good care of my Earth life and my family, from what I've seen."

"No surprise there," Abiona said. She took Dan's hand. "Like you, Daniel, my Kwasi is a good man."

"I only hope Kwasi thinks the same of me."

"I'm sure he does, Daniel."

"Perhaps Calbert and Blake had a Residual Connection," Sohalia said. "It may explain how they created the same poem."

"That very well may be," Daniel responded. "Place the question regarding Blake and Calbert's possible star-twin connection on Earth Forum, Sohalia. I'm sure Dr. Bakari will be glad to look into it."

"Will do."

There was an awkward pause as the group once again, unflinching, eyed Dan, their expressions no different than if they were studying a unique work of art.

The oldest daughter of Olufemi and Sohalia and the youngest son of Kaab and Dia ran up to the group to share something with the adults. The conversation was telepathic. The children stared at Dan, their eyes gleaming with laughter, then they ran off, giggling. Dan looked around at the group, hoping for an explanation.

"They were telling us about a new insect they saw in the backyard," Kaab said.

"Is that why they left laughing?"

"Oh, that!" Dia said. "They find it amusing that you cannot read minds."

Oddly enough, Dan found it amusing, as well.

CHAPTER 44

Earth Forum. Question: "In my studies of Earthlings. I have noticed that mindless, senseless, wicked violence permeates your culture, to the point of being glamorized and glorified. Why is that?"

Answer: "Many Earthlings believe that our obsession with violence is unhealthy in a number of ways. Unfortunately, we have not been able to quell that fixation; in part because the promotion of violence remains a very profitable industry."

Question: "Why does bottom-line profit figure into so many Earthling decisions?"

Answer: "So many human endeavors in the modern world somehow tie back to some form of business. Businesses rely on profits to survive and thrive.

"Unfortunately, this practice often leads to a cold and calculating approach to viewing people and the world.

"Without people factored into business decisions, there is no humanity. Without ecological effect being part of the equation, there is no environmental protection. Without the effects on wildlife and aqualife being respectfully considered, there remains a persistent deterioration of wildlife habitats and an increase in aqualife toxicity.

"Where there is profit, too often there is corruption. Some Earthling businesses are illegal, done for the sole purpose of profiteering with no regard for the damage they do or who they hurt.

"Hearthling priorities are different. Hearthlings care nothing about profit or wealth or material things outside of creature comforts. For

Hearthlings, people, wildlife, aqualife, the environment, and more are first considerations. On Earth, these considerations too often have to be enforced."

*   *   *

The family gathered inside the dining room of Atabey Lodge in an octagon-shaped room with a glass vaulted ceiling and a cream hardwood floor. Panoramic glass windows came down from ceiling to floor, allowing an uninterrupted view of the Atabey community.

Handmade large, round blackwood dining tables with matching cushioned chairs were equally spaced out over the dining room like trees growing on a spiral tree plantation, the natural light pouring in reminding Dan of a cathedral. The mood of the place did the same.

Dan's party was seated at the table nearest the center of the room. They enjoyed a delicious breakfast catered by humans. It was a nice change for Dan, who had become accustomed to IVAs (Interactive Virtual Assistants) catering these events.

It was a lively affair in spite of the normal Hearthling quiet, with most of the sounds being made by clanking silverware. Speech was exclusively directed at Dan.

Seated at his table were Abiona, Ifelayo, Mayowa, Daivika, Funmilayo, Sohalia, Olufemi, Kaab, and Dia.

Dan opened the conversation with a question for Daivika and Funmilayo. "How did you come to live in an underwater city?"

"After our children moved out on their own," Daivika answered, "we did more traveling."

"When we visited Taíno for the first time," Funmilayo added, "we fell in love with this underwater community."

"I can see why," Dan said, sounding star-struck.

"We have plenty of places to go whenever we get nostalgic for land," Funmilayo said, with assurance.

"Our homes are your homes, Mom and Dad," Kaab said. Dan glanced around the table to find everyone in total agreement.

"Sohalia, you're a geologist?" Dan asked Abiona's sister, seated to his left, after a beat.

"Yes."

"You were recently on Mars."

"Yes. I was a member of an archeological dig."

"Find anything interesting?"

"Always, Daniel. If you mean, did we find anything unique for Mars, then the answer is no. Have you ever been to Mars—the one in your galaxy?"

"My people have a long road to travel in science and technology before we'll be capable of similar feats," Dan said, sounding apologetic. "The furthest we've ever set foot from our planet is the Moon."

"The Moon?" Sohalia repeated.

"Earth's natural satellite. The equivalent of our Mwezi, to Hearth," Abiona explained to the group. Everyone nodded their understanding. The group stared at Dan for a moment, as if astounded by this revelation.

"Thank you, Abiona," Daivika said with pride. "She's our resident Galaxy Historian."

"Do Earthlings have Galaxy Historians, Daniel?" Dia asked.

"We do, but we call them 'astronomers.' I'm certain that none of them possess a fraction of the knowledge about our universe that Abiona has about yours."

Dan took their silence to mean they agreed. "Is it true that Hearthlings have colonized all of the planets in your solar system?" Dan asked.

"We have not colonized any planet," Kaab answered. "That would infer forced occupation. We have built communities on every planet within our galaxy, careful not to disturb the natural balance in the process."

"We are interested in learning as much as we can about our universe," Abiona chimed in.

"That, of course, includes the planets themselves," Sohalia said.

"Have you discovered intelligent life out there amongst the stars?"

"If, by intelligent life, you mean beings like you or I, Daniel, then no."

"Are Earthlings doing the same?" Daivika asked. "Searching for other intelligent life within your universe?"

Dan thought about Mae, memories flooding back to him of the two of them searching the airways for signs of intelligent alien life. Dan gazed across the table at Ifelayo, Mae's star-twin. She was enjoying a mouthful of Belgian waffle, her jaws as full as a chipmunk. Her eyes smiled back at Dan.

For the first time, Dan saw Ifelayo as a separate entity from his own precious daughter, despite her identical resemblance. He ached to hold Mae; to hear her voice. The sight of Ifelayo was not an acceptable substitute, for the moment.

"We are searching for intelligent life," Dan said shaking off his yearning. "So far, with no success."

"There are galaxy junkets that happen regularly," Sohalia said, "given by various universities and science organizations for educational purposes. Perhaps you can tag along on one of them, Daniel. I can put in a good word for you.

"I would take you myself, but I will not be returning to space for another few months. I have Hearth commitments."

"Like spending quality time with her family," her husband Olufemi said. That brought a round of laughter from the table and a kiss on the cheek from Sohalia.

"Abiona, is there anything you can do to arrange an off-world trip for Daniel?" Kaab asked. "Being as you are the Pequannock Province Regional Director of Astronomy."

"I will ask. All of our off-world trips are for research purposes. Since there is some degree of risk in space travel, I will need approval from the Exchange Student Program Committee."

"I doubt they will approve," Dan added. "They may not want to risk anything happening to an Earthling exchange student." Everyone nodded their understanding, including the children.

Kaab asked, after taking a sip of his fresh squeezed orange juice, "Are you aware of how our government works, Daniel?"

"Only what I've learned at the Zenith Campus."

"How would you say that politics differs on your planet, from ours?"

"I can't answer that with any authority. What I *can* say is that most Earthlings don't trust our politicians. Sadly, they have good reasons not to.

"The most unscrupulous prey on our fears and distrust for their own selfish gains. Hearthlings, on the other hand, seem to revere their politicians."

"We are bestowed with a *wonderful* responsibility: to selflessly serve our fellow citizens. There is no greater calling, in my opinion.

As governor of Yoruba, it is a charge that I am honored and humbled to have been elected to uphold—one that I cherish and fully accept on behalf of a great planet and noble society.

"Does wildlife and aqualife have votes in your Earthling elections?"

"No," Dan said, stunned by the question. "We can't even communicate with them."

"Pity. They have much to contribute to the well-being of a planet. Some of our most respected board members are wildlife and aqualife officials."

Dan had seen photographs of Hearthling boards in his civics and government class back at Zenith. There were no wildlife or aqualife representatives on the campus that he was aware of.

It was only through firsthand experience that the photographs transitioned from a cartoon fantasy to reality, for him—a reality Dan still had trouble fully comprehending.

"What is most sacred to Hearthlings?" Dan asked the gathering after stuffing a forkful of Greek omelet into his mouth.

"We would have thought you knew the answer to that question by now," Kaab said. "Hearth is most sacred to Hearthlings!"

"We would sacrifice our lives for our planet," Olufemi added.

Dan swallowed. "Would you kill for your planet?"

"We have not known of any occasion when the taking of a Hearthling life was necessary for the sake of our planet," Sohalia said.

"If foreigners such as Earthlings were to invade," Daivika said, "then we would kill and die for her."

The consensus Dan took away from Daivika's declaration of war and his prior conversation with the group was this: Hearthlings don't fear Earthlings, but pity them like lost cousins who cannot seem to find their way—cousins they would exterminate in defense of their planet and all of its inhabitants.

Professor Doba Huaman had emphasized the same thing at Zenith. Dan understood, for the first time viewing the situation with a clear eye. As bad as things were on Earth, in comparison to Hearth, he would protect his home with everything he had if Hearthlings attempted to overthrow them.

This was the way of humans, Earthlings, and Hearthlings alike. Both were bred with a fierce instinct to safeguard their home.

"No Hearthling has willfully harmed another in over 300 million generations, Daniel," Abiona interjected.

"Can you say the same about Earthlings?" Dia asked.

The question was asked in a clinical, nonjudgmental fashion, as a physician might ask a patient about their diet. Dan could only shake his head in shame as an answer.

The mood was quiet and calm throughout the dining room. Dan's table had been the only one having verbal conversations. Dan recovered instantly from his shame.

He had come to know that Hearthlings were not a cruel people. What was relayed to him regarding a war between Hearthlings and Earthlings was not for the purpose of intimidation, or a threat. His dining mates were simply stating a cold, hard fact.

Dan found himself enjoying the peace. A sense of serenity fell upon him. It was not the first time Dan felt tranquil in the company of silent Hearthlings. When had he begun to relinquish his uneasiness during their silence, Dan could only guess.

He was certain it had cemented during his nature hikes with his Golden Meadows Hiking Club—primeval walks that, at times, reminded him of how Hearthlings never began the ominous cycle of contaminating their environment like Earth.

Dan made a conscious decision not to speak unless spoken to. Questions came his way from Hearthlings not seated at their table, telepathically communicated to one of his adult dining companions, who then voiced the thought.

Nothing rude or abusive was fielded. Most questions were mild curiosities about Earthlings and Dan himself. Dan pleasantly answered every one.

CHAPTER 45

Earth Forum. Question: "Is Earthling food organic?"

Answer: "Some of our food is organic. Some of it is processed. Some food is GMO (genetically modified organism). Other food is bioengineered. For precise Earthling definitions on the terms 'organic,' 'processed,' 'GMO,' or "bioengineered,' please visit the Earth Resource Center, where you can find information on Earth agencies that define and implement regulations and policies related to food nutrition and quality on our planet."

*   *   *

Daivika had suggested to Dan that they take a tour of Taíno during breakfast to give Dan an opportunity to see and learn more about their beautiful city. Dan considered it a great idea.

Daivika contacted the tour service. A shuttle coach arrived for them at Heketi Park shortly after breakfast, equally as pristine and luxurious as his school shuttle back at Zenith Campus, with wall-to-wall carpeting and double-file, adjustable plush reclining seats.

Dan was joined by Abiona, Sohalia, Olufemi and Daivika. No one else was interested. The luxurious shuttle was full of excited tourists. Only their reserved seats were empty.

Dan could have done extensive research on the ocean city of Taíno prior to their trip, as he had for every vacation he and his Earth family had taken. Somehow, the same approach did not seem appropriate. Dan wanted a fresh experience unfettered by preconceived knowledge or impressions.

"Welcome to Taíno Tours," the enthusiastic human voice announced over the loudspeakers as they glided east from Atabey Province. "My name is Mayneri, and I will be your tour guide.

"Before we begin, on behalf of Taíno Tours, I would like to extend a special greeting to Mr. Daniel Bluford, the Earthling exchange student responsible for the creation of the Earth Forum website."

Dan was dumbfounded by the eruption of applause.

"Take a bow," Abiona prodded Dan. The applause grew as he did so—applause that included Abiona, Sohalia, Olufemi, and Daivika. Mixed in were a smattering of whistles and complimentary shouts such as "Well done, thank you" and "We have learned so much!"

"Did any of you know about this?" Dan asked his traveling mates.

"No," Abiona said, appearing as proud of Dan as she would Kwasi.

Daivika, Sohalia, and Olufemi shook their heads in response.

"Thank you," Dan repeatedly said with a smile to the crowd. Grateful and embarrassed, Dan graciously took a seat at the climax of their admiration. An interesting thought occurred to him as he sat.

On Earth, the moment would have been captured by a gust of people taking selfies, photographs, and shooting digital recordings, mostly on their cell phones. Hearthlings had the same capabilities, but never behaved that way.

Dan thought he would ask Abiona about it later, before the answer dawned on him. Memory cubes. Hearthlings could literally copy their memories onto memory cubes, the same way Earthlings could transfer their digital content onto websites and devices.

The adulation ceased in waves, like a tide rolling back to sea, leaving a crackling of positive energy in the air.

"Welcome, Mr. Bluford," the tour guide announced. "We hope you enjoy your stay with us."

Dan thanked the tour guide and everyone for such a warm welcome. The Earth equivalent of a murmuring crowd remained for a bit. With Hearthlings, that consisted of the same behavior without the audible murmurs.

"I will point out sites that may interest you as we cruise over this beautiful city," the enthusiastic tour guide continued. "In the meantime, sit back, relax, and enjoy the ride."

It seemed to Dan that everyone did as Mayneri suggested, including himself.

"Taíno is an Aquatic Community of approximately 150,000 square kilometers constructed on the bottom of the North Atlantic Ocean near the Greater Antilles Islands in collaboration with local aqualife and wildlife.

"Taíno is one of only a dozen underwater communities on Hearth. No more are being planned. To build more ocean cities would have an adverse effect on the ecology and environment of the planet.

"Built in 1956, it is the eighth underwater city on Hearth, contained inside of an air-locked, pressurized, soundproof underwater biosphere; soundproof so not to disturb the surrounding aqualife.

"Taíno has the same infrastructure and amenities as any terrain city, with the same stringent environmental sanitation and waste management systems firmly in place.

"Clean air is supplied throughout the city via a specially designed underwater air supply system. Two specially designed hydroelectric power plants keep the lights on and everything else running.

"The majority of our food supply is shipped in, with approximately 12% grown in farm pods scattered about the city. Two desalination and purification plants keep Taíno supplied with fresh water.

"The season is perennial summer, with temperatures ranging from 20 to 30 degrees Celsius inside what we resident Taínos affectionately call "the bubble." Our days are simulated. The natural lighting cycle remains the same all year round: 12 hours of daylight, 4 hours of dusk, and 8 hours of night.

"Some of you may be wondering what evacuation measures ocean cities like Taíno have in place in case of natural or manmade disasters. Ferries like the ones you arrived in, and the shuttle coach you are currently on, are on standby for emergency evacuation. Vehicles can also transport people to the surface.

"Even though the average Hearthling can hold their breath underwater for up to thirty minutes, that ability is of no use at this depth, where the water pressure would crush your body like a tin can.

Citizens of underwater cities are provided with atmospheric suits that will allow them to withstand water pressures at this depth.

"Visitors are not to worry. A surplus of atmospheric suits is available for you, should worse comes to worst.

"About one-third of the population of Taíno and other ocean cities are natives. While you may notice an abundance of plant life and green spaces, there is little wildlife and only domesticated aqualife within the dome. No predators are permitted.

"Since all choices to live underwater are voluntary, few wildlife creatures desire to do so, resulting in very little wildlife being indigenous to Taíno. Should the wildlife who relocated wish to return to land, Hearthlings immediately transport them back."

The tour shuttle hovered over areas of Taíno as the tour guide described what they were seeing, always sharing with the group fascinating information regarding the site history and function.

Green spaces abounded. Outside of the urban areas were patches of groves, small lakes, and streams. Dan had to remind himself constantly that he was in an underwater city. Before Dan knew it, the four-hour tour was over.

"That concludes our tour for today," the conductor said as they landed in Heketi Park. "For additional information about our beautiful city, please visit our website. On behalf of Taíno tours, we wish you safe travels and good health."

CHAPTER 46

Earth Forum. Question: "Hearth has no weapons of mass destruction. Why does your world possess what your people refer to as WMDs?"

Answer: "The prevailing argument is that weapons of mass destruction (or WMDs) exist for our protection, and to create a military advantage. Our enemies will think twice before attacking or going to war against a nation in possession of WMDs, but that's a belief I don't happen to share.

"WMDs have been used more throughout Earth history to exterminate and terrorize people than in defense. I have more faith in humankind than to accept that the bully principle is the only way to keep us safe.

"Unfortunately, Earth is trapped in a global weapons equivalent of a snowball rolling downhill that keeps getting bigger and bigger, discounting the economic incentives involved.

"A full commitment to international trust and the disposal of WMDs is the only solution."

Response: "Who are your enemies?"

Answer: "Nations that wish to massacre our people or overthrow our way of life."

Response: "Why do Earthlings wish to harm other Earthlings?"

Answer: "Some of us are sold on the idea that it is a natural instinct. Others may harm others to feed their egotistical quests for power and conquest. I don't know all of the answers. Perhaps the Earth Resource Center can provide you with more detailed answers to your questions."

Response: "Thank you for your advice. There is no need for me to consult the Earth Resource Center. I have studied this phenomenon at University. The psychology and geopolitical motivations have been thoroughly covered in my classes. I was most interested in hearing from a direct source on the subject. Thank you for your indulgence."

*   *   *

The rest of Dan's stay was a sumptuous blur of conversations, meetings, discoveries, and events. As promised, Daivika arranged a meeting with the Taíno head of transportation, who explained to Dan how their light rail system operated.

The cars literally traveled on rails of light, as Dan had suspected. After their Taíno tour, Dan also expressed interest in learning more about the construction of an underwater city. Daivika made all of the arrangements.

Dan met with urban planners, architects, and designers, and heads of the municipal services, utilities, and ecosystems departments. He met with the lead engineers involved in the dome design and construction and with the lead engineers responsible for the air and water supply systems.

Every component of constructing and maintaining an Aquatic Community was covered. Each person only had time to give Dan a general overview of their contribution to the City of Taíno, offering to send Dan more specific information if he so desired. Dan accepted their generous offers and they made good on their proposals.

Dan was treated to a water taxi tour of the ocean waters around Taíno by Daivika and Funmilayo. They attended an extraordinary concert by a popular Hearth orchestra, and breathtaking live theater and dance performances by local talent at Taíno's beautiful arts and cultural center.

They toured Taíno's outstanding art museum, ate marvelous food (both home-cooked and at restaurants) encompassing every ethnic flavor, And participated in a surprise birthday party for Daivika, Abiona remembering to pack Dan's forgotten gift for her father.

Dan was stumped at how one kept a surprise party a secret from a telepath until he was reminded of how Hearthlings could block anyone else from reading their thoughts.

He took in a fierce football (known as 'soccer' in Dan's country) match between the Taíno Sharks and the land-dwelling Kyiv Vipers at Taíno Stadium. There was no cheating or trash talking or showing up the other team. While the fans were as enthusiastic as any football fans on Earth, there were no verbal or physical altercations by fans of either team.

The Sharks won on penalty kicks. Afterward, not only did the opposing players and coaches warmly congratulate each other, but opposing fans did the same with no residual animosity or arrogance displayed by either side.

Hearthlings were able to evoke the spirit of competition absent the vicious win-at-all-cost malice Dan had so often seen on his planet. It was competition in its purest form.

Dan spent as much time learning about Taíno as he did with Abiona's family, bringing along his EP cube in order to chronicle his experiences. Dan had made it a point to record everything he had learned about the technology, science, and engineering it took to make an "Aquatic Community," along with his personal experiences of his time on Taíno.

He had checked with his professor back at Zenith about the capacity of his EP cube. He wanted to know how much data his cube could hold, and what he would need to do if he needed more space.

Professor Huaman assured Dan that his EP cube could hold more than Earth's largest library. Comforted by the news of virtually unlimited storage, Dan added all of the technical information supplied to him by the department heads he had met. While the advancements on Hearth were well beyond anything on Earth, Dan believed he could at least get the ball rolling once he returned home.

Leaving Taíno was a tearful affair, with all of the families departing at the same time. Dan thanked their gracious hosts with a parting gift of a digital copy of the Beach Boys recording "Good Vibrations." He slept most of the way back to Pequannock Province.

CHAPTER 47

Earth Forum. Question: "Have you discovered any planets besides Earth in your galaxy to contain human life?"

Answer: "None."

Question: "Have you discovered other planets in your galaxy fully capable of supporting human life?"

Answer: "No."

Question: "Knowing that Earth is the only planet in your galaxy capable of keeping you alive, why do Earthlings insist on destroying their home?"

Answer: "Arrogance, short-sightedness, greed, and selfishness. The list goes on. What Earthlings do to our planet defies common sense.

"My fight, upon my return to Earth, will be to make common-sense survival the norm for Earthlings; not the exception."

*   *   *

Back home, there was a day to unpack, settle in, reconnect with friends, and regale each other with stories about their time at Taíno. The next day, they returned to what Dan came to regard as the family routine.

Dan had breakfast with Abiona, Mayowa, and Ifelayo every morning. Abiona escorted the children to their school shuttle on

Monday through Friday, while Dan made entries into his science, engineering, and personal journals. Abiona had virtual staff meetings for most of Monday, as well as impromptu meetings and on-site visits during the week while Dan attended to his Earth Forum website.

On Tuesdays and Thursdays, Dan hiked with his mates in the wild, visiting other parts of Hearth, chaperoned by Abiona or some of his many Pequannock friends. As a member of the Pequannock Province Hearthling Council, Abiona presided over Golden Eagle community issues involving other Hearthlings, wildlife and aqualife.

Dan accompanied Abiona to most meetings. He spent quality time with Abiona when time and circumstances permitted, socializing or having sex. Dan feeling better about having sex with Abiona when the children weren't around. The children spent their time during the week doing homework and hanging out with each other or friends, the novelty of Dan's presence having worn off.

Their weekends were consumed with planned family junkets: outings that were fun for all and often educational for Dan.

There were a variety of events at the Golden Eagle Community Center that Dan attended with Abiona and the children. The family ate dinner together. Dan joined Abiona, Mayowa, and Ifelayo in their meditation circle before bedtime, having become surprisingly skilled at shutting down his active mind.

Abiona tucked in the children and Dan and Abiona retired to separate bedrooms, per Dan's choice.

A few things hadn't changed. The children refused to call Dan anything but Mr. Bluford. Abiona continued to call him Daniel, despite his repeated request that she call him Dan. The house remained the same, including his room, as did the landscaping of their home and much of the community.

Pequannock Province was a clean, safe, and quiet place to live, with people who were content. Then why did Dan sometimes miss his chaotic Earth?

Routine did not mean that Dan was not still learning new things about Hearth almost every day. Abiona put in a request to accompany Dan on an off-world excursion. Her request was denied. All involved in the decision, including the Exchange Student Program Committee, were summarily against it.

"There are still enough dangers involved in space travel that we are unwilling to risk the safety of any Earthling." Abiona read to Dan the damning portion of the report. "We are unable to guarantee Mr. Bluford's safety, and hereby deny your request."

Dan said he would sign any waiver they wanted, to relieve them of responsibility.

"That is not the way it works, Daniel," Abiona said. "We are responsible for your wellbeing. It is a responsibility every Hearthling takes very seriously."

"I understand and appreciate your concern, but I'm an adult, fully capable of making my own decisions and taking my own risks."

"Not as a guest in our home, you are not. We are responsible for you. If that means angering you in order to do what is best, then I suggest you do what you need to do to get the resentment out of your system, because you are not going and that is final."

Dan felt like a child being lectured by his parent. He glared at Abiona, who seemed emotionally uninvested in either her statement or his reaction. Was that her Hearthling way, or was that something she had developed over the years, as a person accustomed to making the hard calls? Dan still could not make the distinction in all of this time of being with her.

Dan resisted the urge to storm out of the room like a spoiled child who was not getting his way. Abiona cupped his face in her smooth, soft hands, an action that always calmed Dan when he was upset.

This time was different. Abiona soul-searched his eyes and Dan waited for her to speak. Experience had taught Dan to be patient, during these moments. Abiona would say what she had to say when she was ready.

"Perhaps you should take a walk, Daniel." Abiona released him after what seemed to Dan to be a few minutes, but was only a few seconds. Dan did as suggested with a huff.

He strolled aimlessly about the neighborhood. Everyone in Pequannock Province knew Dan. Dan knew everyone in Pequannock Province. He encountered neighbors along the way. Nodin and Vaclava dropped by to say hello. Neighbors kindly acted as interpreters for Dan and his wildlife friends. Dan chatted with anyone who was willing, not sharing with any of them his irritation about being denied an opportunity to travel into space.

By the time Dan returned, the serenity of the community had nudged away his frustration. Peace was within him. Abiona greeted him at the door and soul-searched his eyes; this time without touching his face. Abiona smiled and Dan smiled back, then she led him by the hand to her bedroom, where they made love for the remainder of the afternoon.

The next morning, during breakfast, the family announced to Dan that they were taking him on a surprise trip this coming weekend. Try as Dan did, he could not pry any details from any of them regarding the trip.

$$*\qquad*\qquad*$$

It was the fourth Saturday since their return and less than a week after Dan's space travel rejection. Summer weather had taken an autumn turn. They left, in Duke, after breakfast for the surprise road trip.

In less than thirty minutes by air, they found themselves staring down at a place that reminded Dan of the Shanghai Astronomy Museum. It was a building he could best describe as a silver elliptical structure without right angles or straight lines, reminding Dan of the dynamic energy of the universe and the fundamental laws of astrophysics.

"What do you think?" Abiona asked Dan.

"Breathtaking," Dan said after a moment, clearly awestruck by the view.

"Xing Astronomy Museum is the largest museum dedicated to the art of astronomy in the world, Daniel."

Dan recognized the name of the museum. "This is where you work, Abiona?"

The children giggled at Dan's startled reaction.

"This is my office," Abiona said with a smile.

"How big is this place?"

"The Xing Astronomy Museum sits upon a green swath of 50,000 square meters," Mayowa answered, as if quoting from a brochure.

"Our Uncle Olufemi was part of the design team that created this," Ifelayo said.

"Sohalia's husband?"

"One and the same, Daniel," Abiona said. "He told you he was an architect, did he not?"

"Yes, but I never imagined he worked on something like this."

"That is because Olufemi is modest," Abiona said. "Olufemi is one of our most brilliant architects."

"Uncle Olufemi has done great designs all over the world," Ifelayo added.

"He has designed off-world communities, as well," Mayowa said. "Ifelayo and I overheard Uncle Olufemi mention to Grandpa, Grandma, and Uncle Kaab that he was selected as part of the design team for the new Saturn colony."

Dan wondered if what the children had overheard was vocal or telepathic. Mayowa answered as if he had read Dan's mind.

"We overheard Uncle Olufemi telepathically, Mr. Bluford, in case you were wondering."

Dan nodded.

"Olufemi was a part of the Taíno design team," Abiona added. "And may I remind you children that it is impolite to eavesdrop on private conversations."

"Yes, ma'am," the children said in unison.

"When I grow up, I want to be an architect like Uncle Olufemi," Ifelayo said.

"And so you shall, my darling," Abiona said, as if it were written in the stars.

"You certainly are a gifted family," Dan said to everyone.

"As is yours, from what you have told us about your family, Daniel," Abiona responded matter-of-factly.

Everyone remained silent, modesty forbidding them to speak further on the topic. Duke landed in a parking lot composed of eco-friendly permeable locking pavers. Dan recognized the design as one that Single Organism promoted on Earth. Seeing the product being utilized on Hearth made Dan realize that his company was on the right track.

They strolled to the museum entrance, Abiona holding Dan's hand with her children preceding them, looking very much like another happy Hearthling family.

Dan received curious glances from passersby along the way. He had become accustomed to Hearthling first encounter reactions. Besides having a different aura, he understood that, due to his taking Occlumency pills, Hearthlings could not read his mind. Even Hearthlings who had instituted mind blockers still emitted a mental energy. Attempting to read Dan's mind was like dead air, as Abiona had put it.

Still, the Hearthlings were polite, a number of them acknowledging Dan with a nod or a smile while remaining unobtrusive. The fame of being the creator and voice of the Earth Forum website was fading. While still very much active, the Earth Forum had found its place in routine Hearthling life.

As with all Hearthling public and entertainment venues, there were no admission fees or ticket-takers. You simple walked in, the only restrictive factor being capacity. Automatic head counters were installed at each entrance and exit. Hearthlings were strict about enforcing occupancy limits. Safety always a primary concern.

The museum was electric with Hearthling energy; bright and cheerful and bubbling with numerous conversations due largely to the fact a number of the museum workers were IVAs (Interactive Virtual Assistants).

As Dan had learned, in the virtual world, speech is imperative. There are no organic minds with which to connect. Dan took it all in, including gallery exhibits, interactive and virtual, asking questions at every turn and having them answered with accurate and sometimes amused responses.

The family eventually made their way to the Ojo de Dios Auditorium, a Spanish name that Dan knew, translated to Eye of God.

"Here we are," Abiona said to Dan. He looked at Abiona and then the children, not understanding what she meant.

"You will see." Abiona said, answering Dan's unspoken question.

The children were all smiles as they led the way inside. A human usher escorted the family to their seats. The auditorium was already three-quarters full, with more people filing in.

A human announcer marched to the center of the stage: a tall, fit, clean-shaven, middle-aged man with shoulders back, head erect, and chest out. Not at attention, but not quite at ease. He was dressed in what strongly resembled an American white naval dress uniform to Dan. Removing his officer cap revealed a fresh crew cut as he secured the cap under his arm.

"Good afternoon," he said with a commanding voice that reminded Dan of his father. "Once everyone is seated, we will begin." Not budging from his spot, he patiently waited for the few minutes it took for everyone to be seated.

"Before we begin our journey amongst the stars, I would like to ask each of you to buckle your harnesses. Your ride will get a little bumpy, at times. We would not want anyone getting injured." The speaker appeared to be staring directly at Dan when he cautioned this.

Human ushers came around to assure that everyone had properly secured their full-body seat harnesses. The speaker again waited patiently, smiling and glancing around at the crowd.

"I will ask each of you, now, to put on your virtual goggles," the speaker said once the ushers had given him the thumbs up. Hanging from one of their armrests were a pair of onyx-lensed, cylindrical goggles resembling those an Earthling downhill skier would wear.

A roomy VR spacecraft cabin appeared from behind the goggles; one that would be classified as first-class business accommodations on Earth. At the front of the cabin near the cockpit, a tall, fit, well-groomed, middle-aged woman materialized, her bearing and dress the same as the stage announcer. Her officer cap was secured atop her thick hair, which was brushed back into a military bun.

"Ladies and gentleman!" the realistic smiling virtual image announced in a cheerful voice. "Welcome aboard the Veltman! I am your captain and tour guide. Before we embark upon our interstellar journey exploring the neighboring planets and stars, we share a blessing that we call the Silver River Galaxy.

"There are a few items that I would like to bring to your attention. We will not be answering any questions or fielding any comments. In the net pouch on the back of the seat before you is a tablet computer. Please input any questions or comments you may have into the tablet.

"The tablet is also equipped with a mic, if you prefer to dictate your questions or comments. That information will be uploaded into our system, and you can expect a personal reply from one of our experts within a couple of days.

"The Veltman cabin is pressurized and equipped with artificial gravity. This is to allow you to function no differently on this spacecraft than you do on Hearth. At all times, keep your seat harnesses secured during this voyage, for the safety of yourself and your fellow passengers.

"As my co-captain mentioned, our ride will get a little bumpy at times due to forces we encounter that may create unstable conditions. Your complete cooperation would be appreciated on this matter.

"Let us begin with a few basics. A solar system is a star orbited by a group of celestial bodies held to it by its gravitational pull. Our galaxy is home to eight primary planets, dwarf planets, hundreds of moons, numerous stars, comets, meteors, asteroids, and other terrestrial debris.

"This voyage is focused upon our star Sol, Mercury, Venus, Hearth, Mars, Jupiter, Saturn, Uranus, Neptune, and Hearth's moon, Mwezi.

"We will not spend time on dwarf planets or stars, black holes, wormholes, or any of the other associated matter that comprises a galaxy. The Xing Astronomy Museum does offer virtual astrological voyages for any of the areas I mentioned that are not covered on this passage and more. That information is available online or right here, at one of our information kiosks.

"Our earliest space explorers did more than pioneer space travel and chart the stars and planets of our galaxy. They discovered and studied wormholes, black holes, and other space anomalies, chronicling and mastering their sciences, embracing their complexities, and comprehending them on both academic and mystical levels.

"This enabled us to travel to all parts of our galaxy and beyond. We are perennial benefactors of their achievements. If everyone is ready, let us begin our journey into space."

The virtual captain sharply pivoted and marched into the cockpit, closing the door behind her. There were no rumblings or loud noises during the launch, as Dan had expected. The G-force was mild; more like that of an Earth commercial jet airliner rather than the 3gs he had experienced during a simulated spacecraft launch afforded him by NASA.

"We will experience mild turbulence as we ascend," the captain's clear confident voice announced through the cabin speakers. "There is no cause for concern. It is only temporary. Once we clear Hearth's troposphere, it will be smooth sailing for most of our journey."

The captain was true to her word. Once they cleared Hearth's atmosphere and entered outer space, they circled the planet. The hard-shell cabin became translucent. There were gleeful "oohs" and "ahs" throughout the cabin.

Dan ceased, for the moment, to care about the science and engineering behind such feats. He was merely caught up in the magic. Dan looked at Abiona, seated next to him, a smile of satisfaction on her face. Dan had been holding her hand, a practice that had become so common between them that he hadn't even noticed.

To Dan, Hearth from space looked like every modern space photo and video he had seen of Earth, on Earth. It was a big, blue, beautiful pearl that appeared as though he could pluck it from the stars.

Space sounds were broadcast over the cabin speakers: strange, eerie, hollow vibrations, but oddly familiar. Dan was able to discern what sounded to him like ocean waves lapping a shore.

The captain broke in to point out easily recognizable physical geographies. Dan sought out specific places as they circled the globe: Pequannock Province, Naugatuck and Paugussett Forests, and the Zenith Campus. These locales were surprisingly easy to spot, due to clear skies.

The spacecraft traveled from Hearth to Mwezi in a literal blink of an eye. Dan was aware that Hearthlings had achieved superluminal speed (commonly referred to as warp speed, on Earth) long before his arrival. To experience superluminal speed, even in a virtual sense, astounded him.

"There is a common misconception about Mwezi orbiting Hearth," the captain pointed out. "It is more accurate to say that the two bodies orbit each other around a mutual center of mass called the barycenter, a point that lies about 4,700 kilometers from Hearth's core.

"It is the barycenter, not the center of Hearth, that follows an elliptical path around Sol. The orbital pattern of Mwezi, Hearth, and Sol invokes Mwezi's eight phases and the marvels of lunar and solar eclipses. The eight phases or shapes of Mwezi, of course, are: new, waxing crescent, first quarter, waxing gibbous, full, waning gibbous, third quarter, and waning crescent."

They circled Hearth's sole natural satellite, seeing both the light and dark sides of Mwezi. The captain described the planet's atmosphere and geography in a concise, chipper monologue that even an astronomical layman like Dan understood, pointing out Hearthling colonies that populated Mwezi and noting that they existed primarily for research and exploration purposes.

Their celestial voyage preceded throughout the Silver River Galaxy in that pattern, with the captain describing each destination in fascinating detail and making passing mention of dwarf stars and planets within sight of their travels. He inserted enough quips and colorful expressions to break up what could have easily been a dry, comprehensive lecture.

They traveled at superluminal speed between planets and stars, rode along with comets and asteroids, and even entered the gaseous core of Sol, where the temperature could reach 15 million degrees Celsius.

"We hope you have enjoyed your expedition through our solar system. And, as always, in parting, we wish you safe travels on all of your journeys."

As many Nova science episodes that Dan had watched and astronomy events that he attended, none of them compared to what he had witnessed on their virtual tour. The entire spectacular galactic event lasted more than four hours. To Dan, it seemed like less than one.

"Did you like it, Daniel?" Abiona asked as they were leaving the auditorium.

"I didn't like it. I loved it!" Abiona, Mayowa, and Ifelayo laughed. Dan felt as though he were walking on air as they made their way through the museum.

"Mom designed the Veltman Galaxy Voyage," Mayowa said with pride.

"I did not do it alone, dear. My team and I designed the Veltman Galaxy Voyage."

"You and your team did an amazing job."

"Thank you, Daniel. Since we could not take you into space, the children suggested we do the next best thing: bring our universe to you. I only wish I had thought of it."

"It is alright, Mom," Mayowa said. "You cannot think of everything."

"Children are not permitted to space travel, either, Mr. Bluford," Ifelayo said.

"Only adults," Mayowa said. "Mom has been to space."

"More than once, son, as you well know. The Hearth Government controls our space programs. Hearthlings are not permitted to space travel until we are twenty-one. Then we are put through physical training only after we have passed a platoon of psychological tests.

"There are serious risks involved in space travel. Space can be a volatile environment, expanding and contracting, shifting and evolving. Unforeseen conditions occur all of the time. The government works hard to evaluate our space destinations and determine who is permitted to travel, in order to minimize the risk."

"Don't you worry about your sister, Sohalia? She's always in space."

"Sohalia is a responsible adult capable of making her own decisions. I respect and fully support her choices. I also trust our space program."

"Ditto, Mom," Ifelayo said, speaking for her and Mayowa, who nodded his consent.

"Are the tests difficult?" Dan asked after a beat.

"I did not think so," Abiona answered matter-of-factly. "Neither did any member of my family, friends, or colleagues."

"Your entire family has been to space?"

"All except our underaged children."

"I plan on taking a real space trip when I am old enough," Mayowa said.

"Me too," Ifelayo added.

"And you shall, my dears. Until then, virtual journeys will have to do."

"I do not mind, Mom," Ifelayo said. "They are great!"

"This is our third solar system voyage, Mr. Bluford," Mayowa added. "We have also done the Jupiter, Saturn, and black hole virtual voyages. They were fun and educational. Mom and her team designed those, too."

"The black hole voyage is creepy, Mom," Ifelayo said. Mayowa and Ifelayo cringed, then laughed. "I want to do Venus, next. That is another voyage that Mom and her team designed."

"Count me in," Mayowa said to his sister.

"Do real space shuttles have that translucent ship capability?" Dan asked, his engineering curiosity kicking in.

"Tourist space shuttles do, Daniel. Other spacecraft do not. It would serve no purpose."

"One thing I didn't get, Abiona, was why we had to keep our harnesses fastened the entire time. We encountered some turbulent moments as we flew alongside an asteroid and through a meteor shower, and near the atmospheres of Venus, Jupiter, Saturn, and Sol."

"It being a simulation, all of that was controlled. Wasn't it?"

"The conditions were as real as they are in actual space, Daniel. What you were experiencing was mental, not physical. For example: people bounced around in their seats even though there was no actual turbulence."

"Our minds playing tricks on us," Dan said.

"Our minds are who we are, Daniel. Everything we experience or perceive siphons through our minds. There are times when people forget they are having a virtual experience. They attempt to get up and walk around, as they would be permitted to do on a real space shuttle flight, once the captain gave the signal that it was safe to do so.

"They are not on a real spacecraft. They are seated in an auditorium filled with people. Someone could hurt themselves or others if they were permitted to move around.

"We implemented a safety feature for that reason: a centrally-controlled harness release that secures their harnesses until they are safe to be unlocked. You could not have released your harness if you tried."

"I did not know that about the harnesses, Mom," Mayowa said, he and Ifelayo showing their surprise. Abiona nodded.

"Why not tell the passengers, Abiona, about that safety feature?"

"Because people behave better when they believe they are in control. It gives them comfort. Comfort promotes compliance."

Dan thought about what Abiona said, for a moment. As usual, Toni's star-twin was right. The Daniel Bluford in the infancy of the Gaige family relationship would have wondered if the same method of control was being used on him. These days, her candor brought Dan a sense of tranquility.

"The Veltman Galaxy Voyage can be taken from anywhere there is a computer, internet access, and virtual headgear, Daniel. The experience is not as rich as when it is done in the auditorium. We wanted to give you the full virtual space travel experience."

They had entered the grounds surrounding the museum. Outside the museum, their being vocal drew familiar attention from other Hearthlings. Dan stopped, knelt down, and waved the children to him.

Giving them bear hugs, he thanked them again. The children hugged him back as hard as they could. Dan prolonged the hug after the children had released him. The children had become accustomed to Dan's occasional emotional "flare-ups" (as Mayowa had defined them). The children believed it was their jobs to reel him in.

"Okay, Mr. Bluford," Mayowa said. "It is not that big a deal."

"It is to me." Dan released the children after a few more heartbeats and Mayowa and Ifelayo moved on ahead. Dan took Abiona's hand as they trailed the children.

"Is anyone else hungry besides me?" Abiona asked.

"We are!" Mayowa answered for him and his sister.

"I'm starving." Abiona, Mayowa, and Ifelayo stared at Dan. "Figuratively speaking."

They nodded their understanding. They feasted at a place on the museum grounds that specialized in organic veggie burgers, sweet potato fries, and milkshakes.

CHAPTER 48

Earth Forum. Question: "Mr. Bluford, I saw you on the Taíno shuttle tour. You seem to have adopted to the Hearthling way of life. How is that possible, coming from such a different environment?"

Answer: "Great indoctrination by the Exchange Student Program and generous support from the good people of Hearth. Baby steps, on my part."

*   *   *

The observer was correct. Dan felt at home on Hearth, living in the home of Abiona, Mayowa, and Ifelayo as their doppelganger husband and father.

"Daniel! I can read your mind!" Abiona rang out over breakfast, as if Dan had given her a wonderful surprise.

"So can we!" the children exclaimed in harmony.

It was time. Dan had considered the possibility of ceasing his telepathic block medication when in Taíno. Being with Abiona's family made him feel complete, not only as a member of their family but of a community that extended around the globe.

A scheduled dosage was due the day after their return from their trip to Xing Astronomy Museum. Dan made good on his resolution but told no one. He wanted to leave himself room to change his mind. It took a couple of days for the Occlumency pills to wear off.

"I must say, your mind is much more disciplined than our first meeting," Abiona interjected.

"Hearthlings have had that effect on me."

The children stared at Dan for a few seconds, then looked at each other, puzzled. "Mayowa, Ifelayo: don't forget," Dan said, believing he knew the problem, "we can't have mental conversations because you can read my mind. You still have to voice your thoughts for me to understand and respond."

"Right," Ifelayo said with a chuckle.

Mayowa smiled and shook his head. "Of course. We wanted to know how it feels to free your mind."

"Not being accustomed to the experience," Ifelayo added.

Dan thought of Abiona. Dan and the children looked at Abiona, knowing that Dan was seeking help from their mother for a response to their question. Abiona looked back at Dan, continuing to enjoy her breakfast.

Dan took the hint. He thought back on his earliest experiences with having his mind read, beginning his explanation there.

"It's been a journey for me. At first, I was creeped out."

"Creeped out!" Ifelayo said. The children laughed. Abiona smiled at both the children and Dan. "Why?"

"You said it yourself, Ifelayo. I'm not accustomed to having anyone literally read my mind. For Earthlings, it is our most sacred source of privacy. To have anyone get into our head like that ... to be honest, it is intimidating and frightening."

"We still do not understand," Mayowa said.

"Hearthlings are born with telepathic capabilities. For you, it's as normal as breathing. For Earthlings, it is the ultimate invasion of privacy."

The children looked at each other, clearly perplexed. Abiona stepped in.

"Try to image, my darlings, if you were incapable of reading minds."

Mayowa and Ifelayo looked at each other in terror. "We cannot," Mayowa said.

"Bear with me for a moment, sweethearts. Both of you, put up your natural mental inhibitors." The children did as their mother asked.

"Good. Now imagine, if you will, that this was your normal mindset; neither of you capable of reading each other's minds or any other Hearthling, including mine."

The children cringed.

"I know, my dears. Having no telepathic capabilities is a frightening prospect. But it is the norm for Earthlings."

The children thought for a moment, Abiona nodding at them. They and their mother were clearly having a telepathic conversation on the matter.

"We are sorry, Mr. Bluford," Ifelayo said.

"For what?"

"For not understanding your situation more clearly," Mayowa added.

"There's no need to apologize. There's nothing to understand. I'm who I am: an Earthling, just as you are Hearthlings. We are different in some ways, but in most, we're the same."

The children nodded. Dan thought about how this topic would make a good piece for his Earth Forum website.

"It would," Abiona said. Dan was momentarily startled before he realized that Abiona had read his mind. He smiled. The family smiled back at him.

This is going to take some getting used to, Dan thought.

"Do not worry, Mr. Bluford," Mayowa said.

"We will help," Ifelayo said.

"We can loan you books and link you to digital instructions on mind control, if you like, Mr. Bluford," Ifelayo said.

"They will teach you mental exercises on how to discipline your mind," Mayowa said.

"I would like that. Thank you, children."

"Our pleasure," Ifelayo said.

"I can help you with the exercises, Daniel," Abiona added. There was a moment of silence As each enjoyed their meal.

"Thank you, Daniel."

"For what?"

"For trusting me—trusting us—enough to open up in this way. I know this is not easy for you. You will not regret it."

Abiona and the children stood and made Dan do the same. They gave him a group hug that Dan wished could last forever.

*   *   *

Dan was late. Hearthlings in the community kept stopping Dan on his way to the Golden Eagle Recreation Center, shocked they could read his mind.

Dan explained, upon each encounter, that he had ceased taking the Occlumency pills that was blocking their access. He also mentioned to every Hearthling he spoke to that they would have admittance to his thoughts from here on out. This information sparked more conversation from excited Hearthlings eager to learn what it was like for Dan to free his mind, forcing Dan to pry himself away in order to press on to his meeting with The Golden Meadows Hiking Club.

"There he is," Mehdi said when Dan arrived. Mehdi, Gessica, Madison, Seguin, Sahan, Aleja, and Mayneri appeared anxious for their afternoon hike to begin. The shuttle doors were open and ready for departure.

"You are late, Daniel." Gessica said with no noticeable irritation in her voice. "That is unlike you."

Dan tossed his gear into the shuttle.

"You are usually the first one here," Sahan added.

"We were beginning to worry," Madison said.

My apologies, Dan thought. *I lost track of time.*

The group started like a pack of animals suddenly made aware of a potential danger. They gathered around Dan, placing him literally at the center of their attention and commencing to have a Hearthling collective telepathy session, a style of conversation Dan had become accustomed and come to envy.

"Daniel!" Seguin said. "I believe we are able to read your mind!"

Yes, you can, Dan thought.

"How?" Aleja asked. Dan went on to repeat what he had told other Hearthlings on his way to the recreation center, only this time, exclusively through thought. He wanted to practice having more conversations using telepathy, on his end, even though there was no getting around vocal responses.

"Why?" Mayneri asked.

I trust you completely. It's time I showed it.

Dan glanced around at the gathering. All of his hiking mates were smiling, pleased at this revelation.

"You will not regret your decision, Daniel," Mehdi said.

I know.

"We will take it easy on you, Daniel," Gessica said, "so not to exhaust you."

I take it you mean mentally, Gessica.

"Exactly."

In other words, treat me like a child.

The hiking party chuckled at Dan's comment as they boarded the shuttle.

"In a sense, we will treat you that way Daniel," Seguin said. "Using mental energy can be more exhausting than physical."

"Especially for someone unaccustomed to the exercise," Mayneri added.

"Although you are not telepathic, Daniel," Madison said, "you are still expending additional mental energy by allowing others to tap into your mind."

Dan nodded. *I will need to develop mental muscle, in other words.*

"Yes," Aleja said.

"Tell us more about what led up to your decision of trust," Mehdi asked as they buckled in for takeoff. Dan did so on their way to their destination.

The shuttle landed in the southwestern portion of the Naugatuck Forest. Of the four trails leading in the cardinal directions—north, east, south, west—from their clearing, the hiking party decided on the Weyonomon Trail, named after the first Hearthling granted wildlife permission to venture into that part of the forest. It was a seldom-used southern trail that led deep into the bowels of Naugatuck Forest Wildlife territory.

The party was feeling adventurous. Brought on by Dan's coming-out party, Madison joked. The hiking party had secured a special pass from Nodin and Vaclava. They choose the Weyonomon Trail and the wildlife representatives informed their regional family to expect human visitors.

A steady rain had started just before they landed and continued throughout their entire hike; rain that rarely made it to the forest floor through the thick green canopy. Not a bother. They were prepared.

Their normal focus would have been on what they observed during their hike. Today, Dan's Hearthling mates' focus was divided. They were unable to prevent from responding to Dan's every thought.

Dan was astonished at how easily he shifted between speaking and thinking during a conversation. They were rapidly becoming one and the same.

Later, when Dan mentioned this to Professor Bakari, Jabori reminded Dan that he should not be surprised. He had been conversing in the same manner during his time at the Zenith Campus. Dan realized that Jabori was right.

Nodin and Vaclava paid them an unexpected visit to see how they were doing.

"The Earthling's mind is open." Mehdi vocalized from Nodin. Dan disappointed he was unable to persuade the ravens or any wildlife and aqualife to refer to him by any name other than 'Earthling.' Mehdi told Dan he'd explained to Nodin and Vaclava why reading Dan's mind was possible.

"Interesting," Vaclava responded, according to Mehdi. "We find it difficult to understand why it has taken the Earthling so long to do so." Dan went on to explain to the ravens, through Mehdi, what he had told his Hearthling cousins on the matter.

"We do not understand your apprehension," Nodin responded. "But we accept your explanation."

The rest of the telepathic conversation between the ravens and Hearthlings involved details surrounding their hike that Mehdi passed along to Dan. Nodin and Vaclava informed the hikers what to expect from both terrain and non-human life forms as they moved forward, after which, the wildlife representatives took flight, bidding everyone to "Stay safe" and "Contact us if you need anything."

They encountered a large swath of local wildlife; more than usual on their treks, these days. There were beavers, robins, badgers, weasels, deer, bears, coyotes, bobcats, snakes, rodents, eagles, moles, alligators, foxes, hare, otters, frogs, owls, and more; all anxious to get a look at the Earthling they had heard so much about.

Dan had gotten past feeling like a lab exhibit at first contact. The experience always was the same. The wildlife visually examined Dan, with occasional touching here and there. Smelled him. Then observed him for a bit.

Only this time, being able to read Dan's mind, the wildlife made comments or asked questions about him. Dan received all of his information as usual—secondhand, verbally, from one of his hiking mates.

The wildlife they encountered was unimpressed with Dan's new open mind development. The forest residents ultimately became bored with Earthling and Hearthlings alike and returned to their lives.

Onboard the shuttle flight home, conversation was livelier than ever after a longer than usual, spirited walk through unknown territory, the ability to read Dan's mind having melded into the background of their overall hiking experience.

His thoughts often replaced his need to speak. They never took photographs or recorded anything during their hikes, their policy being that they wanted only to commune in tranquil harmony with Mother Hearth.

It was a policy Dan grew to accept, despite his argument that Hearthlings had near-total recall and Dan did not. 'Experience life in the moment and nothing more' was the motto of The Golden Meadows Hiking Club.

The hiking party parted, as usual, after landing in the Golden Eagle Recreation Center parking lot, gathering their gear, making final comments on their latest hiking experience, and mentioning how much they were looking forward to their next hike.

Only this time, they added one change to their normal departure routine: each of Dan's hiking mates gave him a sincere hug, congratulating him for having the courage to trust Hearthlings as they had grown to trust him. They regarded what he had done as a gift.

Dan took a moment, trailing the pack as they headed for home and embracing the affection he felt for his hiking mates.

He was unashamed of the joyful tears welling in his eyes. With his heart full and his mind empty of thought, he had never known such peace.

CHAPTER 49

Earth Forum. Question: "Why is there illiteracy amongst your people?"

Answer: "This is a question that can be interpreted in a number of ways. Illiteracy—or the illiterate—amongst Earthlings can mean lacking knowledge on a specific subject; being uneducated or ignorant. I'm going to assume your question is specifically targeting the inability to read and write.

"My knowledge is limited on this subject, but I'll share what I know. There are a number of reasons for illiteracy on my planet that I'm aware of.

"Generational experience, lack of support or the belief of necessity, disinterest, affordability, poverty, and undiagnosed conditions such as dyslexia are some, and I'm certain there are other reasons. At this time, they don't readily come to mind.

"In my heart of hearts, the only thing truly lacking in the fight to eliminate illiteracy on Earth is international will. I believe that, collectively, Earthlings could abolish illiteracy if we globally committed to resolving the issue. I hope that answers your question."

Response: "It does. Thank you."

*   *   *

Dan was amazed at how little changed after he stopped taking his Occlumency pills. Aside from answering questions or commenting on things, Dan was thinking there was little difference in his relationship with Hearthlings. What surprised Dan was how comfortable he was with having his mind be an open book.

Dan had always been one to cherish his privacy, his mind being the utmost, concerning that tenant. Yet, allowing other minds into his most private thoughts was somehow liberating.

As Dan became more and more accustomed to having conversations generated from both his mental and verbal input, the more natural the experience became. Even his conversations with wildlife and aqualife became less stilted, albeit Dan still required a Hearthling translator.

Dan dove headlong into his telepathic teachings, focusing on mental discipline. One of the first things Dan wanted to learn was how to curb or block certain thoughts, foremost being those involving Abiona.

He and Abiona had made love the day following his hike, while the children were at school. The children were aware that they were lovers. Abiona had told them. That knowledge did not seem to trouble them in the least, extramarital lovers (or consensual non-monogamy, as Hearthlings sometimes referred to such relations) being normal and natural on Hearth.

It bothered Dan and made him uneasy that the children were aware of their carnal relationship. Now that his mind was open, any inappropriate thoughts he might have about their mother would embarrass him to no end.

He discussed his misgivings with Abiona. She understood. What Dan was asking happened to be common practice amongst Hearthling adults—keeping the erotic details of their lives hidden from children.

There were a number of means by which to control one's thoughts. One had been explained to Dan before, that involved placing a mental barrier around his mind. It was an advanced practice in tune with having telepathic abilities that Dan was not ready to try.

Another was what Hearthlings called "Diversion." You would divert a thought to another thought by the use of keywords. "Abiona," for example, would become linked with something innocent, such as "the mother of Mayowa and Ifelayo," so that every time Abiona's name came to mind, Dan's thoughts would divert to her being the mother of

Mayowa and Ifelayo. This would give him time to redirect his thinking, a practice all Hearthlings had mastered by age six.

Memories of their lovemaking would float into his mind like drifting flower petals on a delicate breeze for some time afterwards. That was a common occurrence, for Dan, when it came to sex. He had also added other words like "sex" and "lovemaking" to his diversion vocabulary to trigger the initial thought, "the birds and the bees." Dan practiced diversion at breakfast the next morning. He was amazed how easy it was—or so he believed.

"Why do you think of us every time Mom's name enters your mind, Mr. Bluford?" Mayowa asked.

"Because—"

"Mr. Bluford is practicing his diversion technique," Abiona broke in and answered.

"Hey! We cannot read Mr. Bluford's mind," Ifelayo said.

"That is because I have placed a mental barrier around his mind," Abiona said, "just like I used to do for you two when you were very young, before you mastered the discipline."

"Mr. Bluford is not a child."

"In terms of mental discipline, I am Ifelayo."

"Does this have anything to do with you not wanting us to know about any sexual thoughts you are having about Mom?" Mayowa asked matter-of-factly.

Dan was stunned speechless.

"Yes," Abiona said.

"Adults do that all of the time," Ifelayo said.

"Divert or block those thoughts from us," Mayowa said, clearly finishing his sister's thought.

"You children know about that?"

"Of course, Mr. Bluford," Mayowa said.

"We do not lie to our children, Daniel. Except for the occasional what you may refer to as 'little white lies.'"

"Like when Mom allowed us to spend the night at a friend's house," Mayowa said.

"The same day Mr. Bluford arrived," Ifelayo said.

"Allowing us to believe that you would not be arriving for another week," Mayowa concluded.

"And what reason did I give for doing so along with my apology, my loves?"

"Because we would be restless with excitement if you had not," Ifelayo said.

"Was I correct?"

"Yes, ma'am," Mayowa and Ifelayo replied in unison.

"For the most part, Daniel, we explain to our children why we do not share certain things."

"And say that we will understand when we get older," Ifelayo said, absent the irked tone that his daughter, Mae, would have used.

"Exactly, my darling," Abiona responded with a parental smile.

Embarrassed and ashamed, Dan wanted to leave the table. Not only did he regard his diversion exercise a failure, but he was disappointed in himself for reverting to an Earthling tradition of telling their children 'little white lies' in order to skirt a fact he believed they were not ready to hear.

It was a practice he had come to realize, from his time on Hearth, that Earthling adults used more to avoid the inevitable. Children were going to learn the truth. The only questions were from who, or what, would be the source.

Earthling and Hearthling children shared the same inquisitiveness about themselves, the people in their lives, and the world they inhabited; the difference being that Hearthling adults addressed their curiosity head-on.

The children had nodded their consent to their mother's explanation. Dan found the courage to stay put. The rest of the breakfast conversation carried on as if none of what had been discussed mattered, with Abiona periodically placing a mental barrier around Dan's mind when she saw fit.

Mayowa and Ifelayo shared details of their lives that primarily consisted of school and friends, reporting the information as if it were of vital significance. Dan harbored his disgrace in near-silence throughout the rest of breakfast, listening with interest and only responding as necessary.

His tone was more conciliatory when he spoke. There was nothing the children or Abiona could say or do to break his somber mood.

Dan retired to his room to update his journals after breakfast. Abiona saw the children off to school and paid Dan a visit when she returned.

Dan insisted he was fine. Abiona could tell he wasn't, without reading his mind. She left Dan alone, having a scheduled virtual meeting in a few minutes with her colleagues.

After the meeting, Abiona went to Dan's room to check on him. He was not there. Abiona found him in the study, taking virtual online courses in thought diversion aimed at five year olds. Abiona left him to his studies.

They had lunch together and Dan practiced what he had learned on Abiona. He was better, but still had a ways to go. Abiona bluntly told him so while offering tips that the courses did not cover. Dan said he understood, and he did.

Abiona sensed a difference in Dan from breakfast. He was no longer moping. She saw in him and read in his mind a sense of resolve, a determination to master what all Hearthlings had done with ease.

While Abiona could only imagine what he was going through, her detachment from his experience so far in her past, she admired his fight. It was something a Hearthling would do under these circumstances, a characteristic that this Earthling clearly had, as well.

That night, while the children were asleep, Abiona came to Dan's bedroom and made love to him, their passion reaching a new height. At breakfast, Dan returned to his engaging self.

Breakfast chatter was fun and informative, with the children dominating the conversation. Abiona had jumped ahead in Dan's lesson plan and introduced him to another mental discipline technique called "Hollow." That was a process where you relax the mind to a near-sedentary state while at the same time remaining immersed in the present. It was a process Dan equated as a merging of deep meditation and mindfulness, practices with which Dan had only minimal experience.

By using "Diversion" and "Hollow" together, you gained greater control over your mind, Abiona explained. Abiona helped Dan practice "Diversion" and "Hollow" while they made love and while they basked in the afterglow.

The combined techniques worked. Dan was so relaxed, both methods came to him with ease, like water through a sieve.

While there were still moments when Abiona needed to shield Dan's mind from her children, all in all, he was making considerable progress in mastering his thoughts.

CHAPTER 50

Earth Forum. Question: "Hearth has one form of government. Earth has a variety of governments. Why?"

Answer: "Government is a political system by which groups of appointed officials are given the authority to regulate and administrate within their territories.

"Hearth essentially is one territory. The government is the same no matter where you are on the planet. One Hearth. One people.

"Earth is divided. Many people. The types of Earth governments I'm familiar with are democracy, communism, autocracy, monarchy, oligarchy, plutocracy, theocracy, totalitarianism, fascism, and colonialism.

"These governmental varieties can be explained by the fact that Earthlings the world over have different beliefs, opinions, and histories. In some instances, they are doggedly adhered to as if they were the roads to salvation.

"It's challenging to get Earthlings to agree on anything. On this matter, I speak from personal experience as a Director of Single Organism, a company specializing in environmentalism and geoengineering, back on Earth. I don't ever see Earthlings voluntarily unified under one government system.

"Since I'm far from an expert on Earth governments, I encourage you to take advantage of the wealth of information at your Earth Resource Center on the subject."

*   *   *

In the coming weeks, Dan committed himself to learning Hearthling mind control techniques. With enthusiastic help from Abiona, Mayowa, Ifelayo, Golden Eagle schoolteachers, his former Zenith instructor Professor Doba Huaman, and Dr. Jabori Bakari, Dan had little trouble mastering elementary and intermediate mind control techniques. More than anything, Dan became comfortable with having an open mind; a condition that had come to feel as natural to him as speech.

While Dan did not possess telepathic abilities, he discovered, with help from Dr. Bakari, that he could generate enough mental energy to form a dampening field to block his thoughts. Other Earthlings had mastered elementary mind control techniques. Only a handful had stumbled through intermediate training. None had dared tackle anything more advanced.

This was an exciting breakthrough for not only Dan, but also the "Hearthling scientific community," as Jabori put it. No other Earthling had been capable of achieving that goal. Dan would have the honor of being the first Earthling to succeed, making his name immortal in Hearthling scientific discoveries.

"Your first guinea pig thanks you," Dan had quipped to Jabori for his praise. Dr. Bakari did not get the joke.

The doorbell rang. The children were at school and Abiona was changing to meet colleagues for lunch in Mattatuck.

I'll get it! Dan mentally yelled up the stairs to Abiona, making a detour from grabbing a snack from the kitchen during his break from his advanced mental discipline studies.

"Mr. Bluford. Wonderful to see you again."

Governor Meredith Ellis of Pequannock Province greeted Dan with a cordial smile. Meredith Ellis was the star-twin of Dan's good friend since high school, Wendy Bishop, a First Contact family member that was a NASA astronomer back on Earth. At least, she was a NASA astronomer when last they'd connected.

Dan would not be at all surprised if Wendy hadn't been promoted to a director position by now, as she was on track to become. Both women possessed green eyes, light brown hair, and hourglass figures that belied an average mother of four.

While they shared brilliance, drive, confidence, commitment, and outstanding social skills, there was one area where they vastly differed. Wendy was effervescent. Whenever she entered a room, there was no ignoring her presence. Meredith was poised and modest.

Dan had met Governor Ellis when he first arrived at Golden Eagle. Dan shared in private his star-twin information with Meredith upon their first meeting. The governor thanked him for the news and asked that Dan not make that information public knowledge.

Perplexed, Dan agreed and kept the matter secret. He neither received or requested an explanation regarding the governor's request.

Since then, Dan had only seen Governor Ellis at public events. He had the impression the governor was guarded around him, having been informed by Abiona that Governor Ellis and her husband, Kwasi, were occasional lovers, as Abiona had been with Governor Ellis' husband.

Neither coupling had occurred since Dan had come to live with Abiona.

"Likewise, Governor," Dan replied to Governor Ellis' gracious greeting, returning her smile.

"May I come in, Daniel?" Governor Meredith Ellis never offered Dan the opportunity to refer to her by any other means that was not preceded by her executive title unlike Dan, who near-insisted the governor call him 'Dan.' Like all Hearthlings, the governor preferred his given name, Daniel.

"Of course, Governor." Dan stepped aside. Meredith entered. Dan eased shut the door behind her. Governor Ellis turned to face him in the vestibule, her green eyes as steady and calm as nearby Pulpèkàt Lake.

"Your Earth Forum has been an amazing success and is the topic of debate amongst everyone I know."

"Debate in a good way, I hope, Governor."

"Neither good nor bad, Daniel."

Thank goodness, Dan thought.

The governor pushed forward, ignoring Dan's thought, something Hearthlings sometimes did when they felt no need to respond.

"It is an honor to have the creator of the Earth Forum living in our province."

"You flatter me."

The governor stared at Dan with a blank expression. Dan understood immediately that he had made an Earthling faux pas. Hearthlings did not flatter or exaggerate. It was not in their nature.

"I did no such thing. I merely stated the facts as I saw them."

"My apologies. It is an Earthling expression that does not translate well. Thank you for the compliment."

"You are welcome. Now that your mind is open, how are you getting along?"

Very well.

"Good. Is there anything I can do to help? Anything my office can do, that is."

Thank you, Governor, but I'm receiving all of the guidance I need.

"Excellent. Let me know if you change your mind."

I will.

Dan led the governor into the living room.

Would you like to have a seat?

"No thank you, Daniel. I will not be staying long."

Abiona entered the room, wearing a complimentary plaid executive pantsuit and matching heels, her thick curls long and loose.

The governor and Abiona hugged. They smiled and laughed during their telepathic conversation, behaving like the old friends that they were. Abiona had informed Dan that Governor Ellis and she had been friends since grade school.

I'll leave you two alone, Dan thought, prepared to return to his studies.

"Daniel, please stay," Governor Ellis said. "I would like for you to hear this." Dan did as the governor asked.

"As you know, my term as governor of Pequannock Province is about to end."

"Do you plan to run for higher office, Meredith? If you do, you know you have my full support."

"Even if I run against Kaab?"

"My brother would be the one exception."

Everyone laughed.

"Thank you, Abiona, but I have no plans to run for higher office. My time in office has been amazing. I could not have asked for a better opportunity to serve Hearth."

"Listen to me," the governor said, as if shaking off a bad habit, "giving a preview of my farewell speech. My plan is to step aside from political life and teach at University."

"Our alma mater?"

"Yes. They want me to take over the Department of Government. The current department head is retiring. I have accepted."

"They could not have chosen anyone better."

"Thank you, Abiona. I ask you both to keep this between us, for now," Governor Ellis said to Dan and Abiona, "until I officially announce my resignation."

"Of course," Dan found himself saying in unison with Abiona, feeling as though he was being asked to keep a national secret. Dan supposed that, in a way, he was.

"Congratulations on starting a new chapter in your life," Dan said.

"Thank you, Daniel. Allow me to proceed to the reason why I am here."

Governor Ellis took a deep breath, taking Abiona's hands.

"As you know, the vice-governor will become governor, leaving the vice-governorship open."

"He is a good man."

"Yes, he is."

"A number of fine women will be running to fill his vacated office; all of them qualified." The governor paused and looked deep into Abiona's eyes as if searching for something before she continued.

Abiona was clearly not able to read the governor's mind, based upon her unease in anticipating what was to come.

Dan remembered, from his political teachings at Zenith, that a province governor's term lasted ten years. He also recalled that Hearth has a dual system of government and management; a male and female policy.

It was the yin and yang philosophy of Hearth. That way, Hearthlings got the finest of both perspectives and were most likely to arrive at the best decisions.

Meredith Ellis fulfilled the governmental segment of the female policy. Her predecessor and current vice-governor did the same for the male. He would succeed Governor Ellis once she stepped down. Then the vice-governor position would become available. An election would be held for a female to fill the vice-governor position.

"Abiona Gaige," the governor began, as if she were about to propose marriage, "I would like to nominate you as my candidate to run for vice-governor of Pequannock Province."

Abiona was shaken. She tightened her grip on the governor's hands and Dan rushed to Abiona's side, looping an arm around her waist and placing a steadying hand on her elbow.

Dan had never seen Abiona like this. She was always composed and self-assured during every situation. *Why is this news rattling Abiona?* Dan thought. Abiona and Governor Ellis glanced at Dan, but did not reply. Dan blocked his thoughts with a mind-generated, energy-dampening field. The governor showed surprise that Dan possessed such an ability before continuing.

"I know this is rather sudden. I have given it a lot of thought. In my opinion, you are without question the right person for the job."

"Meredith, I am not a politician," Abiona said once she found her voice.

"Is anyone truly a politician?" Governor Ellis said.

"Yes. Kaab, for one. Everyone my brother came in contact with knew he was meant for government leadership since he was a boy."

"There is no denying that. Your brother is a natural."

"As are you, Meredith. Everyone knew you would become governor one day. It was in your aura."

"Some of us are born to this role, Abiona. Others are forged into this noble profession. You are most certainly one of the latter, my dear friend. I have watched you, over the years, manifest into an amazing Regional Director of Astronomy: someone who has had a global influence in your field; more so than any other acting director."

"Thank you, Meredith," Abiona said. Dan found himself grinning with pride at Abiona.

"Thank you for your global contribution to Hearth."

Abiona nodded, glancing at Dan and giving him a look that inferred he was embarrassing her. Dan stopped smiling.

"You have earned the trust and respect of everyone—Hearthlings, wildlife and aqualife alike—as the elected Hearthling leader of the Golden Eagle community. The wisdom of your decisions sent to our office for approval sometimes left me in awe."

"Those are council decisions. Not only mine, Meredith."

"Yes, but you are the chosen leader of the council, Abiona. You steered them in the right direction; placed them on the right path."

"I disagree."

"Modesty will serve you well in politics. It is a requirement of our profession. Let us not forget that you have the final say as Warden of the Golden Eagle Council. Not once have I had to rescind any of your decisions or proposals for not seeing the big picture, as I have with others."

"I thought you were being kind out of respect for our friendship."

"Hearth well-being eclipses friendships, Abiona—a lesson I believe you know better than you let on, based on what I have seen and heard."

Abiona gave a faint smile. Meredith nodded at her friend. Dan was left to guess at what had been shared telepathically.

"Destiny is relative, as we Hearthlings are fond of saying. Your aura has transformed to prove me right. There was never any question in my mind that you had the fortitude and intelligence for the office. You are a leader and a visionary: two vital qualities every Hearthling government official must have, to succeed at this level.

"Being the vice-governor would be ideal for you. It would place you in the perfect position. I learned so much about what it took to be a good governor as vice-governor, like my predecessor and all of the ones before."

"I love what I do now."

"I promise, you will love the vice-governorship even more."

Abiona initially responded telepathically before verbalizing her comment for the sake of Dan. "I will have to think about your proposal, Meredith."

"Of course! No pressure. Take all of the time that you need."

Abiona held tight to the governor's hands.

"Would you like to sit down, dear?" Governor Ellis asked, appearing mildly amused at Abiona's reaction. Abiona nodded and sat, releasing the governor's hands. Dan helping ease Abiona down onto the sofa.

"I must run. I have office business to attend to. I meant every word I said, Abiona. You are a perfect fit for vice-governor and, one day, governor."

Abiona nodded absent-mindedly, waving goodbye.

"Daniel, will you show me out?" Governor Ellis asked with the same cordial smile that she had when she greeted Dan.

Dan looked at Abiona with concern before responding. "Yes, of course."

At the door, Governor Ellis whispered to Dan, "See that Abiona is okay. I know my recommendation has come as a shock to my friend. I also know she will make a great vice-governor."

I agree, Dan thought.

"Abiona has always been a pragmatist and is rarely one to take a leap of faith. If enough of us encourage her, I believe it will give her the courage to move forward."

I will do what I can, Governor.

"Good." There was silence for a beat. Governor Ellis stared unblinkingly at Dan.

Was there something else, Governor?

"My, you do remind me so much of Kwasi." With that, Governor Ellis left.

Dan rushed back to Abiona, who was still seated in the same place on the couch, looking as dazed as when he left, her hands folded in her lap. Dan sat next to her, gently placing a hand over hers.

"Are you okay?" Dan asked.

"I have to call Kaab," Abiona said with a start, making a beeline for the study.

CHAPTER 51

Earth Forum. Question: "What is faith to Earthlings?"

Answer: "To me, religion needs faith but faith does not require religion. Faith is another word for belief. This is the case when a person believes in one God; an omnipotent, omniscient and omnipresent creator; or a monotheistic conviction erected upon a communal system based upon rituals and rules inspired by warranted divine doctrines.

"Faith, on the other hand, can be expressed through an individual and personal belief system not requiring any specific rules or rituals or collectives. An agnostic could fall into this category: someone who believes in monotheism but does not follow any specific religion.

"Then there are atheists who do not believe in God or religion of any kind: freethinkers who place their faith in tangible proof.

"'Whatever gets you through this world, grab it and hold on tight,' as my father is fond of saying. For Earthlings, sometimes this happens in our darkest hours when we find ourselves at the mercy of fate.

"Wallowing in despair with nowhere left to turn faith becomes our deliverance and keeps us optimistic, believing in the brighter day over the horizon that provides a beacon of light to guide us and a life raft to bring us ashore.

"Faith also attributes to our best moments in life. Meeting a loved one, the healthy birth of a child, achieving a long sought-after goal, faith can give your life meaning and focus. Faith, at its best, can provide a person with a lifetime of positive direction and strength.

"I believe that is why the majority of Earthlings gravitate toward religion and faith. It anchors us; gives us the courage to face the great unknowns."

$*$ $*$ $*$

Dan had attempted to busy himself in his room, writing journal entries while keeping an ear out for Abiona's exit from her office.

He could not take his mind off Abiona. He had never seen his star-twin wife rattled (or, perhaps the word was 'overwhelmed'). For the first time since he'd known Abiona, Dan was concerned.

Abiona had been in her closed office for some time. She had cancelled her luncheon date. Dan respected Abiona's privacy just as she and the children respected his. Still, the urge to tap on her door and ask if she were all right kept gnawing at him. He headed downstairs, determined to follow through on his impulse.

As Dan was marching through the living room on his way to her office, Abiona emerged from her closed-door virtual call with her brother. She appeared to be her old confident and composed self.

Kaab had agreed with his colleague and friend Governor Ellis, Abiona reported to Dan. Her brother believed Abiona would make an effective vice-governor. Kaab had encouraged Abiona to accept Governor Ellis's nomination. He was excited by the prospect and proud that his sister might be joining the fellowship, offering his full support and volunteering to contribute to her campaign in any way that he could.

Abiona asked Dan to remain silent about the governor's offer, albeit with a delighted smile. Dan promised that he would, having mastered enough of his mind to keep his promise. Unfortunately, Abiona had neglected to ask the same of Kaab.

For the next few days, Abiona was peppered with calls from every member of her family, encouraging Abiona to run, accompanied by pledges of their full support. Family members Abiona asked the same thing she had asked of Dan: to remain silent on the matter until she had made her decision.

Despite all of the encouragement Abiona had received, she was still not ready to commit, remaining uneasy about making a career change that she had never envisioned for herself.

Dan was in the mood for a workout to help relieve the stress he had been feeling earlier on behalf of Abiona. He invited Abiona along.

"I could go for a workout right now, Daniel, but I will have to pass. I have a meeting with the Xing Museum team in a few minutes. I am going to grab some water and a snack from the kitchen. Want anything?"

"No, thanks. I'm heading over to the health club. Need anything while I'm out?"

"I am good. Thanks for asking."

Abiona headed to the kitchen. Dan went to his room to stuff some workout gear into his gym bag. By the time he was leaving for the health club, he could hear Abiona's virtual meeting underway, through her office door.

The Golden Eagle Health Club was right next to the Golden Eagle Recreation Center. Both were only a pleasant walk from where they lived.

After sixteen laps on the quarter-kilometer natural outdoor running track, Dan concluded his workout inside the health center with pull-ups, sit-ups, and push-ups. He was enjoying a delicious protein smoothie at the health center café during his extended cool down when he ran into Aleja.

His hiking mate talked Dan into joining her volleyball team in a game at the recreation center. Dan postponed his shower and joined the game. After the volleyball game (where Aleja's team eked out a victory in a very competitive set), Dan showered, changed back into his street clothes, and headed home.

Abiona was in tears and the children were sobbing when Dan walked in. Dan rushed to them. Abiona had been on her knees between the children. They were bound together in a grief hug. Their mother stood, each of her children holding onto a leg and their anguish. Abiona hugged Dan, holding on tightly, her warm tears wetting his face as she wept into his ear.

Dan gradually tightened his hold to match Abiona and felt each child wrap an arm around his leg, linking the four of them together.

Dan waited, his instincts telling him to be patient. Whatever was troubling them would be revealed soon enough. His worst fear was that something had happened to his star-twin Kwasi, Abiona's real husband and Mayowa and Ifelayo's real dad.

Abiona released Dan, dropping her arms around the shuddering shoulders of her children.

"What's the matter?" Dan gingerly asked, feeling the time was right.

Abiona took a deep breath to steady herself. "Magava is dead."

"Your cousin Magava?"

Abiona nodded. "Kaab just called to break the terrible news."

"How old was he?" Dan asked.

"Ninety-eight."

On average, Hearthlings lived past the century mark. Even still, Dan thought, Cousin Magava hadn't looked a day over fifty.

Dan did not know Cousin Magava well. He did remember meeting him at the Taíno family gathering. He was a chubby, affable man of about five-seven with a fetching smile and mischievous eyes.

He remembered taking an instant liking to Magava Owusu, remembering how comfortable Magava made him feel at the family gathering and finding him warm, witty, charming, and smart.

Magava had added his praise about the Earth Forum to the chorus, informing Dan how much he had learned about Earth and Earthlings from the website; two subjects he admitted to not caring much about before his family became involved in the Student Exchange Program.

Magava had called Dan, on occasion, to check on his wellbeing. For these reasons and more, Dan knew he was going to miss Magava Owusu, as he would any member of his Earth family under the same circumstances.

"What happened?" Dan asked.

"Electrocuted," answered Abiona over the sobbing children.

Electrocuted? Dan thought, stunned by her answer.

"Magava fancied himself a handyman."

"Wasn't he a retired software analyst?"

"He was." Abiona let out a couple of weighted sighs. "They were having a section of the house rewired. Magava was bored with retirement and was looking for something to do. His wife said Magava thought he could speed things up if he lent the electricians a hand. She tried talking him out of it, but Magava was stubborn.

"Once he had his mind made up to do something, there was no stopping him. When the electricians were not around, he slipped into one of the rooms they were working on. That was where she found him, electrocuted."

"If Cousin Magava had not fancied himself a handyman, would he still be alive, Mommy?" Ifelayo asked through her sobs.

"Yes, sweetie, Cousin Magava would still be alive if he had not fancied himself a handyman."

"No sense in speculating on the past, Ifelayo," her brother said, able to hold down his sobs long enough to respond. "Cousin Magava made his choices. He lived his life his way. All we can do now is honor and respect him for the man he was, and who will live on in our cherished memories."

Mayowa and Ifelayo collapsed into each other's arms, a parapet of misery in front of their grieving mom. Dan found Mayowa's eulogy for his cousin to be wise well beyond his years; especially from someone in the throes of misery.

The Gaige family mourned the loss of their beloved cousin well into the evening. Neighbors stopped by to offer their condolences, although few knew Magava Owusu. There were virtual calls to and from family and friends, commiserating the loss of someone who meant a lot to them, Dan quietly standing by, consoling Abiona, Mayowa, and Ifelayo as best he could.

Dinner was a depressed affair. While the initial shock of cousin Magava's passing was beginning to subside, along with the tears, sobbing, and weeping, a pall hung over the dining room—one that extended throughout the house.

The Gaige family carried on much of their conversations telepathically, apologizing to Dan for omitting him before filling him in. Dan assured them that he understood, which he did.

"Everyone grieves in their own way," Dan said. "You are Hearthlings. This is your way."

Still, they included Dan in their thoughts whenever they could. To Dan's surprise, the family carried on with their pre-bedtime meditation ritual; one that Dan had become a part of.

Dan was amazed at how the Gaige family was able to calm themselves and find that inner peace they always achieved before sleep. Dan participated but could not still his mind. He could not stop thinking about their misery and the loss of Cousin Magava. He put up his natural mind blockers so as not to disturb the others with his troubled thoughts.

The children slept with their mother and Dan slept alone. He felt alone, unable to sleep, tossing and turning with thoughts of Magava Owusu and the family he believed was still suffering in the nearby bedroom.

*   *   *

Dan knew that Earthling funerals were for the living. Hearthlings did not have funerals as rites of passage for their deceased. They had Transcendence Ceremonies.

This was Dan's first Transcendence Ceremony: a solemn affair celebrating the person's life. Everyone wore handwoven traditional kente cloth, the vibrant, basket-like patterned clothing preferred for the ceremony.

Dan had not wanted to impose. Only blood family members were permitted. Dan was invited not as an Earthling observer, but because he had become a trusted and respected adopted member of Abiona's family.

While the ceremony was as quiet as an empty church, to a listener, Dan had been informed that the service would be given telepathically. They did not break tradition for the Earthling's sake. Dan was not permitted to speak. He simply mimicked whatever everyone else did during the ceremony.

It had only been 48 hours since Magava Owusu's passing. The ceremonial cremation of his body by the state was witnessed only by his immediate family. The use of his ashes had been determined in his will, Magava's option being to create something from his cremated remains, such as jewelry, diamonds, art, glass, or a marine reef. The most popular choices were to mix his ashes with fertilizer to grow something, or turn himself into a tree.

The possibility of placing the remains in an urn or a cemetery did not exist for Hearthlings. There were no cemeteries on Hearth. Creating an altar for someone's remains was considered repugnant and unreasonable.

Cousin Magava had chosen to become a tree, to no one's surprise. He was placed in a copse where a number of his blood family members had decided the same.

Hearthlings have life celebrations. They gathered around Magava Owusu's monument where a baobab sapling was already in place. It was a warm day, humidity mixed with a hint of coming rain, canopied by a pale blue sky spotted with irregular white clouds.

Strings of white baobab flowers dangled like pendulums from the grove of thick-trunked trees that included memorials of Magava's family. Flowers were ready to bloom. There was a tart scent from the flowers in the air. Local wildlife quietly observed, not interfering in any way.

The Hearthlings told stories about their beloved Magava Owusu. They were humorous, sad, romantic, brave, reverent, moral, and then some; the only tenet of a Transcendence Ceremony being that every story must shed a positive light upon the deceased, even if their personal history painted them otherwise.

Their final day of remembrance was not to be a day of crucifixion but life-affirming. In Magava Owusu's case, the life-affirming part was easy. Every family member had attended, each with their positive tale on Cousin Magava's colorful life.

The family held hands in a circle around the burial site of Magava Owusu. The children formed the inner circle nearest the tree. Concentric rings of adults encircled the children in accordance to age. Dan was included. Everyone bowed their heads, each turning on their natural mind blockers before offering a personal telepathic benediction, as Dan would describe it, for Magava Owusu.

Each family member was presented with a traditional "Life Diary," in parting: a cube created by the state, resembling the ones Mayowa and Ifelayo had shared with Dan, containing the deceased memories compiled from his lifelong deposits into their memory vaults.

Anytime any member of the family wanted to spend time with their dearly departed, all they had to do was use the cube. To his surprise, Dan was gifted one.

CHAPTER 52

Earth Forum. Question: "Your world is the same as ours. Why do you not cherish Earth as we do Hearth?"

Answer: "I don't know."

Question: "On April 22 of your calendar year, your world celebrates Earth Day; a day set aside to show support for environmental protection. We do not understand the need for such a holiday. Why must one day be set aside for something that should be a lifelong practice?"

Answer: "Every day is Hearth Day, on Hearth. Earthlings, by-and-large, are not as environmentally-minded as our Hearthling cousins. Earth Day serves as a reminder to Earthlings of the vital importance of protecting our environment for current and generations to come."

There were also Earth Forum questions from wildlife and aqualife.

Question: "All indications are that yours is a predatory society. In the wild, that is expected. It is the natural order of things. Amongst Hearthlings, such behavior is criminal and is legally and morally reprehensible. Why have Earthlings not matured to this state?"

Answer: "Earthlings have evolved as we have evolved. Just as Hearthlings, our journey has led us down the path we travel—a path we are not destined to follow and which remains within our power to change.

"Earthlings have choices. Our free will permits us this. Like Hearthling society, our choices come with consequences; some good, some bad.

"Unfortunately, we have far too often made the worst choices disregarding our humanity, natural environment, and planet.

"I will conclude my answer with this dire warning: Hearthlings can be trusted, but Earthlings cannot. We exhibit egocentricity, greed, and deceit at every turn against each other. The same practices are leveled against wildlife, aqualife, and the natural environment.

"I encourage you and Hearthlings, as well, to continue to distrust Earthlings until we prove, with one-hundred percent certainty, that we can be trusted."

*   *   *

As the old Earthling and Hearthling expression goes, "Time flies when you're having fun." Dan's time on Hearth was nearing an end.

With only a couple of weeks left before his return to Zenith Campus, he found himself working feverishly to ensure that his EP journals were complete. He relished the remaining days he spent with the Gaige family, his hiking mates, Golden Eagle neighbors, and friends, receiving virtual calls ranging from Hearthling acquaintances to Jaheem and Gaige family members, who let Dan know how glad they were to have met him. They wished him all the best of futures for him and his fellow Earthlings.

One of the most touching calls Dan received was from Kwasi's parents, thanking him for doing an admirable job of standing in for their son while Kwasi was away.

Abiona, Mayowa, and Ifelayo were having mixed feelings about Dan's departure, as well. They were sorry to see Dan go, on the one hand, Mayowa and Ifelayo having developed a deep affection for their surrogate father. It was love, but not in the same sense they had for their real dad, but more akin to that of a favorite uncle.

Abiona held a similar sense of affection for her husband's star-twin, her sorrow more in line with saying goodbye to a friend and lover.

While his host family never said anything to Dan, he sensed they were looking forward to the return of the man who belonged in their house.

Word of Dan's leaving had apparently spread throughout the wildlife kingdom. Wildlife that had largely ignored Dan during their hikes came by to wish the Earthling well.

Dan's going-away party was the perfect detour from the sense of foreboding Dan was feeling, knowing that his time on Hearth was nearing an end. It was in the same venue as his welcoming surprise party.

The large, bright, rectangular room was set with the identical elegant dining room décor, with space reserved in the center for dancing. A virtual banner floated near the ceiling that read, "GO IN PEACE, DANIEL." The room was filled with as many well-wishers as the community center could accommodate.

Every member of Abiona's family attended the affair, as well as most of Kwasi's family, the only notable absentees being Achak and Patricia Gaige.

Song after song of Dan's favorite dance music, verbal conversations, and laughter filled the room. Great food, wine, beer, and spirits were served. There were no formal or impromptu speeches were given at the gathering, as one would expect from this type of affair, spotlighting the individual being recognized.

Dan would have it no other way. He always found such treatment embarrassing. The Hearthlings in his life had obviously gotten to know Dan well enough to omit that tradition. There were no tears, but plenty of handshakes, hugs, and one parting gift for the guest of honor: a beautifully handcrafted golden sculpture of Hearth with the engraving, "We do not inherit Hearth from our ancestors; we borrow it from our children."

Despite the festive flavor of the well-organized and attended affair, there was a subdued groundwater mood flowing beneath the layer of celebration.

All were sorry to see their adopted Earthling leave, Dan having had an unexpected influence on their lives by giving them a firsthand prospective of life on their twin planet.

A few Hearthlings admitted to Dan that some had become so comfortable speaking, they found themselves enjoying verbal rather than telepathic conversations when he was not around.

Dan did not know if that was a good thing. Hearthlings laughed off his concern, assuring him that they would return to their predominate telepathic speak in no time once he was gone.

To Dan's surprise, Alvita Agumanu, Dr. Jabori Bakari, and Professor Doba Huaman attended; Dr. Bakari and Professor Huaman insisting that everyone call them Jabori and Doba—especially Dan. Professor Huaman cited to Dan that he was no longer her student, and thereby no longer required to address her as Professor.

While Dan went along with Doba's insistence, he knew she would always be Professor Huaman to him.

An incident occurred early on, while Dan was at Falcon, one involving Jabori and Alvita that continued to nag at him. For some reason, Dan felt his farewell party would be the perfect opportunity to pursue the matter.

"During my first week at Falcon," Dan addressed Jabori and Alvita in the presence of Abiona and Doba, "the three of us were having a conversation in my room about my circumstances."

"I remember," Jabori said.

"Before the two of you left, Alvita summoned my virtual assistant."

"I remember," Al said.

"The two of you had a conversation with my IVA that I couldn't hear. What was it?"

"I instructed your assistant to keep a close eye on you, Daniel," Al said, "and to inform me immediately if your condition worsened."

"I was concerned," Jabori interjected. "You were clearly depressed, Daniel. I was worried that you might slip into a deep depression. If your depression became debilitating, matters could become dire."

"You were afraid I would commit suicide?"

They nodded. "It has never happened before," Jabori said.

"We were not going to permit you to be the first," Al added.

"I see. And if my condition had worsened?"

"We would have placed you in a medical facility for close observation and evaluation, Daniel," Jabori said. "If it was determined you were unfit for duty (to use a military term), you would have been sent home."

"We are thankful it did not come to that," Al said, raising her champagne glass for a toast. "I am so very glad I have had this opportunity to get to know you, Mr. Daniel Samuel Bluford. May your future on Earth be as bright as you have made our days."

"I second that," Jabori said.

"Thank you," Dan said after they all had a sip of champagne.

"We should be thanking *you*," Al said, "for opening our eyes to the wonderful possibilities of what Earthlings can be."

"What Alvita is referring to Daniel," Doba interjected, "is that you and people like you give us hope for your planet. Aside from love, it is my belief that hope is the most powerful force in any universe."

"I can't argue with that, Doba."

"You could, Daniel," Doba said. "Only it would be an argument you would lose."

They laughed.

As Doba or Professor Huaman, there is no denying you are a positive, immovable force to reckon with, Dan thought.

Doba nodded her agreement, having read Dan's mind, along with the others. Abiona led Dan onto the dance floor and Jabori did the same for Doba, Alvita joining them with one of Dan's single Golden Eagle neighbors, who had been eyeing Alvita the entire time.

The party ended at 2:30 a.m. Like a good host, Abiona thanked everyone at the door for coming, with Dan by her side doing the same. In the quiet of the bright empty room with Dan and Abiona, the only remaining humans and Interactive Virtual Assistants cleaning and straightening up. Dan and Abiona held each other close in the middle of the dance floor and slow danced to music that played in Dan's head.

CHAPTER 53

Daniel, your Earth Forum has garnered a place in Hearth history; meaning that it will become part of the curriculum of both Hearthlings and exchange students after your departure. Your request was presented to the Exchange Student Program Committee. We will continue the Earth Forum website once you leave.

I have been selected to step in as interim correspondent until a suitable Earthling replacement can be found. We hope you agree with the committee's decision. Please let us know if you have someone more qualified in mind.

For my part, Daniel, it has been a privilege, an honor getting to know you, and a joy knowing that Earthlings like you exist. I speak for the majority of Hearthlings when I say we believe that Earthlings like yourself will be instrumental in making the change on Earth that is necessary to improve your lot.

'Hope springs eternal' is an expression that Hearthlings and Earthlings share. May its informed waters guide your people to discover their best selves.

Looking forward to seeing you back at the Zenith Campus,
Professor Doba Huaman.

After reading Professor Doba's private communication, Dan answered his final question from the Earth Forum website.

Question: "How would your Earth change if Earthlings adopted a Hearthling way of life?"

Answer: "If, by some miracle, Earthlings would become like Hearthlings, than our societies would strongly resemble yours."

*　　　*　　　*

Dan was leaving in the morning. His packing was done. Everything but his EP cube had been placed in polymer storage boxes designed for long-distance transport, including the Golden Hearth given to him at his going-away party.

Ready for transport back to his old dormitory room at Falcon, Dan was surprised at how little there was for him to pack. The majority of his wardrobe during his stay was borrowed from his Hearthling star-twin.

Besides some newly acquired mementoes and the community's wonderful Golden Hearth gift, Dan would be returning to the Zenith Campus wearing the same clothes as when he arrived at Golden Eagle, having given away his Zenith Campus mementoes to Abiona, Mayowa, Ifelayo, and his hiking mates.

Everything Dan needed to remember about his time on Hearth was captured on his EP cube. Dan was ready, but not ready. While he was glad to be returning to his Earth family, he felt as though he was leaving home.

Dan had joined Abiona, Mayowa, and Ifelayo in their ritual meditation circle before the children were off to bed; something he regularly did these days, especially since he'd stopped taking his Occlumency pills.

He had become good at meditating, shutting down his mind and tuning into his body. The twenty minutes of quiet meditation relaxed him.

Dan decided to retire early when they were done. He had a busy day ahead, and knew he needed his rest. The calming effect of the circle only lasted until he returned to his room. He could not resist the temptation to make a final pass through his voluminous journals before retiring.

Not a day had gone by that Dan had not added to his writings. He had organized his journals into four basic categories for easier reference: Scientific, Engineering, Personal, and Miscellaneous. Dan made minor revisions as he did cursory reviews of each, pleased with how detailed and organized they were. He would have little trouble, if any, comprehending his entries once he returned to Earth.

From what he had read, Dan doubted his colleagues would have any difficulty deciphering his scientific and engineering notes. He planned to keep his personal and miscellaneous notes private.

Dan was about to put away his EP cube for the night when he looked up from his writing desk. He stared out of the window, gazing at a scene his eyes had repeatedly rested upon while his thoughts and daydreams had their way—a view that he had become warmly accustomed to: one of beautiful Golden Eagle homes and clean well-lit streets with its prowling night wildlife and the verdant ranges in the distance east that he had come to know as the Machicomuc Mountains. It was a view he had come to cherish; a tranquil one that made him feel at home.

There was a full Mwezi, filling the night sky like a marauding orb. His eyes settled on the diamond-shaped silhouette of the Machicomuc Mountains. He had taken numerous hikes on that mountain, trudging through its lush forests and fertile valleys and along its clear lakes and unblemished streams.

Memories of those hikes and his hiking mates somehow led him back to the Gaige family, Abiona, Mayowa, and Ifelayo. Dan wanted to do something special to express his gratitude. He just didn't know what.

Abiona came to Dan's room to check on him and to see if there was anything he needed on his last night in their home. She was wearing a loose-fitting pair of men's pajamas—her husband's, she admitted when asked, looking more cute than sexy to Dan.

Making love was out of the question. Neither of them felt right about the idea. Their lives would soon return to normal. Abiona could not sleep, either. She was too excited at having her Kwasi back. Dan was equally thrilled about seeing Toni, Wick, and Mae.

They talked well into the night, Dan mostly about his Earth life and his Hearth life experiences; Abiona about how Dan had changed.

"I don't suppose there is some way we can stay in touch, Abiona?" Dan asked, half-serious. "Like, some intergalactic email or postal service we can use to remain connected."

"I am assuming you are being sarcastic, Daniel. If you are not, you should be. There is no intergalactic email or postal service between Hearth and Earth."

"It would be cool if there was."

"By cool, you mean a good thing, I take it."

"Yes."

"If I were to weigh in on your suggestion in an official capacity, Daniel, there would be nothing 'cool' about it."

"How can you say that?"

"One of the many lessons your Earth Forum taught Hearthlings is that Earth is not ready for Hearth. Your people need to evolve in a number of areas before Hearth would find it beneficial to pursue a relationship.

"That is why the Exchange Student Program exists: in an effort to not only help save your planet, but to open the door for your world to discover ours. Until then, I do not consider it a 'cool' idea."

"Ouch."

"Sorry."

"Did you say, 'in an official capacity'?"

"I did."

"You're already sounding like a government official, to me."

Abiona smiled. "I would make the same call if one of my current staff had purposed your ridiculous idea."

"That's called being a leader, Abiona: being willing to make the tough calls."

"I assume your 'leader' reference is part of a skewed endorsement as to why I should run for vice-governor.

"I have no problem leading, Daniel. My only issue is that I am compelled to be certain of *where* I am leading the inhabitants of Hearth."

"That comes with experience and trusting your gut, Abiona."

"Good instincts I already have, Daniel. Experience is what is lacking."

"Did you have it all figured out at when you stepped in as Regional Director of Astronomy?"

"I did not step in. I was promoted to the position; and no—some things I learned from my superiors. Others, I figured out along the way."

"And, as Warden of the Golden Eagle Council? You had that position figured out from the beginning."

"The same principles apply as my Reginal Director of Astronomy promotion."

"It'll be no different as vice-governor."

"The difference is the amount of lives my decisions will be affecting. Multiply my current choices by millions."

Dan nodded. He put up a temporary mind block. Now he understood. Abiona wasn't concerned about the duties of the office. She was concerned about how her decisions would affect millions of lives.

"Abiona," Dan said, leaning in close as if to share a secret, "someone is going to be making those calls. Why not you?"

Abiona soul-gazed into Dan's eyes, finding there a spiritual connection not unlike the first time that they had made love. Abiona cupped his face.

Dan released his block, but kept his mind clear. Abiona read his mind. Dan had but one thought: an image of a still, blue, crystal lake. He was awaiting Abiona's response.

"I will think about what you said, Daniel."

That's all I ask, Dan thought.

"When you arrived, Daniel, I do not mind saying that I could not see what the Exchange Student Program saw in you."

"Are you serious?"

"Of course. I mean, until you took those Occlumency pills, your mind was as undisciplined as a Hearthling three-year-old. You would not stop with that annoying Earthling sarcasm."

"Sarcasm is not annoying."

"It is to us."

"Why didn't anyone say anything?"

"Because we are polite to our guests. We endure."

"I believe you were being sarcastic just now, Abiona."

"Perhaps," Abiona said with a wry smile. They both laughed. The thought crossed his mind, and Abiona read it.

"Do not worry, Daniel. You will not call your wife by my name."

"How can you be so sure?"

"You have a disciplined mind, now. You can..."

Use diversion to change Abiona to Toni every time your name enters my head.

"Correct. Within a few weeks, you will have forgotten all about me."

"That will never happen, Abiona."

"Promise."

"With all of my heart."

There was an awkward silence, in speech and in mind. The ache of leaving set in Dan's chest. He stood and offered Abiona his hand.

"Would you mind giving me another tour of your home?"

"You already know your way around our home."

"For old times' sake."

Abiona remained reluctant.

"Humor me."

Abiona stood and took Dan's hand. They walked downstairs to the living room. Abiona was about to begin her tour when Dan interrupted.

"What say we go back to the beginning?"

"You mean, back to when we first met in Dr. Bakari's office?"

"Not that far back."

Dan led Abiona out through the front door and onto the curved, herringbone brick, walkway leading up to the front entrance, closing the front door behind him before letting go of her hand. They stood before the two-story luxury brick Colonial with a two-story foyer in relative silence. The full Mwezi added its glow to the night.

"I see," said Abiona, ready to play along. "Allow me to give you a brief tour of our home before you settle in, Mr. Bluford," she began, after opening the unlocked front door.

Dan scooped Abiona up into his arms in a maneuver that caused Abiona to squeal with surprise.

"You're familiar with this tradition, I take it?"

"What tradition might that be, Daniel?" Abiona said, relaxing into the cradle of his arms. She wrapped her arms about his broad shoulders as Dan pulled her closer to his body.

The intoxicating scent of cherry almond that Abiona and Toni shared was not lost on Dan. Her body as weightless as the air around them.

Dan carried Abiona over the threshold, as he had done with his Earthling bride on their honeymoon night. The two of them looked like newlyweds, absent the wedding adornments. They smiled like newlyweds, with unbridled joy, staring at each other with laughing eyes. He carried Abiona down the hall and into the living room, where Abiona gave Dan a sensual kiss.

"Now, if you will put me down, Daniel," Abiona said when their lips parted, "perhaps we can continue your guided tour of our home."

Dan did as Abiona requested. Abiona took him by the hand, reconstructing their tour, mixing the old with the new while being careful not to disturb the children.

They behaved like young newlyweds, making each other laugh at the silly things they said and did. The tour ended in Dan's bedroom, where they eventually managed to settle themselves down, falling into a deep, platonic sleep in the soothing warmth of each other's arms.

CHAPTER 54

Earth Forum. Auto plays a digital message from Dan upon logging in to the website.

"My dear Hearthlings, wildlife, and aqualife family. This is my farewell post. I will be returning to the Zenith Campus in the morning. The Exchange Student Program Committee has asked if they could continue the Earth Forum website upon my departure. I told them I would be honored.

"I cannot begin to tell you what a pleasure and privilege it has been for me to be invited into your home. When you think of my fellow exchange students and me. I hope we will be fondly remembered. I promise that upon my Earth return, I will do all in my power to transform the self-destructive ways of Earthlings.

"Should my efforts and those of fellow exchange students past, present and future succeed, it is my hope that Earthlings will come to know Hearthlings without the need for secrecy, Hearthlings, wildlife, aqualife, and Earthlings moving forward as one.

"You are, in my humble opinion, our best versions of ourselves. I leave your beloved planet with a heavy heart, an Earthling expression reserved for sorry of the most intimate of losses.

"I will also take with me an uplifted spirit, thanks to all you have taught me about the blessing of your beloved Hearth.

To know you is to love you. Love you, I do. Continue to take care of yourselves and each other. I already know that you will."

"Signing off,

Your Earthling brother for life,

Daniel Samuel Bluford."

What Dan omitted from his farewell post was that the Exchange Student Program Committee had wanted to rename the Earth Forum, in honor of its creator, "The Daniel Samuel Bluford Earth Forum." While Dan was moved by the gesture, he felt that maintaining the name 'Earth Forum' would be sufficient.

Dan did relent to a tribute page' to appear on the website after he left so he would not be embarrassed by the sentiment.

*   *   *

The Zenith Campus Shuttle was scheduled to arrive at 8:00 a.m. Dan was ready. Everything but his EP cube had been packed the night before and transported back to his old dormitory room at Falcon, including the Golden Hearth he had received as a parting gift from the Golden Eagle community.

When Dan entered the living room, escorted by Abiona, he was overwhelmed by what he saw. Besides Mayowa and Ifelayo, the Jaheem and most of the Gaige family had made a surprise visit to say farewell. Kwasi's parents were not amongst them.

I don't know what to say? Dan thought.

"Words are not necessary, Daniel," Kaab responded.

"We wanted to be here to see off an extended member of our family," Funmilayo said, walking up to Daniel and placing her warm, soft hands on his cheeks while gazing into his eyes. "You have the light of a Hearthling in you, Daniel. Did you know that?"

"Thank you. With any luck, I'll be able to put that light to good use back on Earth."

"You will," Daivika said. "You possess the aura of a Jaheem, now. You will not fail."

The gathering moved in for a group hug. Dan felt as though he were wrapped in a protective cocoon: one emanating strength, harmony, and peace.

Abiona asked to be excused, after the group embrace. She took Dan by the hand and guided him into her office.

"I needed to speak to you alone for a moment," Abiona whispered to Dan behind the closed doors of her office.

"What is it?"

"I have decided to run for vice-governor of Pequannock Province."

"That's wonderful, Abiona!"

"Keep it down, Daniel," Abiona said in a firm whisper. "Use your mind."

Okay.

"You are the first person I have told."

Why all of the secrecy?

"I will make a formal announcement once Kwasi is home. I wanted you to know of my decision before you left."

Thank you for sharing.

"Our talk last night is what tipped the scales in favor. Someone is going to make the calls. Why not me? I will have to write an acceptance speech, of course. The Golden Eagle Council will need to elect a new warden. I have a successor in mind."

Mehdi Abadi?

"How did you know?"

My hiking mate is an upstanding member of the council. I've heard nothing but good things about him. He would be my choice.

"Do you think he will accept?"

You don't need me to answer that, Abiona. What do you think, future vice-governor?

"He loves this community as much as I do, and the people love him. Like me, he is appreciated and respected by regional wildlife and aqualife. He will accept."

Dan smiled and nodded. *I wish I could stay for the election.*

"The election will turn out as all elections do on Hearth. The constituents will select who they believe will best fill the position."

Then your appointment is a lock.

"Sarcasm, I take it."

Not at all. From what I've seen and heard, not only do your fellow Hearthlings love you, but so does wildlife and aqualife, as you already know.

"'Love' is too strong a word in regards to wildlife and aqualife, Daniel. It's more like they respect and appreciate me, as I have said before."

That still translates to votes, as far as I can see.

"You may be right. Time will tell. I hope you do not mind my saying this, Daniel; but almost everything you have said to me on this matter, I can imagine Kwasi doing the same."

I'll take that as a compliment, Abiona.

"You should."

What would Kwasi have done differently?

"No sarcasm."

Dan chuckled. *I couldn't be prouder or happier for you, Abiona.*

"Thank you, Daniel. That means a lot, coming from my star-twin husband. I have much to learn."

One thing I know for certain.

"And that is?"

You'll have all of the support and guidance you need to succeed. Your family. Your brother the governor, and Governor Ellis. The Golden Eagle community. I'll bet Nodin and Vaclava will volunteer to become a part of your campaign. You know they have major influence amongst their peers.

Abiona smiled and nodded. They hugged.

"Toni will be lucky to have you back, Daniel."

The same can be said about your Kwasi.

Dan and Abiona were making small talk with the rest of the family after having returned to the living room when Dan received a text message that read, "The shuttle is here."

"I guess this is it," Dan said to everyone.

When Dan stepped into the clear morning, he was awestruck by what he saw. The entire Golden Eagle community was there to see him off. He stood stock-still, paralyzed, not knowing what to do. Ifelayo took one hand and Mayowa the other, gently tugging him toward the clear path leading to the shuttle.

"Time to go, Daniel," Abiona whispered into his ear, her hands on his shoulders gently nudging him forward. Dan's thoughts raced as he took baby steps toward the shuttle in a return of his undisciplined Earthling mind having a spasm, as referred to in his teachings.

Dan took a couple of deep breaths, as he was taught, to combat the convulsions, and calmed himself. He stilled and cleared his mind, finding his stride in the process.

Abiona and the children released Dan at the shuttle entrance, his Hearthling family joining the crowd that had gathered close. Dan turned to face them.

He knew that saying goodbye was going to be difficult. Having an entire community farewell made it nearly impossible. Dan closed his eyes, took in a deep meditative breath, then opened his eyes and spoke to the gathering with his thoughts.

I will miss you all. Thank you for your generosity, patience, protection, and wisdom. I am eternally grateful. I will never forget you—any of you. Be well, and continue to live in harmony and peace with each other and your planet. Be forever Hearthlings.

Collectively, each Hearthling placed a hand over their hearts and gave Dan a slight nod, the universal Hearthling sign of a kind thanks. Dan returned the gesture before boarding the shuttle.

On board, Dan was reunited with most of his exchange student classmates. Obed, Nivi, Intan, Waqas, Ella, Jomana, Carlito, Gagandeep, Gennady, and Oliver were staring, wide-eyed, out of cabin windows at the crowd. His was the last stop before returning to the Zenith Campus.

Missing were Amaya and Cardinal Ocampo, both having opted out early to return to Earth, as Dan would later discover. They'd missed their home too much to persevere.

"Wow, Dan! You're sure popular," Oliver said.

"Only a handful of Hearthlings came to see me off," Obed said.

"Me too," Waqas added.

"You must have made quite an impression," Ella said.

"Probably has a lot to do with your Earth Forum website," Gennady commented. "Which is brilliant, by the way."

Dan did not know what to say, so he said nothing. He smiled a modest smile and took a window seat. His classmates, disappointed by his reaction, left him alone.

Dan was going home. At the same time, he felt as if he were leaving home. He stared out of the window at the crowd, fingering his EP cube in his pocket. Dan had photographs and digital recordings on his EP cube of everyone at the gathering. Most, he had taken himself.

Still, he tried to commit each face and name to memory. It was a surprisingly easy effort, using his mental discipline teachings. Abiona, Mayowa, and Ifelayo had already been permanently installed, as were the Jaheem and Gaige families.

His hiking mates, Mehdi, Gessica, Madison, Sequin, Aleja and Mayneri; his neighbors and friends; and even Kwasi's parents had cemented places in his memory, in spite of their absence, thanks to photographs and digital recordings shared by Abiona's parents of the Taíno family gathering.

Nodin and Vaclava sat on the shoulders of Mehdi, the only wildlife representatives present. Dan committed the ravens to memory, as well.

The crowd waved as the shuttle did a vertical take-off. Dan had been focusing his efforts on memorizing the Hearthlings he had come to know in passing. Everyone on the shuttle, including the pilots, waved back.

The ravens took flight, joined by flocks of birds that seemed to appear out of nowhere. They flew in unison, as if intending to act as escorts for the shuttle. Nodin and Vaclava let out a few caws before gliding toward their forest home. The avifauna procession followed their leaders, their way of wishing the Earthling well. He was sure of that, even without a Hearthling interpreter.

The shuttle climbed to its desired altitude, hovered for a moment, then banked east. Dan looked back at the gathering. The crowd had become a speck on the land. A message in sparkling golden letters appeared across the bright blue sky, well within view.

"We will miss you, Dan. Forever your family, the Hearthlings of the Golden Eagle."

The shuttle accelerated, knifing through the farewell message. Dan could not hold back his parting tears.

CHAPTER 55

The shuttle touched down at 10:16 a.m. in front of the Falcon building. Alvita Agumanu was there to greet them with motherly hugs and a dazzling smile, wearing one of her trademark power suits, pumps, and braided crown. A flower-patterned tote bag was slung over her shoulder.

"Welcome back!" the spirited Falcon Student Housing Director said as they gathered in the swarming front lobby with Hearthlings, androids, delivery drones, and exchange students on the move. A once-familiar melody of international voices filled the space. "How was your stay?"

Alvita patiently listened with a sincere smile and appropriate responses as each Earthling compressed their time spent amongst the Hearthling populace into what could be summarized as "good" to "great."

"I trust your return trip was pleasant?" Alvita asked.

Everyone answered in the affirmative.

"Follow me." The exchange students did as instructed like ducklings following their mother. Alvita led them to the elevator lobby.

"I trust you remember how to get to your living quarters from here," Alvita chided.

The Earthlings chuckled.

"Good. Contact me if you need anything." Alvita was off before they could finish their thanks.

Dan made his way to Unit 4A. He found his old dormitory room the same as the first day he had moved in, except for his labeled, packed items, transported from Abiona's home, neatly stacked off in the living room corner. Alvita had informed her flock that they would not have an IVA assistant due to their brief stay, but every Falcon accommodation remained available to them.

Class 3B assembled in the student lounge, as agreed upon, before dispersing to their separate rooms. Alvita informed her flock that they had free rein, with an assigned shuttle at their disposal to take them anywhere on campus.

The day was clear and pleasantly warm. Class 3B unanimously agreed to take a sky tour to reacquaint themselves with the Zenith Campus before they hit the ground. They found the campus was even more beautiful than they remembered. The Falcon building, Wakin, museum, art gallery, library, restaurants, and plenty of green space—even the Zenith Medical Center, where their journey had begun, was a pleasant sight for nostalgic eyes.

Dan discovered that his classmates felt as he did as they excitedly pointed out places attached to memories of their time on campus, as if being awarded prizes for doing so. They were going home, but somehow they unanimously felt as though they were leaving home.

On the ground, they confirmed that nothing had changed except for some new Earthling faces with whom they were not permitted to have any contact. Class 3B was permitted contact other Earthlings who were part of their graduating class—other exchange students who were also scheduled to return to Earth within the next few days.

Dan and his classmates photographed and digitally recorded everyone and everything they encountered, using their EP cubes and behaving like star-struck tourists in the midst of a wonderland.

"That was quite a sendoff, Dan," Obed said. "You clearly made a tremendous impression on your hosts."

They had stopped at Demeter for a late lunch, one of their favorite lunch spots to eat and chat when they were students.

"We connected," Dan said.

"As I mentioned before, your Earth Forum was genius," Gennady said.

"Every Hearthling I knew loved it," Ella said.

"The website helped me acclimate more easily," Intan said, "and become accepted as an Earthling within my community."

Everyone agreed.

"My only gripe was that they never allowed us to communicate with you or have any input on Earth Forum," Waqas said.

"There was nothing I could do about that, Waqas. It was part of the agreement I made with the Exchange Student Program Committee in order for the website to be implemented."

"Ah, politics," Gennady said, "plays a role even amongst Hearthlings."

"I see it more as an agreeable compromise," Dan responded.

"Regardless, it accomplished a lot," Gagandeep said.

"Who's going to take over once you leave?" Carlito asked.

"Does it matter? We won't be here to see it." Dan found himself wanting to drop the subject, feeling defensive and oddly irritated by the realization that he would no longer have any connection to Earth Forum.

Dan suddenly found himself longing for the forests and mountains of Pequannock Province, the Golden Eagle community, his Hearthling friends and neighbors, his hiking mates, the home he shared with Ifelayo and Mayowa and above all else his star-twin wife, Abiona. He missed them for the moment more than he missed Earth.

His classmates sensed his mood swing. Jomana was quick to change the subject.

"Those Occlumency pills were a godsend."

"Tell me about it," Nivi agreed.

"I don't know what I would've done if Hearthlings had known what was going on inside my head every minute of every day," Oliver said.

"My Hearthlings didn't need to know my exact thoughts," Waqas said. "They were good at deciphering what I was thinking."

"Mine, too," added Ella.

"Come to think of it, mine were, too," Carlito said.

"They could read my body language, micro-expressions, voice tics, and aura," Gagandeep said. "You name it and they knew what to look for."

"Looks like they had us all pegged," Oliver said.

Dan had remained silent during their exchange. Everyone noticed.

"What about you, Dan? Were your Hearthlings good at reading you?" Waqas asked.

Dan hesitated before he spoke. "First of all, they aren't *my* Hearthlings. They don't belong to us. They are not our pets."

"Sorry," Waqas said. Looking around, he noticed that everyone else was just taken aback as he was by Dan's reaction. "We didn't know you had become so sensitive on the subject."

"I stopped taking my Occlumency pills."

"What?! When?! Why?!" the trio of Obed, Ella, and Waqas asked, in that order.

"I discovered I had no reason to hide my thoughts."

"You let them into your mind?!" Gennady said.

"I did."

"What was it like?" Jomana asked.

"I remember what it was like before I took the mind-blockers," Nivi said. "I didn't like it. Not at all."

"I felt the same way you did initially, Nivi," Dan said. "Our minds, our thoughts, are our most sacred and private domains. When I let them in—anyone, everyone—I found it peaceful."

"Peaceful?" Jomana said.

"Having nothing to hide was liberating. Hearthlings taught me how to discipline my thoughts. I could naturally block anyone from reading my mind whenever I wanted."

"Sounds like we missed out," Intan said.

"Don't get me wrong. It wasn't easy, but it was worth the effort."

"Could you read their minds?" Obed asked.

"Unfortunately, no. It's too late for us to develop telepathic skills."

"It was like Professor Huaman taught us," Jomana chimed in. "Hearthlings are born with the ability and nurture it early. Earthlings may have the same capabilities, but are unaware. So we lose our window of opportunity."

"If it exists at all," Waqas said.

"Telepathy in infants is an area of study I'm going to make a priority when I get back to Earth," Carlito said.

"Definitely worth exploring," Oliver added.

Everyone nodded.

"Dan, when you were standing outside the shuttle facing all of your—forgive me, those—Hearthlings, you were talking to them?" Gagandeep asked.

"With my mind, yes."

"That's amazing," Nivi said.

"Can you still do it?" Obed asked.

"Yes."

"You're taking that skill home with you," Gennady said.

"Looks that way."

"Who are you going to mind talk with back on Earth?" Waqas asked.

Dan hadn't considered that point. The ideal of having no one around who could read his thoughts made him suddenly feel lonely and isolated.

"I don't know," he answered. "No one, I guess."

The group noticed the curve of sadness in Dan's voice.

"I can't wait to share my notes on Hearthling anthropology," Jomana said, quick to change the course of the discussion again. "And the new music I've written."

"I can't wait to read your anthropological notes," Ella said.

"I can't wait to hear your new music," Gagandeep said.

"We all have plenty to share," Obed said, removing his EP cube from his pants pocket and placing it on the table, "thanks to these amazing devices."

Seeing Obed's EP cube made Dan realize that all of the data he had accumulated on the advances of Hearthling society during his stay, he would not be able to achieve in his lifetime. Furthermore, Dan did not even know where to begin.

"Think we'll ever figure out how they work?" Intan asked.

"I'm certainly going to give it a try, Intan," Dan said, sounding more like his upbeat self.

"You're not alone," Oliver added.

"Let's eat up," Nivi said. "We have a lot of ground to cover on our final visit. Let's not squander our last day sitting on our butts."

The group laughed.

"I wouldn't call enjoying this delicious meal squandering our time, Nivi," Gennady said.

"You know what I mean."

"We do."

They finished their meals while enjoying more conversation wherever it led, continuing their farewell foot tour of the Zenith Campus in no time.

*   *   *

Calypso steel pan music filled the room. It took Dan a moment to realize that it was the doorbell. Dan was bushed after their nonstop whirlwind Zenith Campus tour, delicious dining, and exhilarating conversations, not wanting to miss anything before they left. It was a parting that had spilled over into the Falcon student lounge. Dan briefly reflected on their last moments in the lounge.

It was late. Their conversation had been fluctuating more and more between their time on Hearth and returning to their Earth lives. No one knew what to expect once they got home, and resisted the urge to retire for the night, despite being exhausted.

"We have missed birthdays, anniversaries, holidays, personal and professional milestones, and other events that have transpired within the normal passage of time," Gagandeep said. "Events that have occurred without our presence, with no Earthling realizing we were gone. That, in and of itself, seems strange to me. Stepping back into my own life now seems even stranger."

The mood of Class 3B shifted from joyful fatigue to wistful silence. None of the exchange students knew how to respond. Everyone accepted that they felt the same, making them feel anxious about their future.

As if summoned by some omnificent mercy, Alvita appeared, ordering them to retire to their rooms.

Dan hesitated before answering the door, wishing IVA "Alvita" was there to tell him who it was.

The woman he had tutored in geoengineering, who had tutored him in ancient human societies, and cultures was standing there, wearing casual jeans, white low-cut sneakers, a loose-fitting purple blouse with a matching hijab, and her wedding band as her only jewelry.

Her pecan skin was flawless; her makeup impeccable, as were her big, smoky brown eyes and the teasing hint of an ingratiating affectionate smile.

"Can we talk?" Jomana Ashraf asked.

"Of course," Dan said, stepping aside to let Jomana in.

They stood in the living room in front of the sofa.

"I won't be long," Jomana said, turning down Dan's offer of a seat.

"I have a question for you of a very personal nature. You don't have to answer if you don't want. I'll understand."

"Ask away."

Jomana inhaled, deliberated for a moment, and then exhaled. "Did you have sex with your Hearthling wife? Your wife's star-twin?"

Dan's immediate thought was that it was none of Jomana or anyone else's business. Her clear anxiety made him still that response. "Yes," he said.

"Oh, thank God!"

"What am I missing, Jomana?"

"I did the same with my Hearthling husband."

Now Dan understood. Jomana was looking for confirmation that she was not alone in her indiscretion.

"I wouldn't call what Abiona and I did 'having sex,' Jomana. We made love."

"That's exactly the way it was with me and my husband's star-twin."

"When on Hearth, do as Hearthlings, Jomana. It's their way. We simply adopted it."

"What I don't understand is why I don't feel guilty about it."

"Like we did when we almost committed adultery?"

"Yes. I wanted you, Dan. Still do, actually. Only, now, I can resist the temptation without any guilt or shame, the two emotions that kept us apart, because my attraction to you feels natural, just as my choice on whether or not to act upon it. Do you have that same sense of clarity?"

Dan realized he felt the same about Jomana, although he could not have expressed it as elegantly.

"We're going home tomorrow, Jomana. My advice is that we put this all behind us. Try to forget it ever happened."

"I'll try."

"You'll do it; and so will I."

"My, my, you certainly have become bossy."

"You ain't seen nothing, yet. Wait until you get to know me back on Earth."

Jomana's unbridled laughter turned into that smile that would shame the sun, enlightening Dan of the core for his attraction to Jomana. It was her inner beauty; that radiant glow, like that of his Earth wife Toni and his Hearthling wife, Abiona.

"Friends," he said.

"Friends." Neither was certain who initiated the hug, the sweet, rich scent of jasmine coming from her skin; a warm embrace with no trace of carnal desire, as was Jomana's innocent peck on the cheek. Dan escorted Jomana to the door.

"See you later, Daniel."

Dan started at hearing his given name spoken, making him think of Abiona. "I look forward to it."

It happened in a flash, only seconds after Jomana left. Dan almost didn't recognize the symptoms, it had been so long since his last episode. Dan staggered over to the sofa and plopped down, readying himself for what was to come.

Kwasi and Toni put Wick and Mae to bed without any of their usual fuss. The children were exhausted from a full day of activities, leaving their resistance to slumber nil. Dan heard running bath water coming from the bathroom of their master bedroom when he entered. Toni was humming the song "The Closer I Get To You," Roberta Flack and Donny Hathaway's version being their favorite. Kwasi considered joining Toni for a moment. The moment passed.

Kwasi slipped downstairs and retrieved his laptop. He propped himself up on their bed, addressing work emails by the time Toni emerged from their bathroom.

Toni looked refreshed and relaxed. She wore a rose-red, satin lace, chemise nightgown that Dan remembered. Her espresso skin was aglow from lotion, her nipples budding beneath the satin as if attempting to poke their way through.

Toni sat on her side of their king-size bed, propping up her pillows against the headboard, stretching out, and resting her back against the soft wall she had formed, duplicating what Kwasi had done.

Toni grabbed her laptop from atop her nightstand, flipped it open, and started reading medical journals.

This was more than another Residual Connection with Kwasi. The moment felt like a déjà vu experience to Dan. For the first time, Dan enjoyed seeing his world through Kwasi's eyes.

CHAPTER 56

Dan awoke refreshed. He had made his way to bed after his Residual Connection to Kwasi, feeling good in the knowledge that he would be the one tucking in his children and kissing his wife goodnight from here on out.

He quickly showered, shaved, and dressed, anxious to see his classmates again, his Residual Connection stowed away in his consciousness like prized memories in a steamer trunk. A change of clothes had been left for him while he slept: something from his Earth closet—business casual attire.

They fit him perfectly but felt out of style for some reason. Dan was to meet his classmates in the Falcon dining room for breakfast. On his way out of Unit 4A, he noticed all his packed belongings, including his Golden Hearth gift, were gone.

Over breakfast, Class 3B made plans to get together back on Earth to share notes about their time on Hearth and strategize on what they could do to help save their planet from its worst enemy, Earthlings.

Alvita joined them in the middle of their meal. "Good morning!" she said in a cheerful voice, as if addressing a room of beloved grade-schoolers.

"Good morning," came the ragged responses, some people caught off guard with full mouths.

"I apologize for disturbing your breakfast. You may have noticed that none of your belongings were in your room this morning. That is because they have already been shipped to Earth.

"Once you return, you will know where to pick them up. That information has been left for you by your Hearthling star-twins."

After her announcement, Alvita darted from the room, leaving behind a sobering mood. The exchange students looked around the table at each other, realizing, without words, that this would be their last meal together on Hearth. Obed raised his water glass. His classmates followed his lead.

"Let us mark this moment as a fond farewell to a magnificent past, only to greet the dawning of a glorious new beginning."

"Hear, hear," Ella added. Class 3B air clinked their glasses, finding their way back to the joy they'd felt before Alvita's news.

Their last Hearth meal was done, leaving them full and satisfied. Alvita returned to escort them to an awaiting shuttle. Class 3B was excited and nervous.

"Safe travels, my darlings," Alvita said, giving each a motherly hug as they boarded the shuttle. "Return to Earth knowing that you will forever have a special place in our hearts."

Alvita waved goodbye with one hand as the shuttle lifted off. The other dabbed at her cheeks with a floral handkerchief that matched her floral tote. In silence, they watched their dorm mother vanish from view.

The shuttle landed in an area a few kilometers outside of the Zenith Campus. Their Indoctrination Specialist and Professor Doba Huaman were there to greet everyone with smiles and inquiries as to their wellbeing. Thinking of Dr. Bakari as Jabori did not seem appropriate to Dan, under the circumstances. The exchange Students quieted down when the shuttle took off, watching it in pensive silence until it disappeared from view.

"Follow me," Dr. Jabori Bakari said after allowing the moment to pass, then escorting their charges inside, with Professor Huaman bringing up the rear.

Unlike most Hearthling buildings that welcomed natural light, the building they were marching toward was a large, four-story, concrete and steel enclosed box with no windows or glass or signage of any kind.

"This is one of our Earth Transport Stations," Dr. Bakari announced, pausing inside the pristine entrance hall. It was an impressive modern facility, reminding Dan of a high-end Single

Organism dry research laboratory building, but more advanced than anything Single Organism could have constructed on Earth.

Transparent walls bordered the floor. The room was about half the size of a soccer field; shiny, bright, and to all appearances, spotless.

There were people wearing white (also known as bunny suits) in what Dan could best describe as clean room, attending to some sort of space age-looking capsules; each large enough for a human adult to comfortably fit inside.

"Those are your transport pods." Dr. Bakari pointed toward the capsules. "They are your tickets back to Earth."

Dr. Bakari continued, leading them down the hall and up a wide flight of stairs to the third floor: an office floor of cubicles, private offices, open and private meeting places, a kitchen area, storage closets, and restrooms, again reminding Dan of one of Single Organism's research laboratory buildings.

Hearthlings continued doing whatever it was they were doing, ignoring their Earthling visitors as though they were invisible. Dr. Jabori opened the door to one of the private rooms and asked them to come in. It was a large space that would comfortably seat thirty people around a boat-shaped wooden conference table.

Dr. Jabori asked them to have a seat as he closed the door. The exchange students spread out evenly on both sides of the table near the front of the room, the nanosensors embedded in the office chairs adjusting to their individual comforts, making them feel more relaxed than any massage chair could on Earth.

Dan made a mental note to push this creature comfort technology to top of his to-do list.

"As representatives of the Exchange Student Program Committee," Professor Huaman began, standing next to her husband at the head of the table, "we would like to begin by thanking each of you for participating in our Exchange Student Program. We realize it took a great deal of courage and endurance to stay the course, but you did. It is our deepest hope that your experiences and our teachings will prove indispensable tools in reshaping your planet's future."

"We ask that you remain secret about your Hearthling experience," Dr. Bakari said. "The continuation of the Exchange Student Program is contingent upon your complete silence. Should word reach our

465

committee of Earthlings having discovered our presence, we will immediately severe all contact with your planet."

Leaving us to fend for ourselves, Dan thought.

"That is correct, Daniel," Professor Huaman said, repeating Dan's thought aloud to the class. Dan engaged his natural mind-blocker.

"We ask for your solemn promise," Professor Huaman continued, "that none of you—not a single one of you—breathe a word about Hearth, Hearthlings, or our parallel universes to any Earthling not having been involved in the Exchange Student Program. Not even to those you love and trust the most."

Obed, Gagandeep, Dan, and Jomana promised aloud. The rest nodded their assent.

"You mentioned the exception would be other exchange students," Obed said.

"That is correct, Obed," Professor Huaman responded. "The Exchange Student Program has been going on for centuries. Now that you are members of the club, you will get to know your exchange student alumni on Earth."

"How?" Carlito asked.

"They will contact you, Carlito."

"Does that mean we can't think about Hearth or our experiences here?"

Jabori and Doba laughed at Intan's question. "You can think of us all you want, Intan," Dr. Bakari said. "We have no concern about Earthlings deciphering your thoughts, as long as your *thoughts* do not translate to awareness. Are we making ourselves clear?"

"Crystal."

"Excellent. Are there any more questions?" Dr. Bakari asked.

"What will our star-twins do when they return to Hearth?" Jomana asked.

"Could you be more specific, Jomana?" Professor Huaman asked.

"Will our counterparts go through the same Purification Process we did before stepping back into their lives?"

"Yes," Dr. Bakari answered. "We call it the Reclamation Process on our end. This process does require the same recovery period after such a long journey as the Purification Process but with one additional feature.

"We also purge your Hearthling star-twins of any Earthling habits they may have acquired during their assignment."

All of the Earthlings laughed, believing Dr. Bakari's Earthling purging statement was a joke. The clinical expressions of their Hearthling hosts dispelled that notion.

"Will we need to go through the Purification Process when we return to Earth?" Carlito asked.

"The short answer is no," Dr. Bakari answered. "The launch pad area is as clean as any surgical operating room. Your transport pod is a portable, sterile, environmentally controlled clean room that's 100 times cleaner than your average operating room. Contamination and microorganisms of any kind have zero chance of survival.

"One other thing I would like to mention that was not covered in your indoctrination: your body was purged of toxins, and harmful microorganisms were removed from your systems before your trip from Earth to Hearth.

"Those procedures—along with the normal strain of molecular regeneration due to long distance organic transports—contributed to your weakened state when you arrived at our medical facility. You are healthier now than you have ever been in your life. Literally. Do your best to keep it that way.

"You will be given natural nutrients in the form of a delicious smoothie to expedite the full restoration of your molecules when you arrive. Because of your improved health, you will fully recover in less than an hour."

"Besides returning them to their former lives," Gennady asked, "what else will be required of our star-twins?"

"They will report to the Exchange Student Program Committee on everything they have learned and experienced, to be studied and eventually archived," Dr. Bakari answered.

"Did they have EP cubes with them?" Obed asked.

"They had what we call data cubes to aide them in recording and documenting their entire Earth experience," answered Professor Huaman, "which are similar to your EP cubes. Bear in mind that Hearthlings have excellent recollection."

"We also have the science to record their every experience directly from their minds," interjected Professor Bakari. "As you have already witnessed in the form of memory cubes."

Like most of what Dan had learned regarding Hearthling science and engineering, it was going to take monumental Earthling team efforts to duplicate those magical crystals.

"Are there any other questions?" Dr. Bakari asked.

There were none.

"Any concerns?" Professor Huaman asked.

Silence.

"You will be put to sleep in your transport pods," Professor Huaman continued. "When you awaken, you will be home on Earth. After your brief but necessary recovery period, you will trade places with your Hearthling star-twin at a place and time that will not arouse suspicion. As far as any Earthling is concerned, you have never left."

"While we have elected to assist your planet through the Exchange Student Program," Dr. Jabori said, "Earth and Earthlings are *not* our responsibility. They are yours. We wish you well in improving the fate of your planet and character of your people.

"We will not intervene or save you. Your salvation and that of Earth rest solely upon Earthling shoulders. Fight for your mother. Never give up on your father. Never surrender your future. Know that Hearthlings are with you in spirit and, at times, in flesh.

"Victory and safe travels, family. May Hearthlings and Earthlings one day break bread on the mutual shores of our parallel galaxies. Coexistence is our ultimate goal.

"If there are no further questions or comments, let us proceed to the launch pad area."

Professor Huaman escorted the exchange students to the launch floor, this time with Dr. Bakari bringing up the rear. Their mentors gave them each a farewell hug in the hall framing the floor.

"Go forth and conquer," were Professor Huaman's final words to her class.

"I will leave you with these final thoughts," Dr. Bakari added. "Hearth is not paradise. Paradise is a man-made concept of a utopian existence. Humans are not saints or sinners. Most fall somewhere in between.

"Hearthlings acknowledge and accept all aspects of who we are, relentlessly attempting to improve ourselves in line with the universe which, of course, includes our planet.

"If you learn no other lesson from us, we hope that will be the one that remains at the forefront of your teachings. Be the light that others can follow. Go in peace."

Their mentors stopped short of entering the launch floor area, joining other Hearthlings in the control room. The upright transport pods had been laid flat. They may have been easier to work on in the upright position, Dan surmised.

They were asked to locate the transport pod labeled with their name, and stand beside it. Everyone did so without hesitation.

Dan looked around quickly, locating the transport pod that digitally displayed his name, not interested in the brilliant science and technology, for once—only in the people, the remaining members of Class 3B and the Hearthlings, Professor Doba Huaman and her husband Dr. Jabori Bakari. He saw Jabori for the individual Hearthling that he was, and not the star-twin of his personal assistant, Amiri Hayden.

The other Exchange Student Program Committee members had joined them. Scientists and technicians were going about their business as if this moment were nothing special.

Dan knew that, for them, it wasn't. Trying to save Earthlings from themselves was just another day at the office for the Exchange Student Program Committee and their associates. When Dan looked at the Hearthlings all around their launch site, for the first time, Dan saw himself.

Forever thank you, Dan thought, having removed his mind-block. Every Hearthling paused and stared at Dan, some of them clearly surprised. They placed their hands over their hearts and gave him a brief nod. Dan did the same before he followed the request for Class 3B to climb into their transport pods.

The pod was as cozy as any bed he had ever slept in; as comfortable as the bed he shared with Toni, his Earthling wife, although he did not feel any nanosensors at work to make it so.

The transport lid closed. Dan heard the sound of his pod being vacuumed sealed, a sound he knew well from his work at Single

Organism. Dan checked for the EP cube in his pocket. Still there, safe and secure.

A voice came over the speakers inside the transport pod, asking Dan to count backward from fifty. If he wasn't mistaken, it was Abiona's voice. Dan smiled, basking in pleasant memories of Hearth as he counted down.

A familiar fragrance filled the pod—a floral scent. The fresh scent of lavender and a heavy drowsiness floated Daniel Samuel Bluford into a peaceful sleep.

*　　　*　　　*

Another Exchange Student transport well done, Jabori said telepathically to the lead scientist standing next to him as they stood alone in the control room, looking out over the launch floor where the Class 3B transport pods once were, watching scientists and technicians preparing fresh pods for transportation of the next class of exchange students.

Thank you, Dr. Bakari, the lead scientist responded in kind. *We strive for perfection.*

You and your team have achieved it.

The memory wipes were successful, I trust, Jabori thought.

They were. Reports from our Hearthling operatives on Earth have confirmed that the Earthling Exchange Students of Class 3B have no conscious recollection of us or their time here on Hearth.

Good. We cannot have Earthlings going about aware we exist. That would only create chaos for them.

Not to mention the possible abuses our advances might lead to if they fell into the wrong Earthling hands.

All Hearthling star-twin experiences while they were away have been implanted in their Earthling minds. Echoes of what they have learned and experienced on Hearth lie rooted in their subconscious. They will bubble to the surface in their Earthly future actions and deeds without them ever being aware of their origins.

Have those outcomes been verified, Dr. Bakari?

Overwhelmingly. I know you are new here, but have you not read the reports?

Not yet.

Read the reports and get back to me with any questions or insights you might have. We are always interested in fresh perspectives on how to improve our Exchange Student Program.

The lead scientist nodded his assent. *Those permeations you spoke of, Dr. Bakari, do not include our scientific and technological advances.*

Correct.

All of their EP cube data and Hearthling memorabilia have been confiscated and transported to our Earthling reclamation center per standard procedure, Dr. Bakari.

We will study their EP cube data. It could aide us in discovering new ways to educate future Earthling exchange students.

And the memorabilia?

It will be archived, as will the EP cube data, once our studies are completed.

Did you mean what you said about us breaking bread "on the mutual shores of our parallel galaxies?"

You heard.

I happened to be passing by the conference room at the time, and listened in for a moment.

The likelihood of that happening within our lifetimes is miniscule. I meant it as a possibility if Earthlings survive.

Understood.

Instilled within their subconscious is the best we have to offer their world. I hope that they will use it wisely.

Have you known otherwise, Dr. Bakari?

The exchange students have wisely utilized what we have indoctrinated into them in the majority of cases. A microscopic few have disappointed.

I understand, Dr. Bakari. Such is the human condition. No Earthling has ever left our planet with knowledge of Hearth, Hearthlings, or our advances. These Earthlings have not been the first. If their mission fails and Earthlings continue along their path of self-destruction, then what?"

We will remain vigilante. If failure is imminent, then our Earthling Exchange Students will be returned to us, along with their families, to live out the rest of their days as adopted Hearthlings.

Why only them?

They are the worthy. The only thing that separates them from Hearthlings is their capabilities.

Their inabilities to read minds and auras, communicate with wildlife and aqualife, and so on.

Correct.

Why not tell the Earthlings this, Dr. Bakari? Why not allow them to keep their memories?

Motivation.

I do not understand.

In order to keep Earthlings sufficiently motivated to save their planet, they must believe there is no other option.

That makes sense.

Of course it does.

Is it true, Dr. Bakari, that if Earthlings fail and become extinct, Hearthlings will inhabit their planet?

Not in our lifetime. That will be a decision for a future generation. It is our hope that is one they will not have to make.

You mean, if Earthlings succeed in turning things around?

Correct.

The lead scientist nodded. *Do you think that they will?*

I believe they can.

As do I.

I am curious, Dr. Bakari.

About what?

The exchange student, Daniel Samuel Bluford, the creator of the Earth Forum website. He was the first Earthling, to my knowledge, to have mastered mental discipline approaching that of Hearthlings. He said goodbye to us using only his thoughts.

You are correct in your assessment. Daniel is the first Earthling to show signs of evolutionary progress approaching ours. He may be the Earthlings' first step toward permitting our cousins to become aware of our presence.

Good.

Good? I thought you were ambivalent on the subject of Earthlings and considered them little more than a scientific curiosity of human evolutionary variance. 'The train wreck Hearthlings avoided,' I believe was how you put it.

That was what I believed, Dr. Bakari.

What changed your mind?

The Earth Forum website. I have become an avid follower. It made me view Earthlings from a different prospective. From their prospective. I even had a question I submitted answered on Earth Forum.

Which one?

Hearth has no weapons of mass destruction. Why does your world possess what your people refer to as WMDs?

Good question.

Thank you. I was pleased with the answer I received. Since then, I am convinced that Earthlings are our less fortunate cousins that have gone astray.

It is amazing. We have been at this for centuries.

You mean the Exchange Student Program, Dr. Bakari?

Yes. Yet Daniel is the first Earthling to have ever come up with such an idea. The Earth Forum may do more to move forward Hearthling/Earthling relations than anything we have done in the past.

I can see that.

Evolution is not an exact science, as you well know. Who is to say that Hearthlings could not have evolved as Earthlings, and they as us? Necessitating our becoming their exchange students, in need of salvation for our planet in the process.

We are the fortunate ones of our parallel existence.

We are. It is only fair we share our good fortune. With our help, Earthlings may be able to alter their trajectory toward an alarming future before it is too late.

May the ties that bind be those of cooperation between us, and not restraints requiring cutting.

Well said. May I add that to my farewell speech?

I did not say it, Dr. Bakari.

Who did?

Daniel. He posted it in the comments section on the Earth Forum website. It was one of a number of comments from him that resonated with me.

All the better that I can attribute the quote to Daniel. My first parting quote by one of their fellow Earthlings.

Do you miss the exchange students when they leave, Dr. Bakari?

Some of them, yes.

Daniel will be my first.

Jabori's phone chirped. He checked. It was a text message from Alvita. "The next exchange student class is on their way."

Is everything ready for the next class of exchange students' return journey? Jabori asked the lead scientist.

473

It will be shortly, Dr. Bakari. We are quadruple checking now, to assure the exchange students safe passage home, as usual.

I did not mean to insinuate that your team was not prepared.

I understand. You are simply following protocol. I will assume my station.

As will I.

CHAPTER 57

Dan opened his eyes to the naturalesque sky painted on his bedroom ceiling. Wide awake and feeling refreshed, he looked around the bedroom. Everything seemed new in some strange way. Not new as if recently acquired—more like seeing familiar surroundings with fresh eyes after having been away for a while.

Their firm organic mattress was as comfortable as ever; their bedroom was cozy, thanks to the geothermal heating system. It was a clean, safe place to sleep, perchance to dream.

Toni stirred. Her head rested upon his chest, her ear positioned over his heart. He lay still, not wanting to disturb her sleep. Her breathing was steady and calm. Her thick soft curls held the sweet mild scent of coconut, a byproduct of her homemade coconut milk shampoo. Their polar fleece blanket was pulled over Toni's shoulders and tucked below her chin.

Dan glanced over at the bedside clock located on his side of the bed. 5:27 a.m. During the workweek, the alarm would sound at 6:30. It was Saturday. The weekend. The family would rise and shine at their leisure.

Dan had reclaimed his weekends for family and friends, a condition he had mandated for himself, announcing his proclamation at one of the board meetings. He supported his decision with multiple studies showing that eight-hour, five-day workweeks were not only healthier, but also maximized productivity.

To his surprise, rather than chastising or denouncing Dan for his lack of company commitment, the entire board embraced the idea.

They, too, were feeling overworked and fatigued. The five-day workweek spread throughout the leadership and rained down upon all Single Organism employees.

The board unanimously agreed to enforce a strict five-day workweek policy, making Single Organism the number one place to work (according to the popular newsletter Workforce, the Working Class blog, and Breadwinners Magazine).

While their workweek had been narrowed to five days, hourly restrictions for Dan and the rest of Single Organism leadership were occasionally ignored. Dan had no problem working more than eight-hour days as long as the sanctity of his weekends was respected.

The family had made impromptu plans to drive over to see Dan's parents, who lived only a couple of hours away, for a surprise visit, an idea Dan sprung upon his family in the middle of the week that met with enthusiastic agreement.

Dan lay still, embracing the moment—the quiet of the house; Toni's smooth breathing—knowing that shortly—very shortly—his home would be filled with the happy, healthy sounds of family. He gave thanks for having been blessed with such a life … such a home … such a family.

"Baby, I'm up," Dan said to Toni, kissing his wife on the forehead. Toni rolled over on her side without a word and fell back asleep. Dan slid his feet into his fur-lined scuff slippers and slipped into his cotton robe, leaving the belt untied.

Dan was wearing his favorite grass-green cotton giraffe print pajamas. The giraffe was his spirit animal. He made his way down the soft-lit second floor hallway (the hall lights were digitally set to night lighting), quietly making his way to Mae's bedroom and bowing to a compulsion to check on his children.

As usual, his daughter's bedroom door was open. For whatever reason, their children preferred their bedroom doors left open when they slept.

Mae was clutching her stuffed rainbow-colored unicorn to her chest, her blanket tucked under its head, snoring at her Milky Way galaxy ceiling as loudly as ever.

Harvey perked up just before Dan walked in, awakened from his dog bed on the floor beside Mae's bed. He padded over to Dan, smiling and excitedly wagging his tail, expecting and receiving affection and attention. Harvey accompanied Dan over to Mae's bedside like a K-9 chaperon.

Dan smiled down on Mae, not knowing why; wondering if she dreamed sweet dreams. Dan kissed Mae gently on her forehead, leaving his daughter to dream whatever dreams she was having.

Wick was the definition of 'sound asleep,' in the fetal position, facing the door. Pearl jumped down from Wick's bed and into Dan's arms, as happy to see Dan as Harvey had been, her rarely-slept-in cat bed undisturbed. Pearl mostly slept on the bed with Wick.

Dan hugged and petted Pearl, eliciting satisfying purrs and cheek-to-cheek rubs, furry cheek rubs being an affectionate greeting Pearl had done with her family since she was a kitten.

Wick's breathing was steady and calm, much like his mother. Judging by the disarray of his covers, Dan guessed that his night had not always been peaceful. His son may have been battling demons in his sleep. Dan kissed Wick gently on the forehead, sending his son positive thoughts of pleasant dreams for the remainder of his life. Wick mumbled something in his sleep that Dan could not comprehend.

Carrying Pearl, with Harvey by his side, Dan roamed the living room with The Odd Couple like a new homeowner taking stock in what makes a house a home. Everything seemed fresh and new about the contemporary, custom-built, two-story, 3,000-square-foot home.

Dan ran his hand over the smooth painted walls, modern furniture, wood mantle, and fieldstone fireplace. He visited the kitchen, dining room, entertainment center, and his office, treating each space with the same reverence as he had the living room and taking it all in with a great deal of satisfaction and appreciation.

He stared at the lighted wall aquarium, watching the tropical fish swim carefree and trying to remember the names Wick and Mae had given each of them.

Dan made his way down to the basement. He was less captivated by the game room, home gym, and laundry areas than he had been with the rest of the house.

He opened the door to First Contact, the rustic, wood-paneled room Dan had built for the purpose of contacting extraterrestrial life. Dan set Pearl down on the metal six-foot rectangular table. She sat and watched him, her fluffy tail lazily waving back and forth, her gaze curious, patiently awaiting Dan's next move.

Dan made himself comfortable in the captain's seat, one of two high-back ergonomic chairs. Harvey laid his head on Dan's thigh, excitedly wagging his tail. Dan absentmindedly petted Harvey. His focus was on firing up the state-of-the-art radio transceiver equipment.

Deciding not to use the adult headphones set off to the side, Dan put the transceiver on speaker, adjusted the audio frequency and dialed in the phase eliminator, slid the vintage-styled tabletop microphone close to him, then pressed the push-to-transmit (or PTT) button and spoke.

"Is anyone out there? Over." Dan petted Harvey while he awaited a response.

Dan pressed the PTT button to speak again after waiting a couple of minutes. "I'm broadcasting from Earth. Can anyone hear me? Over."

After about fifteen minutes of calls with no responses, Pearl and Harvey left; Pearl because she was bored, and Harvey due to neglect.

Dan picked up a pocket-sized Rubik cube that he kept on the desk, a distraction he and Mae sometimes used to help pass the time while they waited to hear from extraterrestrial beings.

"What are you doing, Dad?" the voice of his daughter asked shortly after the departure of his only audience. Dan was surprised to find Mae standing in the doorway, wearing her flamingo-pink robe with matching bunny slippers and baggy pajamas, Pearl in her arms, tail-wagging Harvey at her side.

"Attempting to contact extraterrestrial life."

"Without me?!" Mae walked up to her father, her doe eyes making him feel guilty for a sin he hadn't committed.

"Sorry, honey. You were asleep. I didn't want to wake you. Why are you awake so early?"

"I don't know." Mae placed Pearl on the floor. The cat immediately leaped onto the table, reclaiming her previous vantage point. Dan put down the Rubik cube and scooped Mae up onto his lap. "Any luck?" Mae asked, her rich curls holding the same mild sweet coconut scent as her mother's.

"None so far."

Mae slid the microphone to herself, pressed the transmit button, and said, "This is the Bluford family calling any and all alien life. Come in."

"You know, Mae, I've been thinking. Maybe extraterrestrials don't like being called aliens."

"What should we call them?"

Dan thought for a moment. "How about we don't label them before we meet them." Dan leaned forward to speak into the microphone. Mae pressed the transmit button for him.

"Can anyone hear us? If you can, we are the Bluford family. We live on planet Earth. We would like to hear from you. Over."

Father and daughter patiently waited a response. What they encountered instead was dampened white noise.

"Can anyone hear us? Please respond. Over." Mae said. More dampened white noise. Dan tweaked the controls. Mae spoke.

"This is the Bluford family calling from Earth. Can anyone hear us? Please respond. Over."

The two Earthbound space explorers continued to repeat the process unconscious of time or place, expecting to make first contact at any moment.

This time, Harvey became bored with their activity and sauntered away. Pearl stared at them a few minutes longer from the end of the table and yawned before doing the same as her brother.

Dan and Mae remained at it until Toni interrupted them, telling the extraterrestrial pioneers to wash up for breakfast. With Pearl on one side of Toni and Harvey on the other, she gave Dan the amusing impression that The Odd Couple had ratted them out.

Mae leaped down from Dan's lap, bolted past her mom, and ran up the stairs. She moved as fast as a real bunny, Dan noticed, the promise of a hot, delicious breakfast overshadowing her quest for extraterrestrial beings. Harvey and Pearl followed Mae.

Dan turned off the equipment. When he swiveled in his chair to leave, Toni startled him. Dan had assumed that Toni had followed Mae. He almost ran into his wife, who had slipped in behind his chair without Dan noticing.

"Find any aliens?" Toni asked with a slight smirk.

"Intelligent extraterrestrial life—and no, not this time."

"Sorry, baby."

"Are you really?"

Toni laughed. "Actually, I am."

Dan smiled.

"Maybe next time," Toni said.

"Maybe."

"You don't sound disappointed."

"I'm not."

"Usually there's a hint of regret when you come away empty-handed from one of your extraterrestrial life searches."

Dan wasn't disappointed. He had formed a conclusion while he and Mae were probing the universe for intelligent life: one that he shared with Toni. Dan put his arms around Toni's waist, pulling her body against his. Toni placed her soft hands on his broad shoulders.

"When Mae grows out of this hobby, I'm going to give it up."

"Why?" Don't you still believe in alien ... extraterrestrial life somewhere out there?"

"More than ever. I'm simply going to leave the space exploring to the experts: those equipped and educated to do so. First Contact will remain for any of our family to use."

"What brought about this sudden change of heart?"

"Let's call it an epiphany. It's time for this adult to put away childish things. I have all I've ever dreamed of right here on Mother Earth. From now on, home is where my focus will be."

Toni kissed Dan; a passionate kiss that took him by surprise.

"What was that for?"

"For being you, Daniel. The man I'll love forever more."

Toni typically reserved calling him 'Daniel' when she was upset with him. It was nice to hear his given name spoken with honey and not vinegar. They kissed.

"Ahem! Ahem!" they heard from Wick before their kissing escalated into a morning quickie.

Dan and Toni turned to find Wick, Mae, Harvey, and Pearl staring at them.

"There are children present," Mae said.

"Breakfast?" Wick said.

"We'll get right on it," Toni said.

The children and pets made their way upstairs with their parents trailing.

Dan stared at the clean-shaven man in the bathroom mirror, very much liking what he saw. Not so much his face, but the glow that seemed to emanate from his person.

Dan had always been an optimistic person. The man in the mirror was more than that. He was someone happy with his life; someone ethically, morally, and single-mindedly devoted to making the most of his time for the betterment of people and planet. He was looking at the face of a resolute, contented man.

"Dad!" Dan heard Wick yell from the open doorway of the master bedroom. "Breakfast is almost ready!"

"Be right there, son!"

CHAPTER 58

Dan had racked his brain on ways to express his gratitude for all the Gaige family had done. Finally, he landed upon an idea. Dan was permitted early access to his personal Earth cellphone by the Exchange Student Program Committee.

He rummaged through his wealth of stored family photos—ones that he wanted to keep on hand, showing off his family and others that he forgot to upload to his personal Cloud account.

Narrowing his choices to those containing only Toni, Wick, Mae and himself, Dan created a cobbled-together digital family album. It was a parting gift from his Earthling family to theirs. Dan believed that the Gaige family would cherish his present ... discounting Kwasi's feelings, of course.

Not knowing if his star-twin would have the same attitude as his Hearthling parents, Dan asked the Exchange Student Program Committee to deliver the album to the Gaige family after he had left. He had not received a reply by the time Abiona came to get him on his final day, where she found him seated at his desk gazing out of the window, staring at everything and nothing at all.

Dan's Earthling family album was delivered to the Gaige family. The Exchange Student Program Committee saw no reason not to, although they did make duplicates of everything for their files.

*   *   *

Dan walked his children to the bus stop, dismissing Wick's protest of being old enough to walk himself and escort his sister. Mae held onto her father's hand and Wick never left his side. They joined other both willing and reluctant children with parent escorts awaiting the arrival of the Pearson Academy school bus, so named after their private school.

"Good morning!" Sandy greeted Dan and the children, his neighbor having accompanied her young son and twin daughters. The children broke away from their mother to join their school friends after adding a speedy "Good Morning, Mr. Bluford" greeting of their own.

"Good morning, Mrs. Czarnecka!" Wick and Mae said almost in unison before breaking away from their father to join their school-age friends.

Having just arrived, Dan and Sandy stood out of earshot from the ragged group of parents gathered in and around the covered bus shelter.

The crisp Monday morning air provided its own wakeup call with occasional mild breezes, the clear blue sky with a drowsy autumn sun yawning just over the horizon.

All parents who were due on-site were dressed and groomed appropriately for their positions, ready to leave for work once their morning chaperon service was done. Those who worked from home or who were stay-at-home parents were clean and dressed casually. Dan and Sandy fit into the first classification of parents.

"I see it's your turn to accompany the kids, Dan," Sandy said.

Sandy usually accompanied her children to the school bus stop, her husband Marek standing in as parent guide when something unexpected disrupted their routine. Toni and Dan alternated months, accompanying Wick and Mae to the school bus stop. Monthly, because it seemed less confusing than weekly for the children. Theirs was a manner of thinking that caught on with most two-parent households in Golden Meadows who used an alternating method.

"I don't mind," Dan replied. "I enjoy it, in fact."

"Me, too. I'm so glad you pushed for more parents to use the school busses rather than driving."

"It seemed the smart thing to do."

"At first, I thought you were a pain, bringing up how more parents should take advantage of the free Pearson Academy buses the school provides. You brought it up at every community meeting, posted signs on your front lawn, and went door-to-door with leaflets and pamphlets, turning the idea into a crusade.

"As President of the Golden Gardens Council, I thought I was going to have to get a restraining order issued against you to stop your harassing people in the community."

"I understand, Madam President."

"Our community came around, I'm proud to say. Including me. I suppose the real issue wasn't convincing more people to use the school buses. It was getting people to change their routines. We are creatures of habit."

Dan nodded. "People are a lot more adaptable than you give them credit for. Especially when it comes to the welfare of their children."

"So I've learned."

"Hope I wasn't too much of a pain, Sandy."

"You were. Sometimes being a pain is what it takes to yank people out of their comfort zones. Myself included."

"I prefer to think of it, in this instance, as more like nudging. My only concern was—and remains—what is best for the children. Less traffic congestion around the school. School busing has proven safer than driving the children ourselves. More quality time—."

"I know, I know. I still have your materials spelling out all of the benefits of school bussing. Your argument was very convincing."

Dan chuckled.

"From what I've heard, Dan, your materials have found their way into other communities outside of our school district."

"I was contacted by the National School Board Association. They wanted to know if they could use my pro-school bussing materials to help better educate parents on the subject. I gave them my blessings."

"That's great, Dan!"

"It feels good to be a part of positive change, Sandy."

"It most certainly does. I can remember when we had to drag our kids out of bed, most mornings, to ready them for school. Now they're up before we are. They want to make sure they don't miss the bus."

"And the opportunities to spend more in-person face time with their classmates."

"That, too. An additional up side for me as a parent is that I get to spend more quality time with my kids."

Dan looked around. Energetic grade school children were congregating with other children in their age groups. Parents were congregating with parents.

"What are you smiling at, Dan?"

"Enjoying the view."

"Sometimes, Dan, you say things that puzzle me."

"Good."

"Why good?"

"Why not?"

"O-kay," Sandy said, knowing Dan well enough not to be drawn into one of his playful theoretical or philosophical conversations. "It's been a little more than nine months," continued Sandy, on course. "Based upon all that I've seen and heard, the Golden Meadows community is one-hundred-percent behind school bussing."

"That's great news!"

"There's something I've been meaning to ask you, Dan. What prompted your sudden obsession with school bussing? When was it? About a year ago?"

"Sounds about right."

"What made school bussing such a hot-button topic for you?"

"I was getting the kids ready for school one morning when I noticed a yellow school bus go by our house. For the life of me, I couldn't remember seeing a school bus in our neighborhood before. I asked the kids about the bus that morning on the drive to school. They filled me in. I contacted the school that same day."

"You called the school from work?"

"I did. Spoke to the principal, in fact."

"You spoke to the principal about school bussing?"

"Who else should I talk to about it?"

"Good point."

"He was quite helpful. Apparently, only a small handful of kids were utilizing the school bus service that Pearson Academy provided; not only Golden Meadows, but for the entire school district. Most parents were dropping their kids off at school, like you and me, despite the school's best efforts to inform parents about the benefits of using their bussing system."

"That's who you got your school bussing data from?"

"Some of it, yes. The rest was due to my own research. I always like to verify. It's in my nature, and is necessary in my profession."

"Duly noted."

"I felt as though I had to do something about changing our school commute habits, starting with my own family. And, as they say, the rest is history."

"Something as simple as a school bus passing your house prompted your obsession."

"Just goes to show you, Sandy: you never know what kind of spark will ignite a fire."

Sandy nodded.

"I'm sure you've experienced moments like that in your life, Sandy?"

"I have, Dan. Not so much lately, but I have. Why'd you talk me out of mandating school bussing for the Golden Meadows community—amend our bylaws to state that all school-age children are to commute to school using the school provided buses, barring special circumstances?"

"You can't force people to do school busing. Need I remind you of how that played out in our own American history, with forced integration?"

"This is not the same. There were greater social issues at stake in that effort."

"The same principle applies. There would be hardcore resistance if you mandated school bussing. Some would rebel simply for the sake of rebellion, even if they believed bussing was a good idea. You have to let people warm up to the idea in their own way and in their own time."

"I didn't realize you were also a psychologist, Dan."

"Managing people requires some understanding of human behavior, as you well know, Sandy, being a COO and President of our Golden Meadows Council."

Sandy nodded her agreement.

"I have a confession to make, Dan. While your school bussing argument was compelling, I still expected to be able to douse your campaign. Altering people's routines in the manner you were suggesting was bound to create a revolt—one I could use to squash your crusade.

"Which was why I proposed a month-long trial of the school bussing program in the first place: to set fire to the revolt that was bound to follow."

"I, too, have a confession. You knew about the minority of parents who were already bussing their children—the ones you omitted as part of your sample group?"

"I did. Their positions were already established. I wanted an objective sample from those not currently bussing their children to provide me with their unbiased impressions."

"Three-quarters of the sample group you selected were already on board. They were undercover allies if you will."

"You're kidding!"

Dan shook his head to confirm that he wasn't.

"How did you manage that?"

"Some secrets are best kept secret, Sandy. Didn't you ever wonder why I was so thrilled about your trail run idea?"

"No, I didn't. In fact, it never crossed my mind."

"Maybe it was because, on a subconscious level, you knew that supporting school bussing was the right thing to do."

"I don't know about that, Dan. I will say, I'm glad my plan didn't work."

"Me too."

"You stacked the deck in your favor," Sandy said incredulously.

"We weren't making much progress in the community preaching about the favorable statistics, economic, and environmental benefits of school bussing. We knew we had to strike a more intimate chord: one that resonated with every parent's maternal and paternal instincts.

"We believed that once enough parents experienced the pleasure of escorting their children to the school bus stop, watching their children interact with other children and parents connecting with other parents, seeing their children safely off to school, then residents would fall in line. Your trail run granted us an opportunity to prove our theory."

Sandy laughed. "How devious. I see I can add 'politician' to your skill set."

"You don't get to be director of an international corporation without knowing how the game is played. Politics is a large part of our lives whether we like it or not."

"I know who I'm going to nominate to replace me, should I decide to step down."

"You're irreplaceable, Sandy. No one cares more about the Golden Meadows community than you."

"No one's irreplaceable, but thanks for the compliment. I can't imagine life without school buses, now."

"Once you've had a taste, it's tough to go back to the old carpool system, isn't it?"

"That it is. I'm amazed by the ripple effect surrounding this whole school bussing ordeal."

"What do you mean, Sandy?"

"Haven't you noticed? We've had a full house at all of our neighborhood meetings. Not only are more Golden Gardens residents showing up, but they are looking to get involved in community projects. Before, it was like pulling teeth."

"You equate those changes to the increase in school bussing participation?"

"It's the only thing that makes sense when you look at the numbers before the school bussing issue, and after."

Dan had always thought of community as a village; as more than a group of people living in the same area, sharing common ownership. He believed in the communion the word implied. It was an opportunity for camaraderie; a place to celebrate and enrich.

"Community-conscious ripple effect, huh," Dan said.

"Yep." Dan and Sandy high-fived.

"Would you consider becoming president if I decide to step down?"

"That's the second time you've hinted at resigning. Are you?"

"No time soon. My promotion from general manager to COO is gobbling up more of my time and energy than I anticipated. If something has to give, it's going to be my Golden Meadows President position."

"I would need to discuss it with my family, first."

"Do you discuss every decision you make with your family?"

"The ones that affect them, yes."

"One of a number of characteristics we have in common, Dan. That's another reason I believe you would be perfect for the position if—or when—it becomes available.

"Let's join the other parents to see what's going on. I do hope Preston is not talking everyone's ear off about his latest hobby," Sandy whispered to Dan as the two former adversaries approached the ragged huddle of parents.

"What is Preston's latest hobby?" Dan whispered back. "He's had so many."

"Archery."

"Cool. When did Preston start that one?"

"A few days ago. I only have preemptive knowledge because he asked me about building an archery range in Golden Meadows."

"I'll run interference if Preston is doing his thing; create an opening for you to change the course of the conversation."

"Deal."

As anticipated, Preston was dominating the conversation around his latest hobby. The tag team operation of Dan and Sandy worked to perfection, giving others who wished to speak on other matters an opportunity and leaving Preston none the wiser.

The separate congregations of children and parents broke up when the school buses arrived. The families said their goodbyes, the children giving their parents, at minimum, a hug. Some added a kiss. Both were shows of affection delivered per demand or voluntarily, dependent upon the age of the child.

Mae gave both voluntarily to her father. Wick gladly hugged his dad, but resisted returning his father's cheek peck, an action Wick had no problem performing in private, but had become squeamish about doing in public.

Dan made a show for a return kiss by presenting his cheek to his son, playfully beseeching Wick for one little peck on the cheek before he left. Wick finally gave in at the last moment before rushing onto the bus.

Children waved to parents and parents waved back as the buses pulled away. Not a single parent left before the bright yellow school buses were out of sight.

CHAPTER 59

Dan arrived at the Single Organism campus at around his usual time of 7:48 a.m. and walked into his outer office. Amiri Hayden was seated at his station. He sported brown skin, brown eyes, a doorknocker beard, and was fit, meticulously groomed, and stylishly attired.

Dan was drinking his favorite office drink from his 20-ounce stainless steel tumbler: a free turmeric chai latte made with coconut milk from the café on his floor. Free, as was all food and beverage for Single Organism employees, from the food court to any of the café or espresso bars located throughout the campus.

"Good morning, Dan," his personal assistant said in his baritone voice, with a welcoming smile, standing to greet his boss.

"Good morning, Amiri. How are you?"

"Doing well, thanks for asking. And yourself?"

"Couldn't be better. How's married life treating you?"

"Great!"

Dan wasn't surprised by Amiri's response. While Amiri and Ginny had only been married six months, the couple had lived together during their engagement, a choice that had strengthened their bond.

To Dan's surprise and strange relief, Mae's infatuation over Amiri seemed to melt after Amiri said his vows, her childhood crush dissolving like sugar in vinegar on low heat.

"Good. Tell Ginny we said hi."

"Will do. Please do the same for us."

Dan nodded. "What's on today's agenda?"

Amiri and Dan reviewed Dan's daily docket. There were no surprises. His first meeting was with Michelle Tinder, in about an hour. Michelle and Roger Shell had really come around after Dan had given them his teamwork ultimatum, squashing their attempts at individual glory by usurping Single Organism's merited chain of command.

"Send Michelle in when she gets here."

"Yes sir—or should I address you as 'Mr. President,' now?" Amiri concluded with a smile drenched in sarcasm, but mixed with pride.

"You do and you'll be looking for another job, Mr. Hayden."

Dan stepped into his fourteenth floor executive office, leaving the large oak doors open. He was greeted by the fragrance of lavender, his favorite. A vase of deep purple lavender centered on the cubed brushed gold stainless steel coffee table was the source, delivered daily by their in-house florist.

Dan grabbed a square cotton coaster from the coaster caddy on his desk and placed his hot drink on the handmade hardwood desk forming an L. He set down the gift from his parents on his desk near the framed photographs of his wife and children.

The vintage bison leather briefcase he planned to replace soon with an eco-friendly one, per the request of his children. He hung up his coat in the closet and stared up at the handmade contemporary chandelier and coiffured barrel-vaulted ceiling, then looked down at the wall-to-wall seashell carpeting.

Dan roamed his office as he had his house, admiring the décor and furnishings and touching and gazing at familiar surroundings with fresh eyes.

Dan stepped up to the glass exterior of the east wall. The sun had awakened. Oyster-colored, floor-length remote controlled drapes framed the autumn light streaming through the glass. He looked out over the complex.

The Organism was already bustling with constructive activity. He took a moment to recognize his responsibility to not only Single Organism employees, but to all people and planet Earth, making certain every company decision he made or idea he had corresponded to those commitments.

It was his mantra; his living prayer—an obligation to a better future that had propelled Dan to challenge the backsliding Single Organism

Board of Directors to recommit to their original mission statements, expanding their roles in CSR (Corporate Social Responsibility) through philanthropy, activism, and volunteering, not wavering for profit or convenience.

The fight wasn't easy, but he and Seo-yeon Hong would not concede.

One by one, they rekindled the original promises of their purposes in the hearts of their compatriots, harnessing enough votes to oust the stringent bottom-line CEO outsider and unanimously electing one of the founding members to replace him, Seo-yeon Hong, charging her with the task of guiding the family home and returning them to their full commitment of saving the planet through intelligent use of science and technology without cutting corners.

Seo-yeon immediately nominated Dan for the second highest position in the company, President. Dan accepted the nomination after discussing it with his family, stipulating that his acceptance was bound to him maintaining his current position and office location.

The vote turned out to be no more than a technicality. The two of them were putting Single Organism back on course, spearheading the resurgence of the one-hundred-percent green planet commitment by Single Organism.

Dan lifted an award from its place on the mantel. The Golden Earth. It was a beautifully handcrafted golden sculpture of Earth, given to him by the local branch of the international Nexus Foundation in appreciation for his leadership role at Single Organism in helping to protect the environment and promote a cleaner, healthier planet.

Nexus was a planet-first organization headed by worldwide ecological expert and activist for a better global tomorrow Alvita Agumanu, a dynamic leader wholly devoted to the preservation of Earth and the betterment of its inhabitants. She was a bold woman who preferred bright colors and the nickname Al.

The engraving on the award humbled Dan and solidified his pledge: "We do not inherit Earth from our ancestors; we borrow it from our children."

Dan settled in for a routine day. All teams now had a standing rotation of spokespersons to give Dan firsthand reports on the progress being made on their latest project, a requirement Dan put in place that went over well with his research teams.

His meeting with Michelle went as expected. Her report on Eco-Friendly Biodegradable Plastic Manufacturing Equipment was detailed, specific, and professional, highlighting the team's accomplishments and their near-future goals; a copy of which she would email to Dan, as would all of the spokespersons after their meeting with their Polar City Director.

His progress meetings with research department spokespersons took up half of his morning. Roger Shell not amongst them, it not being Roger's turn to represent his group.

Most reports followed Michelle's example. One first-timer needed guidance on what to elaborate on and what to keep out of a precise progress report. Dan was glad to help.

The remainder of his morning involved answering emails. There were three video conferences with clients; two of them new clients. The other was an existing client who needed pressing questions answered. Fielding unexpected requests for info calls from other office directors was something Dan was doing more of, as part of his presidential duties.

Dan had his once-a-week informal catered round table discussion lunch with his department heads and assistant director in a private conference room.

He approved the latest production schedules and two potential new client pitches, answered more emails, and rejected the proposal for a new R&D project due to negative ecological ramifications. But not without offering design suggestions on how to improve the proposal to make the idea feasible for Single Organism.

Then he answered more emails, fielded more unexpected info requests from other office Directors, and paid impromptu visits to R&D Labs C and D, where they were happy to see their Director—as they still considered Dan theirs—and were proud to show him around.

Before Dan knew it, the virtual whistle blew on an exhilarating but exhausting eight-hour workday.

Dan felt drowsy on the drive home. His music mix of modern and old-school jazz from one of his Cloud playlists was too relaxing. He needed a pick-me-up.

Dan took the off-ramp leading to a coffeehouse he favored and pulled into a three-quarter filled parking lot. The place was well lit, lively with conversation and piped in background music. Dan stepped into a short queue to place his order.

"I'll have a tall Ethiopian coffee," Dan said when it came his turn to order. The barista wore a jean apron, pink button-down shirt, and casual jeans. Her tan skin glowed and her brown eyes were bright. Her wavy brown hair was pulled back into a ponytail that reached her round hips. She had a sacred Maori chin tattoo and her nametag read "Aroha."

"For here, or to go, Mr. Bluford?" Aroha asked, her voice as chipper as her smile. Aroha was his barista most times when Dan came to this coffeehouse. She had asked his first and last name once and had remembered it ever since.

"To go, please, Aroha."

"Room for cream and sugar?"

"No thanks."

"Coming right up."

Dan paid for his drink with cash. He placed the change in the tip jar and stepped aside to await his order. He texted Toni to let her know that he had stopped for coffee and would be home soon. Toni texted back, "Can't wait to see you. Love you," followed by hearts and kisses emoji. Dan couldn't explain it, but lately he and Toni had been behaving like newlyweds. Dan texted Toni that he loved her too, but without the emoji adornments.

"A tall Ethiopian for Daniel!" Aroha announced, looking right at Dan. A mischievous glint was in her clear brown eyes, making Dan believe, for a moment, that Aroha knew something that he didn't.

"Thank you," Dan said, taking his drink.

"You're welcome, Mr. Bluford. Have a nice evening."

"You, too."

Dan was always on the lookout for talent. He had considered poaching this energetic young woman from the first time they met. Dan handed Aroha one of his business cards. "Have you ever considered a career change?" he asked, hoping Aroha didn't consider his question some sort of come on.

Aroha smiled back at him. "Yes. In fact, I'm in medical school. I'm studying to become a doctor."

"Great!" Dan said. *Personality and intelligence.* "Listen, Aroha, I believe you would make a great addition to our Single Organism family."

"I don't know," Aroha said with genuine doubt. "I've been here for a while. They've taken good care of me and provide me with flexible hours for my classes."

"Do they offer financial assistance for your education?"

"No. It's not work related, so I don't get that perk."

"We do. Single Organism would be happy to financially support your dream of becoming a doctor."

"Why?"

"Because we're not simply a company that builds things. We invest in people—people that we believe will contribute to the betterment of society, in their own way."

"What sort of job?"

"Off the top of my head, I would say as a host in one of our cafés or an assistant in our medical facility.

"The Organism has its own medical facility?"

"We do. I'm sure we can find a suitable position for you to earn a good living while allotting you time and support to pursue your dream."

Aroha hedged, still uncertain. Dan understood. Making any kind of a career change could be stressful. Aroha placed Dan's business card in her apron pocket. "I'll think about it. I've got to get back to work."

"Hope to hear from you soon, Aroha."

Dan and Aroha smiled at each other like old friends. Aroha moved on to the next customer and Dan left, feeling that he no longer needed the coffee.

CHAPTER 60

Earth Forum. Auto play a video message upon logging in to the website.

"Welcome to a new day for the Earth Forum. Allow me to introduce myself. My name is Doba Huaman. I am a professor at the Zenith Campus, specializing in exchange student education.

"With the departure of our beloved Daniel Samuel Bluford, I will be fielding all the questions you have about Earthlings on the Earth Forum website until a suitable Earthling replacement can be found.

"I will not be attempting to replace Daniel. He was one of a kind, and I do not possess Daniel's intimate Earthling knowledge. What I can deliver to my fellow Hearthlings is the empirical data about our twin universe cousins.

"I am open to any topics or suggestions you might have, just as Daniel was. I look forward to hearing from you soon."

*   *   *

Heavy rain had pelted Golden Meadows since yesterday evening, reminding Dan of a rainforest, for some reason, although he had never been there. The cold drops added an uncomfortable sogginess to an already-cold day, forcing the Blufords to call off their planned Saturday morning hike at a nearby mountain trail by a vote of 3-1 (Dan being the only soul willing to brave the weather for the great outdoors), compelling him to refer good-naturedly to his family as 'fair weather wimps.' The three nays wholeheartedly agreed with Dan's assessment.

Warm and cozy in their game room, the Bluford family alternated between old-fashioned board games favored by Dan and Toni to the online video games preferred by Wick and Mae.

The children were giving their parents a beat-down in a video game where the objective was to navigate your avatar to freedom through a complex maze by overcoming a series of foreseeable and surprise obstacles.

Dan had just finished his floundering effort through the maze with a final time and score that had his children doubled over with laughter when the meditative sounds of Tibetan singing bowls reverberated throughout the game room, interrupting their guffawing. Dan shut off his cell alarm, promptly excusing himself to rush to his office.

In his office, Dan awakened his desktop computer and triple monitor setup. He joined the scheduled video conference and arranged the live camera feeds of each international participant across the spread of his color monitors.

The line-up of participants included Indonesian human rights crusader Intan Nugraha, Indian diplomat Gagandeep Acharya, Swedish sociologist Ella Claesson, Pakistani industrialist Waqas Anwar, Portuguese microbiologist Carlito Macedo, Greenlander eco-activist Nivi Lyberth, Canadian environmental physicist Oliver Martin, Egyptian anthropologist Jomana Ashraf, Russian historian Gennady Kuznetsov, Ghanaian educator Obed Addo, Japanese linguist Amaya Chiba, and Cardinal Gregorio Jayden Ocampo, from the Philippines. Their bright digital faces beamed back at him.

"Glad you could make it, Dan," Obed said. The others added their spirited agreement with Obed. Obed's Accra home office was clearly visible in the background. It was 2:32 p.m. on a Saturday in Dan's part of the world. Obed's digital date and time stamp clocked him in on Saturday at 6:32 p.m.

"So am I," Dan responded to the group.

This was the monthly gathering of the Earthling Collective, an impromptu coalition formed from coincidental circumstances to talk shop regarding the betterment of human beings and the planet.

They had met, by chance, at an International Telepathy Conference held in Buenos Aires about eight months ago. Dan had attended the conference alone at his own expense, curious to learn more about the phenomenon. He was searching for a place to sit in the crowded dining hall of the conference center when he noticed an empty seat at one of the tables and asked if he could join them.

He received such a warm welcome, it made Dan feel as if his question had been superfluous. To his surprise, the gathering was discussing solar fuel rather than the central theme of the conference. They continued their conversation as Dan made himself comfortable.

Dan listened, taking in everyone's ID information from their eco-friendly badges. Dan presented his views on solar fuels when asked for his input. It was an alternative power his company supported and was vigorously researching. This gave his avid listeners a big-picture breakdown on the renewable energy source.

"Who are you?" Intan asked in astonishment. Dan had only volunteered his first name, on his badge, excluding his professional data.

"Dan Bluford," Dan said matter-of-factly.

"Why does your name ring a bell?" Gagandeep asked.

"Have you ever heard of a company called Single Organism?"

"Of course," Ella responded, speaking for the group. "Who hasn't?"

"Wait!" Waqas exclaimed. "Now I recognize you! You're the president of Single Organism."

"Guilty."

"You have nothing to feel guilty about, my friend," Carlito said. "Your company does great work."

"I meant that as a—"

"It's true," Nivi interjected before Dan could finish. "Your company has set the environmental industrial standard for all others to follow."

"My country deals exclusively with Single Organism, when it comes to all of our latest industrial needs," Waqas said.

"As does ours," Ella added.

"We're close to creating an environmentally friendly industry," said Oliver. "Still working on a few holdouts."

"Japan is at the forefront of green awareness, I'm proud to admit," Amaya stated.

"We are well aware of your country's eco-friendly consciousness," Dan responded. "We have a manufacturing plant and a number of offices in Japan that continue to work hand-and-hand with the Japanese government on numerous projects. I see that you're a linguist, Amaya."

"I am."

"Would you consider coming to work for Single Organism?"

"Yes, but not exclusively. I prefer to use my talents where they can do the most good for humanity, and not solely for industry."

"Nobel indeed, young lady," Cardinal Ocampo interjected. "God is clearly with you."

"Understood," Dan said to Amaya. "Please send me your resume. We can place you on retainer, giving you the option to work on the projects that interest you."

Amaya nodded.

"We are attempting to institute environmentally friendly industries in my country," said Jomana. "Convincing those entrenched in the old mindsets that there are better ways to do things is not an easy task."

"True," said Gennady. "Navigating through the minefields of the past toward a better future is never easy."

"Let us pray that God opens the hearts and minds of those holdouts so that they may soon see the light," Cardinal Ocampo interjected.

"Perhaps I can help," Dan said. "If each of you will give me your contact information, I'll provide you with whatever support you need to help convince those in power of the long-term benefits of going green."

Everyone at the table thought that a great idea. Dan passed around his personal cellphone and asked everyone to add their contact information to his "Contacts." Dan grouped their contact information, then sent a prepared text that he had, containing his personal contact information, for the lunch group to add to their address books.

After lunch, Jomana, Carlito, Oliver, Amaya, and Obed accompanied Dan to a "Telepathy For Beginners" seminar for which they had each signed up. The rest of the lunch group dispersed, having registered for diverse lectures or seminars being presented at the same time in different venues.

Dan came away a believer in the dormant telepathic capabilities of people—so much so that he talked the Single Organism board into funding legitimate research on telepathy. The Parapsychological Phenomenon Center was slated for construction at the beginning of next year.

Cardinal Ocampo organized a video meeting of the luncheon group a couple of weeks after their spontaneous assembly at the International Telepathy Conference. Their shared passions for ecology and humanity made them natural allies.

It was then that they decided to make their meetings a monthly affair, floating a time and day that was convenient for all, in each month. That was also when the luncheon group decided on a name for themselves; one suggested by Obed: The Earthling Collective.

"Earthling—" Obed went on to explain, "because we are indigenous members of Earth and the human international society. Collective, because we are banded together in a determined effort to alter the course of human history for the betterment of our planet and humankind."

"How is everyone?" Dan asked the spread of bright digital faces.

Nivi, Intan, Waqas, Ella, Jomana, Cardinal Ocampo, Amaya, and Gagandeep all said they were doing well. Carlito, Gennady, and Oliver chimed in as being fine. As the group rallied around saving the world, they had become instant friends.

Dan could make out a framed group photograph that Obed had taken at the conference, hanging amongst a satellite of other photographs on his back wall. 'TEC,' as they often called themselves, had no charter, mission statement, or formal guidelines. What began as an assortment of like-minded advocates morphed into a combination of those issues and personal relationships.

Sometimes they spent as much time discussing their personal lives as they did collaborating on healthy world solutions. That was fine with everyone involved.

Obed announced his nomination for world's best teacher, to a round of jubilant applause and cheers. It was a response that would disseminate throughout for each member's recognition, accomplishment, achievement, or advancement in their causes or careers.

Intan reported on two recent human rights victories that he was involved in. Gagandeep did the same on the finalization of a hard-fought peace treaty between two nations of generational enemies. Ella asked for assistance on a book she was writing, highlighting the positive effects of going green on everyday life. Waqas updated everyone on his country's latest green manufacturing plant—one that Single Organism had designed and built for them, it so happened.

Carlito gave them an update on his team's research on the negative impacts of plastics on microbial life. Nivi announced a successful effort to clean up the debris left by an abandoned military base on the pristine fjords of Greenland. Oliver gave a brief general report on his team's efforts to refine the global climate model. Gennady and Jomana informed TEC about the big strides made in getting the decision makers in their countries to make firm commitments to a greener future.

Cardinal Ocampo announced the formation of the first organic farmer's co-op market in his region. Amaya reported her selection as Editor-In-Chief of the AILA Review, the official scholarly journal of The International Association of Applied Linguistics. Dan informed TEC that Single Organism's zero emissions mobile power station, with whisper technology for noise reduction, was ready for production.

The Earthling Collective had discovered that, besides being a brilliant anthropologist, Jomana was also a gifted musician, singer, and composer. Jomana graced her compatriots with one of her latest musical compositions: a melodic instrumental piece played on an Egyptian harp, earning her a standing ovation from her video audience.

As had become their tradition, Cardinal Ocampo closed the meeting with a benediction:

"'Love is patient, love is kind. It does not envy, it does not boast, it is not proud. It is not rude, it is not self-seeking, it is not easily angered, it keeps no record of wrongs. Love does not delight in evil but rejoices with the truth. It always protects, always trusts, always hopes, always perseveres. Love never fails.' Let The Earthling Collective remain dogged in our righteous fight for the soul of our planet, with the love of people, nature, and God in our hearts."

After the meeting, Dan found that his family had relocated to the living room, affectionately huddled together on the couch, mesmerized by a wildlife documentary on ravens. Toni was seated between Wick and Mae. A large bowl of green seedless grapes sat on the coffee table in front of them. Dan sat next to Mae, draping a long, strong arm about his wife.

"Once abundant throughout the Northern Hemisphere," the narrator said in a reassuring voice against a boreal backdrop of ravens in the wild, "this stout, cagey, and sharp-eyed bird is now constrained to remote, undisturbed territories, inhabiting desolate deserts and mountains, northern forests, and tundra."

Mae crawled onto her father's lap. Dan scooted over next to Toni. Husband and wife kissed. Dan reached over and palmed his son's head, giving it a gentle rub. Wick and Mae grabbed a fistful of grapes from the bowl.

"Long before being immortalized in Edgar Allan Poe's poem "The Raven," this beautiful, captivating bird was considered a universal symbol of dark prophecy in many parts of the world, unfairly branded as the contemptible harbingers of pestilence, disease, and death on one hand.

"On the other hand, its ingenuity and courageous conduct earned ravens a measure of esteem, as demonstrated in its honorable heraldic roles in the folklore of many cultures throughout history.

"Ravens are intelligent and possess an adept memory, with brains proportionately as large as humans (adjusted for body weight). They are gifted with the ability to mimic an abundance of sounds, including human speech, which they do even better than parrots.

"Their capacity to reason and negotiate new situations is often addressed with human-type responses, allowing them to avoid threats and confront inevitable events."

The narrator paused, allowing the viewers to take in a congregate of ravens launching a flying attack to thwart a predator eagle.

"You may have difficulty telling ravens apart. Ravens have no such trouble. Ravens recognize their preening partners and mates with ease—a mate they will typically be committed to for life.

"Ravens have an elaborate ritual to celebrate their unions," the narrator said as a raven couple performed a courtship flight involving graceful soaring and dazzling aerial acrobatics. The narrator paused again to allow the viewer to enjoy the breathtaking scene.

"Let us hope this couple has a long and fruitful marriage."

ABOUT THE AUTHOR

Michael's passion for literature inspired him to devour everything from contemporary novels to classical prose. As a high school student, he wrote poetry for his enjoyment. That joy blossomed into a zeal that would not be contained. Composing poetry rippled into writing short stories, novels, and screenplays.

Michael has studied English Literature and Creative Writing at Point Park University, Sonoma State University, and Portland State University to improve his craft. He has written creatively for more than four decades and has had poetry and short fiction published in numerous literary publications.

Milton Keynes UK
Ingram Content Group UK Ltd.
UKHW040112160324
439374UK00001B/156